Mother of Valor

Gary Corbin

Double Diamond

PUBLISHING

This book is a work of fiction. Names, characters, businesses, incidents, and dialogue are either drawn from the author's imagination or are used fictitiously, and are not to be construed as real. Any resemblance to actual events or persons, living or dead, is entirely coincidental.

More Valorie Dawes Thrillers

A Woman of Valor

In Search of Valor

A Better Part of Valor

Forthcoming: Under the Banner of Valor

To my mother,

who has always been there for me.

FRIDAY, JUNE 28, 2019

Chapter One

A tall, slender woman in a tank top, tight shorts, heels, and a silver wig sashayed past the parked SUV in Clayton, Connecticut on East Chestnut Street, making eye contact with the man behind the wheel. The model of the car, a Lexus LX, indicated wealth—a doctor or lawyer. Dentist, maybe. The late June sun had just set, but sufficient ambient light remained to allow her to make out the driver's key features: white, middle-aged, well-dressed, and probably lonely. With any luck, she'd found a hard-up suburban dude, prowling for Friday night action after a long work week, who didn't know how much this business transaction should cost.

Perfect.

She stopped, jutted out her skinny little hip, and smiled at the man. He smiled back and nodded. Bingo. Time to negotiate the specifics and close the deal. She sauntered over to the driver's side and leaned into the open window, in a pose that maximized the exposure of cleavage. Cool air washed over her, providing welcome relief from the relentless late June humidity. "Wanna party?" she said, smiling.

"I heard this is the party district," he said, returning her smile. Up close, he looked a little older—don't they all?—and not as wealthy. A businessman, not a lawyer or dentist. Balding, a bit out of shape. Nice suit, tie, tan lines around a missing wedding ring. "I was hoping we could hang out together. Privately?"

"Sounds great. I know a good place." She wiggled an eyebrow and sashayed around the car to the passenger side. He clicked it open. She slid in and reached across to grab his leg. "Whatcha in the mood for tonight, honey?"

"I...I'm new at this," he said. "I'm not clear on how this all works. Do I pay now, or—"

"We'll get to that," she said. "First we work out what you want. While you drive. Take us to 16th and Fir Street."

He started the car, then placed his hand on hers—still on his leg. It remained there when she slid her hand up and squeezed his crotch. Already hard. This one might not take ten minutes. He leaned over and tried to kiss her.

"Whoa! Baby, wait a minute," she said. "No kissing, okay? Come on, don't be so nervous. Drive."

He nodded, said "Sorry sorry sorry," and put the car in gear. Pulled away from the curb. "So, is there like a standard package, a price list? I mean, that's how we do it in my business. Home security stuff, you know? You want alarms, it's X, automatic alerts is Y—"

"Sure, sure," she said. "You tell me what you want, I tell you what it costs. Don't worry, you'll love what I can do for you."

He nodded. "I bet. My ex-wife, she doesn't do anything other than the, uh, 'standard' stuff. Religious and all, you know? So, half the stuff, I don't even know what to call it. What do you call when you, uh, when I, um...when it's not regular front-to-front, but kind of front-to-back...?" Sweat rolled off his scalp, dripping onto his expensive suit. "You know...up the bum?"

"Anal?" She laughed. "Sure, sure. But that's extra." Dollar signs floated in front of her eyes. He might not last past applying the lube.

"You do? Oh, great. How much would...and I assume it's all cash...?"

She laughed. "You're not trying to pay with Bitcoin, are you, honey?"

He laughed too, a nervous titter. "No, no, of course not," he said. "Don't worry, I have cash. So, how much should I..."

She sighed. Her pimp told her always, *always* make them ask for the service first. But with this guy, that might take all night. He was so ready to pop, he might take longer to pay her than screw her.

And he was so desperate, he might pay anything.

"Six bills," she said. "Touching my titties or anything else is extra. And you wear a condom or it's double."

"Six?" He gulped. "Okay, I might be a few bucks short. But my ATM is right up here." He pulled the car over to the curb and unbuckled his belt. "I'll only be a second."

"Dude, hurry," she said. "You're on the clock."

"I sure am," he said, smiling.

She gazed at him, puzzled, for a moment. Then realization struck. She scrambled to find the door handle. Pulled it. Nothing. Tried to unlock the door. Nothing. Turned back and saw his face...in duplicate. The second one being on the Clayton Police Department ID he'd shoved into her face.

"You're under arrest," said Police Detective Robert Grimes, "for prostitution. You have the right to remain silent..."

***

Valorie Dawes opened the passenger door to the Lexus and pulled the young woman by the arm onto the sidewalk. She flashed her badge and ID, then slipped them into the back pocket of her jeans. "Hands on the roof," she said. "Spread 'em. Come on, you know the drill."

The woman complied, cursing but not resisting. Val cuffed and searched her. Not that she could hide much under that skimpy outfit.

"You've Mirandized her?" Val said to her partner, Bobby Grimes, still sitting behind the wheel.

"Of course," he said. "I ain't the rookie here, you are." He stepped out of the car and circled around, taking his sweet time. So typical. The women do the work and bear the risks, the men take the money and the glory. In some ways, Val's situation and the girl's weren't dissimilar.

She spun the woman around, for the first time getting a look at her face. It looked familiar. Slender nose, pointy chin, dark brown eyes. Pale skin stretched thin over bony cheeks. Makeup almost covering faint bruises along her jaw and a scar above her left eyebrow.

"Destiny?" Val said when recognition dawned.

The woman's eyes grew wide, and she cowered a bit. "Do I know you?"

"Another of your high school classmates?" Grimes wise-cracked, opening the back of the SUV. "At the rate we're going, you might have to have your next reunion at city lockup."

"No. Hold on a sec." She kicked the door shut and lifted the suspect's chin with two fingers. Tears wet the woman's face. "Destiny Mathers? It is you, isn't it?"

"What is this, the fucking Masked Singer?" The woman spat onto the pavement. "You want my name, check my ID."

Val cursed and stared off into the darkening sky for a moment. A few months before on patrol, she'd stopped a man from beating Destiny to a pulp in her apartment building. She bent close and gazed into Destiny's face. "How the hell did you end up here?"

"The fuck you care," Destiny said. "Come on, let's go get this over with. I gotta make my one phone call."

Val re-opened the back door, pushed her inside, then slid in next to her. The SUV, repossessed from a drug raid, lacked the usual security features of a departmental cruiser, so procedure required that one of them ride in back with the suspect. "You heard her, Bobby," she said to Grimes. "Let's go."

***

Val booked Destiny at Clayton Police Headquarters and met Grimes on the fourth floor in the Women's Anti-Violence Emergency Squad Office. Mayor Megan Iverson had established the WAVE Squad three months before to stamp out crimes against women. The police chief put Sergeant Brenda Petroni in charge, who recruited Val to the group on day one.

In recent weeks, with violent crime rates dipping, the chief had requested WAVE's help in addressing a spike in prostitution in the city. They focused their efforts on the troubled "Alphabet Soup" District, so-called because the street names progressed in alphabetical order, each for a tree species that no longer graced the district's decaying urban core.

"Another newbie," Grimes told Petroni, a solidly built forty-something woman with short brown curls. "No priors. Dawes says she was an assault victim a few months back, unrelated to her profession."

"So far as I know," Val said. "No indications arose then that she turned tricks for a living. In fact, her attacker's been living in Clayton Cottage for two months."

Petroni smiled at Val's use of the term Clayton cops used for city lockup. "All that means is, he wasn't, or isn't, her pimp. But I get your point. It seems everyone we haul in from the Soup District is new to the game. It makes me wonder if something bigger's going on."

"One thing that's different about this Destiny chick," Grimes said, "is her age. She's twenty. Most of the others have been teenagers—some as young as fourteen."

"Destiny looks younger than her age," Val said. When Grimes scoffed, she added, "At least, she did when I met her."

"Okay, let's look into it," Petroni said. "Dawes, you have a history with her. Think she'll talk to you, or did busting her poison that well?"

Val cast a glance at Grimes, who made a face of disgust, but said nothing.

"It's worth a shot," Val said.

***

Val joined Destiny in a tiny cement-block interrogation room. The chamber reeked in equal measures of sweat and disinfectant, and warm air flowed from a noisy vent near the ceiling. Flickering overhead lights seemed to make the room even hotter.

A tall, uniformed African American cop named Damari Price stood at silent attention by the door. Young, clean-shaven, and fit, with dark eyes always on alert, Price's foreboding appearance often got him tagged with suspect-guarding duty.

"How's she doing, Damari?" Val asked in a low voice.

After a one-shoulder shrug, Price muttered, "A little scared, I think. Like most first-timers."

Price exited to stand guard outside, and Val glanced at the one-way mirror that lined the far wall of the hot, stuffy room. Grimes would observe their interview from another tiny room behind the glass.

"So, Destiny," Val said, taking a seat across a small table from her. "I didn't expect to meet up with you again like this."

"Yeah, well, I must've missed all those party invites," Destiny said with a sneer.

Val sighed. "Okay. I guess I deserve that. How've you been doing since we last saw each other?"

"Fucking peachy, as you can tell," Destiny said, glancing down at her skimpy attire.

"What was that, a month ago or two, in court?" Val asked.

Destiny shrugged. "You say so."

Val waited, and when no more words came, she leaned back in her seat. "Come on, girl. Help me out. How did you get from there to here in such a short time?"

Destiny shot her a sharp, questioning stare. "It's not like 'there' was such a hot place to be, *Officer.*"

In spite of herself, Val smirked. The woman had a sense of humor. "Were you turning tricks back then?"

"Who's turning tricks?" Destiny said, snarling. "Fucking hell. I ain't talking without no lawyer."

Val nodded. "That's your right, of course. Listen, I'm not here to get you to talk about what you did tonight. I'm interested in your story. How this all started. You had a job when I last saw you. What happened?"

"I lost it, obv."

"Okay. And then?"

"Then I fucking got hungry, okay?" Destiny glanced around her as if hoping someone would rescue her from the Idiot Brigade. "I have bills to pay. Rent. The state said I can't get unemployment because I was fired, and that's bullshit, anyway. What options does that leave a girl like me? I ain't a user, so dealing's out. What's left?"

Val took a deep breath. "So, it's just a money thing?"

Destiny scoffed. "You think it's about changing the world or some shit?"

"No, I guess not." Val tapped a pencil on the table, thinking. Somehow, she had to break through to this kid.

She stopped herself at that thought. *Kid.* The woman, three years younger than Val, clearly hadn't enjoyed the benefits of a college education or police academy training. Val, still a rookie uniformed cop, lacked the masterful interrogation skills of her partner, Grimes, or their boss, Sergeant Petroni. But they'd trusted her to tap into something, to somehow relate to this woman. Shared age and gender, perhaps? Intuition? Empathy?

She searched her memory for everything she knew about Destiny, anything that would connect them. Such as the first time they'd met, after her assault.

"You still living at Merrybrook Apartments?" Val asked her.

Destiny made a sour face. "That was Rafe's place." Her attacker and mother's ex-boyfriend.

"So, where will you stay tonight?"

Destiny shook her head in disgust. "I hadn't planned on sleeping. I was planning on working."

"Right. But that's out. So, where will you go?"

Destiny gazed at her in amusement. "Back to the Bar and Grill, is my guess."

Val chuckled. Cops had their pet name for lockup, perps had theirs. "What if I said you had other options?"

Laughter. "I'd say you're a liar."

"I'm serious."

"Yeah, so'm I. We done?" Destiny rattled the cuffs still binding her wrists.

"Who's coming to get you? Anyone?"

Destiny said nothing, just shook her head.

"Your Man isn't upset that you're off the clock, not earning him his eighty percent?"

Destiny locked eyes with her, new respect showing there. "In here, he can't kick my ass. You hear what I'm saying?"

Val nodded, reappraising Destiny's appearance. Her pale skin, almost translucent where the makeup had smudged off, stretched thin over her bony jaw and cheeks. Her eyes appeared hollow and tired. She looked emaciated.

"You hungry?" Val asked her.

Destiny's eyes lit up, her posture straightening. "Always."

"Let me get you some food." Val stood and rapped twice on the door. Price opened it. "Grab her a sandwich and a drink from the machines," she said, handing him some cash. Price nodded and closed the door.

"I'll believe it when I see it," Destiny said.

"That you will," Val said.

Sure enough, Price returned a few minutes later with a tuna sandwich, Coke, and a bag of chips. He stood guard inside the room while Val unshackled one of Destiny's wrists, locking the other to the arm of the chair. "Eat," she said. "That's yours."

Destiny blinked, then tore the wrapper off the sandwich and ate half of it in four bites. She sucked down half the soda in one gulp and shoved fistfuls of chips into her mouth.

"Feel better?" Val asked her.

"I ain't doing nothing for that," Destiny said. When Val shot her a questioning glance, Destiny mimed a humping motion. Price laughed.

Reddening, Val waved her off. "On the house," she said.

Destiny offered her unshackled wrist to Val. "You gonna tie me back up?"

Val shook her head. "I trust you."

The woman's eyebrows rose, her eyes blinking.

"Does your pimp feed you when you're out of funds?" Val asked.

"He likes me to call him my Manager."

"Okay. Does he?"

A wry smile. "Not anymore."

"He used to? When?"

"At first. Like, three, four weeks ago. Says dudes like girls with a little meat on their ass."

"No doubt. I get that a lot, too." Val indicated her own wiry frame, recalled the unkind names boys taunted her with back in high school: Titless Wonder. Broomstick. Lolita. Val-gay-jay.

In a softer voice, she asked, "So, what does he do for you, then? Your manager, I mean."

"Customers."

"Seems like he takes more than he gives on that front. Did I get his cut right? Eighty percent?"

Destiny nodded, thought a moment. "Protection."

"From whom?"

"From..." Destiny fought for words. "Bad dudes."

"The customers he's so proud of sending you?"

No response.

"If he's supplying clients, why do you have to walk the streets?" Val asked.

"It's just...he's got other girls, too, you know."

"Right." Val huffed. "You don't have to repeat what he tells you. It's bullshit, anyway."

"You don't know." She looked away, a sour expression on her face.

"Yeah, I do know, Destiny." Val kept her voice soft. "And you know I know. Don't you?"

She squirmed in her seat, biting her lip. Finally, she gazed back up at Val. "Any chance I could squeeze another sandwich out of you?"

Val waited a moment before answering. "If it means we get to talk some more."

Destiny lowered her eyes, folded her hands in her lap. "We could talk some," she said after a while.

"Better get more," Val said to Price.

He returned moments later. This time, ham and cheese replaced the tuna, with popcorn instead of chips.

"Figured I'd mix it up some," Price said with a smile. He waved off Val's cash. "On me this time."

Again, the food disappeared in under two minutes.

"Feeling talkative now?" Val said.

Destiny glanced at Val for a moment, then at Price. "Aight. Alone, if that's all right."

Price exited, showing respect on his face for Val.

"Okay," Val said, "it's just us girls now. What do you want to tell me?"

SATURDAY, JUNE 29, 2019

Chapter Two

Val shoved the last box of her belongings into the passenger seat of her trusty 2005 Honda Civic. The door wouldn't shut, though—too much stuff. Or had something rusted after sitting idle for five years in Dad's garage? She slammed her hip into it to get it to latch and hoped it wouldn't pop open on the drive to her father's house.

She wiped her brow, a near-pointless exercise in the late June humidity. Only noon, and the temperature had already climbed into the 80s. Sweat soaked her long-sleeve cotton T-shirt and the elastic waistband of her running shorts, the last of her semi-clean clothes until she unpacked. One silver lining of moving into her father's house: at least he had air conditioning.

She hated having to move back in with him. At 23 years old, the idea of living with her parents—or, in her case, *parent*, since her mother left without a trace almost a decade before—grated on her nerves. She had a good job she loved with a steady paycheck, had lived on her own for five years (counting two years in UConn dorms), and enjoyed the independence all of that brought her. But her recent rift with Beth, her longtime roommate and her oldest and dearest friend, was bringing that independent era to a close. Over a silly little thing like almost getting her killed by a psychopath Val had been pursuing. Some people had no sense of humor.

Val got in and turned the key in the ignition, relieved, as always, that the old Honda started on the first try. At least *some* things were reliable. She glanced up at the street-facing window of their living room, as if to say goodbye...except that she still needed to return with Dad's SUV to get her bed.

He'd suggested she sleep in her old one. No way. Not in a million years. Too many terrible memories.

One, to be exact.

She also needed to come back to clean. Beth had offered to help, but Val turned her down. She'd rather avoid the thick tension and the inevitable messy goodbyes. Besides, Beth insisted this wasn't goodbye—just a new chapter of their friendship.

Yeah, right.

On the drive to Dad's, she reviewed her alternatives one last time. She'd tried to find an affordable place on her own, but those didn't exist in Clayton. Not in any neighborhood safe enough for a single woman to live in—even a cop with martial arts skills.

She also considered finding another roommate. For about five seconds. The fact that she had damn near no other friends outside of work—and damn few at work, for that matter—meant living with a stranger, which she refused to do. She barely trusted the people she knew, for God's sake.

The most attractive alternative to living with Dad— moving in with Gil Kryzinski, her former partner/boss and now boyfriend of six weeks—scared her even more than any of the serial killers, gang members, and drug dealers she'd faced in her nine months as a Clayton police officer. Scared her enough that neither of them mentioned it, even once. Gil and Val had agreed not to rush things, which for her meant not even sleeping together yet. As in, not even *sleeping—* sharing a bed overnight. Even though he'd almost completely recovered from the gunshot wound that shattered his hip, which meant he didn't take up 90 percent of the bed anymore. So he claimed.

Still. Too soon for her.

Pulling up in front of her father's house, a modest two-story Cape Cod on Clayton's west side, reminded her of the most compelling reason to move back into Dad's home: Michael David Dawes. AKA, Dad.

Not that she harbored any illusions about patching up their strained relationship. She and her dad fought almost every time they spoke. Which wasn't often. Nor did Val harbor any nostalgia over moving back into the home in which she'd grown up. The opposite, in fact. She hated the place, especially her old upstairs bedroom. A little over ten years before, a family "friend" had raped her in that room, weeks before Val's thirteenth birthday. In her own bed. Which nobody seemed willing to believe, other than her big brother Chad and her Uncle Val. Not her parents, the King and Queen of Denial.

No, the reason to move back home, other than pure economics, was to make sure that her father didn't drink himself to death. Which he'd been well on the path to doing until he re-entered rehab six months before, shocked into it by Val's own near-death experience at the hands of serial rapist Richard Harkins.

However, Chad, her only sibling and the only one who'd always had her back, had pleaded with her. "Dad's slipping back into the darkness," he'd said. "I don't know what triggered it this time, but unless one of us does something, there won't be a next time."

Probably true. Certainly true that, between the two of them, Val had to be the one to step in. She lived closer and wasn't married with two kids. Plus, Val's skills at self-defense and, perhaps, Dad's "never hit a girl" latent sexism—meant he wouldn't, in one of his drunken rages, beat her with his fists the way he once tried to do to Chad.

They hoped. At least, it hadn't happened yet.

Dad's SUV sat in the driveway, meaning he'd be home to greet her. Hopefully sober. 174 days and counting. Every day, a risk that the count would reset to zero.

She weighed her options again. Driving away and never coming back seemed so much more attractive.

Fucking family responsibility!

She heaved a deep breath and began unloading the car.

***

A shrill bell rang—or rattled, more like it—emanating from the cheap plastic cordless phone on the pressboard desk at the end of the lumpy motel bed. Maggie McCloskey's eyes creaked open, and she lay under the musty covers a few more moments, weighing her options. Almost nobody knew she was there, and she didn't feel compelled to answer the call of the few that did. Sooner or later, they'd give up, and she could resume her fitful sleep.

She let it ring five, six more times, and, as expected, the clanging stopped. She let her eyes droop shut again, but the bright sunlight leaking in around the edges of the blinds in the room's double windows cast a red glow through her eyelids. She looked around for her sleep mask. It must have fallen to the floor. She rolled to one side to scan the room, and nearly fell out of bed when the stupid phone rang again.

The digital clock blinked the time at her: 11:30. Almost noon, then. She had checked in well after midnight and hadn't hit the sack until nearly 4:00 a.m. Whoever demanded her attention this morning clearly was unfamiliar with her night owl ways. At fifty years old, she couldn't get by without at least eight hours sleep any more.

But they'd called twice now, which meant they'd call again, and again. Might as well get this over with.

"Yeah, what is it?" She sat up in bed, slid a cigarette between her lips, and readied her lighter, then remembered that she hadn't yet disabled the smoke alarm. Dammit.

"Hey. It's Tanner. Change of plans." His oily voice rasped on the ancient phone's terrible speaker.

But the words perked her up, better than coffee. "Next week's plans? You're calling things off? Why?"

"Not calling things off." He chuckled, a humorless laugh, as forced as any kindness that ever emerged from him. "A shift of gears. We need you in Connecticut, ASAP."

Maggie heaved a deep, frustrated breath, letting it fill Tanner's ears all the way down to Florida. "What about Cleveland? I'm supposed to help them set up shop. They're expecting me tomorrow." She left unspoken that she really needed a day off. Today, in fact.

"Clayton's more important."

"Clayton!" The word spit out of her and launched her un-lit cigarette onto the filthy carpet. "I'd rather eat glass than go there."

Another mirthless chuckle. "Hope you're stocked up on empty beer bottles, then. C'mon, Maggie. Clayton's the linchpin of this whole op. We need our best person there, and that's you."

"Flattery," she said, leaning over the edge of the bed to retrieve her now-broken cigarette, "will get you nowhere, and it sure as hell won't get me back to that hell-hole." She grunted and sat back up on the bed. A stray coil in the mattress poked her ass. How the hell do they expect people to sleep on shit like this?

"That's why we pay you the big bucks," Tanner said, with no apparent irony. "Listen, Maggie. The op there is going to shit. I got word that one of our girls got busted last night...someone not on the books."

Maggie snapped back to attention. "Not on the books? Meaning...?"

"They're running side jobs," Tanner finished for her. "Which means, A, we can't trust them. And B, they're getting sloppy. We can't afford either situation."

Maggie slid her feet into worn, comfy slippers and paced the room, sucking on the broken cigarette. "That's not exactly selling me on this grand opportunity, Tanner." A flat-out lie, for negotiation's sake. Maggie loved swooping in and fixing operations gone bad. In another life, she'd have been a top corporate raider, downsizing companies drowning in debt and bloated, old-school management.

"Listen, this job is perfect for you," Tanner pleaded. "The infrastructure is there, but it needs new leadership. You know the area, you can work your old connections, get things back on track."

"My connections there aren't just old," Maggie said. "They're petrified. It's been almost ten years, Tanner. Anyone I knew then would have jetted out of there long ago." Well, almost anyone. She knew a few people had hung around.

A long silence. Maggie wondered if Tanner had hung up. Finally, he continued with an edge to his voice. "Put it this way," Tanner said. "If Clayton flops, there's no need for you in Cleveland. Or anywhere else, for that matter."

Maggie stopped pacing and bit clean through her cigarette's gummy filter. "Are you saying if I don't take Clayton, I'm fired?"

He sighed. "I'm saying, if you don't go revive our Clayton ops, we might as well just shut down. The money dries up. Not just for you. For me, for Mac, for everyone."

Maggie spit out the last bits of cigarette and sat on the bed again. She'd thought—hoped—that she'd seen the last of that ratty-ass town in her rear-view mirror a decade before. After working behind the scenes for years for reform of the town's stubborn political correctness, she'd left, hoping that fresh opportunities awaited in greener pastures. Where no one knew her or her well-positioned husband, whose corporate success and family harmony would not be threatened by her politics.

Away from those constraints, she'd gained a deeper understanding of the ingrained moral corrosiveness of not just the left, but the so-called "moderates" and the "CINOs"—conservatives in name only, who compromised and frittered away golden opportunities for change. She'd grown to appreciate the value of bypassing conventional, "safe" routes such as elections, which changed nothing, in favor of direct action. Actions that, when successful, convinced the immoral left to cower and the once-quiet majority to rise up against immoral trends such as gay marriage and legalizing drugs.

Returning to the constraining environment of Clayton felt risky. But perhaps she could limit her visibility long enough to fix the local problems and get out. Barring that, maybe enough time had passed. Maybe enough bridges had burned...and maybe, just enough of them remained to build something new out of the ashes.

And maybe, just maybe, she might succeed in repairing a few of those burned bridges. Tap into a few of those old relations. Let the distance of years salve the ancient wounds. Start fresh. Maybe even bring those old relations over to her side.

"Okay," she said, flipping open her suitcase on the bed and stuffing her belongings inside. "I'll be there by nightfall."

Chapter Three

L et me help you with that," Val's father said, propping the front storm door open with a broomstick. The closer had broken weeks ago. Dad had never been much of a handyman.

His face appeared flushed against his long shock of mussed white hair. His round, stooped form, sweating in a loose-fitting T-shirt and baggy gym shorts, looked ready to collapse. He took the box from her arms, grunting at the weight of it. "Damn," he said. "What's in here, your rock collection?"

"Rocks, hell," Val said, deadpan. "Those are bullets...my little ones."

Dad blanched, and she worried that he'd drop the box. "Kidding!" she said, taking it back from him. "I'll get this. Can you grab some of my clothes out of the back?"

"Don't even kid about that," he said. "You know how I feel about guns in the house. And you promised."

"No guns, no bombs, no ammo, I swear." Val bit back an angrier retort, pushed past him, and headed up the stairs. She didn't dare look around. Cleaning Dad's house would be chore number three, right after moving and cleaning her own place.

"Leave that down here for now," he said before she got halfway up. "I, uh, didn't quite finish getting the room ready."

Val stopped, closed her eyes, clenched her teeth, and counted to ten. Twenty.

"Dad. You had a month."

"Sorry. I only need another day or two. I'll be right back." He shuffled outside.

Val trudged back down the stairs. This time, she couldn't avoid taking stock of the living room. As usual, he'd left it a wreck. His old recliner, the leather ripping in strategic locations in the arms and seat, now sat about three feet from the large, flat-screen TV mounted on the wall. Stacks of newspapers, *True Crime* magazines, and unopened mail lined the walls. Takeout containers half-filled with cold Chinese, Thai, and Mexican food covered the coffee table, interspersed with empty soda cans and used plastic flatware. The place smelled like a garbage scow. No doubt the kitchen was worse. She didn't even want to think about the condition of his bedroom. He'd moved into the first-floor guest room after she went off to college, because, she assumed, he didn't want to risk using the stairs in his often-inebriated condition.

He'd promised to clean out the master bedroom upstairs that he'd once shared with Mom. Val had suggested Chad's old room instead, but no go. Dad had converted that into an office after his alcoholism got him "medically retired" from his executive position at Ashford Machine and Dye. After a few years of working from home as a consultant, he quit that, too. Since then he'd filled it with too much junk to even attempt to clean it out. And her old room...no. Just, no.

Which left only one alternative: the garage.

Not a bad option, in the scheme of things. In high school, Val converted it into a private gym, and slept out there more often than in her own bed. It had electricity, heat, and hot and cold water. She even installed a portable shower hose, which Dad never had the gumption to remove. The garage would make a fine apartment once again.

Val tiptoed through the miscellaneous crap littering the floor to the garage doorway, careful not to step on anything, dead or alive, that wasn't carpet or hardwood. She had her hip pressed against the lever of the door handle when Dad reappeared at the front door with boxes stacked high in front of his face.

"A little help?" he called from the steps.

Val sighed. "One second." She pushed her way into the garage. The space remained as empty as when she'd left it earlier that morning. But she'd have to park the Honda on the street from now on. She set down the box of books and hurried back to the front door.

"I'll get the room ready this afternoon, I promise," Dad said, edging sideways through the doorway. "Tomorrow, the latest."

"It's okay, Dad. I'll set up in the garage again." She took the top box from him and kicked a path through the debris in the living room. No more messing around.

"No, honey, listen," he said, trailing behind her. "Give me a few more hours. It's just hard, you know?"

Going through Mom's stuff, he meant.

"It's okay. Take your time." She led the way out to the garage and stacked the fresh box on top of the old one.

"You can't live out here in this drafty old place. It's full of old oil cans and crap, and—"

"There's plenty of room. I like it out here, remember?"

Sadness crawled over Dad's face, and he slumped against the wall. No words.

He remembered.

***

Val unloaded the rest of her stuff while Dad disappeared upstairs, presumably to get the bedroom ready despite her protests. Then she gathered up the takeout containers, old newspapers, and miscellaneous garbage strewn about the living room. One glance at the kitchen told her the ominous task of tackling that area would have to wait.

After loading up her father's SUV with a bucket of cleaning supplies, she drove it to her apartment. She hauled the bed out and tied it to the roof—one small virtue of twin-sized mattresses—then got to work cleaning the place. Beth had come by after all and taken care of the kitchen and bathroom, bless her, and her own bedroom. That left only the living room and Val's bedroom. Piece of cake. She opened the hall closet to grab the upright vacuum, one of the few adult possessions Val had contributed to their living arrangement.

Taped to the handle, Val found a note on letter-sized paper, addressed to her, in Beth's handwriting. She sat on the floor and opened it.

Dear Val,

Honestly, I don't know where to begin. We've been best friends for literally half my life...Where would I be without you?

I'm sorry about the way things ended between us as roommates. I didn't handle it very well. I wanted to sit down and talk with you a hundred times over the past six weeks, but it never felt like the right time.

But deep down I know that timing wasn't really the problem. I've been avoiding you, because I didn't know what to say. You've been going through a lot, and I haven't been there for you. Again, I'm sorry.

The truth is, we've grown apart over the past few years. College changed us. <u>Life</u>

*changed us. Becoming a cop changed you.
But I still love you so, so much—that will
never change. And different doesn't mean
bad—it means we're going in different directions.*

*I'm going to miss you. Not that we'll never
see each other—we will, a LOT, I promise!
But the random, unplanned conversations,
the all-nighters, the spontaneous time...we'll
lose that, and that sucks.*

*So how about let's have a drink soon and
have some girl talk again, okay?*

Love 4ever,

Beth

Val set down the note, leaned against the wall, and let the tears flow.

***

Back at Dad's a few hours later, Val set up her bed in the garage and fashioned a makeshift closet out of a four-foot length of galvanized pipe, some wire, and a couple of hooks she screwed into the ceiling. She even found the old holes in the gypsum she'd used seven or eight years before, the last time she'd transformed the space for full-time living. She arranged her boxes of folded clothes for easy access and even set up her make-up table—something she started using now and again since getting together with Gil. Then, as if summoned, he called her.

"I hope I called late enough for my offer to help to be rendered moot," he said, his voice on the edge of laughter.

"Are you kidding? I waited on all the heavy stuff, just for you," she said in mock irritation. "And you'd better bring dinner. Dad and I are hungry."

"That part, I have under control," he said. "Except my chauffeur appears to be preoccupied with cleaning and organizing. Which means dinner is *Chez Kryzinski* tonight. When might you be able to bring said father over for some quality grub?"

"Ooh, *quality* grub. Your salesmanship is off the charts today. How about seven o'clock? That'll give me time to sandblast the sweat and grit off my skin."

"Don't you dare. I want visual proof that you've been working hard. Seven's fine. Um, I take it, since Dad's coming, no wine tonight?"

"Best not to. Thanks for remembering."

"How can I not? I think of you constantly. I'm counting the seconds, my dear."

"Liar. How many?"

A pause. "Fourteen thousand, three hun—"

"No fair using your calculator," she said, laughing.

"Damn, you should have gone into law. You'd make an amazing prosecutor."

Val blushed, glad he couldn't see her face reddening. "But then I'd have never met the great Chef Kryzinski."

"Touché. See you in...fourteen thousand, three hundred and seventy-five seconds. Seventy-four..."

"Dork."

"Love you too," he said, laughing, and broke the connection.

Val set her phone down, and only then noticed Dad standing in the doorway, holding another box in his arms.

"Um, some ground rules?" she said. "Like, knock before entering my room?"

"This isn't your room, it's my garage." He set the box down on the floor. "I told you, your real room will be ready by tonight."

"You said this afternoon."

Dad crossed his arms. "I'm doing the best I can."

Val bit back a retort that would have escalated the tension more. "Whenever it's ready is fine. I'm comfortable here."

"I'm not comfortable with you here. It isn't right." He pushed out a loud breath of air. "I have a few more boxes to bring down, then I'll be back to work at it. You can use Chad's old queen bed if that's all right with you?"

"That's fine. Listen, it's been a long day. Let's take a break and have some dinner. Gil invited us over—he's an excellent cook."

Dad shook his head and waved her off. "I'll grab a sandwich. You go on ahead."

"Dad, Gil wants to get to know you. You guys have barely met, and he's an important part of my life now. As are you."

He shook his head again, emphatic. "Not tonight. I'm not up for it."

Val's body sagged. "Please? It'd mean a lot to me." She folded her hands under her chin, pleading.

He gazed at her and took another quick, heavy breath. "We'll see. Come find me in an hour. Make sure I haven't fallen in." He laughed. Val wondered what he found so funny.

Two hours later, she ventured upstairs. She discovered him sitting rock-still on the floor of the master bedroom, staring at a photograph. Without looking, she knew which picture had upset him. She sat next to him and put an arm around his shoulders.

"You two look so happy in that picture," Val said.

"Happiest day of my life," he said, his voice raspy.

"Hers too," Val said. "So she often said."

"Pah." He tossed the photo to the floor. "Her happiest day was the day she left. And the next day, and the day after that."

"You don't know that," Val said, shaking his shoulders a little. "I bet she was miserable."

"Then why didn't she come back?" His voice took on a steely edge, the hurt slashing the air like a fiery blade. "No, Val. I drove her away."

"No, *I* did," Val said. "I made you both crazy with my...my *problems*." She inhaled a deep, solemn breath.

"You were just a kid," he said. "It wasn't your fault. No, she left because of my drinking. So she said."

"She drank, too," Val said in a soft voice. "And smoked. And it's not like she was the warmest person I'd ever met."

He shot her a wry smile. "Don't talk like that about your mother."

Val sighed again and pointed at the piles of memorabilia all around them. "Maybe you should get rid of some of this stuff."

"I've tried. It's hard." His face wrinkled into a deep, sad frown. "It's all I have left of her, Valorie. Of that part of my life." He wrapped an arm around Val. "Well. I still have you kids, of course."

"Dad." Despite the tension, she surrendered a weak smile. "This is the first time in ten years we've spoken without trying to kill each other."

"Isn't it terrific? I love this."

Val smiled and wiggled out of their embrace. "Me too. So, let's ride this momentum and get cleaned up for dinner. Gil's making—"

"No, no, I can't," Dad said. "I'm nowhere near done, and I promised."

"Michael Dawes, for heaven's sake," Val said. "The garage is fine for as long as it takes. Okay?"

His smile showed more sadness than mirth. "Careful about lowering your expectations too much," he said.

She bit back her reflexive reply: *I'm used to it.*

Chapter Four

Val stepped out of the shower and towel-dried her short brown hair, hoping the search for her hair dryer wouldn't take as long as it had taken to locate her favorite jeans among her boxes of possessions. Why they'd ended up in the "kitchen stuff" mystified her. By that logic, she'd probably find the hair dryer in the book bin.

Normally she wouldn't care how her hair looked, but tonight, a Saturday night with Gil, might be special. Her father wouldn't budge on his refusal to attend. So much for the family-bonding scheme she'd envisioned. But the silver lining—a romantic dinner alone with the man who loved her—sounded better anyway.

Her phone buzzed. Grimes. Dammit. She considered letting it go to voice-mail. The man had to learn some boundaries.

She reconsidered, though. He'd never called on a weekend night before. 2:00 a.m. on a Wednesday, sure, but not on a rare Saturday night off.

Val pulled on her jeans and cradled the phone to her ear. "What's up, Bobby?"

"Need you downtown," Grimes said. "Major break in the case. We need all hands, ASAP."

"On a prostitution sting?" Val exhaled loud enough for him to hear. Perhaps loud enough for someone in China to hear. "Why? Did someone keep your hundred-dollar bill this time?"

"Funny funny, ha ha. Get down here. I'll explain when you get here."

"Grimes," Val said, pulling on a blouse and pushing her way into the garage. "Tonight's my night off. I have plans."

"Make new plans. Be here in an hour." He hung up.

Val swore and tossed her wet towel to the floor, then stomped on it and kicked it for good measure. That son of a bitch! At least he should explain why she had to cancel what might have been the best night of her life. She slipped out of her blouse, grabbed something far less sexy off her makeshift closet rod, and found a pair of slip-on flats. The change of clothes helped reverse her mood, from light and hopeful to serious and pissed off. Perfect for work.

She phoned Gil while buttoning her shirt. "Bad news."

"Work?"

"How'd you know?" Val glanced in the mirror. Shit, her hair. Still soaking wet.

"We have the same job, remember?" Gil sighed. "All right. I can save it for tomorrow. Maybe then your father will change his mind and join us."

"You're being far too reasonable." But his light-hearted response lifted her mood. "Call you later?"

"You'd better."

She hung up, texted him a heart emoji, and opened the nearest random box, labeled "Food."

Right on top. The fucking hair dryer.

***

About to leave the garage to head to her car, Val stumbled over the box Dad had set by the door. Without intending to, she read the label scribbled on top: "Recycle/Donate." Underneath, he'd scratched through a name. "Rita."

Mom.

Val froze, wondering what possessions of her mother's Dad had relegated to the donation bin. Certainly nothing of great sentimental or monetary value.

She realized she would pass the donation center on the way to work. Might as well help Dad out. She lifted the box— or tried to. Instead, the removable lid flew up into the air, and the box stuck, for some reason, to the concrete floor.

She started to put the lid back on the box, but the contents caught her eye. The top layer consisted of some old women's clothes and scarves that went out of style decades before. Which, of course, could come back into style any minute now. Might be worth saving. She set the scarves on her bed, looked at a blouse, decided against keeping it. Set it aside. Glanced back into the box.

Lying on top, no longer hidden by the dated blouse, sat piles of unopened mail, in familiar handwriting, strapped together with rubber bands. Val picked up the first wad. The envelopes on top and bottom of the bundle faced in—no address visible. She considered reading one, decided against it. Too much like prying. She dropped it into the box.

On impact, the rubber bands, stiff and inelastic with age, crumbled into bits, and the letters fanned out across the top of the box. The one on top was addressed to her father, with no return address. Unopened.

Despite having not seen it in ten years, she recognized the handwriting as her mother's.

For a long minute, she could do nothing except stare, trying to convince herself that they couldn't be what they seemed: letters from her mother to her father. Letters she'd never seen or known anything about.

Val shook out of her stupor and checked the postmark: "Prescott, AZ," dated May 23, 2013. Six years ago.

She pawed through the burst bundle, a few dozen letters in all. All addressed to Michael Dawes in the same hand, mailed from cities all over the United States. The date marks spanned nine years, declining in frequency over time—about every other month in the early years, and only one in 2018. None so far in 2019. Only a few of the ones prior to 2016 had been opened.

She glanced around, made sure Dad hadn't sneaked into the room, and pulled the last opened letter out of its envelope, dated September 29, 2015.

Mike,

When are you going to write back? You promised to keep me up to date on Chad and Valorie. Did Chad go to law school? What did Valorie decide about college? She did go, right? You know how I feel about that.

I enclosed a picture of us. I understand if you don't want to share it with the kids, but I hope you do. They should know what's going on with the rest of the family.

Write to me?

Rita

Val checked the envelope. No picture. She shook it upside-down to make sure. Nothing fell out. Nothing stuck to the inside.

She shoved the letter back into the envelope, tossed it in the box, and sat on the floor, numb. For nine years, Dad had told her and Chad that he'd never heard from their mother— never once. That once she walked out that door, she'd turned her back on them forever. Because she didn't care about the family anymore. Didn't love them. The last time Val asked about her, Dad insinuated that he didn't even know whether she was still alive.

Val now had proof that she was very much alive—and had written multiple times to inquire about them. It didn't make her a good mother, but at least she'd shown some interest in their welfare.

Val got to her knees and scooped all the letters out of the box. She scooted across the garage floor to her own piles of boxes and unstacked the tallest pile. She shoved the letters inside the bottom box, resealed it with packing tape, and stacked the others on top.

She'd need to discuss this with Dad, and soon. At the moment, she needed to get to work.

***

Val arrived at the dull slab of concrete known as Clayton Police Headquarters twenty minutes later, parking her Honda in a visitor spot on the side of the building. She'd need a parking sticker for the employee lot, now that driving to work seemed a certainty for the foreseeable future. She'd miss the short bus commute from her old apartment, where she'd catch up on news and email. Driving sucked, especially in cities like Clayton, designed for the days when only the rich could afford to ride their horse and carriage through the narrow streets.

Always preferring exercise over convenience, Val hustled up the stairs to the fourth-floor WAVE Squad office. When she entered the main area, a rectangular open-air bullpen jammed with clusters of desks, computers, and generations-old mismatched tables and chairs, the animated busyness of over a dozen sworn officers surprised her.

"Dawes! Why aren't you in uniform?" Sergeant Petroni cast her a cross look, interrupting a stand-up briefing to a small team of plainclothes detectives. "I assume you keep one down in your locker. Everybody flies the flag tonight. Come on, hustle. We need to be on the street in under an hour."

"Of course." Val's ears burned. Grimes never mentioned that. Speaking of whom... "Where's Bobby?"

"Down the hall, Interrogation Room B," Petroni said. "He can fill you in when he's done, which ought to be soon. Go change. And wear a vest." She returned to her informal briefing.

Val's heart rate jumped up a notch. Petroni's advice to wear Kevlar—which she did anyway for patrol or street work—meant that whatever operation she had planned, the situation could get dicey.

"What's up, you guys?" Val asked a group of men seated at a table nearby. "Why all the excitement?"

"Some sort of sting," a uniformed officer replied, a stocky, graying veteran named Hodges. An insignia pin portraying a knife and automatic rifle crisscrossed over an eagle identified him as a member of the Special Weapons and Tactics Unit, also known as the SWAT team. Three chevrons revealed his rank as sergeant—a squad leader. "Whores and pimps and money men," he continued. "Something like that. Grimes is gonna fill us all in soon."

"No, right now," Grimes announced, entering the room. "Gather round, people. I've got news."

Val took a seat with the uniformed cops. She didn't know most of them, other than Price, who smiled and arched his eyebrows at her. He seemed pleased, as did Grimes, who bounced on the balls of his feet while waiting for everyone to settle in for his speech.

"Early Friday morning, Dawes and I busted a sex worker named Destiny Mathers. Destiny gave up the name and whereabouts of her pimp, a small-time operator who goes by Rodney Kingman. No relation to the guy in LA." He chuckled and seemed disappointed when no one else got his lame joke.

"Turns out," Grimes continued, "Kingman's rap sheet meant another bust could land him some serious hard time in a place where he already has enemies. We put the fear of God and prison in him, and he talked like a three-year-old. Today, the Vice Squad—thank you, gentlemen," and here Grimes nodded to the plainclothes guys standing near Petroni, "rounded up a handful of Kingman's teammates, so to speak. Other pimps, all of whom share one thing in common: a boss."

"Mob?" Hodges asked.

"Bigger than the mob," Grimes said. "A sex trafficking ring, extending from DC to Boston, maybe farther. These guys lure in underage girls and move them to another city, often across state lines. They've recently moved into Clayton. Tonight we want to push them back out—hopefully, shut them down. At least locally."

"Isn't this FBI territory?" Price asked. "Since it's interstate, and kids, and—"

"We're coordinating with the feds," Petroni said, stepping next to Grimes. "Their operations personnel can't get here tonight, and we need to move fast. We'll read them in as resources come available. For now, the show's ours."

"Which means they'll stop by tomorrow and take all the credit," Hodges muttered. "Typical gold-brickers."

"The operation will take place at this warehouse on Albany Street." Grimes set a blown-up street map of downtown on an easel. A red square indicated the site, a building abandoned years before by a now-defunct shipping company. "As you can see, it's a standalone facility, which means we can surround the entire property. Uniformed officers from Downtown Precinct under the command of Captain Feeley will secure the perimeter. WAVE Squad teams will enter here," and he pointed to the entrance on Albany, "and here," indicating a rear entrance. "SWAT team staff will accompany teams at both entrances."

Grimes covered the map with a building schematic printed on a piece of foam board about three feet wide. "Once inside, we'll work toward the middle, cutting off any means of escape. Dawes, come with me and SWAT Team A, through the front. O'Reilly and Price, you'll take the rear with SWAT Team B. Our informants tell us that our targets are in the office, located on the loft level, here." He pointed to a dotted rectangle off to one side near the center of the old warehouse building.

"Weapons?" Price asked.

Grimes nodded. "They'll be armed. The principals carry concealed handguns. Armed guards will possess rifles, possibly semis. SWAT units will steam 'em out with gas, then we swoop in, wearing masks if need be."

"How many?" another officer asked.

Grimes shrugged. "Best guess? Two to four with handguns, four to six more with rifles."

Hodges whistled. "This could get ugly."

Grimes spread his arms wide. "We'll have them outgunned and out-numbered, at least three to one, and we'll have the element of surprise. It'll be uglier for them than for us."

Val's heart pounded in her chest, and she recognized the look of fear on the faces of the deputies around her. Sure, they enjoyed a numerical and tactical advantage. A fat lot of good that would do for any officer who took a bullet in this raid.

The image of Gil lying on the ground, blood pouring from his shattered hip, sprang to mind. As did the memory of her uncle Valentin, who died a decade before in a shopping mall shootout. The idea that any of the officers in that room—

possibly her—could join them among the ranks of the fallen spooked her into somber silence.

"If there are no more questions," Grimes said, ignoring the hands rising in the back, "let's go."

Val pushed her heavy body up onto her feet. She met the gaze of Hodges, then Price, and nodded at each man. *I have your back*, each said to the other with their eyes. *I hope you have mine.*

"Val?" said a woman's voice behind her. She turned. Shannon O'Reilly, her partner when she'd started on WAVE a few months before, extended her hand. "I just wanted to let you know. I asked for you tonight. No offense, Damari," she said, turning to Price.

"None taken," her partner said.

Val swallowed hard and shook her hand. Shannon had once been Val's mentor, partner, and friend, one of the few she'd made on the force. They'd fallen out over Val's outspoken, somewhat brash approach to nabbing the Schoolgirl Slayer six weeks before, and hadn't spoken much since. "Thanks, Shannon. Good luck tonight."

Shannon offered a weak smile. "We'll have something better than luck tonight. We'll have you."

"Thanks." Val wished she could return the compliment, but Shannon's cautious approach often frustrated her. "Stay safe tonight."

"You too." Shannon bowed her head and stepped back, then sat down to talk to Price.

Val took the stairs to the basement level at a slow pace, her mind burdened by the prospect of danger, and distracted by the odd timing of Shannon's attempt to make up with her. Did O'Reilly fear her own mortality, wanting to make amends in case something happened to either of them?

That brought her father to mind. A number of issues festered between them that they'd never been able to discuss, much less resolve. She considered calling him, then thought better of it. He worried enough already. A call would only send him over the edge—perhaps back to the bottle. Best to keep him out of it.

On the other hand...

She tapped out a quick "Thinking of you" text to Gil and sent it. She didn't mind if he worried a little bit.

Chapter Five

The sun had set, but plenty of ambient light remained, washing the evening sky with a mix of pinks and blues behind the silhouettes of the abandoned industrial buildings on Albany Street. Police in dark blue uniforms and helmets took position on the perimeter of the property, fenced on three sides with weathered chain-link that looked weak enough to knock down with a good, stiff push. Val and Grimes crouched beside their squad car, Grimes on his radio, giving last-minute instructions in a low voice.

Val checked her gear one more time. Sidearm loaded, safety on. Spare ammo, ready. Taser, charged. Club, check. Cuffs, secure. Gas mask ready to wear. Radio on, earbuds in. No one would give away their location through an errant blast of static or voice communication.

"Ready, Dawes?" Grimes said at last. She nodded. He pointed to the warehouse, a two-story rectangle of sheet metal, painted blue fifty years before and now flecked with silver and black. A wide, metallic front door marked the official business entrance, next to a garage-style roll-up unit for loading and unloading. A white rectangle hanging over the door had long ago displayed a corporate logo, lit up during business hours. All that remained now were shards of plastic and a few loose wires.

"Follow me," Grimes said. He followed up with a terse "Moving in" to the rest of the team by radio and led Val in a crouched trot toward the warehouse. A half-dozen SWAT team members followed, rifles at the ready.

When they reached the building, Grimes nodded to Hodges, the SWAT team leader, who tried the door. Locked, of course. He waved them all back, attached something to the door frame, then scooted away. Pressed a button on a hand-held device. Val expected a loud *bang,* so the low-key "Whoof!" sound surprised her. The door swung open toward them, the locking mechanism a smoking, ruined mess.

"Love high-tech explosives, don't you?" Grimes said with a grin. He led them inside, Val on his heels, SWAT team members spreading out into the cavernous space that greeted them. Grimes flicked a switch, and a few bare bulbs hanging from metal rafters provided dim light, just enough to move around. The room spanned at least forty feet wide and twenty feet deep, with no ceiling other than the slanted metal roof. A front service desk sat to one side, more a formality than an obstacle. Gray shelves lined each wall and formed rows from front to back, empty save for some trash left behind by squatters and vagrants.

"We're in," Shannon's voice said in Val's ear. The rear entry team.

"Us, too," Grimes said. "Meet you in the middle." They conducted a cursory search of the room and, as expected, found nobody.

"You want the gas now?" Hodges asked on the radio.

"Not yet," Grimes said. "Let's get a visual first. I want to find those stairs."

Val recalled the building schematic. Behind the room's rear wall, the warehouse had been divided into two levels. At one time, forklifts and freight elevators moved cargo in and out as needed. The manager's office, which their targets had taken over, according to the informants, occupied the front left corner of the second level. Hodges postulated that the gunmen would position themselves up there, with clear sight of the stairs and both entrances. Shannon's team, entering from the rear by the utility rooms and restrooms, should be waiting at the door.

No doubt the gunmen heard them come in. They'd be ready, too.

Val crept to the entrance, this time leading the charge. She glanced through the tiny window. Too dark to see much. Tried the handle. Unlocked. She took a deep breath, checked in with Grimes. He nodded and waved her inside.

She opened the door, and all hell broke loose.

***

Maggie McCloskey navigated her GMC Yukon through the Clayton residential neighborhoods, relying on her memory rather than the car's built-in GPS. She didn't trust devices—or people—that told her what to do, when, and how. When in an unfamiliar place, you couldn't beat a good old-fashioned paper map.

Clayton was not an unfamiliar place.

True, she hadn't driven here in almost ten years, but the city hadn't changed much. Same crumbling streets, same feeling of hopeless poverty and despair. Few children played outside, unless you called roaming street gangs "kids at play." In some ways, it had gotten worse. Her favorite salon had closed, replaced by a sleazy check-cashing service run by the damned Arabs or Iranians. Probably used their exorbitant fees to finance plots against America. Next door, her favorite Italian eatery had sold out to the Mexicans. Burritos and tacos. Cheap crap that made people smell. Disgusting.

Even worse, at least a quarter of the shops along the strip had closed and remained shuttered. Faded painted lettering in picture windows, some half-covered with planks or plywood, spoke of better times in America's past. Before minorities had taken over everything. Proud times. Gone.

The corner where she'd always turned to go home, though, remained the same. The independent gas station and convenience store on one side, run by Zach and Nora Reynolds, deacons in the church Maggie used to attend. Sweet couple. On the other corner, Taylor's Burgers and Shakes. Brig Taylor and his wife often donated their money and time to Liberty Heights High's sports teams.

The Reynolds and the Taylors acted as gatekeepers of sorts: hard-working, honest, church-going folk who paid their taxes, sent their kids to the best schools they could afford, and served their community. Driving on, she passed modest homes with mature landscaping, moss-free siding and roofs, and clean, late-model cars in the driveways instead of on the street. People here still cared. They kept their houses nice, mowed their lawns, flew the flag—and not just on the Fourth of July, five days away. All year-round.

Most of the houses, anyway.

She pulled up in front of the home where she'd lived for fifteen years, the one she and her first husband bought after God gave them their first beautiful son. They'd had such big dreams then. She'd had no idea how hard it was to raise children. Stupid her, though: she'd gone on to have two more, even after learning from the first one how much sacrifice it required. Her own dumb fault for falling in love.

She focused again on the property and sighed in frustration. Weeds choked the front lawn. Paint flaked off the trim around the windows, and the roof needed replacing. Her ex had let the place go to pot. Like their marriage, and everything else he ever touched. Like the filthy, paint-scratched old SUV parked in the driveway, in stark contrast to her immaculate, two-year-old Yukon, its leather seats as pristine as the day she first leased the vehicle.

The entire scene—lawn, windows, roof, SUV—reflected the utter lack of discipline with which he'd lived his life. For that matter, even in how he raised the kids. In their seventeen years together, he never laid a hand on either of them. He "didn't believe" in spanking, or correcting them at all, it seemed. So they trampled all over him, never respecting him, and that bled over into her relationship with them. No doubt he poisoned their minds about her after she left.

She'd considered stopping, confronting him, demanding answers. A scrap of news about the kids, at least. But the condition of the house and yard told her everything she needed to know. He'd neglected himself and the kids as much as his castle. No doubt about it.

It seemed unlikely, then, that he'd help her reconnect with their now-grown children. After all, if they'd stayed close, wouldn't they pitch in with the upkeep? Plus, he'd done everything he could to keep them away from her over the years, out of spite. She'd need to find another way to reach them.

Maggie drove on. She'd lived a life without regrets, for the most part. This was not the moment to start. She had people to see, anyway. Business to conduct. America's business.

Try as she might, the image burned into her memory from the last time she drove away from that home flared into focus. The moment that symbolized her one true regret. A young girl, her face heavy with confusion, watching her mother leave for reasons Maggie couldn't confess. The girl would navigate her teen years without a strong female role model at home, and only a weak man to fill the gap.

It almost made her turn around and abandon her plans.

Almost. She hadn't then, and she wouldn't now.

She drove on, heading east, toward downtown. About a mile from the city's center, she turned north on Albany Street. Her associates had set up operations in a shuttered warehouse a few miles from City Hall in the decaying manufacturing district. Back in the day, it thrived, and the city's port served as a shipping hub in the region. Now, the extent of the city's decline became more obvious with every passing block. Many industrial sites, once the core of the region's blue-collar economy, appeared abandoned, with plywood covering broken windows, back-lit signs now dark and missing letters, parking lots empty. Shards of glass and shreds of garbage littered the streets, clogging the sewer drains. A mess.

A block before she reached her destination, though, the police had shut down the street. Squad cars blockaded the traffic lanes in both directions, blue and red lights flashing. Officers stood at the ready, hands positioned near their weapons, their expressions all business. Yellow crime scene tape circled the entire block.

No, not just the block. Another layer of uniformed police surrounded the old warehouse building itself, weapons drawn. Looking ready...to attack.

A raid! On the local Patriots Pride chapter! How—?

She turned onto a side street, hands shaking. Frustrated, she obeyed the slow speed limit for several blocks until the flashing lights disappeared from her rear view. Then she gunned it, taking the next corner on two wheels, rubber burning on the pavement, and accelerated toward the highway.

A city cop car appeared in the left lane, heading toward her. Maggie pulled over. The cop whizzed by, siren blaring, lights flashing. More help for the crime scene behind her. Moments later, a series of loud *pop-pop-pop* noises filled the air. Gunfire!

She remained on the side of the road, engine running, heart pounding, trying to catch her breath. Had she come straight to Headquarters instead of driving by her old house, they might have trapped her inside, swept her up in the operation. Caught her in the crossfire, even. At the very least, they'd have carted her away to jail with the rest. Unlikely she could talk her way out of it, either. They would run background checks, find too many red flags.

Her connections would have been of no use, then. They'd have cut her loose, despite her many years of loyal service. They'd find others to pick up the slack.

After several minutes, she regained control of her breathing. Her pulse slowed to almost normal, and her hands finally stopped shaking. Too close.

She phoned her superiors in Florida who'd set up this meeting. Told them what she saw.

"Stay in town, but lie low," they said. "Wait for further instructions."

She hung up. Time to find a motel that took cash payments and asked no questions.

Chapter Six

Red lights in the warehouse flashed on and off, blinding Val for a moment, and an alarm blared a repeating pattern of obnoxious blasts. Gunfire erupted in every direction. Bullets struck the metal door with loud thuds, and its tiny window exploded, glass flying everywhere. Men screamed, some in English, others unintelligible amid the cacophony.

"Get back!" Grimes shouted, as if anyone needed to be told. Val's belly hit the floor and she rolled away, bumping into Hodges, clutching his rifle. More lights flickered off and on.

"One shooter down!" Shannon reported over the radio. "Looks like three or four more on Level Two, at least two more on ground level. Let me know when you want in and we'll provide cover."

"Ready, Dawes?" Grimes said.

Another deep breath. "Whenever you are."

Hodges crawled to the door. He held up three fingers, counted down: two, one, then leaned back against the door, pushing it open.

"Now!" Grimes said, and gunfire erupted inside the room again. Hodges rolled backward and then to one side, and Val scrambled in after him on hands and knees. She crawled to the other side, taking cover behind a row of metal shelves filled with cardboard boxes, each large enough to hold an average microwave oven. Grimes and more SWAT team members spilled in after her, each taking similar positions, spread among the dozen or so long, wide aisles. The shelves, metal structures secured with heavy bolts, stretched upward at least twelve feet. The shelves' contents blocked the light emitting from fluorescent shop lights on the high ceilings—the few that hadn't burned out.

"We're in," Grimes said.

"Cover us, we're going up," Shannon said.

The SWAT team members poked their rifles around the corners of the shelves and sprayed cover fire toward the stairs, high enough to avoid hitting any of their fellow cops. Shannon led her team toward the wooden stairs ascending to the next level along the far wall. Extra safety lighting on the stairs, Val realized with horror, made them stand out as targets.

Hodges and his partner ran to join Shannon's team, firing without aiming as they ran, getting about halfway up the stairs before gunfire rained down upon them from above. A screaming Hodges fell and clutched his leg, a dark wet stain oozing into the fabric of his pants. His partner flattened onto the steps, firing wildly above them. The shooting from above paused, and feet pounded on the wooden floor overhead.

Val turned away from the action for a few seconds, steadying herself. She clutched her .38 pistol with both hands, her heart pounding like a drum corps out of sync. Surely they could hear it and would fire on her position at any moment. Her eyes adjusted to the dim light, and she imagined the shooters on the other side could see her as plain as day. She unclenched her jaw, already aching. Breathe in. Count to three. Exhale. Repeat.

A bullet exploded into the boxes above her, splashing a dark and viscous liquid onto the walls, and onto her and Grimes. It smelled like motor oil. Thankfully, not gasoline or something even more combustible.

"They're behind us!" Shannon's panicked voice sounded in her ears. More gunfire, screaming, and pounding feet. Val peeked around the corner of her aisle. Shannon lay on the stairs next to Hodges, sheer terror splashed across her face. Bullets ripped into the wall behind her, above her, missing by inches. Another one struck Hodges in the same leg. He screamed, an agonizing cry.

"We've got to do something!" Val hissed into her mic.

"Got any ideas?" Grimes shot back, his voice a hoarse whisper.

Val traced the gunfire raining on Shannon's position back to its source. Two men crouched behind shelves near the back entrance. Both aimed semi-automatic rifles at the stairs, firing in rapid succession. The slender man in front wore a light-colored T-shirt. The heavier man behind him blended into the dim light in a long-sleeved shirt and jeans. The closer one's shirt glowed in the fluorescent light. An unfortunate choice of clothing in a dark firefight.

She aimed at the slender man's torso, steadying her weapon with her free hand. Fired.

He fell back, clutching his left side, his rifle firing one last random shot as he collapsed onto the floor. His partner dove for cover, knocking boxes off the shelves. That kept him in clear view, and the attack on Shannon's position paused.

"Good shot, Dawes!" Grimes said. "O'Reilly, can you get out of there?"

"Cover me!" Shannon headed up the stairs.

The man in back checked on his partner. Val fired at him. The round lodged into the metal garage-door-style wall behind him, almost as loud as the report from her weapon. He dove back behind the shelves, then crept forward again.

Val guessed that he wanted to get into position to shoot at Shannon and her team again, sitting ducks while pinned down on the stairs. The shelves and their contents screened Val's view of him, but she calculated his position and fired. A loud grunt and clattering of wood and metal on concrete told her he'd dived to the floor. Scrambling footsteps told her she hadn't hit him—at least not anywhere vital.

Moments later, a door opened inward. Not the exit, though. From her memory of the building's schematic, Val guessed: the stairs to the basement, used for cold storage.

A blur moved through the door. The rifleman.

Val sprinted after him, reaching top speed in seconds. A bullet ricocheted off the concrete floor next to her into a box on the shelf. She ran on, faster. She reached the door and gazed into the dark basement. Nobody visible. Weapon drawn, she crept down the stairs. A musty odor pinched at her nose, along with the stink of urine and feces. Like a backed-up sewer pipe.

In the distance, footsteps sounded, along with muffled cries. Female. Probably behind the doors off to one side of the cavernous space. Captives? She started toward the sound.

Movement in the dim light stopped her. Another door opened and closed. Val ran toward it, pulled it open. An even darker space—no, a tunnel, missing from the schematic. At least a hundred yards long, its only light came from the basement area behind her.

Footsteps pounded on the tunnel floor ahead of her. She could just make out the shape of a tall, heavy-set man, holding what looked like a rifle, running away from her.

She lodged her pocket notebook in the crack of the door, propping it open, then turned to follow him. The rifle exploded ahead of her, bullet whizzing by her torso. Had she not turned...

She fired back, and footsteps echoed in the space once more. She ran after him, shot again. The bullet ricocheted off the concrete floor and walls. The man's labored breathing gave away his position as much as his heavy tread. She gained on him with every step. She'd last competed at a track meet over a year before, but she could still outrun garden-variety thugs carrying rifles.

The man reached the end of the tunnel, with Val about forty yards behind him. She expected him to turn and fire, but he surprised her by throwing the rifle to the ground and grabbing something metallic on the wall. A ladder. He hurried up the rungs, pushing a trap door open over his head. He reached up as if to pull himself up and out—

Val, approaching the ladder, readied herself for the leap. As if jumping the highest hurdle of her life, she lunged forward and upward, her right hand holding her weapon, the left stretching toward him. He lifted himself up, his feet dangling from the opening. Val grabbed the man's ankle, but her hand slipped to his shoe, and she feared it would slip off. Her fingers found purchase on his laces, and she yanked them hard, even as her body slammed into the ladder. She bounced off, still holding his foot. He grunted, screamed, kicked at her. Her grip loosened, but her feet found one rung of the ladder. Still, she'd lose her grip if he kicked long and hard enough.

He kicked again. She held on, somehow.

She'd have to use her weapon. But not in the usual way. She wanted him alive and talking.

Careful not to pull the trigger, she lunged upward and drove the barrel of her pistol into the man's groin. He screamed, and his considerable weight landed on Val's shoulders, knocking her off the ladder. He landed on the floor next to her, on his backside. His head smacked hard on the floor. A moment later, his eyes closed, and his body relaxed.

Val checked his pulse. Alive and breathing, but unconscious. She cuffed him to the ladder and leaned against the wall to catch her breath.

***

Val's earbuds exploded with noise moments later, snapping her back to the present.

"Dawes! Where the hell are you?" Grimes's voice shouted in her ear.

"Detained a suspect downstairs," Val said, breathing hard. "I heard women's voices down here. Should I come back up or—"

"Check out the voices. The pansies in charge of this gang surrendered without firing a shot. I'll send backup."

"Copy." Val checked one last time to make sure her suspect couldn't escape, then jogged back down the tunnel.

The basement's main section housed the typical utility appliances of a large building: furnace, water heater, electric panel, and an array of pipes running amid metal joists overhead. Off to her right, unpainted gypsum board with four factory-white three-panel doors created separation for what appeared to be small bedrooms or closets. No light shone from the cracks around any of the doors.

But whimpering sounds came from behind one—no, two of the doors. The two in the center. Val approached the nearer door, jiggled the handle. Locked. But it was a cheap lock, a keyed door handle, no deadbolt. She guessed the opposite handle lacked a keyhole, or had no knob at all. She knocked on both doors.

"Help!" replied a female voice, young—perhaps no older than fourteen or fifteen, from the closer door. Moaning and crying emanated from the other. Weak, sad, and desperate.

Val fished a thin wire out of her belt, already bent into a hook shape for this purpose. She slid it into the crack between the door and frame below the handle, jimmied it to find the latch, and found the right spot.

Seconds later, the first door swung open, exposing a closet about six by eight feet, also with concrete floors and unpainted wallboard. The dim light from the basement shined on a huddled figure, a female of Asian descent, shivering against the wall. Dressed only in her underwear and a camisole, the girl was filthy, with long black hair tangled around her neck and shoulders. The girl, or the room—or both—reeked of urine, feces, and blood. She couldn't have been more than twelve or thirteen.

The girl's eyes widened at seeing Val, and she curled into a tighter ball. "Don't hurt me," she said. "Please."

"I'm not going to hurt you," Val said. The girl winced, and Val guessed that her captors told her the same thing, countless times each day. "I'm Officer Valorie Dawes from the Clayton Police Department. Are you hurt?"

The girl sniffled, shook her head, then nodded. Only then did Val notice the blood splotch between her legs. Poor girl had her period—maybe her first—in this room.

Or... Val shuddered at what the men might have done to her to cause her bleeding. She stepped closer and crouched next to the girl, resting her hand on the girl's shoulder. "Would you like to get out of here?"

She nodded. Val helped the girl to her feet and placed her police jacket over her shoulders. It hung to her thighs, thankfully covering her stained underwear.

"What's your name?" Val asked.

"Vanessa."

"Vanessa, I'm Val. You're safe now," Val said in a low, soothing voice. "We've arrested the men who did this to you." Or killed them, but no need to shock her with that. "I'm going to check the next room over, okay?"

The girl nodded. "Britney's in there. Maybe another girl. I don't know her name."

Footsteps echoed on the staircase. Val led Vanessa out of her tiny prison and greeted Damari Price, entering the basement. "Help me with the other rooms. Vanessa, hang tight a moment, okay?"

Price nodded and ran to the door nearest him, at the last moment leaping and kicking the doorknob. The force of his blow loosened the knob and sent splinters of wood flying. Price howled in pain, holding his foot and swearing.

Val shook her head and held up her wire jimmy. "This is easier," she said.

Price scowled. "Do I look like a fucking burglar to you? Where'd you get that, anyway? Damn, that hurts."

"I made it. Comes in handy in times like these." Val jimmied open the door next to Vanessa's, where she'd heard moaning a few minutes before. Vanessa's prediction rang true: two girls, also about twelve or thirteen, lay huddled together against the back wall. It stank even worse than Vanessa's room.

"Which one of you is Britney?" Val asked.

A white blonde wearing a plain white T-shirt and panties jumped to her feet. "About fucking time. I heard shooting. You kill those motherfuckers?"

Val blinked, exchanging a wary glance with Price. "Let's just say it's safe to come out now." She turned to the other girl. "How about you, young lady? What's your name?"

"T-T-Tasha." She rubbed her legs for a few seconds, then stood. Val nearly vomited. A Black girl with tangled dreadlocks halfway down her back, Tasha couldn't have been older than ten. She wore a white chiffon ballet dress, stained with urine and feces, that barely covered her privates and hung like draperies on her skeletal form. "C-can w-we leave n-now?"

Val nodded, choking back tears. "Yes, you can go home now, Tasha," Val said. "You're free."

Chapter Seven

The raid netted seven official arrests, plus one that needed to wait. An ambulance brought the guy Val shot to Mercy Hospital, and his prospects for recovery appeared grim. Val didn't look forward to the paperwork, debriefs, and mandatory psych reviews she'd later endure for that. But all of that had to wait for the moment.

Grimes remained on-site until they completed a search of the premises, directing teams to different parts of the building. After handing over the imprisoned girls to medical staff, Val and Price donned latex gloves and searched the basement and tunnel. They found a locker in one of the unoccupied rooms that contained girls' clothing—lots of it. Dozens of outfits of various sizes, ranging from torn jeans and popular-branded T-shirts to short skirts, high heels, and crop-tops, filled the lockers. "Hooker clothes," Price said, holding up a leather bustier. "Not exactly age-appropriate."

"What *is* the appropriate age for a girl to become a sex worker?" Val snapped. "Come on, help me find something they can wear home." She guessed at their sizes and found some Levis, sandals, and cotton tees. They bagged the rest as evidence after a forensics team dusted the rooms for fingerprints.

Grimes greeted them at the top of the stairs and pulled Val aside. "Dawes, we want you and O'Reilly to head to the hospital and debrief the girls. We figure they'll be more at ease talking to women." He paused a moment. "Are you two gonna be okay working together on this?"

Val heaved a deep breath. She wanted to spit out an immediate "yes," but the word stuck in her throat. She spied Shannon across the room, chatting with a few lingering SWAT team members, her eyes darting toward Val. Shannon looked as uncertain about their pairing as Val did.

"Sure," Val said after too long of a pause. "Not a problem."

"Good. Meet me at HQ after for a debrief." Grimes turned to leave.

"Bobby, can't that wait until morning? It's going to be a long night." Val gestured toward the dark skylights overhead, which, in late June, meant it was well after 10:00 p.m. Gil's lasagne had long since gotten cold, but he'd still be up, awaiting word from her.

"Sleep when you're dead," he said, snickering. "We've got work to do."

Val clenched her jaw and exchanged eye rolls with Price. "He'd better bring coffee and donuts," Price said with a half-smile.

"If not steak and eggs," Val said. "I ate a granola bar for dinner."

Shannon waved at Val, then pointed to the door. Val nodded and met her there.

"Okay if I drive?" Shannon asked, holding a set of keys.

"Don't you always?" Val said, then regretted the sharp tone. "I mean, yeah, sure."

Shannon winced. "I just thought, since you rode over with Grimes..."

"Right. No, it makes perfect sense. Let's go."

***

The trip to Mercy Hospital took less than ten minutes, but felt like hours. Shannon gushed about how well the raid had gone, and Val contributed an occasional "yeah" or "mm-hmm," and not much else. Mercifully, Shannon ran out of platitudes by the time they pulled into the hospital's visitors' lot.

"The girls are in the trauma wing," Shannon said as they approached the front door. She stopped before triggering the automatic opener and turned to face Val. "Are we okay, you and me? You're quieter than usual."

"Yeah, yeah," Val said. "Tonight was intense."

Shannon crossed her arms, frowning. "It feels like it's more than that. Something...personal."

Val stuffed her hands in her back pockets, rocking on the balls of her feet. She met her former partner's gaze, found the hurt there, and sadness replaced the irritation inside her. "Yeah, well, things didn't really work out for us, last time we worked together. I felt...mistrusted, I guess. Disrespected."

Shannon's gaze fell. She licked her lips and scratched the sole of her shoe on the pavement. "Fair enough. I held some things back from you—under orders, though. Not by my choice."

"So, you're throwing Brenda under the bus?" Val scoffed and stared up at the stars. "Nice."

"We needed to find out who was leaking—"

"And you thought, sure, it *could* be my partner." Heat rose in Val's voice. "So let's not tell her what we're up to, see how that goes. Right?"

"No!" Shannon fumed, uncrossing and recrossing her arms. "Brenda explained all this. We made it appear we were pinning it on you to flush out the true culprit. Which worked, remember?"

"I remember." Val threw her hands up in disgust. "I also remember you snitching to Petroni about every mistake I made while learning this job. In your mind, that included me refusing to obey a vague 'order' to conduct an illegal search. Good times, Shannon."

Shannon started to object, then shut her mouth again. After a long pause, she nodded. "We'll agree to disagree about the search. As for the rest, for the hundredth time, I apologize. Please don't continue to hold this grudge against me."

Val scowled. Hundredth time? Bullshit. The two women hadn't exchanged a dozen words in the six weeks prior to the pre-raid meeting.

But they had business to conduct, and they needed at least a semblance of cordiality between them.

"I accept your apologies. All of them," Val said. "Let's proceed under the assumption of mutual trust and respect. After all, these girls deserve our very best."

"Agreed." Shannon reached out, both arms wide. Val cleared her throat, hunched her shoulders, and turned away a bit. "Oh, sorry. You're not a hugger. I forgot."

Val bit back her retort. No one who'd spent ten minutes around Val could miss that she still suffered anxiety over being touched, especially by strangers. She allowed only a few people in her innermost circle that privilege. Shannon no longer fell into that category.

"It's okay," Val said with a nervous shrug. "Let's go find out what these girls can tell us."

***

They started with Vanessa, the Asian girl who they'd discovered first, alone in her own filthy basement closet.

"I'm Detective O'Reilly, and this is Officer Dawes," Shannon said when they joined Vanessa in the hospital examination room. Shannon remained standing, and Val sat on a nearby rolling stool so she could take notes. The room, all white and antiseptic, smelled like bleach and was about ten degrees too cold. Medical charts on the wall displayed the internal organs of male and female figures from the knees up to the chin.

Vanessa remained seated on a padded bench, sipping from a carton of chocolate milk. An empty, rolled-up McDonald's bag rested next to her. She had cleaned up and gotten dressed in loose-fitting jeans, tennis shoes, and a Baltimore Ravens sweatshirt.

"Vanessa, right?" Shannon said. "What's your last name?"

"Kumari." Vanessa finished her milk. "Can I have another one of these?"

"Sure thing." Shannon glanced at Val.

Val glared back, not budging. She wouldn't run Shannon's errands anymore. "There's a machine down the hall. You need money?"

Shannon sighed, a noisy expulsion of air and frustration. "I'll be right back."

"And some chips?" Vanessa asked. "Barbecue?"

Shannon grimaced, then forced a smile. "Absolutely." She disappeared into the hallway.

Val smiled at Vanessa. "They didn't feed you very well in that little prison, did they?"

Vanessa dropped her empty milk carton and McDonald's bag in a nearby trash can. "Th-they s-said they wanted us s-skinny." Her eyes welled with tears.

"They were not nice men."

Vanessa shook her head, eyes widening.

"How old are you, Vanessa?"

The girl bit her lip, then answered in a low voice. "Thirteen. Almost. My b-birthday's in a f-few weeks."

Val's heart twisted into a knot. Vanessa was the same age Val had been when Milt, a friend of her parents, raped her. She'd never imagined that a girl could suffer a worse fate at that age. Vanessa clearly had.

"Where are you from, Vanessa?"

"Towson, Maryland."

"Near Baltimore, right?" Val said. "A friend of mine went to Towson State."

The girl nodded. "My s-sister goes there."

Val smiled and jotted down some notes. "Have you called home yet? Your parents must be worried sick about you."

"I t-talked to m-my d-dad. He-he's c-coming l-l-later tonight."

Val noticed the girl's stutter increased when she talked about her home and family. "Flying up, I hope?"

Vanessa nodded.

Shannon returned with the requested drinks and snacks. "I got you a Snickers bar, too. Everyone likes Snickers, right?"

Vanessa smiled and tore open the candy wrapper, taking a huge bite and chomping with unfettered glee. "I love Snickers," she said with her mouth full.

Val showed Shannon her notes. Shannon sat next to Vanessa and rested a hand on the girl's shoulder. "Can you tell me anything about what those men did to you?"

Vanessa froze in mid-bite, the candy hanging from her lip. Tears flowed down her cheeks like rain. "I-I t-told the doctor. Th-they s-s-said I wouldn't h-have to—to—umm," and she broke down, burying her head in her hands. The candy bar's chewed end stuck in the girl's long, straight hair.

Nice work, Shannon, Val groused to herself. Smooth.

Shannon, oblivious, pulled the girl in for a hug, patting her shoulders and muttering in her ear. She freed the candy from the girl's hair and handed it to Val. "Sorry, so sorry. It's okay."

Fighting the revulsion rising within her, Val moved closer, sitting on the other side of Vanessa. She patted the girl's arm.

With unexpected abruptness, the girl sat up, breaking Shannon's embrace. "It's not okay! It fucking sucks!" She stopped and stared at them, covering her mouth. "Sorry for swearing." She wiped away a few tears.

"Not a problem," Shannon said. "Cops hear that sort of thing all the time."

"We don't mean that it's okay what they did to you," Val said. "Believe me, we know it wasn't."

"Yeah, yeah." Vanessa rolled her eyes. "You're an adult, so you *know*. Sure."

"No, not because we're adults," Val said. "Because as women, we've experienced some pretty nasty stuff ourselves."

"Not this! Not what we went through!"

Val and Shannon exchanged sad glances. Shannon's gaze seemed to plead with her: say something!

Val thought for a moment. She knew what she needed to say. It wouldn't be easy.

However, having fewer ears in the room, particularly ones she no longer trusted, would make it easier.

"Shannon," Val said, "would you mind giving us the room?"

Shannon stared at her, mouth agape, then closed her mouth and stood. "Sure. Whatever. *Partner*."

Val ignored her sarcasm and waited until she'd shut the door. Then she held Vanessa's hand and met her gaze. "Vanessa, I'm going to tell you something in confidence. Something I've told very few people, ever. If I do, can you promise to keep it a secret?"

Vanessa stared back, her eyes hardening. "Will you keep my stuff secret, too?"

Val sighed. "Honestly, I can't. So I won't ask you to, either. I'll tell you anyway, okay?"

Vanessa nodded, sniffling. Waiting.

Val drew in a deep breath. Here goes. "When I was your age—almost exactly your age—a man...raped me."

Vanessa's eyes grew wide, and she gripped Val's hand harder.

"He was a family friend," Val said, "a man my parents trusted to keep me safe while they were attending to an emergency with my brother. He came into my room, my own bed, and overpowered me. There was nothing I could do. Then, he threatened me, saying if I ever told anyone...well, he made it clear I shouldn't do that. He said that if I did, everyone would think that I was a slut. That it was my *fucking* fault."

Vanessa gasped. Val smiled. "Sorry for swearing."

After a moment of holding her breath, Vanessa let out a tiny giggle. "Sorry. That was funny."

Val laughed, too, and tension flowed out of her. "I guess it was, kinda, huh? Anyway, for a long time, I never told anyone, or hardly anyone. So this man...he got away with it. Totally. Now, he's God-knows-where, probably abusing some other girl. All because he convinced me to keep my mouth shut. Which I was glad to do, you know? I mean, whoever wants to talk about something like that?"

"It sucks," Vanessa said, crying again.

"Totally," Val said. "Beyond."

"So beyond."

"Infinitely beyond."

Vanessa gazed into Val's eyes, her face contorting as if to cry again. Then her expression changed into a resolute frown, a look of utter determination and courage. "Those fuckers. They're not getting away with this."

"No, they're not."

"They threatened me, too. Said they'd cut my...you-know-what off."

Val recoiled. She could imagine a few things that could mean, none of them good. "No way they can do that now. Unless they go free, I mean."

"If I tell you what they did," Vanessa said, "will they...will you and the courts and everybody kill them?"

Val smiled. "Probably not." Connecticut had banned capital punishment five or six years before. "But I guarantee you, if you *don't* tell us what they did, they will get away with it."

Vanessa sat up straight in her chair. "No way," she said. "Okay. I'm ready."

Val readied her pen and notepad, then set them down. She wouldn't need notes.

***

Val found Shannon a half-hour later, emerging from a room similar to Vanessa's, a few doors down the hall.

"Britney, the blonde girl, is from Rochester, New York," Shannon said. "She's thirteen. Her 'roommate' Tasha, the Black girl? Ten. Ten goddamned years old!" She shook her head. "Anyway, she's from Atlanta. What about Vanessa?"

"Twelve, from Maryland," Val said. "Shannon, they've got girls from all over the eastern seaboard, *except* around here. Doesn't that strike you as weird?"

"Destiny, that girl you and Grimes busted the other day. Isn't she from Clayton?"

"She's only lived here for a few months," Val said. "She's moved here from Memphis to be closer to her mom, who's serving time upstate. At least, that's the story she gave me."

"So, four girls, four different states," Shannon said. "Grimes says that the perps are from all over, too—from Ohio to Florida and everywhere in between." She blew air out from loose lips. "You know what that means, don't you?"

Val shook her head. "Not following you."

Shannon grimaced. "It's interstate. As in, federal. As in, Bureau of Investigation. They're going to take over this case, sure as sugar."

Val tossed one shoulder up, let it fall. "Makes sense, doesn't it?"

"Yeah, but hell. Fucking FBI. Once again, we do all the work, they grab all the glory."

Val rolled her eyes. "There's plenty of glory to go around tonight."

Shannon's cell phone chimed an Irish jig. She answered. "Hey Grimes, s'up? Oh, really?" She made wide eyes at Val. "So, seven, then. Any word on the rape kits? Right. Okay, well, I'll tell her." She hung up and crossed her arms. "Bad news," she said.

"From the forensics team?" Val said. "Oh, wait. You said seven. Don't tell me they let one of the guys go."

"Not exactly," Shannon said. "The eighth guy, the one you shot...died a few minutes ago."

Val fell back a step, like a ton of bricks had fallen on her. For the second time in her short police career, she'd killed a man. A criminal, yes. Scum of the Earth, no doubt. But a human being.

"Fuck," she said, and dropped into a nearby chair, drained.

Chapter Eight

After taking a few minutes alone to collect her thoughts and emotions, Val rejoined Shannon for a silent ride back to Headquarters. All hopes of returning home for some shut-eye before filling out mountains of paperwork vanished with the death of the man she'd shot. Even the cretins at Internal Affairs would stay up late for the opportunity to grill her over when, where, and why she pulled the trigger. Never mind that it was a planned, armed raid on a known criminal hotspot.

But even that had to wait.

"The guy you ran down and cuffed to the ladder is waiting for you in Interview Room 403-B," Grimes said before Val could sit down in WAVE headquarters. "I'll observe."

"Didn't you already take care of that?" Val said, surprised. "Why wait for me? You're a better interrogator, anyway."

"I took the first four," Grimes said, "and I need a break. Anyway, I thought you might want the experience, since you're the one that caught his sorry ass."

"Fine," Val said. "Give me a minute to prepare."

"Take as long as you need," Grimes said. "Are you done yet?" He laughed and popped a hard candy into his mouth. The aroma of peppermint mixed with stale coffee wafted over her.

"What did the others give up?" Val asked. "Anything I can use?"

"Not much that we didn't already know," Grimes said. "All of them claim that someone else is in charge, but nobody can 'remember' the bosses' names. Even the local boss. An epidemic of criminal amnesia. I guess we need to go check the water pipes for lead…or stupid drugs."

"Then they lawyered up, right?" Val said.

Grimes nodded. "The ambulance chasers haven't arrived yet. So get in there before they do. Nothing shuts up a perp like a paid mouthpiece."

Val sat at her desk and jotted down a few notes, but Grimes's warnings and his continued hovering made her feel rushed. She folded the page of notes and stuffed it into her back pocket. "Let's roll," she said.

She entered the interrogation room moments later, a cramped, rectangular room with a rickety wooden table in the center. On one side of the table, her suspect slouched in a stiff wooden chair, his hands and feet cuffed. The chair, bolted to the floor and far too small for him, looked like someone salvaged it from a 1950s middle-school classroom. The suspect faced a one-way mirrored wall, behind which Grimes and perhaps others observed and recorded the interview. Bright overhead fluorescent lights flickered on the other three walls, solid shrines of light-green concrete block, emanating cold indifference.

Val stood across the table from the man, who still hadn't looked at her. His thick frame spilled out in all directions: elbows bent at his sides like wings, legs bowed under the table. An orange jumpsuit hung on him like he'd been trapped inside a parachute. Sweat dripped off stringy, dark hair, bushy eyebrows, and the stubble of his sunburned, leathery skin. The room stunk like the boys' gym lockers her soccer team had to use after some of their high school meets, and had even less air circulation.

"So, Mr. Tyler Paxton, is it?" Grimes had supplied little more than the man's name, age (thirty-one), and short rap sheet. He didn't look up, even then. "I'm Officer Dawes."

Paxton sat stone-cold still in his chair.

"You're a pretty good runner for a man your age."

That earned a glance and a smirk.

"Did you ever run competitively?"

He exhaled a loud huff of air that smelled like tobacco and looked away.

"I'll take that as a no. Too bad. I'm sure Granville, Ohio High School could have used you."

That resulted in an eye roll, nothing more.

"Or were you a Denison College boy?"

He spat. A definite no.

"Yeah, I figured you more for an Ohio State kind of guy," she said.

"Ha!" Paxton clammed up as soon as the sharp bark of a laugh escaped his mouth.

"Did you bring Vanessa here?" she asked. "Granville's near Cleveland, isn't it?"

"What am I, your fucking Ohio geography teacher? Buy yourself a goddamned map," he said. His voice, a raspy tenor, carried a hint of a Canadian accent.

Val sat in the chair across from him, hands folded on the table. She waited until he looked up. "Tyler. Can I call you Tyler?"

"Can I call you Officer Flaws?" Paxton snapped, a smile curling on his lips.

"Good one," Val said without missing a beat. "That's one I haven't heard. I've heard Does, Doesn't, Doll, and my favorite, Dogs. You boys, you're so clever with names."

"What the fuck do you want?" he asked. "I ain't talking."

"Of course not. I don't expect you to, or even want you to." Val yawned and covered her mouth. "Fact is, I go home right after this. So if you just clam up, I get to sleep in my nice, soft bed within the hour. You, though—you won't be so comfortable tonight. Or tomorrow. Or for the next twenty to fifty years, if you live that long. You know what they say about the life expectancy of child sex traffickers in prison? 'Solitary, nasty, poor, brutish, and short.' Emphasis on the nasty and short."

He glowered at her. "You're making that shit up."

She shrugged. "Nope. Thomas Hobbes coined the phrase 300 years ago. And the penalties? Sorry, no. Kidnapping in Connecticut gets you ten to twenty-five. Same for child sex trafficking. You're a felon on probation, so add illegal possession of a firearm. Then for the big one—attempted murder of a police officer—add another ten to twenty-five. Soonest you'd get out on parole would be, let's see...2043?" She leaned back in her chair. "What kind of job do you think a 55-year-old triple felon would land then? Assuming, again, you live that long."

"I didn't kill no cop!"

"Attempted. You know that gun you fired in my general direction?" Val tapped her badge. "That's on film, Ty-boy."

"Don't fucking call me that!" Paxton lunged at her, but the chains held him back.

She smiled. "Sure thing. What should I call you?"

"Don't call me nothing. Officer *Flaws*."

"Ouchie. That hurts so much."

"What the fuck's your problem?" He tugged at the chains again, rattling them as loud as he could. "Dumbest damn interrogation I've ever been in."

"Oh, right. You've been here before." Val pulled out her notes. "Three, no, four priors. Second felony. I forgot to take that into account in my prison math. So, my guess is, no parole until 2055, maybe later." She gave him a level stare. "With any luck, you may never get out. Alive, that is."

"Bullshit. I was just hired for security a couple of days ago. You can't prove I did any of that kidnapping shit."

"Under the RICO statute, I don't have to," Val said. "Just that you were part of the conspiracy. Which, obviously, you were."

"Fuck off. I was not."

Val shrugged. "You were there. Oh, I admit, you *almost* got away. You ran, Ty. Which makes me think. Maybe you're telling the truth about being a recent hire."

"Damned straight."

"Anyway," she said, "it doesn't matter what I believe. You clam up here and you go down with the others on the triple-felony charge. Multiple counts, too. Oh, that also changes the sentencing math...let's see, three times two times ten times—"

"Wait, what?" Paxton sat up a bit. "What's all that got to do with me?"

She cocked her head and put on a puzzled frown. "Tyler. Come on. They taught you math in Granville Elementary. Three counts each of kidnapping and sex trafficking—"

"I didn't do nothing to those girls!" he shouted, banging the table with his handcuffs. "I never saw 'em before you opened up those doors. All they told me was, don't let anybody in, even cops. *Especially* cops. And fucking liberals."

"Yeah, cops and liberals, the worst," Val said. "They *hate* seeing young girls sold into sexual slavery. Imagine."

"I *told* you, I didn't know *nothing* about no *girls*," he said, his voice rising again.

"So, who did?" Val asked in a conversational tone.

"I got no idea."

"Hmph. Not very helpful."

"I don't know nothing. I swear."

"Okay," Val said, standing. An idea occurred to her. "See you in 2055. Oh, and by the way, Pedro says he'll wait for you."

Paxton froze in his seat, gripping the edge of the table with whitening fingers. "What the fuck?"

Val smiled down at him. He'd bought into her little fiction. Good. "Pedro. Your partner in 'security'? He walked out of here ten minutes ago with some guy in a suit. I guess he decided he didn't want to go to prison for the rest of his life. Probably figured you'd get smart like that too, but—"

"He talked?" Paxton leaned forward, the tendons in his neck taut, his pronounced Adam's apple bobbing in his throat. "Fucking Pedro?"

Val took a breath, glad she remembered the other shooter's name right. "I recall he has kids somewhere, kids he probably wanted to watch grow up. Changes your perspective, I'm told, once you have babies, right?"

"Pedro named me?" Paxton's sweat poured over his face, turning redder by the second. "Pedro *hired* me! He's the guy that pays me, that little twerp!"

"Pedro's one of the bosses?" Val said, letting her surprise show.

"He's *the* boss," Paxton said through gritted teeth. "Of everything. The whole platoon."

"Platoon?" Val's ears perked up at the use of military jargon.

"That's what they call the unit. Pedro's the captain. I'm a goddamned foot soldier—still a private. Still on fucking *probation*. They ain't even decided whether I'd stay on past this week. And he says I'm the one that took those girls? Jesus!"

"A case of the pot calling the kettle black?" Val sat down again.

"That piece of shit-scum!" Paxton pounded the table again. "I ain't going down for him. No way!"

"I don't blame you," Val said. "I mean, you've only been there a week or so, right?"

"Four days!"

"That's a terrible trade, thirty years of prison for four days' work," Val said. "Sounds like you're getting screwed."

"I ain't taking the fall for no fucking Pedro!" Paxton yanked at his chains again. "I ain't even gotten paid yet!"

Val nodded and gave him her best sympathetic gaze. "Tell me more about Pedro and his little platoon," she said.

***

Grimes intercepted Val on her way to the WAVE office, grinning ear to ear.

"Great work, Dawes!" He slapped her on the back with a little too much exuberance. "Way to make that guy sing!"

"What'd you learn?" Shannon asked, standing in the doorway. She waved them inside and shut the door, then led them to the long meeting table where a bleary-eyed Brenda Petroni sat, sipping coffee from a Styrofoam cup.

"Pedro, aka Peter Soto, is the ringleader of this outfit," Val said. "I believe he's still in custody?"

"Sure thing," Brenda said. "Nobody leaves until a judge gives the order, which won't happen before Monday."

"When you say 'this outfit,' do you mean there's more?" Shannon asked.

"There are cells all over the eastern seaboard," Grimes cut in before Val could answer. "That's why none of the girls or perps are local."

"Except Destiny, sort of," Shannon interjected.

"I meant the underage girls you found in the basement," Grimes said. "I'm betting dollars to donuts that we'll find cells in every girl's city of origin. Rochester, Atlanta, and so on."

"My theory is, they move the girls as fast as they can to another city, out of state, where they force them into sex work," Val said. "After they've broken them by keeping them locked up and starving, that is."

"That checks out," Shannon said. "All three girls went missing in the past week. I bet we'll find girls from the Clayton area in one or more of the other cells, and so on."

Brenda nodded. "Great work, guys. What physical evidence do we have to back it up?"

"We haven't verified it yet, but we seized phones, computers loaded with email, and papers and files from their office," Grimes said. "Plus all their weapons, which we can trace to points of sale. I doubt many of them came from Connecticut stores."

Shannon's face darkened. "Which means the feds will definitely take this one over," she said.

Brenda's expression soured. "No doubt. But that's the rules, gang. Okay, do your follow-up...tomorrow. It's almost 2:00 a.m. You've all earned some sleep. Go get it."

As the others stood to leave, Shannon held up her hand. "What about our UOFs?" she asked.

Val groaned. The department mandated that officers file UOFs, or Use of Force forms, within 24 hours of any incident involving weapons or hand-to-hand combat with a suspect.

"You have..." Brenda checked her watch. "Nineteen more hours to finish them. As a courtesy, I asked downtown to open a UOF record for each of you on the system, with the basics already filled in. All you need to do is fill in the details for your particular situation. Except—who fired the shot that took down the DOA?"

Dead on Arrival. Val's stomach grew queasy. She'd been told he died during surgery. "That'd be me, Sergeant."

Brenda sighed. "Yours is a little more involved. O'Reilly, as the Officer in Charge of the raid, you'll need to sign off on that one, too. But tomorrow's fine." She took Val's elbow in her hand and held it in a light grip. "You okay, Val?"

Val swallowed hard. The lump in her throat wouldn't go away. "I'll be fine."

Brenda held her gaze for another few moments, then let her hand drop. "Okay," she said, nodding. "I'll need you here by 10:00 a.m. I think I can hold off the Internal Affairs guys until then. Get some sleep, okay?"

Val nodded, but she knew that wouldn't happen.

***

Arriving home a short while later, the concrete floor and unfinished walls of the garage struck Val as way too similar to the hot, cement-block room in which she'd left Tyler Paxton an hour before. She'd always kept her living quarters spare and simple—*Spartan*, Beth always called it—and the drabness never bothered her.

Until now. Tonight, the stark surroundings kept the events of the past few days fresh in her mind. A sex-trafficking ring, right there in Clayton, and she'd waltzed right into the middle of it. Even shot and killed a man, one she'd never met. She wondered what sort of desperation drove a guy into working for a syndicate that imprisoned little girls into a depraved, miserable life. Talk about desperation.

After an hour or two of tossing and turning, Val gave up on sleep. She turned on the light and searched her still-unpacked crates for something to read. She found nothing that sparked her interest.

Ah, but Dad had stowed some more boxes in the corner. Maybe she'd find something good in there.

She opened the top box and found it crammed with boys' clothes—Chad's stuff he'd outgrown and never threw out. Another held sports gear and memorabilia: her brother's Little League championship team photo, a charity golf trophy—her Dad's? Her jiu-jitsu belts, from white to brown, and a *gi* she outgrew several years before. No books.

A second box felt heavy enough, and sure enough, it held books—her brother's college textbooks. Way too much political science and finance crap. She set it aside. A third held a mish-mash of old school supplies, baseball cards, and obsolete chargers for long-ago-discarded electronics.

The fourth and final box held no books, but plenty of treasure.

Right on top sat a shoebox, with "Family Photos" scrawled on top in Dad's handwriting. The steady hand of his pre-alcohol-addiction days, that is. She lifted it out of the storage bin and set it on her lap, then peeled off the lid and grabbed a handful. A 4"x6" framed copy of her college graduation photo sat on top. Chad's *Yale Law Review* photo rested underneath, also framed. High school photos filled the next layer, a mix of hers and her brother's. Beth's, too, for some reason. Those must have come from Val's old room.

Then, a photo of a tall brunette in a knee-length dress, holding a baby girl in her arms, and the cherubic face of a small boy hugging her knees. Everyone wore their Sunday best. "Rita - Chad - Val's first Easter, 1996," read the inscription in her dad's handwriting on the back.

She almost set the picture down, but found that she couldn't. She leaned back against the wall, studying the photo. Dad had taken it, she guessed, in the front yard, a sunny day in April. Rita—Val refused to call the woman who abandoned her "Mom"—looked so young, almost as young as Val's current age of twenty-three. Which couldn't be true. Rita was older than that when Val was born. But she *looked* so youthful. Val always thought of her as being so old, like Dad. As kids do, she mused.

The other unusual thing about the picture: her mother looked *happy*. Val couldn't remember her ever being in a good mood unless she'd downed a few drinks. Even then, Rita wasn't so much happy as boisterous. She had a drunk's laugh, loud and unselfconscious.

Come to think of it, she couldn't remember Rita laughing when she hadn't been drinking.

She tossed the picture back into the box and pawed through the others. Photos of Chad and Val at various ages, mostly before their mother left. Annual school photos. A few with Rita, almost always smoking or holding a drink. Precious few of Dad—he almost always hid on the other side of the camera.

Then, toward the bottom of the box, she found some newer ones. As if they'd been hidden there on purpose. One of Uncle Val—his police service headshot, one she saw every day in the lobby of Clayton PD Headquarters, in the photo gallery of the fallen. A candid of Uncle Val and Dad together, dated 2008. Another of a very pregnant young Rita and three-year-old Chad at the Dinosaur Park in Rocky Hill. She'd later grow to love the Dinosaur Park. The idea of missing out on a trip there—even before her birth—made her burn with jealousy for a moment. She turned the photo over to read the inscription. "September 1995," it read. Three months before Val was born. She smiled.

Then she studied the handwriting again. Long, elegant strokes, in cursive. Her mom's handwriting. At the bottom, more of her handwriting—an inscription, in tiny letters. "With M.M."

M.M.?

Her blood ran cold. She only knew of one person in her parents' circle of friends with those initials.

"Uncle" Milt, the man who'd raped her ten and a half years ago.

What was Milt doing with her mother and brother at Dinosaur Park—without her father?

Sunday, June 30, 2019

Chapter Nine

Val reported back in to work early the next morning—a few minutes after 8:00 a.m.—something she avoided most Sundays. But she wanted to get the UOF report done before everyone else showed up so that she could focus on the case when the rest of the team arrived.

Which she *almost* accomplished. But Brenda Petroni rolled in around 9:15 with surprise written all over her round face.

"Didn't I tell everyone 10:00?" Petroni lifted an empty coffee pot and grimaced. "And why isn't this full of paint remover, as usual?"

"Sorry, I didn't expect anyone yet." Val saved her file and jumped up to help with the brew. She yawned and scooped coffee grounds into a basket-shaped paper filter.

"Lucky for you I'm in a good mood, or you'd be facing the kangaroo court at high noon." Petroni filled the coffeemaker's reservoir with bottled water and peered closer at Val. "Did you sleep at all?"

"I'll make up for it tonight when my paperwork is done." Val placed the coffee filter into the basket and pushed the "brew" button on the coffeemaker.

"How are you feeling?" Petroni pointed to an empty chair and sat next to it. "About...you know. The shooting and all."

Val took a few seconds to respond. "It all happened so fast. In the moment, I didn't think about it. He represented a threat to the team, and I reacted. It wasn't until I learned of his death that it hit me."

She paused and swallowed. "I've only been a cop for nine months, and already, for the second time, I ended a man's life. He was a criminal—a gangster—so better him than one of us. But still." Val sat, her body heavy and without energy.

"I get it. He was a fellow human being."

"A living, breathing soul," Val said. "He probably had family and friends who loved him, and who miss him this morning. I—I know what that's like, Sergeant. All too well."

Petroni spoke in a quiet voice. "I know you do, Dawes. Which is why the department has psych protocols."

Val groaned. "Not Dr. Cyrus again."

Petroni smiled and patted Val's arm. "I know Chris Cyrus isn't the softest and cuddliest of psych counselors. But he does valuable work and gives us excellent results."

Val fumed in silence. Cyrus counseled her when Clayton PD first hired her, and again after her prior two shootings, one of which ended in a fatality. In her case, some might argue his results had been anything *but* excellent. But pressing that point would do her no good if she wanted to remain on the WAVE Squad. "What should I do while I wait for him to clear me?"

Petroni shrugged. "Take a day or two off...after today, that is, which I promise will be a short one."

"Tell that to my wife," said a male voice. Bob Grimes shut the WAVE office door behind him and tossed a gray suit jacket onto his desk. "She's convinced I'd rather be here than at home and that I don't remember my kids' names or birthdays."

"Okay, I'll bite," Petroni said. "Name them."

"Er...Brooklyn is...twelve?" Grimes shook his head, grinning. "And Bobby Junior was born in October. I'm almost certain of it."

"Don't you have *three* kids?" Petroni said, smirking.

"Hush, or I'll name the next one after you. When's the staff meeting, boss? Do I have time to get my UOF filed?"

"Going by your past UOFs, that shouldn't take you more than a minute," Petroni said. "How many rounds did you fire, anyway?"

"Twelve," Grimes said. "Based on the number of bullets left in my second magazine."

"Twelve minutes, then. Yes, I promise. You'll be playing golf by noon, at the latest."

"Awesome," Grimes said. "My tee time's at one. That gives me time for lunch."

"Sergeant," Val said, "are you sure about that? Don't we need to follow up on the leads we gathered last night? That ought to take a few days, at least. If we wait until tomorrow, won't some of those trails go cold?"

Petroni sighed. "I was going to hold off on telling you guys until everyone got here. I guess it doesn't need to wait. I'm about ready to burst anyway." She stood, and both Val and Grimes gave her their full attention.

"The FBI is taking over the case," Petroni said. "They'll be taking copies of our files and will conduct some follow-up interviews over the next few days. Otherwise, we stand down."

"Typical!" Grimes slammed his desk with an open palm. "Typical FBI. Fucking Bullshit Interlopers. You're right, Sarge. My report won't take a minute."

"We won't have any role at all?" Val said. "In a case situated right here in Clayton?"

"Local support," Petroni said. "Running down leads as they need help, answering questions—"

"Serve as their fucking errand boys—and girls." Grimes nodded at Val. "Screw that. They can get their own damned coffee. Speaking of which..." He stomped over to the coffee machine and poured a cup from the still-brewing pot.

"It's not like we have a choice," Petroni said. "The fact is, it's an interstate sex trafficking case. It falls under their jurisdiction, like it or not."

"So, we do all the hard work, put in the blood, sweat, and tears, and they steal the glory." Grimes sipped his coffee and grimaced. "By the way, how's Hodges doing?"

Val recalled Hodges, the SWAT team member, bleeding and writhing in pain on the warehouse stairs. She'd almost forgotten about him in all the excitement since.

"Stable," Petroni said. "Lost a fair amount of blood and will need surgery on his knee. But they expect a near-full recovery."

Val swallowed some guilt over that. She and Shannon had spent hours at the hospital the night before, interviewing victims. But neither had looked in on their fallen colleague.

"So, get your paperwork done, and go home after we debrief. Then forget about this case." Petroni turned to Val. "And please. Get some rest."

Val ambled over to her desk and stared at the computer screen. Forget? Rest? Never going to happen.

***

Despite a short night's sleep, Val had too much nervous energy to attempt daytime slumber. She needed, more than anything, to confront her father over what she'd found in the garage. But that had to wait until Dad returned from his Sunday morning Alcoholics Anonymous meeting—assuming he'd gone. If not, they'd confront that instead. Neither of those scenarios fit Val's emotional state at the time she left the downtown precinct.

But she thought of a better alternative.

She drove straight to Gil's, a 1960s ranch-style home about a mile from her old apartment. She found his sturdy, six-foot-two-inch frame relaxing in a wooden Adirondack chair in his modest front yard. Gil's thick, wavy black hair looked damp, as if he'd just towel-dried it after a shower. A rough stubble dotted his chin. He wore khaki shorts, sandals, and a plain gray T-shirt, revealing a thin sheen of sweat on muscular arms.

Gil grinned, set down an oversized New England Patriots coffee mug, and waved at the empty chair next to his. "Next time, call first, and I'll heat up some leftovers," he said once she got out of the car. "Assuming you don't mind lasagne for breakfast."

"Sounds dreamy," she said, hurrying up the walk. "Extra garlic?"

"Dees phrase, 'extra' garleek, vee have no word for dees in our language," he said in a garbled East European accent. "How many kilos make extra?"

Val laughed, sat on the arm of the chair, and wrapped him in a tight hug. "You smell like you ate kilos of garlic. Is there more coffee?"

"Not until I taste your lip gloss."

Val caught her breath, and her heart beat faster for a few seconds. Then she planted a soft smooch on Gil's lips. Even after six weeks of dating, every kiss brought on a hitch of anxiety, a product of spending far too many years avoiding physical contact with men. Fortunately, Gil's tender embrace always left her heart swimming in warmth.

She pulled back and stared into his dark brown eyes. She'd read somewhere that a man's eyes always reveal his true feelings. He radiated calm and joy at that moment.

"That's all?" Gil said. "You must not want much coffee." He kissed her again, his tongue dancing between her lips, his powerful arms holding her tight. She draped her arms around his broad shoulders, and his hands slid down to her hips. A shiver followed a light caress down her spine. "Maybe we should go inside," he murmured into the nape of her neck.

"Is that where the coffee maker is?" she said, grinning.

He laughed. "Never let it be said that Valorie Dawes lacks focus. Okay, come on in and enlighten me as to why you graced me with this surprise visit."

Val hopped up and handed him the crutches leaning against the wall. "What? Can't a girl visit her boyfriend without having an ulterior motive?"

"Please, tell me you have an ulterior motive." Gil's eyes widened. "One that I can get behind."

"Hush," she said, blushing. She opened the door and led him inside, noticing that he carried his crutches instead of using them. He sat on the black leather sofa and leaned the crutches against the matching love seat. She took his empty coffee cup into the kitchen, refilled it with the hot, dark brew in a pot three-quarters full, and fixed herself a giant mug as well.

"I heard about last night's raid," Gil said. "How's Hodges doing?"

"He'll live, but he'll never beat me at hurdles." Val joined him on the sofa. "Or even you. His knee is a mess."

"Crap. Well, I'll refer him to my rehab team." He paused. "There's something you're not telling me."

Val expressed a loud gust of air and shook her shoulders. "We arrested seven. The eighth guy, I...shot. He..." She shuddered, swallowed hard, and tried to speak. Couldn't.

"I'm sorry, honey." Gil held Val's hand. "How are you feeling about it?"

Val shrugged. "Kind of numb. He was a bad dude, but still a human being, you know?" She stared at her feet, grateful for Gil's silent, understanding company.

After a minute, she met his gaze again. "That's not all." She drew a deep breath and cleared her throat. "We found three girls. *Young* girls—ages ten to thirteen. From all over the East Coast. From what we can tell, the men were..." She paused. "Forcing them into prostitution."

"Jesus. In Clayton?" Gil squeezed her hand tighter. "You okay?"

"I want to cut their damned balls off," Val said.

"I've got a rusty butter knife."

"Don't tempt me. Anyway, the feds swooped in this morning and took over. We're done with the case."

Gil sipped his coffee. "Bastards let our guys take the bullets, and they go stealing the headlines."

"Yeah. Anyway, that's not what I wanted to talk about." She set her mug down and folded her hands. "I discovered something in Dad's garage." She told him about the inscribed photo of her mother, taken by Uncle Milt.

"You're sure?" he said in a low voice. "It couldn't be anyone else?"

"I know of only one other person with those initials." She hesitated. "Mickey Mulroney."

"That asshole of a detective in South Precinct?" Gil scoffed. "Yeah, it ain't him. Have you asked your dad about it?"

Val shook her head. "I'm wondering if I should. On the one hand, it *might* have been an innocent outing. Milt was their friend, close enough that we treated him like family. Even called him 'Uncle.' Until..." Her voice trailed off.

Gil waited a few moments before replying. "And now, you're afraid of how your dad will react."

Val nodded. "He's been really good about staying sober and going to meetings. I'd hate to trigger a setback."

"What does your brother think?"

Val slapped her forehead with an open palm. "I'm an idiot. I haven't even asked him."

"That seems like a pretty safe first step." Gil thought for a moment. "Tell me if this is an impertinent question." He paused, took a deep breath. "Did Milt have anything to do with your parents splitting up?"

Val pondered that. "Possibly. I asked my dad a million times, 'Why did Mom leave?' He never gave me a good answer. 'Mommies and Daddies fall out of love,' blah, blah. As for my mother, I haven't heard from her since the day she left. Chad and I suspect that the whole incident..." She paused to make sure Gil knew what she meant by "incident" without having to say "when Milt raped me" out loud. "Even though they never acknowledged what he did, we believe it caused a huge rift between them. That led to more drinking, which made things even worse. Maybe Mom blamed Dad for bringing Milt into our home, exposing me to that danger."

"Even though she never believed you?"

Val sighed. "Yeah, that part doesn't make sense."

"Seems like Dad would feel more guilty than Mom."

"Which could explain why his drinking got so bad," Val said. "After a while, they stopped hiding their fights and mutual animosity. Eventually, Mom couldn't take it anymore, and she left."

"Eventually meaning, about a year after it happened, right?"

"Right. So not very long." Val lay back in her seat, hands folded across her stomach. "Of course, I blamed myself for letting it all happen."

"Val," Gil said, worry in his voice. "You know better now, right?"

"Intellectually, sure. Emotionally..." She closed her eyes, fighting tears. The couch cushions shifted beneath her, and the weight of Gil's body shifted close to hers on the sofa...but, other than his hand on her wrist, not touching.

"Look," he said, "I'm no expert on any of this. But it ought to take a lot more than guilt over your being assaulted by this guy to induce a mother to leave her kids. Are you sure there isn't anything else?"

"No, I'm not sure. As I said, Dad never gave me a straight answer. Probably trying to protect me." Val barked out a hollow laugh. "Against what, though? Not a damned *rapist.*" Saying the word made goosebumps rise on her skin.

"I'm sorry this happened to you," he said.

Val shrugged. "The worst part is, I was just moving past it a little, making some small amount of peace over it. Being with you has helped so much." Gil smiled at her, and she kissed him, a soft, lingering caress of tender lips. She leaned back against the sofa, expelling a whoosh of air. "I wish I could forget about it. But if anything, I'm more obsessed about finding out what happened than ever."

Gil nodded, a somber expression on his face. "How can I help?"

Val leaned forward, pulling him as close as strength would allow. "You're doing it. Exactly the right thing."

He squeezed tighter and held her for several minutes.

"So," she said, leaning back from him. "Want to take a road trip?"

Gil shot her a puzzled grin. "Where?"

Val stood, still holding his hand. "I think," she said, "that it's time you met my brother."

Chapter Ten

Maggie turned off the TV in her shabby little motel room, fighting the urge to throw the remote into the garbage. Of course, morning-after media coverage of the raid focused on how "heroic" the cops were, the horrific conditions in which the "criminals" kept the girls, and how the raid shut down a huge "threat" in the community. Idiots. So enamored of uniforms and flashing lights, the sheep would buy anything that made them feel like they were living in a cop show.

She opened her suitcase to unpack her wrinkled clothes. Last night had been too much of a shitstorm to get around to it. Even then, the local news got it all wrong. Little did these numbskulls know where the true threat lay. Or, rather, they didn't *want* people to know. Because the gullible morons in the liberal media were, themselves, part of the problem. Them and their over-reaching, nanny-state partners in government. They believed in the stupidity of their viewers, and in that sense, they believed right, in her opinion.

Of course, there was plenty of stupid to go around. The fools her organization had put in charge of the regional operation had gotten sloppy. Mistake number one: recruiting and retaining a local, exposing themselves to predictable breakdowns. They'd gotten greedy, keeping the girl, Destiny, for themselves, not sharing her or her earnings with the network. A cardinal principle: all resources support the central cause.

Maggie laid out her blouses on the spare bed and plugged in her travel steamer. She could create more steam faster with her sour mood than with the stupid gadget. She wished she could afford a hotel that did this as a complimentary service for guests. But not in this tight-fisted organization. They didn't believe in expense accounts.

Which led to the group's second mistake: being penny-wise and pound-foolish. For example, treating the girls like cattle instead of valuable, fund-raising assets. Locking them in disgusting little rooms without proper food or shelter made for bad TV. Now, public opinion would unite against them. All the good work done here, lost.

Mistake number three: keeping so many staff onsite. Too many eggs in one basket. Another cardinal principle violated: keep it lean and dispersed, always.

With eight men down, that left, according to her information, only four employees free. At least two of them disappeared into the wind, running like scared little babies. Good riddance to them. They were replaceable.

On that note...

She opened the folder on the nightstand by the bed and scanned the top page, a list of new local resources to recruit. Her number one job was to make contact, to find insiders that could help prevent future disasters. Collaborators who could tip the organization off, enable them to secure or destroy assets before the enemy seized them.

Ironic that the raid occurred on the very night that Maggie arrived to commence her mission.

Oh, well. A major setback, but not irrecoverable. She'd encountered worse in other cities, where she'd inherited much less groundwork to build on. Here she'd already built a network. History. Connections.

The steamer hissed and emitted a damp cloud onto the dresser. She aimed it at her most wrinkled blouse, letting the steam act as an iron—smooth enough to make it wearable in a day or two. Then she turned on her burner phone and speed-dialed the first name on the list.

"Mulroney."

She closed her eyes, took a breath, and counted to ten. Did nobody understand discretion anymore? She couldn't imagine answering a call from an unknown number and announcing her identity like that.

"Did you receive the information?" she said in a monotone. Experience taught her never to show excitement or emotion in recruitment or negotiation.

"Yeah. I looked at it." Clayton Police Detective Mickey Mulroney sniffled, a sound that nearly made her gag. "I'm interested."

"Are the terms to your satisfaction?" She finished one side of the blouse and turned it over.

"Well..." The detective emitted another crude noise, like the smacking of lips. Good God, man. Put the donut down for ten seconds. "The compensation could be a little more generous."

"I see. Well, I apologize for wasting your time, then." She set the steamer down, then brushed her hand over the mouthpiece. Let him think she was hanging up.

"I didn't say it wouldn't work," the detective added, his words rushed. "I just mean, well...I'm taking an enormous risk here, and, you know..."

"And the future of the country isn't worth sacrificing a few shekels and taking risks for. Yes, I understand you," she said. "Perhaps my search for true patriots has hit a dead-end here." She hung the blouse on the shower rod and considered her other options in the department. Not many. Few, if any, possessed Mulroney's combination of attributes: a decade or more from retirement, angry at being passed over for promotion, and with a long, if tenuous, connection to her past, thanks to her late brother-in-law. She needed to play him with care here.

"No, no. I'm not saying that. Look, I'm in, okay? And not for the money. What you guys are after is overdue. *Way* overdue."

She smiled, relieved. "On that, we agree. So, you'll help us?"

"Any way I can. But I can't access the files on what went down Saturday night," he said. "That info is all on a need-to-know basis, and the fibbies swooped in and took it all out of house. Rat bastard feds, always—"

"That's understood." She returned to her laundry. "That's not the type of information I'm after right now." She noted the revelation about the FBI taking over the case. That was important, and a nice freebie from the unaware detective.

"I'm confused," he said. "I thought you wanted updates on planned raids and stuff."

"Yes, of course. Always. But that ship has sailed here, has it not?"

After a few seconds of silence, he responded. "I guess so."

"At the moment, we have other needs you can help with." She chose a second blouse to steam.

"Like what?" Doubt crept into his voice. "I told you last time, I can't go busting guys out of jail. That's over the line, and they'd haul my ass—"

"Let the lawyers take care of that," she said, growing impatient. "I'm looking to expand the network a little. I wondered if you knew of any other of your colleagues who'd be willing to join the cause."

"Clayton cops? Uh, I dunno, maybe I can give you some leads."

"Excellent. Don't restrict your scope to your own department. Other cities, county sheriffs, state...even a federal agent, perhaps?" Some of the steam bounced back at her, scalding her fingers. She swore and set the steamer down again.

"Oh, okay. Sure, I got contacts all over. Let me think on it. How should I get them to you?"

"Do you have access to secure internet?"

"Sure, sure. The precinct's network—"

"Don't be a fool," she said. "I mean, secure *from* the prying eyes of the government."

"Oh. I'm not all that good with computers." His voice brightened. "Hey, my son could help me. He's great with this stuff."

"No!" She shook her head. Dumb, dumb, dumb. *He* should be doing her laundry. He didn't seem capable of much else. "If you can't find a secure private network, then we'll use the next best thing. Find public Wi-Fi, like at a coffee shop."

"What? I don't understand."

"It's called hiding in plain sight. Using public sources makes you almost as hard to track down as a secure network."

"Oh, I get it," he said. "Everyone uses those networks. It's a needle in a haystack."

"Right. Just remember to pay cash for your coffee and never use the same place twice. Now, I'll send you a code to scan. That will bring up a secure site where you can enter the information. Got it?"

"Cool," Mulroney said. "Wow, you guys are so organized."

She hung up, clucking her disdain. With soldiers like Mulroney on the front lines, sometimes she wondered how the government didn't collapse of its own foolishness.

Then again, he probably never touched a pile of laundry in his life. Maybe he wasn't as dumb as he seemed.

***

After a quick lunch, Val drove her Honda to Chad's house in Danbury, with Gil riding shotgun. The drive took about an hour, and they battled good-naturedly over control of the radio station. "Michael Bublé, really?" she complained with a grin. "Five minutes of that and I'll fall asleep at the wheel."

"One more minute of gangsta rap and I'll hip-hop out the window." He pressed the "search for station" button again.

They compromised on a harmless 80s station and sang along to the tunes they recognized, and otherwise caught up on office gossip. Her air conditioner struggled to keep pace with the heat and humidity building outside, even on its maximum setting. At one point, Gil rested his hand on her thigh, adding even more clammy heat to her leg, and she brushed it away without thinking.

"Something I said?" He play-frowned at her. "Or am I singing that far off-key?"

"Oh, sorry." She blushed. "That was sort of an autopilot response." She reached over and held his hand for a minute.

"Something else bothering you?" Gil asked after a while. "You seem quieter than usual."

Val nodded. "I hope you'll forgive me, but I need to tell you the reason I wanted you to come today."

"Besides the pleasure of my company?"

"That, too." She paused another moment, collecting her thoughts. "Chad and I haven't been getting along so well lately, because...well, I feel he forced me to move in with Dad."

"He guilt-tripped you," Gil said, "but if I recall, the final decision was yours."

"Whose side are you on?" she snapped.

"I calls 'em as I sees 'em," he said, smiling, but with steel in his eyes. "Anyway, I think it was a good decision. And it's not permanent, right?"

"Right. But it's caused a lot of friction between us. It's weird, because we've always been close. He's one of the few people I ever told about the rape. After Mom left, Dad's drinking got worse, so Chad—just a high school kid at the time— looked after me. We used to say it was him and me against the world."

"You'll get back there," Gil said. "I know you will."

"But today, we're not," she said. "And I know my temper can get a little short, so I'm hoping you'll keep your eye on that and, if it's not too much to ask, step in when you see that happening?"

Gil eyed her sideways, biting his lower lip. "It sounds like a bit of a mine field," he said. "But okay. I'll tread lightly, but if I see you spiraling, I'll speak up."

She nodded and wondered how soon she'd need him to intervene—and if he'd live up to that promise.

Chapter Eleven

Val and Gil arrived at Chad's sprawling, four-bedroom brick ranch a little after 2:00 p.m. New shrubs and rose bushes dotted the perimeter of the house. Like all the neighbors' properties, trim, golf-green grass filled the remainder of the quarter-acre yard. Chad's BMW sat next to his wife Kendra's Lexus in the driveway, both surrounded by puddles of soapy water, as if they'd just finished washing them.

"Nice rides," Gil said. "Your brother's law practice must be going well."

"Don't all corporate lawyers rake in the big bucks?" she said with a wry smile. "Another reason he didn't become a cop."

"Besides it being a shitty, dangerous job?" Gil laughed. "We should ask if their security department is hiring."

"Daddy! Auntie Val is here! Auntie Val is here!" Val's niece bounded out of the house in a purple one-piece swimsuit. She treated the puddles like hopscotch squares, generating tidal splashes with both feet and giggling as only six-year-olds can do. By the time Val's feet hit the pavement, the adorable little imp looked like she'd swum from the house to the car.

"Ali!" Val threw her arms wide, then enveloped her favorite pint-sized human into a crushing hug. In moments, Val, too, was drenched. "Let's get inside before your dad grounds us both for playing in the rain," she said, tousling the little one's hair. Ali laughed and dragged her by the arm through most of the same puddles, despite the presence of a dry sidewalk running parallel to their wet path.

"Wait for me!" Gil pushed the passenger-side door open.

"Omigod, I'm so sorry!" Val picked Ali up and carried her piggyback to the car, then set her down and helped Gil with his crutches. "Ali, this is my, ah, *boyfriend,* Gil." Her ears reddened. She hadn't thought through how she planned to introduce him, and the situation caught her flat-footed.

"Hello, Officer Kryzinski." Ali followed her formal greeting with a curtsey, even pretending to hold the hem of her invisible dress far above the wet ground. Then she jumped up and down and squealed in delight. "You're just as hunky as Mom said you'd be! Can I help hold your crutches?"

Val reddened, but Gil grinned. "Okay. You grab the right one and make sure it doesn't get wet, okay?" He winked at Val. "She's adorable," he mouthed to her.

Noise by the house drew their attention.

"Come on inside, you little fish," Chad called from the doorway. "You too, Ali." His lopsided grin, Big Bang Theory T-shirt, black-rimmed glasses, and unruly mop of shaggy brown hair qualified him as the poster child for Nerd of the Year. He traversed the wet driveway in sandals, splashing as much as Ali had, and extended his hand to Gil. "I'm Chad, Val's older brother. You must be Gil."

Gil accepted the handshake, trusting Ali to hang onto his crutch. "We've sort of met. At one of Val's many award ceremonies. I've changed my look since then. I was in a wheelchair at the time."

"Of course. Please, come in out of this heat and I'll get you something to drink."

"Can Auntie Val sleep in my room?" Ali said in a pleading, sing-song tone.

"I think Auntie Val and Uncle Gil would rather sleep in the guest room," Chad said. Val blushed at the "uncle" reference, and Gil grinned. Chad ignored them both. "Besides, you have school in the morning. I know how Auntie Val likes to keep you awake all night."

"I promise I'll sleep!" Ali said. "Please?"

"Next time," Val said, blushing again. She hadn't shared with Chad the status of the physical side of her relationship with Gil...or the lack thereof. "We need to make this a brief visit."

A slim, pretty woman in her late twenties, with auburn hair, green eyes, and perfect skin greeted them at the door, tall glasses of iced tea already in hand. "I'm Kendra," she said to Gil. "Welcome to our home."

"I see where Ali gets her good looks and manners." Gil accepted the glass of tea. "Certainly not from these Dawes characters."

"I could have left you home, you know." Val gave his ribs a playful punch.

"Don't you dare even suggest such a thing," Kendra said, helping Gil across the threshold. She guided him around a scattering of baby toys to their dark, cushy sofa and helped him get comfortable. "Ali, please find a convenient place for Mr. Kryzinski's crutches."

"I'll hide them in my secret, super-safe Wonder Woman closet!" Ali dashed down the hall, crutches still tucked under her arms.

"Someplace a little closer, please," Kendra called after her, then surrendered a sheepish grin and disappeared after her. Somewhere in the back of the house, a baby cried. "I need to change Dar's diaper," she called moments later. "Go on ahead without me."

"Come on, I'll give you a tour," Chad said. He led them into the kitchen, then out to the spacious backyard, where Ali reappeared to show off her trampoline and swing set.

"What, no golf green?" Val clapped for one of Ali's acrobatic flips on the trampoline.

"Who has time to golf? It took me a month just to set up the play equipment."

"Fancy stuff, though," Gil said. "When we were kids, my brother and I had a basketball hoop that fell down twice a week. Half the time, one of us held it while the other took free throws. See all these bumps on my head? My brother was a terrible shot."

Chad laughed. "Next summer, we're thinking about putting in an above-ground pool and giving Ali swim lessons."

Val sighed. "All the things we wanted as kids and never got. Nice, Chad."

He walked them back through the kitchen and down the stairs to show off his "man-cave," a workout room with weights, a treadmill, and a large-screen TV.

"So, Val," Chad said, "how's the move going?"

Val cocked her head and gave Chad a take-no-bullshit glare that made him cringe. "Rocky and uncomfortable. But you knew that would be the case when you suggested it."

"I only tossed it out as an idea because, well, you needed a place, and Dad needs support, so—"

"It's *fine*, Chad." She glared at him again. "And *temporary*."

"Of course. I appreciate it, Val. As does he, I'm sure. How is he adjusting?"

"Not well," Val said. "It's been a roller-coaster ride for him. It's forced him to sort through some stuff—emotional and physical—that maybe he wasn't prepared for."

"Such as?" He led them back upstairs.

Following behind him, Val glanced at Gil, who nodded encouragement. "I discovered some memorabilia he'd stored in the garage—"

"Wait, you're going through his stuff?" Chad led them back to the living room, where Kendra rejoined them, holding fourteen-month-old Dar in her arms. "Bad idea, Val."

"Not on purpose. I'm living in the garage for now—don't shake your head at me." Val sat with Gil on the sofa. "It's complicated. Anyway, I found some old pictures of Mom, and one of them shows you, very young, with her at Dinosaur Park. She's clearly pregnant with me, and a note on the back said, 'With M.M.' I wondered if you remembered anything about that day?"

Chad shook his head. "Naw. I was, what, maybe three years old? I remember going again later, with you and the whole family." He glanced at Kendra, then looked away when she frowned at him.

Val smelled a rat. She could always tell when he was holding something back. "So, who's M.M., then? Any theories?"

Chad paused, avoiding Kendra's furrowed brows, then wagged his head again. "No good ones."

Val fumed and squeezed Gil's hand, hard.

"Bad theories work," Gil said, taking the cue. "If you've got one."

Chad started, as if he'd forgotten about Gil. "I'm not sure what I've got qualifies as a theory at all."

"Tell me anyway," Val said.

"Come on, Chad," Kendra said. "How many people with those initials do you know?"

"A dozen. Don't you?"

Kendra rolled her eyes. "Name one."

Chad stared at the floor, his tongue running back and forth over his lower lip. Dar fussed a bit, and Chad took him from Kendra. "You okay, little guy?" He pushed a yellow pacifier back into the boy's mouth.

Val sighed. "Chad. Why is this so difficult for you to answer?"

"Can you say hi to our company, Dar?" Chad wagged Dar's hand at them, and he spit his pacifier onto the floor with a sharp giggle.

"Darwin Michael Dawes," Chad scolded him in a playful tone, "now why would you do that?"

"Takes after his aunt," Gil said, a twinkle in his eye. "I can never get her to stop spitting on the floor."

Ali bounced back into the room, once again soaking wet. "Who wants to play Chutes and Ladders with me?"

"In a few minutes," Chad said. "The grown-ups are talking right now."

"What are we talking about?" Ali sat cross-legged on the floor.

"My mother's secret past," Val said before Chad could sugar-coat it, the way he always did. She smirked and continued in a hoarse whisper, "As an international spy."

"Cool!" Ali said.

"Ali," Kendra said, glaring at Val, "why don't you go change into some dry clothes?"

Ali moaned and trudged down the hall, complaining under her breath about "never being allowed to do *anything*."

When Ali disappeared out of earshot, Val picked up the thread. "Chad, why does talking about Mom make you so uncomfortable?"

"Everything about your family's past makes Chad uncomfortable," Kendra said. "I keep telling him we all have horse thieves and bootleggers in our family trees. But he seems determined to allow our children to grow up ignorant of their ancestry. Aren't you, darling?" She flashed a faux-sweet smile at him, and Val detected an undertone of hard frustration in her expression.

"No," he said. "I prefer to focus on the brighter future of our progeny, rather than the dark misdeeds of our forebears. What's so wrong about that?"

"The problem is that those 'dark misdeeds' are part of our story, what makes us who we are today," Val said. "Wouldn't you agree, Kendra?"

"Absolutely." Kendra sat in a plush recliner with Dar on her lap. "So, what do you know about this 'M.M.' guy?

"Only that he was a friend of my mother's," Val said. "Any ideas?"

"Well, there's that Milt guy," Kendra began.

"And that cop friend of Uncle Val's," Chad interjected. "Mulroney or something?"

Val nodded. "I didn't know Mickey and Uncle Val were friends."

"Your uncle trained Mulroney, I think," Gil said. "So, they had a bit of a history."

"How long ago?" Val stole a glance at Chad, who seemed relieved, as if he preferred that the conversation focused on this Mickey guy, rather than Milt.

"Twenty years or more?" Gil shrugged. "Way before my time. We could look it up."

"The timing of that matches," Chad said. "Around the time you were born."

"Uh huh." Val cleared her throat. "Milt was around even longer. He and Dad go way back, don't they?"

"Not sure," Chad said.

"Wait, I thought Milt was your mom's friend?" Kendra said, bouncing Dar on her knee. "That's what your dad told me."

"What?" Val's face curled up into a puzzled frown. "That's weird. I thought he worked with Dad. Chad?"

Chad shrugged. "He was friends with both of them," he said. "He and Dad used to golf together."

"And play cards and watch football," Val said. "However, if Mom knew him first…"

"I don't know about 'first', but they were definitely closer," Kendra said. "After our wedding rehearsal dinner—well, your dad was pretty drunk," she said, reddening.

"As always," Chad mumbled.

"Anyway," Kendra went on, "he said something about wishing your mom should have been there. But she didn't show, he said, because of that 'asshole boyfriend of hers, Milt.' Don't you remember that, Chad?"

"He was drunk, like you said," Chad said.

"*Boyfriend*?" Val bolted up in her seat. "Boyfriend as in, a boy who's a friend, or as in, lovers?"

"Could be either," Chad said, louder. "Or neither. A figure of speech from an angry drunk."

"It seemed at the time he meant boyfriend as in 'old flame,' or…" Kendra paused, withering under Chad's baleful stare. "Or…I'm not sure if he meant anything by it at all."

Blood pounded in Val's ears. Gil reached over and patted her arm, then took a deep breath, indicating that she should, too.

Screw that. "You're saying that my mother and Milt once dated?" Val said, her voice tight. "Like, before she married Dad?"

Chad tilted his head to one side, and he held up a hand to silence Kendra, who'd opened her mouth to speak. "Possibly. I kind of got that impression from stories they sometimes would tell."

Something about his explanation still seemed…incomplete. Val pressed on. "Or, *after* they were married?"

Chad's gaze met hers, and his face fell. "Now that you mention it…I'm not really sure. I've been so consumed by hating him, I never gave that element much thought."

"Fuck!" Val's breathing became fast and shallow. Kendra's eyes widened, and she glanced at Dar, then back to Val, pleading in her eyes. "Sorry," Val said. "Chad, you're telling me that the man who *raped* me ten years ago was also our mother's secret lover?"

"P-possibly," Chad said. "Again, I don't know."

"Holy sh—sorry," Val said, glancing at the now-sleeping Dar. "Holy *cow*. How long have you known this, Chad?"

Chad swallowed hard, his nervous glance shooting between the two women on either side of him. "I—I don't *know* anything. Kendra's guessing, as am I. As for how long...well, like Kendra said. Since our wedding." His voice fell to a whisper. "I'm sorry, Val. I should have mentioned it sooner."

"Val," Gil said in a quiet voice, "When is the last time you, or anyone in your family, interacted with this Milt guy?"

Val took a moment, steadying herself. "So far as I know—and have believed all of my life—a few weeks after he raped me. He showed up at a soccer game. My uncle confronted him—at that point, he was the only one I'd told. I didn't tell Chad until several months later." She stole a glance at Chad, whose glum glare sent the clear message: *See. I'm not the only one who keeps secrets.*

"When Uncle Val saw Milt, he went a little berserk. He slugged him and threatened him, said he'd send him to prison," Val went on. "Before he could prove anything, Uncle Val died in that supermarket shootout. On..." Her voice shook. "On my birthday."

Gil squeezed her arm. "When did Mom leave?"

"About a year later," Chad said.

Shaking, Val stood over her cowering brother, still seated in an easy chair, head bowed. "Chad, tell me. Did Mom run away with Milt?"

Chad took a long moment to answer. When he lifted his head, his face was wet with tears. "I don't know. I never got to ask her, and I've never heard from her again."

"Dad has," Val said, her voice steady.

Chad sat back, surprise washing over his face. "He...he told you this?"

Val shook her head and sat next to Gil again. "She sent letters. I...read one of them." Her voice quivered. "She wanted to see us. Dad kept her away."

"Oh, my God," Kendra said. Tears welled in her eyes, and she put an arm around her husband. "Chad. I'm so sorry."

Chad shook her off, staring at Val. "Did you ever tell Mom about the rape? About what *he* did to you?"

Val sighed. "No. But I think she already knew. And *that's* why she had to leave."

Chapter Twelve

Val and Gil drove home with the sun to their backs, blazing hot over the Berkshires' rolling green hills. They'd stayed at Chad's for less than an hour, declining his polite but insincere dinner invitation. After all, what remained for them to discuss? Val almost changed her mind when Ali appeared in the driveway, her face as long as the Wonder Woman cape clasped around her skinny little neck. But too much tension remained, ready to explode. Val and Chad needed time apart—her to cool off, him to sort through whatever feelings of guilt he harbored for keeping important secrets from her. For far, far too long.

"Are you going to be okay to drive?" Gil asked after she jerked the car to a stop at the first traffic light. "How about we stop somewhere, take a break? Talk a little?"

Val considered the idea and nodded. "I could go for some ice cream. With lots of disgusting mix-ins." She sped out onto the main drag, heading toward the Interstate.

"You mean like a Menchies?" Gil laughed. "Wouldn't junk food like that send shock waves through that perfect, healthy body of yours?"

"Nothing compared to what Chad just did. Got any better ideas?"

"Take the next right," he said. "Whenever we visited my aunt here in Danbury, she brought us to an amazing frozen yogurt shop run by an old German grandma-lady. She gives the best hugs. I think you could use one right about now."

Val followed his directions and, minutes later, they relaxed at an outdoor table, shaded by a bright red umbrella. "Delicious," she said, spooning frozen yogurt loaded with chunks of chocolate and peanut butter into her parched mouth. "You still owe me a grandma hug."

"I guess she doesn't work on Sundays." Gil's smile crumpled. "But I'll hug you anytime."

"How about now?" She set her ice cream down and scooted her chair next to his. He wrapped her in a tight embrace, warm and wonderful despite the awkward positioning of their bodies and the heat of the afternoon.

"I don't understand something," Gil said once they returned to their half-melted treats. "How could your entire family have kept so many secrets from you? Wasn't there anyone else—your own grandma, for instance—to break the silence?"

Val shook her head, swirling the gooey mix-ins together in her paper dish. "My dad had only the one brother—Valentin—who, as you know, died on my thirteenth birthday. My mom was an only child. Both sets of grandparents died before I was born."

"Holy smokes, Val. Does anyone in your family live long enough to collect a pension? What am I gonna do when you widow me at fifty?"

Val opened her mouth to reply, then caught the full, perhaps unintended implications of Gil's offhand remark. "Widowed" implied marriage. Even joking about it meant he'd given the idea at least subconscious thought.

That felt good. *Really* good. But did he mean anything by it? More than a joke?

She played it cool for now. "Getting a little ahead of ourselves, aren't we?" She scooped ice cream from her bowl. "Besides, look who's talking, Mr. I'll-Take-Your-Bullet-Anytime."

"You say that like it's one of my many faults," he said with a chuckle, his voice light. As if he hadn't just suggested they spend their lives together.

"It is. A fault we share, and you know it. Hell, what are the odds either of us makes it to fifty in this job?"

"Good point." Gil pushed his yogurt aside and took her hand. "I already know who I want by my side when some bad guy plugs me."

The warm feeling returned. So he *did* mean it.

"Plug you *again*? Hell, no. Next time, no way I want to be there." She laughed and squeezed his hand. "Every day until then, though...you bet I do."

Gil leaned closer and brushed her lips with his. Val took his face in her hands and pulled him in, tasting the sweet remnants of ice cream on his lips, exploring his teeth and tongue with a hunger she didn't know she had. He returned the kiss, caressing her face with a gentle hand, his tongue dancing on hers, his warm breaths the only sound in her ears.

After several seconds, she tilted back a few inches, drinking in the wonder swimming in his dark brown eyes. "Gil," she said, her voice breathy, "I don't think I can sleep in my dad's house tonight."

He took a deep breath, caressed her lips again with his. "You're always welcome to stay with me."

"That sounds...nice." She gulped. "But maybe just sleep this time, if that's okay."

"*Just* sleep?" he said with a wry smile. "Nothing else?"

"Of course. Sleep, and talk." She laughed, and after a moment, he did too.

He pressed his forehead against hers, and she smelled the minty chocolate mix-ins on his breath. "We do have a lot to process," he said.

Val nodded, and their lips joined again. Softly this time, but for much longer than before. Long enough for their ice cream to melt.

She no longer needed a hug from any German grandma.

***

The entire hour-long drive home, Val struggled to concentrate on her driving, her mind whirring with anticipation. Her Honda drifted over the white lines separating the lanes more than once, the bumpety-bumps of the rumble strips shaking her back into focus. Gil glanced at her each time, but said nothing, his hand resting on her knee. More than once, she considered reneging on her proposal to spend the night, and suppressed the urge. She wanted this, dammit. Him. Closeness. Intimacy.

She parked in his driveway and collapsed in her seat, expelling noisy air and shaking the tension out of her shoulders. Gil squeezed her thigh, and she covered his hand with hers, offering a bleak smile. "We made it," she said.

"Never doubted you for a moment." He gave her a gentle kiss. "Can I interest you in some dinner and wine, my sweet?"

Val pulled him in closer, mashing their lips together, tongues dancing together to music playing in perfect synchronicity in their minds. When he started to break the embrace, she held him so that his eyes remained inches from hers, drinking in the adoration she found there.

"Is that a yes or a no?" Gil said.

She laughed, too loud, a release of some of the tension building inside her. "If you're offering some of that homemade lasagne you bragged about this morning, it's a yes."

"With wine, and salad, and garlic bread." He punctuated each word with another soft kiss.

"Hmm. Garlic isn't good for after-dinner smooching."

"Then we should get that in now." He covered her lips with his.

Only the heat of the day, raising the car's temperature to uncomfortable levels, forced them inside Gil's air-conditioned house, cooling their amorous mood for a few moments. Val assembled a salad while Gil sliced focaccia into chunks, rolled them in melted butter and garlic salt, and tossed them onto his backyard grill. "Best toaster in the land," he said with a grin.

"At least you're not barbecuing the lasagne."

"Hmm. Now that you mention it..." He wrapped two big slabs of the pasta in foil and hobbled back outside.

It was delicious, of course. They dined in the living room, sitting side by side on the sofa, with loaded plates resting atop portable tray tables. "You're a grill master," she said after the first bite. "Smoked lasagne. Who'd have thunk it?"

"My dad grilled everything," Gil said. "Even salad."

"So, your dad taught you how to cook?"

He nodded. "And my mom. She was Italian, second generation. We celebrated every holiday with food—even ones from other countries and religions. I didn't realize other Catholics didn't celebrate Rosh Hashanah until sixth grade." Gil chuckled, then went quiet.

A lump rose in Val's throat. Gil had told her about losing his mother to cancer two years ago, his father six months later. "Died of a broken heart," according to Gil.

"Have you spoken with your brother lately?" she asked him. They'd been close before the loss of their parents.

Gil shrugged. "We still talk on the phone about once a month. Ish."

Val heaved a sigh. "I'm sorry. I know this is hard to talk about."

He pushed his plate aside and took Val's hand. "We both have some tough family memories."

Val's lump doubled in size. She dropped her gaze, and her vision blurred. "I'm glad your family is—was—close. My family's kind of fucked up."

"All families are." Gil squeezed her hand harder. "Even close ones."

She nodded and nibbled on her bread. Delicious, but thoughts of the strained relations with her meddling older brother, alcoholic father, and estranged, absent mother destroyed her appetite. She rested her face in her hands, pressing her eyes to keep the tears from flowing.

Gil scooted closer and wrapped his arms around her, kissing the top of her head while she rocked from side to side.

After an eternity, Val broke away from the embrace. "Dinner's getting cold," she said, sniffling.

"Cold lasagne's the best." He popped a chunk of bread into his mouth. "Hmm. Maybe not cold focaccia, though."

She laughed. That goof. Gil always knew just what to say.

But her mind wouldn't behave itself. Memories of her mother walking out the door for the last time, cigarette in hand, and her father's grief and rage for the next decade refused to go away.

"Did I say something wrong?" he asked.

She sighed. "My stupid brain won't shut up."

"I'm here to listen, if you want to talk."

"I can't get it out of my head," Val said. "My mom, leaving that day, never coming back, never knowing what happened to me a year before."

"You never told her?" he said around a mouthful of lasagne.

Val tried to swallow a small chunk of lasagne. "I hinted, but...no. I never told either parent outright. I was too ashamed, too afraid of what Milt might do to me."

"And Chad didn't either?"

She shook her head. "I made him swear never to tell anyone, on pain of death."

"And he knew you could deliver," Gil said with a wry smile.

"Also, Mom was only there for another year after it happened," Val continued. "Physically, anyway. Mentally, emotionally...well, the drinking was really bad, Gil. *Really* bad. For her, and for Dad. But if Mom was involved with Milt..." She shuddered, fighting nausea, imagining that big, grotesque man with her mother.

"It's hard to imagine," Gil said in a soft voice, "that she wouldn't hate his guts."

"Quite the opposite. She always defended him," Val said. "I, of course, hated him, never wanting him around, even before that day. My uncle warned him to stay away—*I* had just told Uncle Val—but he died before he could do anything." Tears flowed again, dropping onto her lap. Her heart ached like it was about to split in half. Like it was all happening again.

"You're sure your uncle also never told them?"

Val shrugged and sucked in a deep breath. "He said he wouldn't. I believe he kept his promise. Again, he didn't have to keep it long."

"And Milt...you don't think he ever admitted it to her?"

Gil's words hit her like a thunderbolt, shocking her out of sadness. "That never occurred to me, because I didn't know they were a thing. Why would he? No, he couldn't have. She wouldn't have gone off with him if he had...would she?"

Gil heaved a heavy gust of air. "I don't know, Val. She's your mother. But no, I agree. That's not feasible. Is it?"

Val shook her head. No. *No.* NO! It was not. Not even a teeny, tiny bit.

***

Their food had gone cold while they talked. Despite that, the lasagne and garlic bread were still delicious.

"How about I heat this stuff back up?" Gil said. "Unless you're not hungry."

"Let me." She needed to move, shake her emotions loose a bit.

When she returned with the reheated food, the conversation turned to more pleasant, mundane things, and their appetites revived. Bellies full, they sat closer on the couch watching TV, his arm around her, his other hand caressing her thigh. The light touch sent shivers of warmth up her back. She returned the gesture, at once appreciating how strong and firm his leg was.

"How about some dessert?" he asked, his voice deep and soft.

"I'm too full."

Gil dropped his voice a register. "I was thinking of something a little sweeter." His eyes widened, a teasing smile creasing his face. His lips grazed hers, then he pulled her toward him. An instant later, she straddled his lap, knees bent, her arms draped over his shoulders. He leaned in and kissed her neck, sending shivers down her entire body. Their mouths joined while his hands roamed over her back, her rump, then under her shirt, stroking northward until reaching her bra strap. When it unclasped, she froze for a moment, muscle memory kicking in: *Make him stop.*

But she didn't want it to stop.

"You okay?" he asked. "Should I not—"

"No, no," Val said through heavy breaths. "I mean...yes. Keep doing that. In fact...wait." She sat up straight, locking eyes with him, taking another breath. Then, in a single fluid motion, before she could change her mind, she pulled her shirt and bra over her head and tossed them aside.

He emitted a tiny gasp, then plunged his face into her chest, kissing her cleavage, then the softer, pale flesh of the breasts, edging closer to her aureoles with his wet tongue—

"Can we go somewhere, um, more private?" She noticed for the first time the open windows and abundant lighting of the living room.

"I thought you'd never ask." He lifted her, then grunted in frustration. "Sorry. In my condition, I won't be able to carry you over the threshold."

Val laughed and scooped up her blouse and bra, standing and helping him to his feet. "Then I guess we're even on that score." She handed him his crutches and helped him into the bedroom, pausing at the side of the bed. "Gil, I'm...I mean, I don't...have any experience with any of this. Outside of, well, you know. Which doesn't count."

"That's okay. We're taking it slow, remember?"

"So, it's okay if we don't..."

"Have sex tonight? Yes. It's okay." He smiled and pulled her in close for a warm hug. "There are lots of things we can do short of actual sex."

Her face warmed, half out of anticipation, half out of embarrassment. She didn't even know what she liked among those "other things." She leaned back another moment. "I didn't plan for this, so...I'm not, um, prepared."

Gil nodded toward his bedside table. "I have supplies, if that's what you mean."

"Not just that. I mean, I haven't been to, like, a spa, or anything." Her face reddened more.

He laughed. "Good. I prefer the natural look. In fact," he said, nuzzling her neck again, "one thing I love about you is that you're, what's the word? Authentic. That's what makes you beautiful."

She sat on the bed in front of him and leaned back, her body shaking. Don't chicken out, she told herself. Say it.

"Undress me," she said, and closed her eyes.

Monday, July 1, 2019

Chapter Thirteen

Val awoke with the first light of morning, a dim ray reflecting off a cherry-framed mirror atop its matching nine-drawer dresser.

Wait a minute. She didn't own a nine-drawer dresser, much less a matching mirror. Where the hell—?

She sat up in bed—not hers. A king-sized bed, with an actual wooden frame and headboard. A man slept next to her on his back. A big, hunky, handsome man.

Val smiled. Ah, yes.

The blanket fell away, and cold air washed across her bare tummy and breasts. She scooted down under the covers, trying to remember everything that happened the night before. The canoodling on the couch, then the bedroom. Gil's hands roaming over her body, all of it feeling natural and good—unlike the few times in the past when she'd allowed a boy to touch her, and only for a moment, until shame and fear would wash over her. This time, unlike those times, she wanted the touching to continue, and it did. Unlike those times, she wanted to explore, too.

"You okay?" Gil mumbled, eyes still closed.

"I'm...perfect," she whispered, and draped an arm across his chest.

"You sure are." He smiled and rested his hand atop hers. "Time's it?"

"Sun's coming up, so...five-ish?"

He groaned. "Too early."

"Yeah. Go back to sleep." But Val couldn't sleep, herself. Her mind drifted over the night before, the kissing, the exploring, the thrills overcoming her fears. Almost stopping, dozens of times, but trusting him and allowing it to continue.

A new panic seized her. Had she trusted him too much? She'd drunk several glasses of wine—okay, two or three—and fallen asleep in his bed. A lesser man might take advantage.

No. Not Gil. He wouldn't. He couldn't.

Right?

After several minutes: "Gil?"

"Yo."

Val heaved a deep breath, afraid to ask. "Did we...I mean, how far did we...I mean, we...*stopped*, right?"

Gil opened his eyes, drawing her closer. "We never even got naked. Check if you want."

She could feel her own panties still on her body. She ran her hand down his side. Boxer briefs, present and accounted for. She sighed in relief and cuddled up against his sturdy frame.

"I think my eighth-grade health teacher, Mrs. Balboni, would call it third base." He kissed her forehead. "Which is about two bases beyond what I expected."

"A baseball analogy, really?" Val shook her head. "What does that mean, anyway?"

He chuckled. "You prefer football? Lots of first downs, no touchdown."

She swatted his nose, then rolled on top of him, sitting up, not caring that the covers fell away again. His eyes dropped for a moment, appreciating her naked breasts. "I remember we spent some time in this position," she said.

Gil winced, but placed his hands on her waist.

Dammit! His hip, still recovering from reconstructive surgery. "Sorry. Too much, too soon?"

He grinned and ground his hips against hers. "You nearly killed me, but hey, if you're so inclined, please, *please* do it again. So totally worth it."

Val pushed back, feeling him hardening against her. "Mmm. Yes, I am so inclined. You sure it doesn't hurt too much?"

He shook his head, grimaced, then laughed. "I'm a lousy liar, aren't I?"

She lay down, holding his shoulders and resting her face on his muscular chest. A few wisps of black, curly hair tickled her nose. "I might need to shave you."

"Promises, promises."

"Oh, so you'd like that?"

"Very much. Especially if you did it in the shower with me."

Val froze, her body going rigid down to her toes.

Gil sighed. "Sorry. Pushing it too far?"

She shrugged. "I've just never..." She sighed, too, and forced herself to relax. "Which doesn't mean I shouldn't." She raised herself up again and rubbed his shoulders, thinking about how that would feel. Her body answered with a shiver and goosebumps.

He brushed his hand against her cheek, a sad smile forming on his lips. "All in due time."

She kissed his fingers. "You're sure? I'm not making us go too slow? If you need someone who's more willing, more exper—"

Gil pressed his finger against her lips. "Sh, *sh.* None of that." He caressed her cheek again. "What I need is Valorie Dawes. On her schedule, in her comfort zone. Okay?"

Her heart filled her chest, making it hard to breathe. "I have another question."

He nodded. "Sure. Anything."

Val lay down, arms wrapped around him. "Can we do this again tomorrow?"

The way he held her at that moment gave her the answer she needed.

***

Val's father was still in bed when she returned home for a rushed change of clothes, so she left him a quick note on the fridge, asking if they could "chat a bit" that evening. She almost added "about Mom," but figured that would put the kibosh on the plan and might prompt him to end his four-month sobriety streak.

Grimes greeted her at the WAVE office with a half-empty coffee pot and poured her a cup into a chipped "Clayton Owls" mug, a souvenir of a now-defunct minor league base-ball team. "You look way too chipper for a Monday," he said.

Val thought again of waking up with Gil, and the prospect of doing the same the next morning. "I'm like this every day," she said with an impish grin. "Happy to be alive."

Damari Price emerged sour-faced from Sergeant Petroni's office. Despite his slumping posture, his Clayton PD uniform appeared pressed and clean as if it still hung on the rack.

"OK, let's get rolling on this meeting," Petroni said.

"Without O'Reilly?" Grimes asked.

"She'll join us once she returns from Evidence Control. The feds will arrive any minute for evidence transfer, and I want to be ready. Price, copy the arrest files on Patriots Pride to a thumb drive. Grimes, we need all the background data on the group, same format. Dawes, you—"

"Is this the Women's Auxiliary Volunteer Escapee office?" A smirking, late-thirties man in a dark blue suit and a crew cut, six feet tall and built like a block of granite, threw the office door open and strolled into the room as if he owned the place. Val would have classified him as white, except his skin glowed orange, like a bad spray-on tan. An Asian woman of about thirty with short black hair and a smarmy smile entered two steps behind him. She, too, could have been built from Lego blocks, and her suit looked like someone cut it from the same skein of cloth as the man in front of her.

"That's the Women's Anti-Violence Emergency Squad to you, J. Edgar Hoover," Grimes snapped. "And next time, knock before you enter."

Granite-guy sneered at him. "The name's Aaron Forrestal. You, Baldy, can call me Special Agent, or simply 'sir.' This is Agent Hannah Powers." The agents both flashed badges and tucked them back in their pockets in under a second. "Where's the Joe in this dump?"

"Here." Price held up the almost-empty pot.

Forrestal wrinkled his nose. "I mean the good coffee."

"For you? Down the hall, second door to the left," Grimes said. "You'll recognize the symbol on the door of a stick figure in a dress. Third door for you, Agent Powerful."

Forrestal's eyes narrowed, and he crossed his arms. "Maybe you local dicks drink out of the toilet. In the Bureau, we task smart-asses like you to fetch our lattés." He sat in an open chair, propped his feet up on Grimes's desk, and pointed at Petroni. "You got the evidence transfer ready? Come on, hustle. I'm illegally parked."

"Dogs off the furniture, *Special Agent* Forrest Gump." Petroni smacked his legs with her forearm. Had he not caught himself, Forrestal would have landed on the floor. "You'll get your evidence once we've got it ready."

Val gazed open-mouthed at the obvious ill will exploding among the professionals around her. The other agent's eyes widened and she met Val's gaze, as if she, too, couldn't believe what had just transpired.

Powers's superior officer showed no hesitancy in returning fire. "Stonewalling already? Tsk, tsk." He leaned back in his chair, leaving his feet on the floor. "This won't look good on our report, but hey, have it your way."

"Be sure to mention what flavor of coffee you expected served on a tray to your delicate little hands," Petroni said. "In fact, you should open your report with that." She shook her head. "The Hartford office warned me you were abrasive, but damn, man. Don't they teach manners at Quantico anymore? Or is charm school now an elective course?"

Forrestal stood and extended a hand, newfound respect in his eyes. "You must be Petroni."

"*Sergeant* Petroni." Brenda accepted the handshake, only for a moment. "Is there anything else you need, *Special Agent* Forrestal?"

"Like I wrote in my email to you: evidence and a briefing. A little cooperation might be nice, too."

"Can I get a hand with this?" Shannon O'Reilly pushed the door open with her butt and backed into the room, dragging a dolly loaded with archive boxes, taped shut and stacked three high. "There's six more down in the—Oh. Hello. Sorry, I didn't know we had company."

"What have we here?" Forrestal read the filing label on the top box. "Mendez, P. As in Pedro, the man in federal custody because of this weekend's raid?"

"Who's asking?" Shannon inserted herself between Forrestal and the pile of boxes.

Forrestal flashed his badge again with a heavy sigh. "The Special Agent now in charge of this case. Don't bother unloading those here, Detective. I parked my car out front." He nodded to Powers, who scooted around Shannon and held the door open.

"What the hell?" Shannon said. "This is under Clayton PD jurisdiction. You want a peek, you submit the paperwork, and after I take a look, I'll *maybe* think about sharing it with you." She grabbed the handle of the dolly and pushed it toward her desk.

Forrestal lay both hands on the boxes, stopping her. "Don't make it ugly, Detective. Sergeant Petroni, please inform your staff as to proper protocol surrounding evidence handling and jurisdiction in a federal investigation."

All eyes turned to Petroni, who looked like she wanted to vomit. Val held her breath, hoping that the sergeant would, as usual, back up her staff and, at the very least, insist on some sort of evidence-sharing arrangement.

Petroni glared at Forrestal and shook her head in disgust. "You're a real asshole, you know that?" She tossed her hand in the air. "He's right, it's theirs. Give it to them, Shannon."

"What?" The word escaped Val's mouth before she realized it. "You're going to cave? Just like that?"

Petroni turned her angry glare in Val's direction, her face reddening like hot coals. "I have no choice. It's their case now. We're obligated to turn over all evidence we've collected immediately. You got a problem with that, take it up with your congressman."

"Thank you, Sergeant," Forrestal said. "We appreciate the spirit of partnership—"

Grimes swore and tossed his entire cup of coffee, mug and all, into the garbage can, where it landed with a loud *Bang!* "This is so fucking stupid! You idiots," he said, waving an arm at Forrestal and Powers, "don't understand the first thing about partnership and what we bring to the table here. We're not your fucking errand boys. You want this shit hauled down to your car? Do it yourself. You want local help? Forget it. Here, give me your business card so I can block your number on my phone!"

"Can it, Grimes." Petroni turned to Shannon. "Transfer all the boxes of evidence, here and in your car, to the agents.

Price and Dawes, help her. Then get back up here so we can brief them on what we know. Grimes—my office. *Now.*"

Val and Price eyed each other, heaving deep breaths. "Yes, ma'am," they said in unison.

Shannon sneered at the agents and let go of the dolly. "Sorry, I strained my back getting these in here. You'll need to push the cart downstairs yourself. Oh, and the elevator's out of order. See you on the street, guys." She walked out the door with an exaggerated limp. Val and Price hustled after her, closing the door behind them. Sure enough, Shannon abandoned her limp and sprinted toward the elevator. "Keep them inside!" she called back, pressing the call button. The elevator dinged a moment later and Shannon ducked inside.

The doors closed, and Val chuckled, Price joining in a moment later. Voices inside the WAVE office indicated that the FBI agents weren't finished complaining to Petroni about the lack of cooperation they'd encountered.

"I hate politics," Val said, shaking her head.

"Me, too. Especially bureaucratic politics," Price said. "Now I guess we're supposed to wait and escort these bozos down to Shannon's car?"

Val shrugged. "As long as we don't have to buy their damned lattés."

***

The agents emerged from the WAVE office a few minutes later, with the much-smaller Powers pushing the dolly behind Forrestal's arrogant stride. He marched straight to the elevator and pushed the button. The call light blinked on. "Out of order, my ass," he said, snarling.

They rode down in silence. Val, feeling sorry for Powers, helped her wheel the heavy cargo down the steep access ramps to the street. The agents loaded the boxes into their illegally parked black sedan—sporting a parking ticket with Shannon's signature, Val noted with a wry grin. Meanwhile,

Val and Price each grabbed another box from Shannon's trunk and set them on the ground next to the FBI vehicle.

"I'd help you load," Shannon said, "but my back—"

"Fuck you and your bullshit injuries," Forrestal said. "Get the hell away from my car." They sped off moments later.

"So much for our briefing," Price said, "and my thumb drive."

"We can't let that guy take over," Val said, "no matter what Petroni says. Forrestal's an idiot, and I don't trust him."

Shannon laughed. "Thanks for the insight, Captain Obvious."

"What do you suggest we do?" Price shifted his gaze from Val to Shannon. "We got direct orders."

"People are coming into Clayton and selling young women into slavery," Val said. "We're the Women's Anti-Violence Emergency Squad. If this isn't a Clayton emergency, I don't know what is."

"Glad you feel that way," Shannon said. "Price? You in?"

Price shrugged. "If we can convince the boss."

Shannon smirked and wiggled her eyebrows. "Leave that to me. Now, come help get the rest of the stuff out of my car."

"More?" Price cocked his head. "I thought we were supposed to—"

"Hush." Shannon hustled to her car and reached into the back seat. "Petroni said to give them all the *boxes* of evidence we'd already collected. She said nothing about any new or loose items, or anything in bags." Shannon handed each of them a glossy, four-color brochure. The front cover contained photos of angry protesters carrying the American flag and a variety of guns. Phrases on their red, white, and blue clothes shouted nationalist, racist, and anti-immigrant slogans.

"Where did this come from?" Val asked.

Shannon smirked. "From an archive box in the back of that warehouse we raided. It seems our sex trafficking buddies are also involved in right-wing politics."

Val flipped through the brochure, her mind whirring. What connected the criminal ring to these crazy right-wing groups? And why?

One thing she knew for sure: there was no way she would leave this case in the hands of the dubious competence of Agent Forrestal. Even if it meant defying her boss's orders.

Chapter Fourteen

The burner phone vibrated, tumbling around on the table like a dying bug. Out of habit, Maggie checked Caller ID, even though only one person had this number, and that person would block his outgoing number. Still, she recognized it, and his voice when he said her name.

"Tanner," she said. "You're late."

Tanner scoffed, the abrasiveness of the sound magnified by the phone's cheap speaker. "Now you're my timekeeper?"

Maggie counted to five and steadied her breath, fighting the urge to snap back at him. "You either respect my time, or you don't. What the hell, you're paying for it, so perhaps I should celebrate your foolishness."

Tanner's response—a string of pornographic curses that would make a sailor's skin crawl—elicited only laughter in her. "Mother fucking bitch!" ended the minute-long spiel.

"Are you done?" she asked in a calm voice.

He seethed a moment, then said in a steely voice, "For now."

"Good. So. Are you going to send reinforcements, or do I need to get by with the shits-for-brains who didn't get rounded up by Clayton PD's finest? Let's see, I think Calvin and Randy were out getting pizza. Jasmin and Marisa were screwing each other's brains out somewhere instead of re-cruiting new talent like they were supposed to be doing. Yeah, real leadership potential we've got here."

"We'll send you some guys," Tanner said, his voice thick with resentment. "It's going to take a few days. You'll need to find a new headquarters."

"*I* will? My friend, that sounds like operations. I'm strictly organizing, messaging, and partnerships. Keep me away from admin and payroll."

"We have no choice." Tanner's voice softened. "Maggie, you know how essential Clayton is to our plan. You need to get it back on its feet, and fast. We still want our event to go off as planned."

"July Fourth?" Maggie laughed. "That's three days from now. Not gonna happen. Not with three-quarters of the team behind bars. No, we need to regroup and—"

"Not an option. It's too late to change plans. We need to make our statement, and there's no better date than Independence Day."

"That's idiotic. There's no way—"

"Get it done, *Maggie*." He spit out her name like an epithet, then hung up the phone.

***

Val sat in the soft upholstered chair, gripping the armrests to focus her tension. The man sitting across from her, Dr. Christopher Cyrus, smiled in that fake-concerned way of his, as he had in their previous meetings. Their first encounter resulted in him approving her psychological fitness to serve when she entered Clayton PD almost a year before. The second and third set of sessions followed her prior two shootings, where he'd tied her up in knots during his painstaking probes of her resulting mental state. Both times, he seemed reluctant to allow her back on the streets on patrol.

Cops weren't supposed to have two post-shooting evaluations, much less three. With three in her *first year*, Val would be lucky to keep her badge, much less return to active duty.

"We meet again," he said, as if reading her mind. His New York accent—or perhaps, New Jersey—sounded harsher than usual, made even more pronounced by his slow speaking cadence. "I've been thinking about you."

"Yeah. I guess I kind of missed you, Doc." She smiled to punch the joke, hoping a little humor might ease the tension between them.

Not so. Cyrus's dark, brooding eyes gazed over the horned rims of his glasses, perched midway down his long, pointy nose. His bushy hair, still black and full on his weathered head despite his age, bright pink lips, and pasty-white skin made him appear clownish. Val put him in his early sixties, based on the date of his Yale undergrad diploma, framed and on prominent display on the light gray walls. A photo on his desk showed a gray-haired woman bearing a pleasant expression. Well, good. Cyrus needed a patient wife.

"I was hoping to see you again," Cyrus said in that slow, ponderous baritone. He glanced at the notepad resting on a tiny table next to his thick padded leather recliner. A chair that looked more comfortable than hers. "Although not under these circumstances."

Val gripped the arms of her chair tighter. She kept her voice as calm as she could, trying to keep it light. "Why's that, Doc? I confess, these meetings bring me a lot of stress. I'd rather avoid them."

He laughed, a honking sound that grated on her nerves even more than his condescending demeanor. "You're not alone in that regard, Officer Dawes. But it's a fair question." He crossed his legs and folded his hands together around his knee. "I make it a practice to review my files, both the outcomes and the logic behind my recommendations, six months after closing them. As you know, I've had multiple occasions to do that in your case."

Val stiffened. Here it comes.

"I do this not to persecute you, but to fulfill my obligations to the citizens," he went on, "and to the leadership of the department. They expect me to act as a bit of a gatekeeper, to ensure that we don't return officers to active duty who present a danger to the public."

"Is that what you think I am?" Val couldn't keep the defensiveness out of her voice. "Dr. Cyrus, I assure you that the opposite is true. In each incident where I've drawn my weapon, I acted in self-defense against a man who was firing *at me*. In this most recent case—"

"I understand," he said, nodding. "Your fellow officers' accounts of this weekend's raid corroborate your report. You were in a situation of grave danger."

She exhaled and loosened her grip on the armrest. "It was a good shooting."

Cyrus nodded again. "So it appears. That is a matter for Internal Affairs. My concern is about *you*, Officer Dawes." He fixed her with a steady, unblinking stare.

It unnerved her. So intense, so authoritative. Val's chest tightened, her lips dry. She licked them and fought for words. "M-me, Doctor?"

He smiled, and this time it seemed genuine. "Yes, you. In the space of under nine months, you've shot three men. Two of them died."

A heavy weight settled over her. Her tongue felt thick and sluggish, her throat tight. "If you're trying to make me feel guilty, Dr. Cyrus, you're succeeding."

"Not at all. But I am gratified to hear that you're feeling that way."

Val's annoyance grew. "Gee, thanks. So glad that my feeling like shit is making your day."

Cyrus laughed again, surprising her. "I wouldn't go that far," he said. "However, it is an important thing for me to know. Officer Dawes, psychiatrists have studied the effects of police shootings on officers' psyches for decades. Probably not enough," he said, almost to himself. "But we understand some things. Shootings are traumatic events, both for the victims and for the shooters. Do you understand?"

"Of course," she said, again fighting annoyance at his condescension. "Lots of cops suffer PTSD after a shooting."

"Exactly," he said. "There are less obvious effects as well. Did you know that an officer who has fired his or her weapon at a person is far more likely to fire it again than an officer who hasn't?"

She nodded, growing wary of the direction he'd taken. "I am aware. Some of that is circumstantial, though. Officers assigned tougher beats in more violent areas find themselves in more danger, more often."

"True. But repeat shooters are responsible for about half of all officer-involved shootings. That's an unusually high concentration, don't you think? On the other hand, nearly 80 percent—"

"Never fire their weapons in the line of duty. Yes, Criminology 101. Your point?"

Cyrus paused and studied his notes again with a furrowed brow. "My point, Officer Dawes, is that if I approve your return to duty, the odds of you firing your weapon again in the next three years are...well, one can't say with precision, but—"

"If someone aims a gun at me, yes, I'll return fire," Val said, her voice steely. "Otherwise I will not. Dr. Cyrus, don't the circumstances merit consideration here? A gang member, a serial rapist, and an armed sex trafficker tried to kill me. Because of my reflexes and superior marksmanship, I'm here today and they're not. Would you prefer the opposite be true?"

His gaze dropped to his lap. "I'm not attacking you, Officer. I'm evaluating you. At the moment, what I'm finding troubles me."

Val leaned back, calming herself as her sensei taught her. Deep breaths, clearing her mind, imagining scenes of serenity. Blue skies, calm lakes, the scent of pine needles on a backwoods running trail. Happy moments from childhood, from before the days of Milt and the disappearance of her mother...

"There is a complicating factor, in your case," Cyrus said, breaking her concentration. "I'm certain you know the event to which I refer."

She stared at him, alarmed, leaning forward again in her seat. Did he know about Milt? About her mother? Was he somehow connecting those events to her reaction to situations of danger on the streets?

"Please, let's not assume," she said, trying to match his tone and manner. Academic, polite, condescending.

"Right, right. Better to speak plainly. I refer, of course, to the death of your uncle."

Oof.

Cyrus's words slammed into her like a freight train, slamming her back into her chair. Of course he'd connect that to her seemingly trigger-happy record. "You think I'm taking revenge for my uncle's death against Clayton's sex offenders?" she asked in a whisper. "Seriously?"

He attempted a smile, failed. "It's something we need to explore. Certainly that event, too, impacted you in, ah, *unfortunate* and traumatic ways."

She chewed on her bottom lip, nearly biting through, or so it felt. "How," she said, "do you propose to evaluate my fitness for duty based on something that happened to me as a child? An event that, I should point out, I spent three years in therapy as a teenager to work through. Or is that not in your files?"

His eyes widened in surprise. "It is not," he said. "Interesting."

After a moment of victory, Val's heart fell. *Interesting* didn't always mean "good" to Dr. Cyrus.

It often meant the exact opposite.

***

Back in the WAVE office, Val found Shannon, Grimes, and Price poring over the Patriots Pride brochures Shannon had snagged from the sex traffickers' headquarters. They'd taped the brochures, suspect mug shots, and other evidence reports onto the whiteboard and drawn dotted lines between a few of them. But only a few.

"This is bold," Val said. "What if Petroni sees this?"

"She went home with a migraine," Shannon said, "leaving me in charge. And officially, we're researching the prostitution cases. One hundred percent local."

"Maybe ninety-nine," Grimes said with a laugh. "But I was never so good with math."

"What have you got so far?" Val asked, drawing closer to the whiteboard.

"Not a lot more than we had this morning," Grimes said. "The biggest piece we've found is that most of these girls all arrived here within the last three months, the exception being Destiny Mathers."

"So, it's a new operation," Val said. "And Patriots Pride?"

"Registered with the state as an advocacy group in February," Shannon said. "About a month before the underage girls started showing up on our rap sheets."

"The guy they call Pedro, the big boss, immigrated from Puerto Rico in February, too," Grimes said.

Val rolled her eyes. "He's not an immigrant, then. Puerto Rico's part of the US."

Grimes shrugged. "Yeah, whatever. He ain't from Connecticut."

Price looked up from his laptop. "Found something!" He stood and drew a dotted line from Pedro's mug shot to Tyler Paxton's. "Pedro served time with Paxton's brother in Ohio a few years back on a small-time burglary and assault case at a jewelry store. Pedro got paroled, but the big brother got into some weird Nazi gang crap that got an inmate killed and earned him life without parole."

"So that's how they got hooked up," Grimes said. "Looks like his 'I just met the guy' story is a bunch of BS."

Val glanced at the whiteboard again. Something didn't add up, but she couldn't put her finger on it.

"The question is whether the political connection is material, or just coincidence," Shannon said. "The rap sheets of the other guys we busted are all over the map. We hauled in one of the guys last year at an Antifa riot for busting windows. Two are illegal immigrants—Mexico and Jordan—with criminal records in their home countries. Each one requested political asylum, but disappeared before their cases got processed."

"So, do they share a political ideology, or are they simply fringe actors, looking for acceptance in a new organization?" Val asked.

"Or, is it just a coincidence?" Grimes said. "The one thing they all have in common is that they're part of this sex trafficking group."

"Maybe they all share a different common trait, then," Price said, taking his seat again. "Maybe they all know vulnerable women and are good at recruiting."

Something in what Price said clicked in Val's mind. She peered again at the whiteboard to confirm it.

"I don't think so, Damari," Val said. "Do you see why?"

They all stared at the makeshift diagram. "No," Price said.

"Me, either," Shannon said. "Lay it out for me."

Val walked to the whiteboard. "What *don't* we see that we should? Or, rather, that we *would*, if these guys were 'recruiting' sex workers?"

"Connections," Grimes said, snapping his fingers. "None of the girls knows any of the guys."

"Exactly." Val crossed her arms and faced the group. "So, the question we have to answer is, where are these connections being made? And who's behind them?"

"And," Shannon said with a sigh, "we have to answer those questions out of sight of the FBI."

"And our boss," Val said.

Her final remark was met around the table with glum silence.

***

The bullpen session with the team ended Val's workday, drained her energy, and left her in a despondent mood, one she didn't want to share with Gil. She needed some busy work to transition her mental state, and the stack of boxes in her father's garage—her interim bedroom—presented the perfect distraction.

She tackled a box labeled "Memorabilia/UConn," a euphemism for junk she didn't know what to do with. Old history books and English Lit anthologies—why did she still keep those? A notebook full of criminology research papers she'd once fancied might be good enough to polish up for publication seemed juvenile now and went straight into recycling. A box of clothes Val once hoped would return to fashion went into the Goodwill pile. Except one: a white blouse she bought to wear on a date with a guy Beth had fixed her up with. Val canceled at the last minute after discovering the guy posted pictures of her on Instagram he boosted from her Facebook page. She still liked the blouse—its tapered cut flattered her fit torso and even showed a little skin. She imagined Gil would like it, too.

Dad had piled a few more boxes in the garage, stuff he'd packed up from upstairs. He left a note, saying he'd move the boxes up to the attic in a day or two and that the room was "almost ready." He added that he'd gone out to dinner with Chuck Noble, an old pal Val remembered from her youth. She smiled. Good for him, getting back out there socially. It had been too long.

However, the boxes blocked the path to her makeshift closet. Clueless Dad. She pushed the first one toward the corner, but the cardboard had grown weak, and the box's contents spilled out the bottom, all over the garage floor.

Val cursed and wondered how Dad got the flimsy container into her space in the first place, then grabbed one of her empties and started stuffing Dad's belongings into it. She paused over a few old photos, including a framed picture of a young Mom and Dad sipping champagne at a fancy restaurant. The label on the back read, "Mike and Rita, First Anniversary," in handwriting Val didn't recognize. The photographer's, no doubt. Then one each of Chad and Val on their first day of kindergarten, four years apart. She grinned at their awful haircuts—Chad in a mullet, of all things, and Val in a pixie cut that made her look like an underage flapper from the 1920s. Then another picture of Mom and a preschool-age Chad in his Easter best—

No, wait. The young boy, about three or four, bore a family resemblance, but it was not Chad. The photo was too new, and the boy sported curly blond hair, rather than Chad's straight brown locks. Mom looked older than she should—somewhere in her forties, her wavy brown hair shorter than Val remembered. Mom also sported wire-rim glasses in the photo, rather than the black-rimmed ones she always wore to read, and deep wrinkles framed her eyes. Plus, Val didn't recognize the scenery: an adobe house with a red rock bed for a front lawn, with jagged, snow-capped mountains in the background.

She checked the back of the photo for an inscription and found none, except a date: April 1, 2014. The picture was a little over five years old, then. Meaning the boy in the photo would now be around nine, give or take a year.

Who was this boy?

Val didn't like the possibilities that sprang to mind. Not one bit.

Chapter Fifteen

Maggie stood up from the makeshift desk in yet another cheap motel room and stretched, wincing at the snap-crackle-pop sounds emanating from her back and neck. Everything ached. She blamed it on spending too much time in a stiff chair too short for comfortable keyboarding. Maggie rubbed her eyes, bleary from concentrating on computer screens in the room's dim light. She'd worked right through dinner and gotten nowhere.

Stupid Tanner. The man had no idea how to put together reliable teams, especially in their line of work. A person can't just pop an ad on Craigslist for people willing to round up young girls. The motel's slow, unsecured Wi-Fi network ruled out accessing the usual websites and chat rooms where she'd connected with potential Patriots Pride leaders in the past.

She tried contacting some of her old associates in the area, guys who had organized efficient teams and kept her involvement invisible to her "respectable" friends and family. But too many years had passed. The more successful ones had moved on to bigger opportunities. The rest had "retired," either through age, burnout, or jail time. She'd gotten lucky finding Mulroney. Hopefully, he'd find more luck recruiting candidates among the uniformed rank and file.

There was a name Maggie hadn't tried—a young, female cop who'd gained some celebrity in recent months. A young hero, revered by the local press for her bravery and track record, despite her inexperience. Still young and impressionable, perhaps her celebrity could lever others to the cause if she could be turned. They'd known each other once. But it had been almost ten years.

She couldn't cold-call her. Recent attempts to reach her through back channels had hit a brick wall. Maggie needed a fresh angle, one that involved a more subtle approach. Learning the girl's vulnerabilities, her motivations, and which buttons to push.

But that could take time. Time Maggie might not have.

She sighed. Men like Tanner expected everything, gave nothing. Women were nothing more than slaves and sex objects to them. Fodder for their self-aggrandizing schemes.

Correction: not just men like Tanner. All men, including both of her ex-husbands—oops. One completely useless ex, and one soon-to-be-ex...who, come to think of it, might yet prove useful.

Maggie sighed again. She wanted to avoid relying on him. She couldn't give in now after everything she'd done to distance herself from his narcissistic, arrogant perversions and his manipulative charm. That meant admitting failure, and that she couldn't succeed without him, after all.

No. Not acceptable. There had to be another way.

She considered her next-best option, one she'd resisted all night long: her son. A successful businessman, with children of his own, with so much to lose if the world continued down its present course. They'd been so close once. In his youth, he'd worshipped the ground she walked on.

Until that ground became the path away from him. The path of separation and regret that she'd forged out of dumb passion for a man who had done nothing but disappoint her. Could her son find it in his heart to forgive her? And, perhaps, open the door to patching things up with her daughter?

Maybe. Again, it might take too much time, at least for current purposes. Long-term...well, that's different.

She decided: yes, she'd cultivate that long-term option, even as she worked on other short-term possibilities.

Maggie returned to the desk in the dingy room, her nose wrinkling at the smell of mold and dust arising from the well-trod carpet, and checked her various email accounts. No word back from anyone, not even Mulroney. She'd need to press him again, make sure he understood the urgency of the situation. How much she needed inside help, how lucrative this could be for him.

Three days. Not much time.

She cursed and picked up her new burner phone. Dialed the number from memory, stabbing each numeric dot on the phone's keypad with an angry digit, and pressed, softly this time, "Send." He wouldn't recognize the number. Would he pick up?

Two chirpy tones later, he answered, using their well-rehearsed security phrase. "The National Firearms Act is not a revenue measure..."

"But an attempt to usurp police power reserved to the States, and is therefore unconstitutional," Maggie responded in monotone. "It's me. How's the kid?"

"Mags! I've been trying to reach you," said John Milton "Mac" McCloskey. "What the hell—"

"Don't call me 'Mags.' I've told you a thousand times, I hate that nickname." She squeezed the phone hard enough to crack the plastic case. Almost. "Unless you want me reviving *your* old nickname...?"

Mac grunted into the phone. "Did you call to give me a hard time, or is there a business reason for reaching out? Tanner says you're back in Connecticut."

"Yes—Clayton, actually, of all places." She swallowed a little more pride. "I...might need your organizational skills up here. Is Sammy well enough for you to travel?"

"He's fine." Chewing sounds came over the wire. Lucky bastard, already eating dinner. "As I wrote in the email, he probably just caught a cold from another kid on the playground. He asked about you today."

"Good. Find him a sitter and get your ass up here."

"Whoa," Mac said. "I can't—"

"If you talked to Tanner, you know things here are desperate." Maggie lit a cigarette, took a deep drag, and exhaled blue smoke right onto the "No Smoking" sign. "Fucking cops scooped up almost all the top soldiers and half of the meatheads. If we don't line up some fresh troops, all the work they did here for the big event is toast." She took another drag, then stubbed it out when she noticed the smoke detector on the ceiling in the corner. She dragged her chair over to the corner, phone still pressed against her ear.

"I'm knee-deep in responsibilities here, helping with the Orlando event. A much bigger one, as you might have heard."

"I've heard nothing." She stood on the chair, pulled the smoke detector from its base, and removed the battery. "Which means you don't have problems, because then I *would*'ve heard something. In fact, Tanner told me that this one is numero uno. The tip of the spear, so to speak."

"Oh, yeah? Why?"

Maggie let out an exasperated sigh and climbed down from the chair. "Think about it. Where did the American Revolution begin? New England. It's symbolic. Poetic even."

"I've never been one for poetry."

That nearly set her off. She counted to five, calmed herself, sat on the bed. "Come on, man. Help me out here. You have resources here that could make a difference." Fucking jerk, making her beg.

"If they're even still around. It's been a long time since I've been back."

"Yeah, me, too. But they need new leadership here, Mac," she said, warming to her clinching argument—an appeal to his vanity. "Why be a flunky in Florida when you can run your own operation here? You've always wanted to be the top man."

"You'd let that happen?" His voice registered both hope and doubt.

"We'd run it together. Like in the old days." She blew another cloud of smoke into the air. "So, what do you say? Will you help me? I can pick you up at Bradley Field, set you up in a room—"

"What, a husband can't share a room with his own wife? I mean, you said I could be on top." Mac laughed, a hearty roar this time. So fucking funny. "C'mon. This could be our way back to normal."

"With you and me, there is no normal."

He laughed, not so hard this time. Polite laughter. "The boy would like to see you, and I don't have time to find a sitter. So, he'd have to come too. The only question: would he stay with you or me?"

Maggie rolled her eyes. "You, obviously. You're the one that wanted full custody. Fine, I'll rent you a double. Email me your flight info. See you tomorrow." She ended the call without waiting for a reply.

Dammit. Bringing the kid. One more problem to manage. Once again she felt pangs of regret for having a third child late in life...and then felt pangs of guilt for that regret.

She pushed away both emotions. She had business to conduct. Mac would just have to find a day camp for him somewhere. Sammy liked his bow and arrow set—maybe an archery camp.

Or...

She *did* have some burned bridges to rebuild.

She smiled and lit another cigarette.

***

Val had just started her car when a noisy SUV pulled into the driveway behind her. Dad stepped out of the car, appearing not to notice Val until she popped her driver's side door open and waved at him. "You're blocking me in."

Dad stared at her for a moment, eyes widening. "Oh, geez, I'm sorry." He hustled back toward his car. "I'll get out of your way. You going out tonight, I take it?"

"Gil's making me dinner," she said, hoping that was true. "Um...speaking of which, how was your evening with Chuck?"

"Nice. We had pizza. It's not the same without beer, though." He offered a lopsided grin.

"I'm proud of you for resisting the urge."

Dad ducked his head. "Thanks, honey." An awkward silence prevailed for a moment. "Oh, I just remembered, I gotta go pick up some milk at the store." He shuffled toward his car.

"Wait a second," Val said. "I need to ask you something."

He paused, keys inserted into the door lock. "If it's about the room—"

"It's about the stuff in the garage." Val swallowed hard, formulating a question in her mind. She didn't want to appear confrontational, but how else could she ask this?

"That's temporary," he said. "I'll get that up into the attic tonight. I just needed someplace to stick it while I finish cleaning up. Have you checked out the room? It's so close to done, I only need—"

"That's okay," she said. "No rush. Look, I didn't mean to pry, but I accidentally opened one or two of your boxes, mixed them up with mine, and...I, uh, got confused." Her hands shook. They'd finally started to get along well, but this could blow it all up again.

"Oh, that's okay." His lip trembled a bit—one of his tells when he felt guilty about something. "It's all mostly old junk anyhow..." His voice trailed off, and his gaze fell to his feet.

Val stepped closer and leaned against the hood of his car, still warm from the drive. Surely he could hear the loud pounding in her chest, the blood racing through her veins. But he showed no sign of it. She cleared her throat, folded her arms. "Dad, I found some letters and pictures...from Mom."

His breath caught in his throat, making a little "hic" sound. "You're s-sure that's what you found?" he said. "Sometimes that old stuff can be...confusing, like you said. Might *look* like one thing, and turn out to be something completely different, once you know the truth." His voice faded to a whisper, and he faced the car door, leaning into it for support.

"Hey." She rested a hand on his arm. "Why did you hide her from me?"

He glanced at her, tears welling in his eyes. His eyelid fluttered and his mouth twitched, as if forming words, but none came.

"Dad? Was Mom trying to stay in touch with Chad and me all this time?"

Dad stood stone-cold still for a moment, then blew a long breath out between tight lips. He leaned his elbows onto the roof of the car and buried his head in his hands, rubbing his face. When he pulled his hands away, his face was red and wet.

"Valorie," he said. "Your mother left us at a bad time, with no warning. She didn't want to be part of this family anymore. No amount of letter-writing or sending pictures was going to change that."

"So you've always said," Val said, her voice sounding thin and tense, "except that you never told us about the letters and pictures. Why?"

"I...she...Val, you've got to understand," her father answered, tears flowing down his cheeks. He faced her and reached out to her, holding her by the arms. "Her leaving hurt me pretty hard, too. Like a knife to the gut. When those letters came, it just drove the blade even deeper."

Val choked back tears, seeing how hard this was for him to talk about. "I understand why you might not want to read them," she said. "But why not let Chad and me know about them? About her wanting to stay in touch with us? She still wanted to be our mother—"

"Rita wasn't a well woman," Dad blurted out. "She hurt us, and she would have hurt us again if I had let her. She would have hurt *you*, especially, Val. In ways I—I can't describe, but trust me. I know her and what she was up to. If I'd let her get to you—"

"Dad!" Val knocked his hands away and gripped him the same way he'd held her, and shook him once, hard, her voice rising. "You blocked my mother from communicating with me. I was a teenage girl. I needed my mother. How in the hell could you do this to me?"

Dad's mouth gaped open, then closed, and opened and closed a few more times. He wagged his head, tears dripping onto his shirt. "Val, listen, I'm sorry. It wouldn't have been good, okay? It would have been bad—so, so bad. You have to trust me, okay?"

"Trust you?" Val tossed back her head and laughed, an angry sound she didn't recognize coming from herself. "For ten years, you lied to me about my mother—even let me believe that she might be dead. You insisted over and over that she wanted nothing to do with us anymore. Now you expect me to *trust* you?" She pushed him away, and his body fell into the side of the SUV, his car keys falling to the pavement.

"For fuck's sake, Dad. I'm twenty-three years old, a college graduate, and a gun-toting sworn law enforcement officer. Don't you think you could've found at least one opportunity since, oh, say, my eighteenth birthday to tell me *my mother isn't fucking dead and might want to see me?*" Her voice reached a fevered pitch, and a couple of neighbors across the street stopped to stare. Val glared at them, and they looked away.

Her father remained crumpled against his vehicle, wiping tears from his face, glancing at her every few seconds. A few times, he tried to speak. Each time he broke down again, crying.

Finally, he straightened, blew his nose into a tissue that materialized from nowhere, and wiped his cheeks dry with his sleeve. He turned his bleary gaze to her and took a calming breath. "You're right, of course." He offered a crumpled smile, a cock of his head.

Another long, awkward silence passed.

"Well," she said, "we should chat more about this. Right now, I need to get to my boyfriend's house."

Dad smiled and wiped away a few more tears. "I'm glad," he said. "Not about you leaving right now. I mean about you having a boy who loves you."

"Man. He's thirty-four."

"Right. A man who loves you. I'm glad about that. I wondered sometimes—"

"You need to move your car." She picked up his keys and handed them to him. "Please."

"Oh. Right. Right." He chuckled and blew his nose again. "On it. Look, enjoy your date tonight. How about we have dinner tomorrow? I should have your room ready..." He winced, and she realized she must have scowled at him, as she was wont to do when he rambled.

"Sure. Let's plan that. And Dad?"

He paused with his car door open. "Yeah?" Hope tinged his voice.

Val leveled a serious stare at him. "We're not done. Talking about Mom, I mean. I...have more questions."

He grimaced, got in the car, and drove away.

Chapter Sixteen

On the drive to Gil's, Val's phone rang. Her brother. She put it on speaker. "S'up?"

"Val, first, I'm so sorry about Sunday," Chad said. "And about holding back from you all these years. I feel horrible about it all."

"Apology accepted." Val nearly ran a red light and had to stop short. She caught her breath and continued, "You said 'first.' What's second?"

Dead silence reigned for several seconds, and Val wondered if he'd hung up. But her phone still showed the call as connected.

Finally, Chad took a shaky breath, let it out. "Mom called me about an hour ago. She...wants to see us."

"Wait, what? She's *here,* in town? Where's she been? When did she get back? Why? How did she find you?"

"I don't know, I don't know," Chad said. "I'm as floored as you are. All she said was that she wants to get together and meet her grandkids." He paused. "She...asked about you, too. How to reach you and all."

Val's breathing stopped, and for all she could tell, her heart, too. She pulled over and parked in the lot of a shabby strip mall housing a nail salon, a check-cashing place, and Sal's Beverage Mart—ironically, Dad's favorite liquor store before he went sober. "What did you tell her?"

"Nothing," he said. "I told her I'd check with you first. She understood, but she really wants an answer."

"Holy crap. This is all too much. Way too much." Feeling self-conscious about their conversation in such a public place, she turned the phone off speaker and held it to her ear.

"What's too much?" Chad said. "The thing about Mom, or is there more?"

"Isn't that enough?" Val shook her head and gazed down the row of cars in front of the liquor store. An SUV that looked a lot like Dad's sat there, parked at an erratic angle. Maybe she should go inside, make sure he's not buying liquor.

"Sure, sure. What should I tell her?"

Val frowned, focusing on the cars, her head aching from concentrating on too much at once. "I don't know, Chad. Of course I should say yes. But you know, Dad was pretty freaked out by all this. I told him he shouldn't have kept her from us all this time, and he sort of lost it, saying she was bad for us...he wasn't making much sense."

"Listen, we can't let their breakup keep Mom from us," Chad said. "That's between them, right?" His voice sounded uncertain, even fearful. When she didn't answer, he went on, "So...you want to join us tomorrow? With Mom?"

"Tomorrow?" Val's hand shook so much, she nearly dropped the phone. "That's...too soon. For me. I need some time. To process. It's too much, too soon. Sorry, Chad."

"Hey, no prob," he said. "I get it. I'm going to go ahead without you if you don't. I...I can't pass up this opportunity."

A blonde woman in her fifties exited the liquor store and drove off in the SUV. Not Dad's, then. Phew. "I understand. You do what you need to do. As for me..." She restarted her car, but didn't move it yet. "I can't. I have to work, anyway, and Dad and I are having dinner tomorrow night, so...maybe later this week, okay?"

After a long pause, Chad sighed. "Okay, little sister. Understood."

They hung up a few moments later, after which Val sat in her car, wondering if she should patronize Sal's Beverage

Mart herself. Only the buzzing of her phone startled her out of her dazed reverie. A text from Gil: *Are you coming over? Dinner's getting cold.*

With the sun hanging low on the horizon and her heart heavy in her chest, she fired up the engine and nudged her car out of the lot.

***

How Val made it to Gil's, she had no idea. Her brain operated on automatic pilot, or the car steered itself, or aliens beamed her Star Trek–style to his place. All plausible explanations, given her mental state.

Gil greeted her in the driveway, concern written all over his face. "What happened?" he asked, holding open the driver's side door.

Val shook her head, tossed her hands in the air, then plopped them back on the steering wheel. "You may need to get me drunk tonight."

"That bad, eh?" He held out his hand. "C'mon. We've got half a bottle of Chianti in there to get us started while you tell me everything."

They sat on his couch, sipping the Chianti, and she insisted he tell her about his day first while she unwound. He'd worked out at the gym, where he lifted 110% of his target weight on the bench press. Once home, he took second place in a timed online chess tournament while cooking dinner.

"You're the only man I know who can actually multi-task," she said with a grin.

When his stories ran dry, she recapped what she found in the garage, Dad's lame explanation, and her call with Chad. Except that she no longer sipped the wine, she gulped it. Gil obliged her with generous refills, even opening a second bottle, and fed her a delicious African peanut soup he'd made from scratch. She mopped up the last drops with a chunk of fresh bread and finished her third glass of wine, holding her hand over the top so he wouldn't refill it again.

"So, tell me about this mysterious, long-missing mother of yours." He pulled her close. "What's she like? Or, what *was* she like, as you remember her?"

"Distant," Val said. "Not just physically, and not just for the last decade. Mom was never warm and cuddly—not with me or Chad, not even with Dad. Very old-school, Puritan New England. Which is weird, because you think of that being typical of people of, say, British heritage. Mom was Spanish, although she didn't talk about it much."

"Spanish as in Latina, or as in Madrid?"

"Spanish as in Barcelona. Her grandfather lived there." Val snuggled in. Gil felt so warm and soft, despite his muscular build. "He fought the fascists and fled to America when Franco prevailed. Mom rejected all of that family lore and tradition, though, even Americanizing her name. She was baptized 'Margarita,' but always preferred Rita, and hated when my Dad called her by her formal name. Of course, he only did that when they argued."

"Did they fight a lot?" Gil stroked her shoulder with his thumb. It felt so, so good.

"When they were sober," Val said. "They both drank too much, although usually when entertaining friends or celebrating some event or other. That is part of the reason I got raped."

"They passed out, or...?"

Val shook her head and picked imaginary lint off of Gil's sleeve. "They'd all drunk way too much, starting at dinner. Chad broke his arm showing off some martial-arts trick he'd learned, apparently not well enough. Mom and Dad took him to the hospital, leaving Milt behind to 'take care of me.' He took care of me, all right." Her throat constricted, and she couldn't talk anymore.

"Sorry, I didn't mean for you to relive this all over again," he said.

"It's okay." Val's voice came out raspy, and she cleared her throat. "The thing I don't get is, if she was having an affair with Milt...why did he come after me? And why didn't she believe me about what he'd done? It makes no sense."

"So, you *did* try to tell her?"

Val looked up at him, frowning. "I...hinted at it. Milt threatened even worse things if I told anyone, and I believed him. Neither she nor my dad picked up on my subtle hints, or chose not to. They insisted I was just upset about Uncle Val's death—which I was—but..." She shook her head. "Anyway. I went to counseling, and for the first year I didn't even mention Milt. It was all about Uncle Val. By the time I opened up in therapy, Mom was gone."

"What was your dad doing all this time?" Gil held both of her hands, his eyes locked on hers.

"Drinking," she said. "Both of them. More and more. And fighting. Naturally, I thought it was all because of what I'd 'let' Milt do to me—yes, that's how I thought of it at first. The fact that none of us spoke a civil word to each other, except Chad and I in private, only drove that point home even harder." She glanced at her wine glass, still empty, and resisted the temptation to ask for more. Don't go down that path, girl.

"You haven't heard from your mother since?"

She heaved a great sigh. "Thanks to my father."

Gil nodded, stroking her hands with his thumbs. "So now she's coming to town and wants to bypass his blockade. How do you feel about that?"

She searched inside herself and found only foggy grief and anger where she'd hoped to find lucidity. "I don't know. So many things, I guess. Part of me wants to see her so bad, and another part doesn't believe that she tried. I mean, if my mother really wanted a relationship with me, why wait nine years to come back to town?"

"Great question," he said. "I have trouble waiting nine *minutes* to see you."

Val laughed, tension rolling off of her shoulders, and wrapped her arms around his neck. "You're wonderful, you know that?"

Gil chuckled and returned the embrace, pulling her body across his until she landed in his lap, their lips touching for a long moment. His hands slid up her back, then down to her hips.

At that point she pulled away, grabbing both of his hands between hers. "I...I'm not in that space right now. Mentally, emotionally. I'm sorry."

"It's okay," he said. "I didn't mean to, you know, get something started here. I'm trying to figure out how to best be here for you."

She smiled and leaned back into him. "Hold me," she said. "Just hold me."

Tuesday, July 2, 2019

Chapter Seventeen

Val's phone belted out the chorus of the old Dolly Parton tune "9 to 5," the ringtone she'd set up for emergency work calls. The noise jolted her out of bed, and she fumbled for her jeans on the floor of Gil's dark bedroom, pushing the phone against her ear. "Dawes here," she hoarse-whispered, glancing at the clock on the nightstand. 2:55 a.m. Dammit! She'd gotten maybe two hours' sleep.

"Val? Bobby Grimes. How soon can you get downtown?"

She yawned, despite the mix of frustration and excitement building inside her. The last time Grimes had called off-hours, they raided the sex trafficking ring's headquarters. She padded out to the living room, jeans still unbuttoned around the waist. "At this hour, fifteen minutes. What's going down?"

Grimes grunted. "Feds rounded up another gaggle of working girls outside Hartford and decided our jails had more available capacity or something. Forrestal claims it's all related to the prostitution ring, but we won't know until we debrief them all. Which Special Agent Orange insists has to be ASAP. With him involved, the only way we get any evidence is if we help collect it. Are you cleared to go back to work?"

Val took a long breath and heaved it out without hiding her annoyance. "Desk only. Dr. Cyrus hasn't OK'd me to carry a weapon yet."

Gil appeared in the bedroom doorway in his boxers, leaning on a single crutch and squinting in the dim light. "S'up, babe?" he said, yawning.

Grimes chuckled. "Whoa, Dawes. Is that a man's voice I hear? Sorry if I interrupted something."

"Just make sure there's coffee," Val said through gritted teeth. She hung up and offered Gil an apologetic smile. "Duty calls. I have to go in."

Gil sighed, a grimace overtaking his sleepy face. "At three in the morning? This can't be good. How can I help?"

She sidled up to him and held him tight for a long moment, savoring the return hug. "Get healthy so we can add you to the squad."

He grunted. "I was hoping you'd say, punch Grimes in the face." Disappointment and worry lined his face.

"I'll be fine. It's just interviews. No raids tonight." She tried to soften the message with a laugh, but it sounded forced.

Gil's glum expression confirmed it.

***

By the time Val reached Headquarters, Grimes had laid out an interview schedule for everyone on the team. The plan allocated a half hour for each pair of officers with each woman they'd arrested. "Our job is to find out where these young ladies came from and how they got here," he said. "The FBI will plug it all into their magic data machine and correlate it with info they've gathered in other cities. We're looking for specifics, they're studying for patterns."

Val and Grimes set up shop in a cramped, stuffy interview room, dim with unreliable overhead fluorescent lighting, with the ubiquitous one-way mirror taking up one wall. They alternated between the roles of questioner and observer, starting with a white woman of about sixteen who gave her name as Tiffany. No last name, no legal ID, and no help, either.

"The fuck we wasting our time here for?" Tiffany complained after refusing to answer even the most basic of questions. "I ain't done nothing wrong and I ain't got no lawyer."

"Soliciting sex for money is still against the law in this state," Grimes answered in a bored tone. "Of course, it might not be where you're from. Ohio, is it?"

Tiffany glared at him, then laughed. "Nice try, dude. I know my rights. I ain't gotta tell you nothing, and I ain't gonna."

Val detected a hint of an accent, tried to place it. Not Ohio. "Smart girl. You've been in trouble before?"

The girl sneered. "No. You?"

Val made a show of considering the question, taking a moment to reply. "My high school vice principal might make a case for that. Mr. Barnick. Do you know him?"

At the mention of that name, the girl started, then recovered and shook her head again.

Val played a hunch. "So, Tiffany Barnick, how long have you—"

"My name ain't Barnick," Tiffany said, her voice heated. "I mean—none of your fucking business, what my name is. I ain't talking to nobody. Y'all are wasting your time."

With that outburst, Val recognized her accent. "West Virginia. Let me guess. Wheeling? No, you're pretty savvy. A big-city girl. Morgantown? Your daddy's a professor? In the law school, maybe?"

Tiffany stared at her, a deer caught in the headlights. "How the fuck—?"

"Lucky guess," Val mouthed to Grimes, who appeared as surprised as Tiffany. To the girl, she continued, "My history prof at UConn was a proud Mountaineer. He always surprised me with the things he'd say. I always thought of folks from that part of the world as being really conservative, but not him. He was a rebel."

Tiffany scoffed. "Everybody assumes a person with a Southern accent is a redneck Klan member. Lots of us ain't. My daddy voted for Hillary Clinton—" She caught herself, shook her head. "Nope. I ain't saying nothing else without no lawyer in the room."

That ended that interview. While they waited for the next girl, Grimes said, "Nice bit of trickeration there, getting her to open up a little. We'll run her profile against missing persons in Morgantown. Shouldn't be too many law professors with runaway teens."

"What I don't get is why she'd run away from that, and why she's so reticent to talk about it," Val said. "And how does this connect to the Clayton bust?"

Grimes shrugged. "That's what we're supposed to find out."

Val made a sour face. "Why are we always busting the girls when it's the men running the ring we're after?" she said. "Yet they always walk out of here scot-free. Why?"

"The men walk because they lawyer up before we dig up any real dirt on them," Grimes said. "We're hoping to scare some of these kids into giving us something we can lever against the men. Sure, it seems unfair, but that's the game we've got to play."

The next few girls offered no helpful clues, either. One refused to say anything other than her name, and Val guessed her age at seventeen. Her fake driver's license pilfered the identity of a seventy-year-old California woman in hospice care. Another couldn't have been older than fifteen, maybe younger, and she did nothing but cry throughout the entire interrogation. Val tried to console her, but the girl rebuffed her attempts. A third only spouted slogans such as "women rule, men drool," and "all men are rapists." All shared a common theme: men sucked.

"This is pointless," Val said during their next break. "Why don't we just call their parents and ship them home?"

"We will," Grimes said, "if we can figure out the who and where. Damn, you're grumpy when you don't get your beauty sleep."

"I still say we're locking up the wrong people," Val said, ignoring the jibe. "These girls are the victims of the sex traffickers, not the organizers."

"Clayton PD's not running this show, remember? The feds are." Grimes drained the cold remnants of a paper coffee cup and tossed the empty in the general direction of the trash can. He missed by three feet.

Val yawned, irritation growing. "So tell the feds they screwed up. Where the hell are they, anyway?"

Grimes grinned and pointed at the mirrored wall that separated them from an observation room. "Taking notes. On everything, Dawes. Know what I mean?"

Val caught his meaning: On her, as well as the sex workers.

Screw it. Time to send them a message.

"So, the FBI's strategy is to blame the victims? So-o-o *smart.*"

A rap on the glass wall startled them. The overhead speaker spit static for a moment, then a male voice. "Whose side are you on, rookie?"

Val grimaced. Agent *Fucking* Forrestal. "Whichever side sends you back to the cave you crawled out of." She caught Grimes's eye and waved toward the door. "This is pointless. And I need a bathroom break."

Grimes beat her to the door and rapped on it twice. It opened, but instead of a Clayton uniformed cop greeting them, the doorway filled with Forrestal's black-suited, square-shouldered frame. "Where the fuck do you think you're going?"

"To take a leak," Grimes said.

"Both of you?" Forrestal laughed. "You two piss together? How romantic." He pushed his way into the room, backing them up and blocking their exit.

Grimes sneered. "For you, that would pass for romance. But hey, maybe you saved me a trip. Your face is nothing but a fucking urinal."

Forrestal turned as red as a fireplace poker, pushing Grimes backward, the door closing behind him. "Watch yourself, Paul Blart, or you'll be on the wrong end of these interviews in a New York minute." He softened, the condescending sneer returning. "Word on the street is, you like vice duty a little more than you ought to."

"Eat shit and die, Feeble Brained Insect," Grimes said, spittle flying. He leaned into the agent, grabbing his shirt and tie.

"Boys!" Val stepped between the two snarling men, pushing them apart. "Go measure your penises somewhere else. It's an hour until sunrise and we have too much work to do to waste time with this horseshit."

Forrestal yanked his arm out of Grimes's grip, pushing him by the shoulder for good measure. Grimes stepped back, his breathing heavy, but otherwise calmer. The two men glared at each other for a moment.

"So," Grimes said in a calm voice. "You gonna let us go tinkle, Teacher? Or shall we piss on your shoes?"

"Bobby." Val rolled her eyes.

"Fine, go," Forrestal said, disgusted. "You might as well, given how little you've gotten from these girls. Fucking amateurs."

"What's going on here?" Brenda Petroni stood in the doorway. Wearing no makeup, her already-ruddy complexion glowed an even brighter red, her eyes blazing. She took one step into the room, holding the door open.

"We were just about to take a break," Val said, "before resuming these *fascinating* interviews."

"I gathered that," Petroni said. "So why the hell does this resemble a WWE match more than a debrief? Haven't you guys learned even the slightest bit about interagency cooperation?"

"Abbott and Costello here have some, ah, *opinions* about how this debrief ought to be run," Forrestal said.

"Summarize them for me," Petroni said to the agent.

Forrestal stared at her, mouth agape. "*What?*"

"Show me what a good listener you are," Petroni said in a patient tone, "and summarize their professional opinions to me in your own words. I'll ask them to do the same in a moment, don't worry."

"I don't take orders from you, Angie Dickinson," Forrestal said. "This is an FBI operation. We make the rules here." He made his way toward the door.

Petroni stopped him by grabbing his arm. "Pepper Anderson."

Forrestal blinked. "Say what?"

Petroni smiled. "Angie Dickinson was the actor. The character's name was Pepper Anderson. Attention to that sort of detail, Special Agent, separates good police work that leads to convictions—"

"To the shoddy FBI crap," Grimes cut in, "that gets cases thrown out by federal judges."

Forrestal's face burned hot again. "Don't even presume to school me on investigatory procedure, ladies. I've closed more cases and made more arrests—"

"Nobody cares, Agent," Petroni said. "We're all on the same team here, right? With the same goal—shutting down this sex trafficking ring and putting their organizers behind bars. You asked for cooperation when we started this thing, and now I'm asking it from you. So, since you don't think it's part of your job, I'll ask my staff to answer my question. What's your beef, Grimes? Dawes?"

Val and Grimes exchanged glances. She nodded once and cleared her throat. "If we want to shut down the sex trafficking ring, why focus on the sex workers? The girls don't know squat, and even if they did, they aren't giving anything up. We need to aim higher." She fought the urge to lower her eyes, instead keeping them fixed on Petroni's.

"Sounds logical to me," Petroni said. "Agent?"

"I don't need to explain our process to you people," he said. "Again: our operation, our rules. You guys wanted to play, so we invited you into the sandbox. You want out, say so, and we'll find other local partners."

"Not in Clayton, you won't," Petroni said. "And I'm not being stubborn—that's just the way it is. We're the only game in town."

"The sheriff—"

"Operates under a written agreement to defer to our jurisdiction within city limits," Petroni said. "As per state law and city ordinance."

"Federal law—"

"Doesn't matter in questions of local jurisdiction, and you know it." Petroni relaxed, sitting on the edge of the table next to her. "So, can we both stop the bickering and get back to business? My officers have a point. What's your strategy here?"

Forrestal huffed and spun away from her. "It's a proven method," he said after a few moments. "Round up the visible miscreants, get them to talk, work our way up the food chain. Or don't they teach that at police academy in Connecticut?"

"They do, but is it working tonight?"

Forrestal threw up his hands and faced them again. "It. Takes. Time. It's a numbers game. If this batch doesn't produce, we go find more. Sooner or later, someone talks. It works. Trust me."

Grimes scoffed.

Val shook her head. "So, your answer to 'Why are we blaming the victims?' is to harass more victims?"

"If that's what you want to call it," Forrestal said.

"Sergeant?" Val spread her arms, begging Petroni for a reply.

"I'm with Dawes," Petroni said. "It isn't working, and it won't, because it's wrong-headed. We need a new strategy."

"So, you're telling me," Forrestal said, his voice rising, "that you won't participate in tonight's interviews? You're shutting me down? What the *hell* are we going to do with all those whores locked up in there? Thank them, give them each fifty bucks for their time, and send them home?"

"Sex workers," Val muttered.

Forrestal whirled and glared at her. "Come again?"

Val sighed. "Professionals call them sex workers. Not whores. That sort of locker room slang is beneath you."

Forrestal shook his head at the ceiling in disbelief.

"To answer your question," Petroni said after a pregnant pause, "we'll finish tonight's suspect interrogations, as promised. But the next roundup had better have some male faces in it, or I'll send them all back on the street faster than you can say JB Fletcher." She smirked, catching Val's eye, and Val nearly burst out laughing.

"Fucking amateurs," Forrestal muttered, and stomped out the door.

***

Maggie picked her way through the array of taxis, rideshare vehicles, and personal cars that clogged Bradley International Airport's arrival gates. She growled aloud in frustration. Bad enough that the small airport had allowed the slimmest strip of asphalt possible for finding and picking up exhausted travelers. These morons made it even worse by parking at odd angles in random spots, including around tight curves and alongside shuttle buses already too wide for the pavement provided. By the time she found the right exit, her nerves were as fried as overcooked bacon at a cheap diner.

To top things off, her soon-to-be-ex's 7:00 a.m. plane was late. Twenty more minutes, according to the airline's website. She'd have to circle around and do it all over again. Dammit!

She stopped for a cigarette alongside the airport access loop, resting against the car's rear fender. Though the sun had risen less than an hour before, the day had already grown warm and would reach into the nineties, with matching humidity. Perfect weather for the struggling tobacco farms she'd passed on the way in. Maggie saluted the farmers with the glowing butt in her hand, then stomped it out on the side of the road. She blew one last lungful of smoke in their direction in tribute. Without tobacco, God knows how shot her nerves would be.

Maggie looped around again, this time finding a tad less chaos in the arrivals area. She spotted her ex and their handsome son standing on either side of a large suitcase. No smaller case for the boy, dammit! She'd specified that Sammy would need his own. The boy and his father would part ways soon. She'd made vastly different plans for each of them.

She pulled over to the curb, popped the lever to open the trunk, and powered down the passenger-side window. "Get in," she said with no further greeting. "Put the kid in the back seat—not the bag! Luggage in the trunk, for God's sake!" She hissed air between gritted teeth. Mac reinforced the correctness of her decision to leave him every day, it seemed.

"Hi, Mommy!" Their nine-year-old slid across the back seat and wrapped her neck in a hug from behind, nearly choking her. "I missed you!" Sammy's bright blue eyes shone through shaggy bangs that hung over his eyebrows, almost to his cheeks. He looked like he was wearing a sandy-colored mop.

"I missed you too, Sammy boy." She pulled his hands away from her throat and kissed them. "Did you have a fun flight?"

"Yeah! The waitress gave me free Cokes and *two extra* bags of pretzels! And I got to watch a whole movie for *free!*" Sammy's grin widened and he bounced on the back seat on his knees. "I want to fly again tomorrow!"

"Sammy was great." Mac thumped his oversized frame into the passenger seat. He reached one arm across his body to scratch his opposite shoulder blade, then buckled in. Mac looked tired, his eyes bloodshot, his face flushed. "Sam, remember what we call the nice ladies on the plane? Not waitresses, but..."

"Oh, leave the kid alone." Maggie put the car in gear and darted out into the mad crush of vehicles zipping by them.

"Jesus!" Mac grabbed the handgrip near the doorframe, his knuckles white.

Maggie rolled her eyes. What a pussy. "We're going to be late to the meeting you set up, thanks to said pilot. Not a great way to start."

"We have plenty of time," Mac said. "The hotel's only a half-hour away. Sammy, buckle your seat belt, okay?" Mac's voice seemed slurred, like he'd had a few too many free vodka tonics on the plane.

She snuck a glance at his eyes: bloodshot. She grimaced. His hepatitis C had gotten worse.

"I hate seat belts!" Sammy resumed his bouncing, somehow landing his butt on opposite ends of the seat with every bounce. "Mommy, tell Daddy I don't have to!"

"Buckle up for safety, buckle up," Maggie sang, a tune she recalled her first husband singing to their kids many years before. "Wear your seat belt please…"

"Put your mind at ease, buckle up!" Sam finished the song, slid over behind Mac, and snapped his belt into place.

"Now, these people," Maggie said. "You've worked with them before?"

"Some," Mac said. "Bosco, anyway. He vouched for Smiley."

"Smiley?" She shook her head. "The hell kinda name is that?"

"Hell if I know," Mac said, loosening his grasp on the hand grip. "I suspect it's some kind of prison nickname."

Great. Fucking ex-cons.

"Does our hotel have cable TV?" Sammy asked.

Mac heaved a deep breath, pressing a fist into his thigh. "Hey, Sam, why don't you put on your headphones? They're in your backpack, with the iPad. Go on, watch that SpongeBob movie we downloaded."

"SpongeBob is for *little* kids," Sammy said, pouting. "Can I watch Avengers?"

"Sure," Mac said. Facing Maggie, he pressed a finger to his lips and jerked his head toward the back seat. Once Sam had his iPad on and earplugs in, he cleared his throat. "We'll have to bring him with us, Mags. He's got his electronics. He'll be fine."

"Nice," Maggie said, her voice laced with sarcasm. "Park the kid in front of a screen. Super-A parenting program you got there, Mac."

"Beats abandoning him and jetting off to Connecticut!"

Maggie shook the wheel in frustration. "Really? You want to have this conversation in front of the boy?"

"He's fine," Mac said. "You can't hear us, can you Sammy?" No response from the boy, who stared rapt at his screen.

"All right, then, the team," Maggie said, calming. "By day's end, we should have six more guys and gals to help with the event. But none are management material."

"I've got that in hand," Mac said. "You know Bosco?"

"From the Philly job? Heard of him." She fought off a sigh. Bosco had a reputation for being a few bricks short of a full load. "That's it?"

"He'll lead the event team with me. Smiley will help you on the street."

Maggie threw him a look, mustering as much disgust as she could. "Remember who's in charge here," she said with a growl.

"Plus," he went on in a cheerful tone, "Tanner's sending a dozen new girls in—from Maine, I think."

"Today, I hope. These stupid feds nearly wiped us out." She thought for a moment. "I don't like this division of labor much. I'm more of a logistics person. Speaking of which, I've got a lead on a new space."

"Good. Where?"

"I'll show you later today," she said. "Assuming Tanner wired the money like he promised."

"If I know Tanner, it's there," Mac said with too much enthusiasm.

Maggie bit her tongue. She did know Tanner. And she knew better than to trust him.

Chapter Eighteen

Val and Grimes returned from their nature break bone-weary from lack of sleep, interagency squabbling, and the run of fruitless interviews with the arrested sex workers. Val's focus lagged, and she longed for Gil's warm, comfortable bed.

"So, we just go through the motions with these women?" Val sipped lukewarm black coffee from a stiff paper cup. "What's the point?"

"You're probably right that we won't get anything of value from these girls." Grimes swirled his own cup and didn't seem to notice when it spilled onto the floor. He sat with his feet up on the table. "But you never know. Maybe we can pick up little bits here and there, put together a pattern that leads somewhere. Not that these federal bozos are smart enough to do anything with it."

"Watch your step, Grimes," Forrestal said over the speaker.

Grimes rolled his eyes and waved one hand over his head. "Send in the next victim."

A few minutes later, a uniformed officer escorted in a thick-waisted, light-skinned Black girl wearing a halter top, leather mini-skirt, and boots over fishnet stockings. Her garish mascara had smeared under her eyes, and gaps showed in her bright red lipstick. Thick makeup and straight black hair curling around her jawline failed to hide bruises on her face and shoulders.

"Getting rough in there?" Grimes asked when she'd taken a seat.

The girl stared at him, toying with her hair. "Beg pardon?"

Grimes pointed to her shoulders. "Looks like someone's used you like a punching bag a few times. Did that happen here? I can file a report, look into it—"

"Mind your own fucking business," the girl snapped. "I'm fine."

Val and Grimes exchanged glances, eyebrows raised. Val, still standing, picked up her file and browsed through it. "Angel N. White," she read from the top of the page. "How'd you pick that name?"

"I'm named for my grandma," Angel said. "You got a problem with that?"

"No, no, I like it," Val said. "It's clever."

The girl scoffed, turned away, said nothing.

"The arresting officer didn't find a driver's license in your possessions," Val said. "You don't own a car?"

Angel sighed and shook her head. "Who needs a car? Expensive toys that pollute the planet," she said, as if by rote.

Val picked up on her tone, filed it away for the moment. "So, you flunked the driver's test?"

"Fuck no." Angel laughed, a can-you-believe-this-shit sort of chuckle that shook her whole body.

Val nodded. "So, you've never taken it. Because you're not old enough?"

Angel leaned forward, as if to protest, then stopped herself short. "Dammit, you're gonna prolly find out whatever anyways. Yeah, I'm fifteen. Sixteen next month. Now don't go lecturing me with all that 'Why-aren't-I-in-school' bullshit. You ain't my daddy." She sat upright in her chair, indignant.

Val exchanged glances with Grimes. He signaled with a nod: keep going. She sat next to Grimes, but kept some distance between them. "When's the last time you spoke with your father?"

Angel shot her a puzzled glance. "The fuck that has to do with anything?"

"Where do your parents live?" Val repeated her interrogation mantra to herself: *Don't let them get to you.*

"What the hell does that matter?"

Val smiled at her. "Because we're required to call them. You're a minor. They're responsible for your legal defense. Which you'll need, unless you plan on spending the next few months enjoying the county's hospitality behind bars."

The girl froze for a moment. "What? *Months*? For what?"

Val shrugged, shaking her head. "It's stupid, I know. My partner here will attest to how much I complain about the bass-ackward nature of our prostitution laws. The women get arrested and abused, the men go off scot-free. Makes no sense, right? But what can I do? None of you girls will tell us anything about the pimps who steal all of your money and knock you around for coming up short some nights. Never mind that it's because some dickhead john stole your purse—"

"No shit!" Angel nodded with vigor, smacking her palm on the table. "Preach!"

"I can preach all night," Val said after a moment's pause, trying not to show her surprise. "It won't do any good unless we can make some of these scumbags pay instead of you girls. But hey, you do you. If you don't want to tell us anything, you can go back to Black Bars Hotel and sleep on the piss-covered floor until someone cracks your head open again. No skin off my nose." She closed the folder, stood, and stretched, and kept an eye on Angel. "Let's call in the next one, Bobby."

"Wait a second," Angel said. "I never said I wouldn't talk. You never asked me nothing except where my damn daddy lives!"

Grimes held up his hands as if in surrender. "Technically true, Dawes. You should ask her something."

"Your actual name?" Val returned to her seat. "The one on your birth certificate."

The girl's face fell, and she stared at a spot on the table. "Alyssa Dixon."

"Hometown?"

"Richmond, Virginia."

Grimes's eyebrows shot up. Val caught his meaning: a new city in the network. "What brought you to Clayton, Alyssa?"

The girl shrugged. "Guy named Tanner."

"Tanner what?" Grimes said. "Is that his first name or his last name?"

"Fuck if I know," Alyssa said. "He was hanging out at the under-21 club with some white chick, Jackie or Julie or something. My girlfriend Wanda said he had some Ecstasy and she wanted to buy some from him." Alyssa's eyes darted away. Val guessed Wanda was fictional, but let it go. Alyssa continued, "Jackie got to talking about how we could make easy money and help save the country. Uh, Wanda asked him how, and this Jackie chick talked about how The Man was keeping women and Black folk down with their cops and taxes and shit. I'm like, yeah, that's straight talk, for a change. She offers us some liquor from her flask, and we're like, shit, yeah. Next thing I know, I wake up in a van, wearing a blindfold and handcuffs. Then we pull up in this dogshit little town—I mean, here, in your *fine city*." Alyssa's voice trailed off.

"Wanda too?" Grimes asked in an innocent tone.

Alyssa blinked at him a few times, then went wide-eyed. "Uh...no. She musta got away."

"So, tell me about this Tanner guy," Val said. "Old, young, Black, white? Is he still here in Clayton?"

"He's an old white dude, probably forty or fifty," the girl said without irony. "Kinda tall, about six feet? Skinny guy—wiry, my dad would say. He combs his hair back over a great big bald spot. Some weird splotches of color on his face, some sort of skin condition."

"What about this Jackie woman?" Grimes asked.

That startled Alyssa, and she glared at him as though he'd appeared out of nowhere. "White chick, kinda chunky, with like, blue hair. I don't remember anything else."

"Okay. Where might we find them?" Grimes asked.

Alyssa shrugged again. "I got no idea. I ain't seen them since Richmond. No, wait. Tanner drove the van here, or was in it. When they dumped us off at the warehouse, I heard him talking to some guy he called Pedro."

Val recognized the name: one of the men they arrested during their Saturday night raid. "Us? How many other girls were there?"

"Two or three? Only one from Richmond. Bella. I ain't seen her since that night, either."

"Since the ride in the van, you mean?"

Alyssa shot her a sour look, then nodded. "She got to talking with Tanner about some political shit. Like, Keep America White or some such, working for pay. When we got out of the van, they brought her somewhere else. I got no idea where."

Val's eyes connected with Grimes's for a moment. "They didn't discuss the political stuff with you?"

This generated another how-stupid-are-you roll of the eyes, and no comment.

Val paused, sorting out the girl's story in her head. "So, they offer you a job of sorts, and don't say what it is. Then they drug your drink, spirit you four hundred miles north, promoted White Supremacist politics...and you stayed? Why?"

The girl shot her a disbelieving stare, mouth agape. "The fuck, you think I got the kind of money I can just hop on a plane back to Virginia?" She shook her head. "I try something like that, Pedro and them would kill me before I even got close to the airport. They got trackers on our cell phones and God-fucking-help us if our battery goes dead. Besides, what's the fucking point? My momma and daddy don't want me at home. I only get *in their way*." She spat out the final words with a sneer.

"I'm sure they're worried about you," Val said. "And is this life here better than what you had there, even with their neglect?"

Alyssa heaved a deep breath, exhaled. Tears trickled down her cheeks. "I guess not."

"We can talk to them, let them know that you're safe," Val said. "Don't you think they'd want to hear from you?"

Alyssa shrugged, sniffling.

"When was the last time you spoke with them?"

The girl concentrated a moment, shrugged again. "Month or so? I sorta lost track." More tears.

"They've got to be worried," Val said. "Don't you think?"

Alyssa wiped her face dry with the back of her hand. "P-prolly, sure." Grimes offered her a tissue, and she thanked him. "I guess, if you want to call my parents, that'd be okay."

Moments later, Brenda Petroni escorted the girl to her office where they could track down her parents.

"That was interesting," Grimes said. "They find kids with neglectful parents, then try to lure them away with promises of drugs and money—and careers in right-wing politics? Let's keep on this track, see what else turns up."

"Don't waste your time, or mine," Forrestal's voice boomed over the speakers. "Stick to the objective: find this Tanner guy and his cronies. Leave the political science to the professionals."

Val rolled her eyes and shot the mirrored wall a sarcastic salute. Grimes covered his laughter with an open palm.

Over Forrestal's objections and frequent griping between interviews, Val and Grimes elicited similar stories of abduction from the next several young women. Many also shared tales of finding a sympathetic adult—as often as not, a woman—promising freedom from "oppressive" rules and discipline. Others spoke of the adults offering a better life from neglectful parents. A few repeated Alyssa's second-hand tale of political recruitment.

"This must be connected to those White Supremacy pamphlets O'Reilly confiscated in the raid," Grimes said. "Somehow the Patriots Pride folks are involved in this sex trafficking thing. My question is, who's driving the train here? Are the Nazis using trafficking as a cash cow to fund their protests? Or are the traffickers using politics as bait, or as a smokescreen?"

"Leave the analytics to the people who know what they're doing, please?" Forrestal's voice crackled overhead. "Jeez Louise, guys. It's not a long enough night, you need to prolong it with your half-baked political theories? Just interview the damned suspects!"

A sharp tone, like speaker feedback, pierced the room, followed by someone clearing their throat. "Sorry about that," Sergeant Petroni said. "This is Petroni. Disregard Special Agent Forrestal's direction on that. Keep doing what you're doing."

"Sergeant Petroni!" Forrestal bellowed. Val covered her ears, too late. "You do not have the authority—"

"My staff, my facility, my orders." Petroni's voice rose over the speaker as well. "You don't like it, go complain to the ghost of J. Edgar Hoover. Or find staff to conduct the interviews yourself. That's final. Grimes, Dawes—go home. You're done for the night. Forrestal, you and Powers, my office. Now."

Val and Grimes grinned at each other. "Last one out the door buys breakfast," Grimes said.

Val, taking the stairs three at a time, beat Grimes's elevator to the first floor by two minutes, where she waited for him in triumph. "I'll take a rain check on breakfast," she said. "I've got a busy day ahead. And I need sleep."

***

Against her better instincts, Maggie drove them straight to the sleazy motel where her estranged husband rented a room for their organizing session. The two-story pastel-vinyl-sided chunk of drabness overlooked the state highway halfway back to Clayton. It smelled of an ongoing war waging between carpet mold and cheap disinfectant, and at the moment, mold had gained the upper hand. The room itself consisted of a 15' x 20' rectangle with all of its tiny windows placed high on one exterior wall. Dim fluorescent lights flickered from the drop-ceiling of crumbling overhead tiles that someone should have incinerated decades before. Mac chose the place for its low price, easy access, and promises of discretion should any law enforcement types come prowling around. Perhaps most important, the motel was willing to deal in cash—meaning no paper trails.

They set up Sam in what the manager labeled a "breakout room," more of a walk-in closet with a small table and folding chairs. They supplied the lad with a coloring book, crayons, and a family-sized box of pre-sweetened dry cereal. With his iPad and headphones, he hopefully wouldn't overhear or understand the discussion underway in the adjacent meeting room.

Ten minutes later, two of the new hires ambled in. Bosco, a tall, wiry man with long, greasy light brown hair tied back in a ponytail, leathery tanned skin, and a straggly beard, looked anywhere from thirty to forty. Bosco did not dress to impress: he wore torn jeans and a T-shirt from a heavy-metal concert at least a decade old. He spoke in a voice suggestive of hearing loss—overly loud, as if he couldn't hear himself over his own uproar. "Mac!" Bosco wrapped Mac in a weak hug. "How long's it been, man? Ten years? You ain't changed a bit. Still fat!" He howled at his own joke and slapped Mac on the butt.

"Bosco, this is my better half, Maggie," Mac said. Maggie scowled at the "better half" moniker, but Mac ignored her. "She'll be heading up our street ops. Maggie, Bosco Nicorelli."

"I haven't decided who's managing what yet." Maggie shuddered at Bosco's wide-armed offer of an embrace and scooted away before any part of him landed on her. "Your companion here is...?" She glanced at the quiet, heavy-set woman standing behind Bosco with her arms folded across her chest. The woman's blue-and-orange hair sprayed out in all directions, as if a tie-dye T-shirt had exploded around her head. Her tight-fitting tank top showed off the considerable array of tattoos covering her arms, shoulders, and neck. Oversized red-framed glasses with yellow lenses made her eyes appear as large as salad bowls, and the bored scowl on her face could stop the advance of twenty U.S. Marines.

"Jackie," the woman answered in a dainty voice. "Most people call me Smiley."

Maggie turned wide-eyed to Mac. "This is Smiley? I thought..."

"That I was a man? Yeah, I get that a lot." Smiley grinned for no apparent reason, and then Maggie understood the nickname. "So do you, no doubt."

Maggie shrugged off the insult. That was the least of her concerns. The woman's caustic smile revealed brown, crooked teeth and a soul of pure evil, in Maggie's eyes. But she never expected Mac to recruit Mother Theresa, either.

Maggie sat at a bare, six-foot folding table in the center of the room and waited for the others to follow suit, then addressed Jackie. Er, Smiley. "Mac said you had experience...and recruits?"

"Enough," Smiley said with a nervous grin. "Of both. They're being trained as we speak."

"You need to train them to fuck for money?" Mac asked. "I should think that would be almost instinctive."

"There's lots these girls need to learn," Bosco cut in, sitting across from Maggie. "How to spot a cop, for example. How to make the john say what he wants first. How to, you know, get the session over with quickly." He grinned, and his breath, a horrid mix of coffee, cigarettes, and sewer pipe, wafted over Maggie. She gagged before she could stop herself and covered her mouth and nose.

"There's also the issue of keeping them from running," Smiley said.

"Putting the fear of God in them if they do," Bosco said.

Maggie turned her head away to avoid the wave of stink breath heading her way. God bless Mac for taking Bosco as his aide and giving her Smiley and the street operations, after all. She turned to Mac, sitting next to her. "I thought the girls were in transit?"

Mac shrugged. "I'm always the last to know."

"They are," Smiley said. "Tanner starts the orientation on the road, in the van. Then they spend a day in a facility. Speaking of which, do we have one?"

"No, not yet," Maggie said. "I'll get on that right after this meeting. What about the girls' managers? On-the-street guys. You know what I mean."

"Pimps," Bosco said with a nasty grin. Another tidal wave of aerosol shit flooded across the table. "Yup. They all walked within 24 hours of the raid. Most of 'em are waiting on us to get going again."

"Then let's talk about the event," Mac said. "That's where we're most behind. Where are we on that?"

"Word's gone out on social media—Discord and Gab," Bosco said. "Don't worry, it's all hyper-secure. The night of the Fourth, during the fireworks and leading up to them, we strike. During the day, we'll have hundreds—no, thousands—of people marching, ready to take back this country. They've been told to remain peaceful unless provoked, but to be ready in case we're attacked."

Maggie turned away from his awful breath again, fighting the urge to vomit. She addressed her question to Mac, though she doubted he knew the answer. "You've secured all necessary locations? Meeting points, marching routes, all that?"

"Yeah. I mean, it's not like we're applying for fucking permits," Bosco said, erupting into a raspy, loud laugh that Maggie feared would shatter the windows. "People are scouting out spots and getting the word out. They'll be ready."

Mac cleared his throat and held up a hand to silence Bosco. "Speaking of recruiting, how's your insider work going? Any luck infiltrating the boys in blue?"

Maggie smiled, her pride swelling. "I found a pretty senior guy who's lining up like-minded colleagues, ready to crack 'Antifa' heads as necessary. I'm working on finding more."

"Antifa?" Bosco's hands trembled and he patted his shirt pocket, as if searching for cigarettes. "Those bastards are bad, man. Fucking terrorists. My cousin got into a fight with one—"

"We'll be ready for them, don't worry," Mac said.

Maggie hid a smile behind her hand. No point explaining to Bosco that the officers would find "Antifa members" whether or not any showed up. "All right. Jackie—er, Smiley—keep me posted on the progress of our recruits. I'll secure a facility that can house them. What's their ETA?"

"Six o'clock tonight," Smiley said.

"Nine hours," Maggie said. "It's going to be a busy day. Let's get on it!"

Chapter Nineteen

Val arrived at the physical therapist's clinic a few minutes before Gil's appointment ended. She somehow resisted the urge to camp out at a nearby café and pour triple-shot espressos down her throat. Her head pounded, but sleep would serve her better than caffeine.

Followed by a week or two straight of cuddling with Gil.

She waited in a stiff, metal-framed chair for a few minutes, and considered asking the receptionist if he'd be out soon. Before she made it out of her seat, Gil limped into the waiting area, carrying his crutches.

"Val!" His eyes grew wide, his mouth forming a small "o." He stumbled backwards, then grinned and righted himself. "I thought—"

"You think too much." She enveloped him in a huge hug. "No way I'm missing out on getting the straight skinny from your doctor on how you're doing." To the receptionist, she added, "He always sugar-coats the prognosis, the little liar."

"He won't need to, today," said a tiny, thirty-something Black woman in scrubs behind him. Dr. Kimbreaux, his therapist, slid around him and patted him on the shoulder. "Gil's making terrific progress. Record-breaking, in many respects, all things considered."

"Doc says I'm almost ready to go back to work," Gil said. "Desk duty, at least, right?"

"Assuming they'll take your ornery old self back," Kimbreaux said. "However, fixing your attitude is outside my job description."

"We're cops," Val said. "Ornery is a job requirement." Then, to Gil, "That's wonderful! We should celebrate."

Gil hugged her again. "Lunch? I'll buy." He kissed Val and squeezed her hand. "Then after we can swing by HQ and get my reinstatement paperwork moving."

"Perhaps later this afternoon?" she said. "I really need some shuteye. I haven't slept since I saw you last. What was that, 3:00 a.m.?"

"I'd love to join you," he said with a twinkle in his eye.

"I'll leave you two to your 'sleep' plans," Dr. Kimbreaux said with a sly smile. Val buried her face deeper into Gil's chest so the doctor couldn't see her blush.

Gil caught her up on the prognosis on the drive to his house. His hard work at home and at the gym between therapy sessions had paid off, strengthening the muscle tissue and allowing his injured pelvis to heal ahead of schedule. "So, instead of early August, we're looking at mid-July for my return to duty," he said. "Maybe even next week!"

"That's amazing," Val said in a dull voice. Her headache had worsened with the heat, humidity, and the sun's bright glare.

"Gee, don't go all overboard with excitement," Gil said with a frown.

"I'm sorry, Gil. I can barely keep my eyes open." She slammed on the brakes when the taillights on the car ahead of them glowed red, and Gil lurched forward in his seat. "Sorry. I'd love to hang out with you today, but..." A yawn overtook her and, try as she might, she couldn't make it end.

He rested a hand on her thigh and squeezed. "I know. I'm just so excited. Look, come over to my place, get some rest, and when you're ready—"

"If I stay at your place, I won't sleep much." She grinned. "So, as tempting as that sounds, I can't. The minute I wake up, though, I'll head your way. I promise."

Gil smiled, squeezed her leg again. Warmth spread from his touch throughout her body. Damn, that felt so, so good. How much better it would feel with his arms around her, holding her, kissing her—

"You don't have to take me to HQ. I'll be fine." He patted her knee. "Hey, I know it's a long shot, but I'm going to ask to be detailed to the WAVE Squad. I want to work with you again."

"That would be wonderful." Val's heart brimmed with joy. "But I don't know of any vacancies yet."

"Details, details," Gil said. "Let me work my magic on the bureaucracy. You get some sleep. We can make plans to-night, over dinner."

Val sighed, turning onto Gil's cul-de-sac a little too fast. "I can't tonight. I promised Dad. How about after?"

He didn't answer for a moment. Then he forced a smile and glanced away. "Of course. After dinner's great. Will you be staying...?"

Val pulled into the driveway and put the car in Park, motor still running. She returned his smile with one far more genuine. In her opinion, anyway. "If you'll have me."

"In so many ways, honey. In so many ways." A devilish smile replaced his sad one, and he gave her thigh another gentle squeeze.

Val's heart raced. He'd made his intentions clear, and Val wanted it as much as he did, despite her trepidations. She helped him to his front door, his body pressed against hers. She marveled at how her body responded, with longing and desire rather than the revulsion she'd always felt when other boys touched her. Part of her wanted to go inside with him that very minute, to end her procrastination and let this new chapter of her life begin.

But exhaustion won out. Val also wanted to enjoy the experience, not risk falling asleep in the middle of it. She kissed him goodbye at the door and drove away, anticipation of the moment growing with every passing second.

Val hoped to fall straight into bed when she got home, but Dad greeted her in the living room with a hearty smile. "Valorie! Perfect timing. I made a fresh pot of coffee, and your room is all ready for you to move in. Let me show you!" He guided her by the arm toward the stairs.

"Sorry," she said, and meant it. She shook free and trudged toward the garage. "I've been at work since 3:00 a.m. and I desperately need to hit the sack."

"We're still on for dinner, right?" Dad said.

"Yes. To talk. Not just eat and gossip."

"I understand."

Val looked him square in the eye. "The truth this time. All of it. About Mom, and Milt, and...everything. Right?"

He stared at his feet. "Everything," he said in a low voice. "I promise." After a moment, he sat on the bottom stair. "*And I show you your room?*"

She laughed, tension flowing out of her. "Sounds awesome."

Minutes later, she lay under the covers in her garage-as-apartment and fell fast asleep.

***

Maggie secured their new headquarters space on Clayton's decaying east side, a three-story brick warehouse building with close proximity to the bohemian "Alphabet Soup" District. Besides its proximity to the red-light district, the space included private first-floor "offices" where the sex workers could provide their services. She tasked Smiley with furnishing the space with cheap thrift-store purchases and rentals, then moved on to the more strategic item on her to-do list: recruitment.

She entered the westside coffee shop a few minutes early for her 11:00 a.m. appointment, expecting she'd need to wait for her meeting companion to show. He surprised her, though, by standing and waving to her before she cleared the threshold. The tall, barrel-shaped man sported wavy, salt-and-pepper hair, slicked with sweat against his ruddy, pock-marked skin. Despite the day's heat, he wore an ill-fitting gray suit and black Oxford shoes that, together with the haircut, screamed "cop" to anyone with an ounce of sense. So much for discreet.

Maggie hustled toward the table, but a slender, pink-haired creature in a form-hugging sleeveless T-shirt blocked her path. "Welcome to The Claytown! Can I find you a seat, or are you here for a meet-and-greet?"

Maggie glared at the girl, a human pincushion of metal piercings and body art. She would be pretty if not for all the self-induced skin mutilation. "My colleague apparently started without me," Maggie said, indicating Mickey Mulroney with a wave of her hand. "Could I trouble you for a cup of black coffee?"

"Americano for the Americana, coming right up!" The barista bounced away, exchanging greetings with other patrons on her way back to the bar.

Maggie shook her head in disgust. The girl was about the same age as her estranged daughter. Hopefully they shared no traits in common, other than age.

"Maggie May, how the hell are you?" Mulroney extended a pudgy hand.

"Sh!" She glanced around, hoping nobody noticed them, and gave his hand a quick shake before sitting across from him. "Keep your voice down, you idiot. I thought you cops understood the meaning of the term 'undercover.' For God's sake!"

Mickey leaned back, grinning. "No one here knows me. That's why I picked this place. Plus they have a well-earned rep for great Joe. Damn, this cappuccino is amazing!"

"Yeah, yeah." Stupid coffee freaks in this world. Another scourge of the politically correct, Volvo-driving, liberal elites. Whatever happened to good old Folgers? Maggie set a small notepad and pen on the table. "I hope you have encouraging news for me."

Mickey smiled, sipped his coffee again, and patted his breast pocket. "This'll make you smile. More than smile." He chuckled with far too much pride for such an unaccomplished man.

She cocked her head, counting the seconds. "Are you going to share, or are you having too much fun making me wait?"

Mickey leaned back in his chair and folded his hands behind his head. "I am kind of enjoying this, actually. Far more important, however..." He slammed his chair back on all fours and leaned his elbows on the table. "Did you bring what makes *me* smile?"

"Of course." The fool. What kind of riff-raff did he typically deal with? The quickest way to failure in business was to stiff one's partners. Only a moron with a death wish would try something like that. "Once I see what you brought, you'll be well-compensated."

The waitress returned, set her coffee down, and asked if she wanted cream and sugar. As if she hadn't insisted on coffee, black. Maggie managed a polite "No, thank you," and waited for the strange creature to leave.

She turned back to Mulroney, who stared without shame at the girl's retreating ass. She rapped the table, recapturing

Mulroney's attention. "Come on, at least share some data with me. How many?"

Mickey glanced left and right, then lowered his voice. "Seven solid, plus five definite-maybes I'd bet the farm on. Four possibles, and I'm working on more."

"Including you?" Maggie sipped her coffee. Yuck. Pure mud. She'd suffered through crap this undrinkable in New Orleans once. She pushed it aside.

He shrugged. "I'm one of the seven, yeah."

"So, six for real, and a gaggle of names you pulled off the personnel file."

Mickey snorted and slapped the table, his face reddening. He spoke in a low, angry hiss. "Don't belittle the work I've done. These guys are committed. They believe in the cause and are ready to risk their damned jobs to give our side a chance. *And* they'll be in position, on duty no less, when the time comes. You think this is easy, getting those strings pulled? Huh? Because you can go do it yourself if you—"

"Calm down. I'm just checking. It's my job." She waited for his breathing to return to normal before continuing. "You said 'guys.' So, no contact with any of the women on the force?"

Mickey scowled. "The broads in CPD are a bunch of left-wing lezzies, all too afraid to take risks that might hurt their careers. You know that as well as I do."

Maggie rolled her eyes. "Not all of them, surely. And you know who I mean, in particular."

Mickey drew in a quick breath and shook his head. "I ain't seen her. She's on that special women's task force. Lezzie libtard central, if you ask me. Not a real cop on the entire squad."

Maggie scowled. Coward. Afraid of talking to a twenty-three-year-old girl, for God's sake.

"You should talk to her," Mickey said after several moments. "She might respond better to a woman."

"Fine, then." Maggie sighed. It was just as well. Mulroney's bedside manner left a lot to be desired. He'd probably push her further away rather than bring her into the fold. She reached into her purse, pulled out an unmarked letter-sized envelope, and counted out twelve hundred-dollar bills. She stuffed the bills back into the envelope and returned the rest to her purse. "Okay, give me the list."

Mickey's lips pursed in anger. "We agreed on two thousand up front."

"That was for ten or more names. You've found me six."

"Bullshit! I'm giving you *extra*. And I'm putting them into position. I've more than earned my full amount!"

Maggie smiled and patted his arm, setting the envelope in his hand. "Then consider this a down payment. When we're all done, there'll be plenty more where this came from. Besides," and she shifted her tone, laying on the saccharine, "we're doing it for the cause, not the money. Right?"

Mulroney stared at her for a long moment, then slapped the list onto the table and stood. "I'll get you four more names, solid, by tonight. More tomorrow. You make sure you do your part, got it?" He grabbed the money, stuffed it into his pocket, and slammed the contents of his mug down his throat. "Since you called this meeting, coffee's on you." He pushed past some patrons waiting for the restroom and stumbled out the door of the café.

Maggie picked up her mug, thought better of it, and slid the so-called coffee away. Damned Mulroney. Now she'd have to do this the hard way.

Chapter Twenty

Walking along the shoreline, soft waves lapping on the white sand, Val's hand clasped Gil's. To her surprise, he walked with confidence beside her, without crutches, or even a limp. He turned and lifted her, and she gazed down at him, the muscles of his sun-tanned arms and chest rippling with easy exertion, his smile wide with joy. She craned her neck closer to kiss him, and the awkward angle caused them to tumble into the warm surf. She laughed, and he rolled on top of her, kissing her neck, unclasping her bikini top, and she wondered if she should stop him. Such a public display—

A shrill, insistent chirping sound dashed away the sunshine, sand, and gentle waves, and Val woke to the much less inspiring environs of her makeshift garage bedroom. Rays of bright light snuck in around the blackout curtains hung over the windows, casting an uneven gloom over the humble space. She sat up and found her phone, which she'd forgotten to silence before her daytime slumber. Caller ID showed a Clayton PD prefix. "Hullo?"

"Dawes. Grimes here. Did I wake you?"

Val yawned in response. "Whassup, Bobby?"

Grimes's breath filled her ear, a sound of irritation and impatience, his two most signature qualities. "Vice squad transferred another couple of girls over to us, and Petroni wants you and me to debrief 'em before she decides whether to rope in the feds. You game?"

Val groaned and plopped her head back onto her pillow. "Seriously? There's nobody else?"

"I guess Shannon O'Reilly has a sick kid, and Price turned off his phone. We're it. Come on, can I count on you?"

Val heaved a deep breath and considered it. "What the hell. I'm awake. See you in twenty."

She missed that mark by ten minutes. No way she could go in again without a shower.

Grimes had a cup of coffee waiting for her in the observation annex of the interrogation room where their first subject waited. The woman glared at them, cross-armed and cross-legged in the uncomfortable chair facing the one-way mirrored glass. "This gal says she works for a pimp named Tyler Paxton—correction, *worked*," he said. "That's the guy you ran down during the raid on Saturday, right?"

"Why wasn't she hauled in with the others?" Val sipped the bitter black brew. She wondered whether Grimes even remembered that Val took her coffee with cream. Attentiveness to details about his partner did not count among his greatest attributes.

"Those girls hailed from the Hartford area, remember? This one's local, from the Alphabet Soup District." Grimes downed his coffee, grimaced, and set his empty cup on her desk. "Ready?"

Val took one more sip of her drink and tossed the rest in the garbage, where it belonged. "Let's get some answers."

The pencil-thin young woman had light brown skin and long, straight hair streaked black and green in horizontal rows. She continued the color themes with emerald tints around her eyebrows, broad arcs plucked to a millimeter in width, green eyeshadow, and black lipstick. A shade shorter than Val's five-foot six height, she wore a tight halter top, a black leather skirt, and dark green fishnet stockings that disappeared into black boots trimmed in green. She gave her name as Jade and claimed to be eighteen.

"I want to make it clear from the get-go," Val said,

ignoring Grimes's disapproving glare, "we're not after you. We're after some information."

"And if you don't supply it, we'll charge you for solicitation, which means you rot in here until your pimp comes by to post bail," Grimes said. "Which will be very difficult, because his ass is rotting in the men's section as we speak."

Val wondered if Grimes checked on Paxton's status prior to the interview. She'd assumed he'd posted bail within hours of his arrest.

"What kinda information?" Jade chewed on something, God knows what. The guards would have relieved her of any sort of gum or candy when locking her up. "I already told you my pi—boss's name. What the hell else you need?"

"Where are you from, Jade?" Val asked.

Jade shot her a surprised glance. "Uh, Detroit. Dearborn, to be exact. Why?"

"Interesting. What brought you to Clayton?" Val said, nonchalant.

Jade laughed. "Fucking work, what else? Ain't no jobs in Detroit."

"You came all the way to Clayton to work as a prostitute?" Grimes said, laughing. "What, nobody in Detroit likes sex?"

Jade scoffed and shook her head. "Can't do sex work in your own backyard. What if your old man or his buddies come buying? Fucking game over, you hear what I'm saying?"

Val held up a hand to keep Grimes silent for a moment. "So, you *chose* sex work as your profession?"

Jade laughed. "Yeah, the job of President of the United States was already taken. I went with Plan B."

Val and Grimes exchanged a quick glance. Seems every prostitute in Clayton came armed with the same joke, or some version thereof. Jade, at least, seemed willing to talk, and Val pressed the point. "We're interested in how this entire network works, how a girl gets recruited, et cetera, et cetera. Who signed you up and brought you here?"

Jade eyed her dark green fingernails, each of which extended an inch beyond the tips of her fingers. "Dude's name was Jacob. No, Jason. Something like that. Met him at a party, me and some other girls. He was kinda good-looking, real muscular, you know? Super hot car, a Jaguar or some such. Dressed super fine, too. Like he had money."

"What did this Jason fella tell you?" Grimes said. "Let me guess: a pretty girl like you could make a lot of scratch on the East Coast. Modeling, maybe?"

"More or less," Jade said, some of the vivacity draining from her voice. "Except he didn't say it'd be East Coast, or anywhere, really. Just talked about the money and the 'opportunities' for a girl like me."

"He was convincing?" Grimes said.

Jade chuckled. "Enough to get me in his bed, drinking his booze, and...you know. Stuff. Wait, am I gonna get in trouble for saying that? Being under twenty-one and all?"

"We're not interested in that," Grimes said, with a conspiratorial glance at Val. "If he gave you booze or drugs, that's on him, not on you. Are you still in touch with this Jason guy?"

"Pfft! I ain't heard hide nor hair from him in two months. Get this: he promises all this shit. I say, okay, sounds good. He gives me some drinks and some pills, and the next thing you know, I wake up in a shitty little room with a couple of other girls. One of em's fucking some fat guy, and he looks over at me and says, 'You're next.' I'm like, fuck this, and I try to get out of there, but the goddamned door was locked from the outside. Son of a bitch raped my brown ass, and I do mean my *ass*, the kinky motherfucker. Dude did all three of us and still had a hard-on the size of the Empire State

Building. Fucking hurt like fire down there for days."

Val drew in a shaky breath, exhaled. "I'm sorry to hear that. Could you identify the man? If that happened here, I promise you, we'll—"

"Do nothing, as always," Jade said, spittle flying. "Lying fucking cops. To answer your question, I got no idea what town I was in. I never saw the light of day in that place. We ate, slept, fucked, pissed, and shit in that tiny room. We were lucky if they changed the smelly ass water in the pail we squatted on to relieve ourselves. Musta been twenty, thirty guys a day coming through, using us, and they didn't even give a shit that we hadn't showered all day. I tell you what, I doubt most of them bathed, either, the way they stunk."

Val blinked, mouth agape. The girl's unexpected rant, uncharacteristic of the sex workers they'd brought in over the past several days, caught her off guard with its vitriol and level of detail—so much so, she hadn't written a single word on her notepad. Nor, from the looks of things, had Grimes. She hoped the techs captured it all on tape. "How long were you there?" Val asked when she could compose herself again.

"A week, maybe? Then off to another place just like it, except this time, they gave us new clothes each day. If you can call it clothes. Mostly used underwear, or maybe a skirt and a halter top. There were two or three of those places, all of them disgusting."

"How did they move you around?" Grimes asked. "Were you conscious for it?"

"One time I was," Jade said. "I figured out how they were drugging us. Most days they barely fed us, said the guys didn't like fat girls. Then they'd all of a sudden give us some real good food, like steak or fried chicken. After you eat it, you go out like a light and wake up in some new hell-hole. So the last time, I gave another girl my dinner and faked going to sleep. They dumped us on the piss-covered floor of a shitty old van and drove a while. Then they dragged us into a new place for another round of the same thing."

Bile rose in Val's throat. She forced it back down, fighting the urge to vomit. "When did you arrive in Clayton?"

Jade gave that some thought. "About a month ago? When we got here, they told us, 'Good news. You ain't gotta live in these shitty rooms no more.' But we gotta go find our own business. Gave us a quota, and all that. If we miss quota, we go back to the rooms. Nobody fucking wants to do that, so you bet your ass we found ways to market our goods, if you catch my drift."

"Did you ever try to run away?" Val asked. "If so—"

"If so, I'd be a dead-ass tramp instead of talking to you here today," Jade said. "Besides, the work's not so bad once you get used to it. I mean, those stinking fuck rooms, that was bad. But finding our own johns and doing 'em, hey, it beats fucking farm work. At least they don't beat our asses, most of 'em. They give us decent clothes, hook us up with some quality blow and weed now and then. Some spending money, nice hotels. If we make quota, that is."

Val's jaw dropped, and she widened her eyes in Grimes's direction.

"Stockholm Syndrome," he whispered, giving his head a tiny shake.

More like Battered Woman Syndrome, Val recalled from Psych 101. "That's crazy," she whispered back, not bothering to correct him.

"I heard that." Jade sat up straight in her chair. "Let me tell you something, Miss Prissy-ass Cop. I know you don't approve of what I do. Big fucking deal. It's not the career I dreamed of, and I won't do it forever. At least when I land on my back, I get something for it. When you put out for your man, what the fuck do you get? Huh? A little jewelry, or some grocery money?"

Val, too shocked and angry to reply, could only clear her throat, and even then, she choked on it. She glanced at Grimes and wondered if he could sense her humiliation. From his self-satisfied smirk, he seemed to enjoy her discomfort over Jade's rant, and that only made her angrier.

"Fucking white-ass, middle-class motherfuckers," Jade continued. "You think your pussy's too pure to let it work for you. But tell me this: how often do your bosses make you do shit you hate? What do you do then? Do you tell them to go fuck off? Do you pull out your guns and blow their fucking heads off? No, of course not. You bend over and take it, like I do. Except in your case, you don't even get off once in a while. God damned holier-than-thou sons of bitches!"

"I think we're done here." Grimes walked to the door and rapped on it twice. "Thanks so much for your help."

"Yeah, we good." Jade held out her cuffed wrists for Val to unlock them.

The door opened, and a uniformed officer escorted Jade back to her cell.

Grimes turned to Val, his expression full of concern. "That was rough, eh? Hope that didn't get too personal for you."

Val waved him off and waited for him to exit. She bent over in her chair, heat rising in her face and neck. The woman's horrific tale spooked her, and the jabs about her job situation and her so-far nonexistent sex life hit too close to home. What Jade described was far removed from a normal, healthy sex life. But nothing in Val's life related to what the woman had experienced—except the one thing she wanted to forget. The woman, and her story, seemed alien, almost fictional.

That complete lack of a connection, the total lack of relatability to a fellow woman, victim, and human being, haunted her in ways she hadn't expected.

Chapter Twenty-One

After a few more uneventful interviews, Val returned to the WAVE Squad office, where Sergeant Petroni greeted her with some unwelcome news.

"We need all hands available this week," she said. "Extra shifts wherever possible. I'll tell you why, but keep this under wraps. Don't talk to anybody outside of the Squad, and assume that nobody you talk to knows why. Understood?"

"Why all the secrecy?" Val said.

Petroni pointed to her open door, and Val got up to push it shut.

"Anonymous tipsters alerted us to the possibility of violence taking place on the July Fourth holiday," Petroni said. "I'm talking organized, armed militias, hoping to make a statement on Independence Day. A 'Strike for Freedom' is the language being used, or so I understand."

"Whoa. Here, in Clayton? Why?"

Petroni held up both hands, palms-up. "Something to do with a purported Revolutionary War event. An attack on an armory or some such?"

"You mean Shay's Rebellion? That happened in Springfield, after the war was over. People wanting to overthrow the Continental Congress."

Petroni chuckled. "You must stay glued to the History Channel. Anyway, with this crowd, facts don't always matter. Bottom line, we need to staff up for this thing."

"There's one problem," Val said. "Cyrus hasn't cleared me for street duty yet."

"Not exactly true. He wouldn't clear you to carry a weapon. It's not up to him to decide how we deploy you."

Val's brows knitted together. "Street work kind of requires being armed, doesn't it?"

Petroni shook her head. "Not necessarily. We often assign unarmed officers to various duties outside this building. As with them, what I want from you is your presence, in uniform, as a reminder to the public that we're there, in force. I want your eyes, ears, and intuition on this. You don't need a gun for that."

Val considered it. "No, I don't suppose I do, and if I'm partnered with armed officers..."

Petroni grinned. "I think, Officer Dawes, that we've got ourselves a plan. Now, go home and get yourself some sleep."

***

When Val arrived home, her father's SUV sat in the drive-way, the rear passenger door open. Two bags of groceries lay sideways on the back seat. She sighed with mixed emotions. When sober, Dad always drove a little too fast. She repacked the wayward onions, tomatoes, dry spaghetti noodles, and salad dressing into the bags and carried them inside.

She found her father busy in the kitchen, chopping garlic and humming to himself. He glanced up, and his face fell in embarrassment. "Oops. I guess I forgot about those." He took the groceries from her and gave her a quick hug. "I thought I'd get an early start on dinner. My specialty of the house..."

"Spaghetti and meatballs," they said in unison, and laughed.

"I'll help with the salad." She grabbed a couple of tomatoes.

He waved her away. "No chance. You relax. This dinner's on me. Anyway, it's going to be a few hours. Go on, now. I'll call you when it's ready."

Val didn't need to be told twice. She headed straight to the garage and climbed into bed, with only a sheet for bedcovers on the warm afternoon. She expected to fall right to sleep, and her heavy eyelids and weary body seemed willing. Only the occasional clink of plates and spatulas interrupted the perfect quiet of the day.

But the silence only allowed her mind to wander. The jabs from Jade, the sex worker, still stung. The whole encounter left her feeling even more insecure about her relationship with Gil—particularly on the physical side, where her apprehensions dictated the terms. For whatever reason, Gil put up with it—for now. How long could that last?

After two hours of tossing and turning, she gave up. Besides her overactive brain, she couldn't get comfortable. After two nights at Gil's, her ancient single bed now seemed lumpy and small. Her head still in a fog, she pulled on a sleeveless T-shirt and shorts, considered applying make-up to cover the dark circles under her eyes, and opted out. This was dinner with Dad, not a date with Gil. Minutes later, she rejoined her father in the kitchen.

"How was your nap?" he asked, tossing chopped greens into a wooden serving bowl.

"Unsuccessful. How can I help?" Hands on hips, she stretched her back. That, at least, felt good.

"Too late to help, too early to eat." Dad added chopped tomatoes, carrots, and onions into the bowl. "How about a tour of the new bedroom while we wait?"

"Sure." She followed him up the stairs, and he stopped at the closed door to what used to be her parents' private enclave.

"Close your eyes," he said. "I want you to get the whole effect at once."

She chuckled and did as he requested. She let her imagination wander, recalling its state the last time she'd peeked inside: a queen bed with a thick cherry frame, piled with Dad's clothes amid a tangle of pillows and blankets that hadn't been washed since the collapse of Rome. A matching nightstand and dresser, each with a burned-out lamp. Dust-covered photo frames, turned face down, used as coasters for a dozen or so coffee cups containing murky brown liquids. Laundry everywhere, and the smell of mold.

The door swished open and he took her arm, guiding her into the room. "Okay. Now."

She blinked her eyes open, and inhaled a quick, audible breath. No mold, no piles of dirty clothes. A golden oak bed, queen-sized, with a comforter that she would even describe as feminine. A vacuumed, off-white carpet. Every surface, clean and spare.

"It's beautiful, Dad," she whispered.

"Thanks," he said in a raspy voice, and wiped away a tear. She wrapped him up in a tender hug, holding him for several heartbeats.

Then, over his shoulder, she noticed the photos.

Most of them seemed innocuous enough: two pictures of Val—one with Dad at her high school graduation, and one with Beth, both of them eight or nine years old. Beside them, a photo Val took of Chad holding a trophy after his team won the league championship. Of course, her favorite photo, of Uncle Valentin, took center stage in front of a make-up mirror.

And then a picture she hadn't expected froze her in place and cut through her foggy-brained exhaustion. She tightened her grip on her father and stopped her breathing for several moments.

"What's wrong, honey?" Dad pulled back from her.

Val walked toward the 6"x9" framed photo, stopping a foot from it. She picked it up and cradled it in her hands, staring at it until her vision blurred.

"I'm sorry," Dad said. "I thought, since you'd asked about what happened—"

"Sh!" The command came out harsher than intended. Whatever. She blinked away tears and gazed up at the ceiling, regaining her composure. Then she looked down again, confirming what she'd seen a moment before.

A picture of Val as a little girl, holding the hand of a woman she hadn't seen in nine years—not even in a photograph. Tall and slender, the woman's wavy brown hair framed dark eyes and olive-toned skin. She smiled at Val with obvious love in her eyes.

After a minute, she set down the photo and said a silent, bittersweet hello to her long-lost mother, Rita Dawes.

***

Maggie's eldest son answered the door seconds after she rang the bell, an unsure smile spreading across his face. He'd matured so much since she'd last seen him, having lost the baby fat in his cheeks, and he'd adopted a more conservative cut for his sandy-brown hair. His early years of practicing corporate law—information she gleaned from stalking his wife's social media accounts, using a fake persona—had taken a toll on him. Dark circles appeared under his eyes, making him look exhausted, even at this dinnertime hour. Otherwise, he looked the same as she remembered. Handsome and fit, with an affable charm that fit his pleaser personality.

Chad gave her a tight, brief hug, then stepped back. "Come in, come in," he said, his words rushed. "Dinner is almost ready. The kids are dying to meet their grandma."

True to his words, the grandchildren—a cute-as-a-button six-year-old girl and a chubby, drooling toddler of a boy in a blue onesie—laughed and sang and ran in circles as he introduced them. Ali gave Maggie a tour of the sprawling, four-bedroom brick ranch, focusing on her own room, of course—a den of female superhero worship, from Wonder Woman to Captain Marvel. Among them all, one 9"x11" framed photo took center stage on the girl's dresser. Maggie's own daughter. No longer a sassy thirteen-year-old, but a grown woman, her enshrined photo surrounded by newspaper clips and cop paraphernalia.

She shook her head in dismay. Good Lord. This little grandchild had so much to learn.

They chatted for a while in the living room, the whole family gathered in a circle of sofas and easy chairs. Maggie's son and grandkids remained engaged, while her daughter-in-law Kendra sat stiff and reserved, like she wanted to flee, and often made excuses to leave the room. She checked on dinner (three times), changed the toddler's diaper (twice), and then took a call "from work" (on her silent phone). Whatever. No doubt her son poisoned that well ages ago.

"Dinner's ready," Chad said at long last. "Mom, won't you sit at the head of the table?"

"Can I sit next to Gramma?" Ali asked. So. Darn. Cute. Of course she can.

"How long are you in town?" Chad asked while serving her a thick slice of tenderloin.

"I'll be in the area for at least a few more days," she said. "It depends on how long this relocation effort takes."

"Mom is setting up a new field office for her company in Clayton," Chad told his wife. "I didn't catch the name of the firm…?"

"D&M Enterprises," Maggie improvised. "We specialize in logistics and public events management. May I try a few of those steamed green beans, please? They look tasty."

"They're best with lots and lots of butter!" Ali picked one up and chomped on it. She made a face and set it back on her plate, half-chewed.

"What sort of events does D&M manage?" Kendra asked, breaking her silence.

Long-practiced euphemisms sprang to mind. "Corporate gatherings," Maggie said. "Annual company-wide gatherings, that sort of thing."

"Who are some of your clients?"

"No one you would have heard of," Maggie said. "They like to keep a low profile."

"I'm confused. I thought you said the company did *public* events," Kendra said, brows furrowed.

"Public as in outdoors," Maggie said, her mind spinning. "Picnics, team-building, that sort of thing." When Chad appeared ready to ask another nosy question, she changed the subject. "May I have some more sour cream for these delicious potatoes?"

It worked. Chad either dropped or forgot his question. They made uncomfortable small talk for a bit, punctuated by long silences and Ali's jabbering on about stupid boys at school. Then Maggie honed in on the business reason for this trip.

"How is your law practice going?" Maggie asked Chad in a cheerful tone. "Have you made partner yet?"

"Oh, God, no," he said. "I'll be a staff attorney for at least a few years. It's mostly contracts for now. Things are going well, though, and I hope to move into litigation at some point."

"Contracts, how interesting," Maggie said, hoping she sounded sincere. "That's right up your alley. You've always been great at finding common ground between people." Keeping the peace at home, for example, with divorcing alcoholic parents and a rebellious younger sister.

Kendra broke into a loud coughing fit into her napkin, then rose from the table. "I should check on dessert. Your favorite, I'm told. Peach cobbler."

"Yay!" Ali cheered. "Wif ice cream, too, Mommy?"

"We'll see," Kendra said, hustling off to the kitchen. "Finish your vegetables first."

"So, no criminal law, or, say, civil litigation?" Maggie asked. "Estates, divorces…"

"No, I avoid that stuff like the plague," he said, his voice uneasy. "Too messy." Chad glanced away, then back up at her. "Why do you ask?"

"No reason. Just…curious." He was lying. Why? Maggie smiled and chewed another bite of tenderloin. Moist and succulent. "This is delicious," she added to break the growing silence.

"Things are good with you, then?" He sipped his wine, wiped his lips. "There are no, uh, legal issues in your life prompting that inquiry?"

"Well," Maggie said in a rush of air, "nobody's ever free of the judicial system in the world of business. And…" She caught herself, shook her head, and smiled at Ali, transferring her green beans onto her little brother's plate while Chad sat by, oblivious. "Chad, dear, we haven't spoken in nine years. Do we want to spend all our time talking about work?"

Another long period of silence, other than the clinking sounds of plates and the opening and closing of cupboards in the kitchen. The oven door thudding shut. Forks being counted. Water running in the sink.

"If you *want* to talk about it, though—"

"I may need some legal advice in the coming days," Maggie blurted out. "Relating to…well, my husband and I may, ah, need to split up some assets, both personal and business…"

"Ah." Chad frowned, moving food around on his plate. "Hence the questions about family and civil law. Well, I might be able to advise you a bit on the latter. As for the divorce legalities—"

"Even a referral." She shrugged. "It would mean so much to me."

"Of course. Whatever I can do to help."

"I wouldn't ask, but...well, let's just say, I don't expect this to be a congenial separation." Maggie paused for effect. "In fact, I anticipate an all-out attack."

"Wow, Mom, I'm so sorry." His eyes widened. "Of course, I'm glad to—Young lady! Leave Dar's plate alone. Eat your mashed potatoes. Sit. Now." He glared at the adorable little girl, who resumed an angelic pose in her chair.

Time to change the subject. "Have you spoken with your sister lately?" Maggie kept her tone casual.

Chad focused on his plate, taking his time to cut a piece of meat into bite-sized pieces. "Now and then," he said. "With my work, and hers, we don't always get to catch up. But the kids love her."

"She's my favorite auntie!" The little girl bounced in her seat. "Is Auntie Val coming for dessert, Daddy?"

"Not tonight, honey." He turned to Maggie. "I, uh, told Val you were coming."

"I'd like to see her. Do you think she'd be receptive?" Maggie's heart rate accelerated. So much rode on how she navigated these waters.

"I don't know. Probably."

"Probably?" Maggie chuckled. "She hasn't seen her mother in nine years, but only probably?"

"I don't know how to read her anymore," he said, his voice low. "Val and I aren't as close as we used to be. In fact, we're kind of...not fighting, per se, but not getting along so well lately."

"Would you be able to put me in touch with her, at least? An address, a phone number?"

"I suggest you call Dad. He can help you."

Maggie stared at him in surprise. "Your father? Last time he and I spoke, they weren't on speaking terms. Granted, that was at least five years ago."

"They've reconciled a bit."

"Does she still live in the area? Near her father, I mean?"

Chad started to answer, stopped, set down his fork, and drained the rest of his wine glass.

Maggie waited, her head cocked. He glanced at her, then away again.

"Holy...is she living *with* him?"

His face—no, his entire head and neck—reddened, and he wiped sweat off his forehead.

"I can't believe it," she said. "You're right, then. I know how to find her."

"Please don't tell her I told you—"

"You didn't," Maggie said with saccharine sweetness. "So neither of us needs to lie."

"Here's dessert!" Kendra reappeared, carrying a pan of hot peach cobbler. She paused, noticing their half-full plates. "Oh, I'm sorry," she said. "Too soon. Well, as soon as everyone's ready."

"I'm ready!" Ali sang. "See? All my beans are gone."

Maggie laughed. This girl could charm the most cynical mobster out of his ill-gotten gains. Easy to see why Valorie loved the little imp.

That gave her an idea.

Chapter Twenty-Two

While Dad finished preparing dinner, Val took a long, hot shower, luxuriating in the steamy, well-appointed comfort of her familiar childhood home. She'd lived a subsistence lifestyle for the last five years and had forgotten the joys of a spacious bath, plush towels, and an endless hot water supply. It made her think of Gil's home and how comfortable she felt there—and not just in his arms. It felt…easy. Like she belonged.

Changing clothes in her garage room—she still wasn't ready to adopt the upstairs bedroom as her own, despite her father's urging—she streamed an historical TV documentary on her laptop, just to have some background noise. She paid it little mind at first, until the narrator mentioned Patriots Pride. She finished pulling on a pair of shorts and turned up the volume.

"Patriots Pride, like many of the Tea Party's splinter groups, complained that the Party had 'gone mainstream' as early as 2012, just two years after its founding," the narrator said. "Here's founder Tanner Williams."

The screen showed the face of a middle-aged white man, with unkempt shocks of white hair crowning his head, bright blue eyes blazing with intensity. "The problem with the Tea Party and the Republicans in Congress is, they're all talk and no action," he said. "All they want to do is raise money. We want change—real change in America—back to the true freedoms promised by our Founding Fathers, like the right to bear arms and conduct commerce without government intrusion."

Founded in 2012, the narrator continued, Patriots Pride claimed that the country had veered in a dangerous, socialist direction since Reconstruction. They advocated "taking back America" from the "immigrant criminals" and the "communist politicians" like "Barack *Hussein* Obama."

Val shook her head. Perhaps they'd lost track of who ran the government these days. 2019 wasn't exactly the Year of the Liberals. At the very least, President Donald Trump and Senate Majority Leader Mitch McConnell might dispute the Commie label.

"Val?" Dad called from the kitchen. "You hungry? Dinner's ready!"

"Coming!" Val said. She pulled on a maroon top that might hide the wayward splashes of spaghetti sauce, then sent a quick email to her work account—a reminder to look further into Patriots Pride. Something about their crazy-looking, wild-talking leader sparked the flickering of an idea—a possible connection to the rumors of an "event" on Thursday.

It would probably amount to nothing. "But," she said out loud to herself, "you never know."

***

"I'm so sorry about the photograph," Dad said for the hundredth time, slicing warm garlic bread onto a serving plate. "I thought, since you were asking—"

"It's fine," Val said, for at least the ninety-ninth time. "It surprised me, is all."

"I didn't mean to spoil the mood for dinner," Dad said, setting down the knife. "I feel sick about it."

"Please, don't." Val lifted the serving bowl filled with thick marinara sauce and walnut-sized meatballs and carried it to the dining table. "Tell me some things about her. Not the big stuff yet. Just some things to help me remember. Did she ever hold a job, or pursue any hobbies, or anything?"

Dad sat at the table and waited for Val to take her seat across from him. "Your mom worked as a restaurant hostess when we met. In fact, that's how we met. Then I, uh, became kind of a regular customer."

Val laughed. "You flirted with the hostess? How gauche."

"She was beautiful," Dad said, his voice distant. "She exuded such energy, and a regal sort of bearing. I knew she had much greater things ahead of her."

"That's so sweet," Val said. "What else did you like about her?" She picked at her salad.

Dad smiled and poured water for both of them from a glass pitcher. "She was a great cook," he said. "Although she liked when I cooked for her, while we were dating. She struck me as creative and forward-thinking, even progressive." His tone shifted, losing some of its light cheerfulness. "Once we got married, I discovered her views were, shall we say, a bit more traditional."

"In what way?"

"As in, men work, women raise the kids and go to PTA meetings, that sort of thing."

"Until they don't," Val said under her breath, chewing a mouthful of salad.

"Valorie—"

"I'm just saying, I don't remember her doing a lot of that," Val said. "Other than taking us to the Dinosaur Park a few times, she didn't seem all that interested in the whole mothering thing."

Dad drew in a deep breath and set down his fork. "Your mother loved you very much. She always bragged about you to our friends—how smart you were, how pretty..."

"Come on, Dad," Val said, rolling her eyes. "The truth."

"It *is* true!" He frowned and took her hand in his. "I know you hate to hear it, but you *are* a beautiful girl—ah, woman. Both your mother and I always thought so. So did your uncle M—uh, Uncle Val."

"Let's move on," Val said, glad Dad stopped himself for once from saying Milt's name. That would have ruined her appetite. "I don't remember much about her, except she always seemed so serious. So *tense*. When she wasn't drinking, I mean."

"She had a lot on her plate," Dad said. "I was not the easiest guy to be married to. I was a workaholic, and you know how I've struggled with alcohol. Much worse than she did. Much worse." His voice went quiet.

"I'm proud of how well you're doing. I know how hard it is." She returned the hand squeeze.

"Thanks, Valorie. That means a lot." He paused, held her gaze another moment. "All of this does. You being here tonight, moving back in here to help..." A sad smile crept across his face. "It gives me strength."

Val nodded, waited. After a long moment of silence, she let go of her father's hand. "Let's dive into this pasta, shall we?" They passed the serving dishes back and forth, filling their plates, and each took a bite or two before Val cleared her throat to regain his attention. "So, what happened nine years ago?"

Dad set down his fork, wiped spaghetti sauce from his face with a paper napkin, and met Val's eye. "It all began years earlier," he said. "Your mother and I had, shall we say, some conflicting ideas about how the world works. Different...*assumptions*."

"Assumptions?"

Dad waved a hand near his face in circles, as if trying to grasp words out of the air. "About...people. Society. P-p-politics."

Val shot him a nervous glance. Dad only stuttered when on the brink of relapse. "Politics?"

"Your mom viewed government as the enemy, and to her, the police are—what was the phrase? 'The armed wing of a fascist state,' or something like that," he said. "Anyway, she and your uncle used to argue...oh, Lord, how they'd quarrel." He chuckled and rubbed his chin. "When you and Chad were little, they nearly came to blows one time over some dumb political argument. A local tax bond, I think."

"I don't follow how this led to you two breaking up."

Dad sighed. "What I'm trying to say is, long before she left, we drifted apart," Dad said. "First, it was over your uncle. Valentin represented all the wrong things to her: over-reach of government authority, violence, Big Brother. It got to where she couldn't stand to have him around. She only allowed it because of how much he adored you."

More than Mom did, Val groused to herself.

"Then when we started talking about saving so we could put you kids through college...well, she, uh, held some different views about all that." Dad coughed, sipped his water, and stuffed some pasta into his mouth.

"Different, how? She didn't think parents should pay for their kids' education, or something?"

"Not exactly." Dad spent a long, long, *long* time chewing. Which seemed unnecessary for spaghetti.

"So, what did you feel about that?" Val asked in a neutral tone. She set down her fork. The pasta seemed so thick and heavy now. Too hard to swallow.

"I felt we should save as much as we can to send you both to the best possible schools we could afford," Dad said. "Of course, we hoped you'd each earn scholarships and financial aid—"

"And Mom?" Resentment grew inside her. How could her mother disagree with that? "She felt what? We shouldn't go to college?"

"She thought…how can I put this? She definitely was on board with Chad's ambition to become a lawyer," he said. "I mean, that made so much sense."

"Okay." Val waited. "As far as me wanting to become a cop? That didn't align with her politics, I take it?"

"That was part of it," Dad said. "Look, Valorie, you were what, twelve, thirteen years old when she left? What teenager really knows what she wants to be at that age?"

"Fourteen. I seem to recall you weren't too thrilled with the idea of me being a cop, either."

"I lost my brother in the line of duty," Dad said into his plate.

"Right. So, where's the disagreement between you and Mom?"

Dad opened his mouth to speak, but nothing came out. He took another bite of pasta, then some garlic bread. A sip of water. He glanced at Val again, still silent.

Then it dawned on her. Val pushed her chair back from the table and tossed her napkin into her lap. "She didn't want me to go to college at all!"

Dad fought for words again, this time using both hands to grasp at the air around him. "Let's just say her views about women in the workplace are—were, anyway—a little antiquated."

"For crying out loud, Dad. In the twenty-first century?"

Dad cocked his head, once again speechless.

Val's temper flared. All those suspicions she'd harbored about her mother favoring her brother no longer seemed so outrageous and childish. She stood and paced the room. "But you two didn't split up over a disagreement over my chosen vocation. Did you?"

Dad licked his lips, then dropped his gaze. "No."

Val waited. And waited. And waited a little longer.

"Your mother and I, she didn't want to...Valorie, I'm sorry. Some of this is too personal—"

"Yeah, you grew apart. Emotionally and, um, physically?"

Dad shot her a surprised look, his mouth again moving without producing a sound.

"She was having an affair," Val said, recalling the photos she'd found.

Dad froze, alarm spreading over his face. "I-I can't say for sure—"

"With Milt," Val continued, her voice rising. "With the man who fucking *raped me* when I was twelve years old! Holy shit, Dad, please tell me I've got this wrong!"

Dad's mouth failed once again to produce words. Sweat broke out on his brow, and his face flushed red.

"I'm right, aren't I?" Val gripped the back of her chair. "About Mom, and Milt?"

"We were never sure he...did what you said, at least in our minds—"

"For Christ's sake, Dad! The *fact* that he raped me is *not* in question. That is the God-given truth, and I'm sorry if that's too hard for you to believe. What I am asking is whether he and Mom—"

"Yes," Dad said, nodding. "They were having an..." Again he couldn't finish. Tears flowed down his face, and he wiped them away with his napkin.

Val waited, toying with the food growing cold on her plate. Rage battled with disappointment for control of her emotions. Not only had her father confirmed her worst fears, that her mother had an affair with Val's rapist. But also that he'd known about it, and hid it from her for over a decade.

***

After excusing herself to the bathroom, Val splashed her face with cool water, dabbed it off with a towel, and took in her reflection in the mirror. The whites of her eyes reflected a dull pink color, not quite bloodshot, as much an artifact of her lack of sleep as her emotional state, she supposed. She searched her face for any resemblance to her mother and found little, other than her slender nose and fine cheekbones. That suited her. She wanted nothing to do with her mother at that moment. The thought of her made her stomach churn, and she leaned over the toilet, expecting to vomit. None came. Only some painful cramps, perhaps marking the start of her next period.

Val washed her hands, fixed her hair, and returned to the dining room. Dad seemed to have calmed as well. Val sat, took a sip of water, and collected her thoughts. Finally she spoke, in a low, even voice. "I'm sorry Mom did that to you. And I'm sorry for yelling. I was upset. Not at you. At her."

Dad nodded, wiped his face with his napkin, and blew his nose. "Me too, honey."

"I have another question," Val said after a long silence. "About the letters. The ones Mom sent. They were in those boxes, in the garage."

Dad sat up in his chair, breathing hard. He nodded. "What about them?" he said in a raspy voice.

Val worked hard to keep her tone even, not wanting to get confrontational again. "Why did you hide them from me?"

Dad puffed his lips, breathing for several beats through his nose. "When she left, she…said some things. About how I, and this family, ruined her life. Her words, not mine." He paused a moment. "How she needed a new start. A clean break." He pressed his fingers against his closed eyelids, as if trying to stop the flow of tears. "I knew the real reason— and she knew that I knew." He met Val's gaze again and seemed to seek something from her. Understanding? Approval? Val could give neither.

"When she wrote to me the first time, all she wanted was a divorce, and money," Dad said. "That was the last straw for me. I called a lawyer and told him that all further communications would go through him. I vowed to never read a single word from her ever again. I was angry, and spiteful, I guess."

Val nodded. "Sure. I get that. Not the healthiest response, but I understand how you must have felt." She leaned across the table and took his hand. "Why didn't you burn them?"

The wave of guilt spreading across her father's face told her the truth before he spoke the words. "More than once," he said in a raspy voice, "I did."

Chapter Twenty-Three

The remainder of dinner passed in awkward silence, broken up by occasional "please pass the salt" or "more pasta?" Val's attention wandered to the Patriots Pride documentary she'd heard earlier that evening. She wondered how their political activism linked to their sex trafficking. Their traditional conservative values seemed to contradict the promotion of such promiscuity.

"Got plans for the Fourth?" Dad asked out of the blue, breaking her concentration.

"Working a double," she said. "You?"

"The usual," he said with a smile. "Parade and fireworks. I'd hoped maybe you could join me, but...I guess not." Their awkward silence resumed.

But tensions gradually eased between them, and after dinner, Val insisted on cleaning up the kitchen. "You cooked. It's only fair," she said. "Relax for a bit."

To her relief, he didn't argue—she needed a few minutes alone. She took her time, rinsing each plate, bowl, and fork before loading them into the dishwasher. Then she scrubbed, dried, and stowed the pots and pans, wiped down the counters, and packed away the leftovers in the fridge. The physical activity helped calm her down, and her spirits lifted enough that she no longer feared spoiling the romantic mood she expected to find at Gil's.

She poked her head out into the living room and found Dad snoozing in his favorite recliner. She tiptoed into her garage bedroom and grabbed her keys, but got careless, and they dropped with a loud jangle to the floor.

"Hey, are you leaving?" Dad appeared in her doorway before she could scoop the keys back off the floor.

Her face warmed. "Gil invited me over."

He nodded, his lips set in a half-smile, half-frown, sadness moistening his eyes. "Of course. Silly me. You don't need a room here. What was I thinking?" He dropped his gaze and turned away.

"Dad, please. Listen." She rested a hand on his shoulder. "I love the new bedroom. I just wanted to spend some time with Gil tonight."

The doorbell rang, its Winchester chimes echoing throughout the house. Dad swallowed hard, his face filling with dismay. "There's your young man now," he said, his voice breaking.

"I don't think so," Val said. "He's not even supposed to drive yet."

"Well, I'm not expecting anyone," Dad said. They stood there for a moment in silence.

The doorbell rang again. "Dad? Are you going to answer the door, or should I?"

"Yeah, yeah. Of course." He trudged back out to the living room. Val followed, careful not to crowd him, something she'd long ago learned made him nervous.

Standing in front of the door, Dad gathered himself. Tucked in his shirt, rebalanced his glasses, smoothed back his hair. The doorbell chimed for the third time.

"Dad, anytime now..." Val stepped closer, reached for the handle.

He waved her back with annoyance, then swung open the heavy door...and gasped. "What the hell are *you* doing here?"

Val craned her neck to get a look at whoever had paid this unannounced visit, but the person had retreated too far back for her to see. "Dad? Who is it?"

"Aren't you going to invite me in?" said a woman's voice.

Val froze. She recognized that voice, though it had deepened and aged since she'd last heard it. Heard it right in that very doorway, nine years before, telling Val she wouldn't understand, before heading out to her car and driving away.

"Yeah, yeah, of course," Dad said. "Come on in." He stood aside and waved her in.

The woman strode in the door at a brisk pace, head held high, like she still owned the place. Which, Val realized, might be the case—she never learned the terms of her parents' divorce.

Still. It had been nine years. It showed in the wrinkles around the eyes, the sprinkling of gray in the roots of her auburn hair, the laugh lines around her eyes. Otherwise she looked the same as always: slender, confident, with bright brown eyes and a piercing gaze.

"Valorie, darling," her mother said, as if she'd expected Val to be there. "So good to see you. I hoped you'd still be home."

Dad whirled to face Val. "You invited her here?" Anger spilled into his voice. "What was all that bullshit before, then, asking me about her, as if—"

"Dad, I promise you, I did not—"

"Relax, Michael. I invited myself over," Mom said. "By the way, your son says you owe him a call." She turned away from Dad's frozen-still frame and spread her arms wide, facing Val. "Well, don't just stand there. How about a hug for your mother?"

***

Val's body went rigid, her heart racing, while her mother wrapped her wiry arms around Val's shoulders. The old woman smelled of tobacco, hairspray, and cheap cologne. Choking, half on the aroma and half from shock and anger, she broke the embrace and backed up a step, holding her hands out to block Mom from approaching again.

"No!" Val said. "No way. You don't walk out on us without explanation and then pop back in unannounced nine years later, demanding hugs. No. Uh-uh." She retreated to the sofa and sat, her arms wrapped around herself, her whole body shaking with surprise, anger, fear, love, spite—

"Oh, Valorie. Let's dispense with all the drama, shall we?" Mom said, her tone both teasing and condescending. "I told you why I left. Or didn't you get my letters?" She crossed her arms and glared at Dad, who hung his head and looked away. "I see. Well, darlings, it looks like we have a lot to talk about. Right after I hit the loo. It was a long drive from Danbury. Pour me a drink, would you, dear?" She glided toward the hallway, sniffing the air and wrinkling her nose.

"There's...no liquor in the house," Dad said after an eternity. "I'm...in the program...again. S-sorry."

Mom paused and rolled her eyes before disappearing down the hall. "Of *course* you are. Make me some coffee, then?" A moment later, the bathroom door banged shut.

Val and Dad stared at each other, shaking their heads. "I'm going to kill Chad," Val said after a long silence.

"Me first. Did you know they've been talking?"

"He said yesterday that she called him out of the blue," Val said. "I...haven't found the right moment to tell you. I'm guessing neither has he."

"He l-left me a message earlier today, but I haven't listened to it yet. I-I was busy getting dinner ready." Dad leaned against the open door frame, exhaling a heavy breath. "I can't believe this."

"This is insane." Val stood and closed the gap between them. "You aren't letting her stay, are you?"

He heaved a loud breath, made a face. "I don't want to see her. Do you?"

"I don't know if I'm ready." Despite the warm night, goosebumps rose on Val's bare arms. "I don't even know what to say."

The bathroom door swung open down the hall and loud footsteps warned of Mom's return.

"Don't worry," Dad said, his voice barely a whisper. "She'll know what to say."

"Mike, darling," Mom said before she became visible again, "I've changed my mind. Be a dear and go get us some wine, would you? You know what I like."

"Mother!" Val spun to face her, anger spiking. "Didn't you hear him? He's in the program. He shouldn't even step foot inside a liquor store, much less bring it home. For God's sake!"

"It's not for him, it's for me," Mom said, sitting back on the sofa. "Besides, it's you I want to talk to. We have some catching up to do!"

"Oh, f-fuck this!" Dad dashed out the door, slamming it behind him.

Fuming, Val raced to the door, then stopped and glared at her mother, unsure if she should leave her alone in Dad's house. "That was cruel. What were you thinking?"

Her mother only shrugged and glanced away.

Val flung the door open. With luck she could intercept Dad in time. But no—his car was already peeling rubber down the street. Before she could reach her car, only a trail of blue smoke showed the path of his escape—no doubt, toward a liquor store.

"Let him go," Mom called after her. "He'll be back when he cools off. Come inside and chat."

Her anger flaring, Val hustled inside, slammed the door shut, and stomped toward her mother. "Get out of here!" she shouted. "Out! Right now!"

Her mother's face reflected a mixture of frustration and amusement. "Don't be rude," she said. "We wouldn't want your father buying wine for no reason, would we?"

Val pointed an accusing finger at her face. "You selfish idiot," she said, spittle flying. "If he goes off the wagon tonight because of you—"

"Drunks don't fall off the wagon because of other people," Mom said with a drawl. "They do it because they're weak. A word that fits Michael Dawes to a T." She smiled, a saccharine smile that nearly made Val vomit. "Not you, dear. Come, sit. We have so much to talk about."

"Like what?" Val shouted. "Like how you abandoned us nine years ago, and left me to deal with the aftermath of being raped by that scumbag you ran off with? Huh? How about we start there?"

Her mother cast a glance at her, an expression of "oh-not-this-again" lining her face. A face that had not fared well with time—raisined from too much sun, age spots appearing through her makeup, nicotine stains on her lips and hands. Her eyes, rheumy and bloodshot and surrounded by black bags. Holding it all together, a look of disdain and impatience—her trademark expression. "I'll let that ridiculous accusation slide, for old times' sake," she said, "so long as you don't repeat it until Milton gets an opportunity to explain his side—"

"He doesn't have a *side*!" Val screamed, waving her arms in frustration. "And don't say his name again, or I'll—"

"Don't say his name?" Mom laughed. She could have been Mary Poppins, correcting one of her wards' poor grammar. "Don't say the name of my *husband*?"

***

Val's shouted response stopped in mid-air, her mouth open wide. Her mother's announcement knocked her backwards, as if she'd punched her. "Husband? You married that rapist son of a bitch?"

Mom's face flushed red, and she stood, pushing Val aside. "I should slap your face for saying that," she said, "except that I despise him now as much as you do. Which is why he won't be my husband for long."

Val's mind spun. This all seemed too surreal. "You're divorcing him? Already?"

Mom laughed, a haughty sound that would send dogs running for cover. "Eight years is nothing to sneeze at. It felt like twice that long. But we're not here to discuss M—ah, *him*, are we, dear?"

Val turned a 180, throwing her hands up into the air, then paced the room. "Hell if I know. Why *are* you here?"

Mom smiled, serpent-like, and a chill ran down Val's spine. Mom shrugged. "To see you, my dear. Can't a mother inquire as to her daughter's well-being?"

"If you cared about my well-being, where the hell have you been for nine years?" Val wanted to go on, but her throat grew tight, and tears welled in her eyes.

"It was all explained in the letters."

That knocked some of the wind out of Val's sails. Fucking Dad, withholding those! She drew in a deep breath, exhaled it, and sat on the sofa. "I only learned of those letters a couple of days ago, and I'm way behind on my reading. Consider this your opportunity to explain. You have my full attention."

Mom sat next to Val, her slender hand on Val's wrist. "Where should I begin?"

"How about at the beginning?" Val crisscrossed her legs on the couch so she could turn and face her mother. "Why did you leave? To run off with Dickhead McCloskey?"

Mom chuckled and waved that notion off. "Because of him? No, no. I mean, yes, Mac and I did go off together. You've pieced that part together correctly. I, like an idiot, thought I'd found my second chance at love." She laughed. "Such a fool."

"So, if not just for him...?" Val held her breath, not sure if she wanted to hear the response.

"We had ideals," Mom said. "We'd made plans. We were going to change the world." She shook her head. "Hard to believe that a forty-year-old woman could be so naïve, isn't it?"

"You left your family for some sort of social or political *cause*?" Val shouted, incredulous. "Like what? What could be more important than the family you left behind here? For Christ's sake, Mom!"

Mom's face softened, and the beginnings of a tear welled in one eye. "We can get to all that later," she said. "Suffice to say, I faced a hard choice, and...sacrifices had to be made, Valorie. For the greater good. If I wanted to be with Mac—and I did—it meant leaving you and your brother behind. You can't imagine how difficult that was for me."

"Try me," Val said. "I spent three years in therapy dealing with all that shit. And calling him 'Mac' doesn't soften the blow here, Mother. You ran away, abandoned Chad and me and Dad, and you did it with the man who raped me." Her voice grew thick and raspy, and it hurt to speak. "Who fucking *raped* me. How could you?" She held her mother's gaze for a long moment, and Val could no longer hold back the tears. They splashed down her face, hot and salty.

Mom fidgeted in her seat, licking her lips. "As I said, Mac—"

"*Don't!*" Val held up her hand. "Say. His. *Name.*"

Mom nodded. "He...claimed something different happened. I believed him. And Valorie, you never actually said it out loud. That he...abused you, I mean. We tried and tried to get you to tell us what happened, but you couldn't. *That's* why we sent you to therapy—to find out what was wrong. For over a year, we waited and waited, and you never told us. You admit that, right? That you never spoke the words?"

"I was...not even...*thirteen,*" Val said, her words barely audible. "He threatened me. Said he'd...if I talked he'd...Mother, I was *scared* of him. And of you. What you'd think. How you'd react. It all just..."

Then words would no longer come. Her head, her throat, her heart and soul ached, right to the core, and her body would no longer support her. She collapsed back onto the sofa, fighting tears and struggling to breathe.

Mom watched, impassive, waiting.

"Well," her mother said after Val's breathing returned to normal, "I was hoping we could talk about some other things. What's going on in your life—your career, are you dating, that sort—"

"We are *not* going to 'catch up' on things!" Val sprang up on the sofa, anger refueling her body. "Not until you acknowledge the truth of what I've told you already. Of what *he* did—your soon-to-be second ex-husband. God, I can't believe any of this!"

"I'm not sure we can trust the memory of a thirteen-year-old girl over that of—"

"*Get the fuck out of here!*" Val grabbed her mother by the meat of her wiry arms and dragged her across the living room, both of them stumbling along the way. "Leave this house and do not return. Do not call me. Do not write. Stay away! Do you hear me?"

Mom heaved several deep breaths, shaking Val's hands off of her. "I see," she said. "So that's how you feel. What a pity." She grabbed her purse from the credenza and opened the door. "Here I thought perhaps you'd at least be curious to meet him."

"I've *met* the shit-face too many times, and I don't need to hear any silly claims about how he's changed, or—"

Mom laughed. "Not Mac, silly. Of course you've met *him*." She smiled, her eyes narrowed, and her face took on that serpentine look again. "I was talking," she said, "about your baby brother."

Chapter Twenty-Four

Despite her cool exterior, the meetings with her son and daughter left Maggie drained of emotion and energy. But her day was from over.

She returned to the motel and went straight to Mac's room. Knocked in her unique sequence and pattern, the one that told him she was alone and safe.

He pulled the door ajar and retreated. "It's open."

Which meant someone was in there with him—Bosco, who looked even more strung out than earlier that morning. Same torn jeans and smelly rock and roll T-shirt. Smellier, even.

"Just in time," Mac said, sitting at the tiny dining table next to his bed. Bosco occupied the only other chair.

Maggie set down her purse and sat on the far side of the bed, away from both men. "In time for what?"

"The update. Hey, you live in a fucking barn?" Bosco said.

Maggie glanced at the door, still ajar, and kicked it shut. "Where's Sammy?"

"Sleeping in your room," Mac said. "Smiley's watching him. How'd it go?"

"Magnificently. My daughter sends her regards." She laughed, as did he. "Don't let her get too close to you. Not if she's armed."

Bosco roared with laughter and poked Mac in the ribs, blowing foul breath and spittle between his brown teeth.

Mac waved him off. "Is she on board? For Thursday?"

Maggie lit a cigarette. "She'll get there."

"Fuck," Bosco said. "That's another one."

"Another what?" Maggie exhaled, then double-checked to ensure Mac had disabled the smoke alarm. "Problems?"

"Thanks to the efforts of your daughter and her pals, we're understaffed," Mac said. "Even borrowing from Hartford, we need a couple of dozen more foot soldiers to carry off the plan, if we stick with it."

"They didn't arrest that many."

"A bunch of the other chicken-shits eighty-sixed us when they found out about it," Bosco said.

"What about Mulroney and his insiders?" Mac asked.

"Getting there." Maggie blew a smoke ring over the bed. "What was that about 'if we stick with the plan?' What are you suggesting?"

The two men eyed each other. Bosco ducked his head in submission. Mac inhaled through his mouth and folded his hands on the table. "We came up with another idea."

"As in, a backup plan, or a total shift in strategy?"

"As in, we don't have much choice," Mac said.

"Spill, then." Another smoke ring.

"First, we use the girls," Mac said. "Deploy them downtown."

"As foot soldiers?"

"Nah," Bosco said. "As whores. The cops'll go nuts."

Maggie rolled her eyes. "Wow, what a strategy," she said. "Fucking genius. How long do you think it'll take CPD to round up a couple dozen girls in mini-skirts? Ten minutes?"

"A few hours, which is plenty. Anyway, that's part one," Mac said. "Then, the Big Bang!"

Bosco rubbed his hands together, his eyes glowing. He looked ready to explode with excitement.

"You know the annual fireworks display the city puts on?" Mac said.

Maggie nodded.

Bosco could no longer contain himself. "We're gonna attack the barge!" he said, jumping to his feet.

Maggie sat up in bed and took another deep drag, glaring at Bosco until he sat again. "What good would that do? Besides making a loud noise."

Mac slow-clapped. "Exactly. We create a huge distraction, creating chaos, focusing the cops on what the hell just happened. They'll send all units down there, and we can hit the Armory with a much smaller squad, and bingo! Easy-peasy."

She mulled it over. "Hmm. That might work. Hell, we should've thought of that in the first place. So, how do we do that? The 'Big Bang,' I mean. Won't that require even more people?"

Mac and Bosco exchanged glances again. "Well," Mac said. "Just one."

"One person?" Maggie stubbed out her cigarette and brushed ashes off of her blouse. "How is one person going to get past all the security with enough explosives to detonate all that and then escape—oh, shit." Blood drained from her face. "They're not going to escape, are they?"

Mac took another heavy breath. "That's the part we can't discuss with the crew. Or Mulroney."

"How will you get someone to volunteer if you don't tell them?"

Silence.

"Jesus, Mac. You're not going to tell them?"

"As you often say, Maggie," Mac said, "sacrifices may need to be made."

Maggie sank onto the bed. She'd made many sacrifices in her past. But never had she played God.

"Well," she said, "then I guess we'll have to make sure we don't get caught."

***

After her mother left, Val sat for a few moments on the sofa, shell-shocked. Baby brother? With Milt, the man who raped Val, even while carrying on an affair with her mother? Whom her mother had *married*? *How* was any of that possible? Did Dad know?

Which reminded her: Dad was out there, somewhere, buying her mother alcohol. He shouldn't go anywhere near a liquor store, much less bring any home. Val had to stop him.

She called his cell phone. It rang...in the kitchen, dammit!

That spelled all kinds of trouble: she couldn't call him, or track him, and he couldn't call anyone for help.

Please, Dad. Please. Just turn around and come home.

Two fretful, agonizing minutes later, she dialed Gil and explained what happened. "Should I go looking for him?"

"No. Stay there in case he comes back with liquor," Gil said. "I'll dial up an Uber and come over."

"I can't just sit here and wait." Agony burned in Val's chest, where, no doubt, her heart had already ripped itself in half. "I have to do *something*."

"Do you have the number of his sponsor?"

"No. But his phone's here. Maybe I can break into it, find him." She put her phone on speaker next to her dad's and tried a few obvious passwords, but none worked, and his phone's security locked her out.

"I'll call in some favors and ask the department to put out a watch for him, have patrols keep an eye out," Gil said. "It's not technically legit, but how bad could they punish a crippled guy on medical leave?"

"I hate to think," Val said, her mood lifting.

"Where might he have gone? You can call a few bars and stores, ask around."

"Gil, you're brilliant. Or I'm an idiot for not thinking of that." Val grabbed a notepad and scribbled down a few places to try. "Here I am, thinking I could become a detective."

"Nobody thinks straight when they're upset," he said. "Call around some places. I'll be there in ten minutes."

She called Sal's and a few other liquor stores close by. None remembered selling anything to anyone matching Dad's description. Or, rather, *everyone* met Dad's general description: middle-age, gray-haired, average height and weight, desperate for a drink. She needed to show them a photo, somehow. She wished she knew his friends, even their names. But they'd had so little contact in recent years.

Then Val had an idea. She dialed one of the few non-work-related numbers on her Favorites list that didn't involve food delivery. One she hadn't called often in the last six weeks. It rang two, three, four times. Her heart sank. It would go to voicemail—

"Val?" Beth's voice sounded distant, strained. "Did you get my letter?"

Letter? Oh, hell. She'd never reached out since finding Beth's note in the apartment several days before. Of course Beth would want to talk about all of that. *Before* Val asked for a massive favor. Shit.

"Yeah," Val said. "Thanks. It was really sweet."

"I didn't expect you to call this soon," Beth said. "Have you gotten a deposit check from the landlord yet? I thought maybe that would be a good time to have that drink, maybe talk about some things…"

"No, I haven't," Val said. "Look, something has come up, and, well, I was wondering, if you're not doing anything right now, if I could ask you for a huge, unreasonable, ridiculous favor?"

Beth laughed. "What is wrong with you, girl? I've never known you to beat around the bush so bad. Come on, out with it. What do you need?"

Val took a deep breath, then another. "My dad...I think he's out buying alcohol, or drinking. I wondered if you could help me find him?"

"Find your Dad? How? I have no idea where—"

"I'll give you a few places. Just pop in, show them a photo if you don't see him—"

"Where the hell would I get a picture of your father?" Beth's tone grew irritable. "For God's sake, why don't *you* go looking for him? I'm not dressed, I'm half-drunk myself, and I have...*company*." She paused, and Val understood: she was in bed with a guy. Dammit. Beth had broken off her engagement with Josh six weeks before, and it hadn't occurred to Val that she might already have a new boyfriend.

"Hold on a sec," Beth went on, and it sounded like she'd covered the phone with her hand. Muffled voices, Beth's and someone else's, carried on some sort of argument.

Beth came back on. "Fuck it, all right. Send me the deets. I'll let you know what I find."

"Beth, you are an angel! Oh, thank you thank you thank you," Val said, relieved. "I will so make this up to you, I promise. You are too good to me."

"Yeah, love you too, bitch." Beth laughed. "I'm the biggest dope in the world, except for you. But what the hell, it might be fun playing detective. Hold on." She covered the phone again, and a man's muffled voice asked something in the background. "Okay. Send the pic. I'll send the boy-toy home."

Val sent Beth a photo of her father and a list of nearby bars and liquor stores. Then her phone rang again, an unfamiliar number.

"Dawes!" The booming voice of Sergeant Travis Blake, her former supervisor and occasional patrol partner, pounded her eardrum. "Kryz told me what's up. Glad to help. Anything's better than doing my kids' homework for them. What do you need?"

"Travis, my dad's off the wagon, or is about to be, and...I need some help finding him."

"Done," Travis said. "Send me a photo and his vehicle info. I'll twist some arms, get an all-points out on him. Liberty Heights area?"

"Yeah, the north end, probably. You're a prince among men."

"Tell that to my wife after I forget our anniversary again. Hey, are you working Thursday?"

"Aren't we all?"

"I was hoping I could snag you for sentry duty at the Armory with me," Travis said. "We're short a few guys."

"Ask Brenda. If I can shake free, you've got me."

"Awesome. Hey, by the way. That crazy old duck, Mickey Mulroney, asked about you the other day," Travis said in a low voice. "Some weird political shit. I didn't think you'd be interested. Has he called you?"

"No, and you're right, I'm not," she said. "I met him once. He struck me as a dinosaur. What sort of political shit?"

"All I know is, he's one of those conspiracy theory lunatics," Travis said. "It wouldn't shock me to find white robes in his closet. Anyway, heads-up. You're on his radar."

"Thanks." Val texted what she could remember of her father's vehicle info to Travis, along with the same photo she'd sent Beth. The whole time, Travis's words rang in her ears, and she wondered why, of all people, Mickey Mulroney had her on his radar.

Chapter Twenty-Five

Gil's arrival interrupted Val's worry, a welcome sight on an otherwise miserable night. His gait seemed almost normal, just the hint of a limp, and he looked delicious in a tight-fitting black T-shirt and jeans. She savored his warm hug, then escorted him to the sofa, where they held each other some more.

"I was hoping I'd see you tonight," Gil said. "But not under these circumstances."

"Likewise," she said. "Sorry I've been leaning on you so hard lately. It feels like you're always bailing me out of some emotional crisis or another."

"That's what I'm here for. Hey, while we're waiting, how about you show me your room? This being my first time here and all."

Val led him to her space in the garage. He took it all in, leaning his shoulder against the door frame. "You used to hang out here as a teenager, too, right? Lifting weights and practicing martial arts?"

"And sleeping. I couldn't stand being in my old room after everything that happened there." Val's throat tightened. She sat on the bed and patted the spot next to her.

Gil eased himself down and wrapped his arm around her. "Lots of history here for you," he said after a long while, his voice hoarse. "I'm surprised at how well you're doing, living back here again. I'd be a wreck."

"Trust me, I *am*." She shuddered out a sigh. "Gil, this whole thing, moving back here, is a mistake. Now it's led to my dad falling off the wagon again—"

"A, you don't know that, and B, it wouldn't be your fault. It's on him to stay straight, not you."

"You sound like my mother," Val said with a bittersweet smile.

"If anyone's to blame for knocking him off his stride, it's her, not you." Gil stopped and slapped his forehead. "Which, holy hell, how are you feeling about *that*?"

"It was weird. It was almost like she wasn't my mom. She was more like some strange long-lost relative, an old crazy aunt or something, who popped in for a visit, unannounced. She screwed with our minds for a half hour and breezed out like a freaking hurricane. I didn't feel any sort of connection to her, or love, or anything like that. I kept thinking, *what the hell is she doing here?* You know?"

Gil nodded and rubbed her shoulder. It felt so damned good.

"Mmm," she said. "You've got quite the touch, mister."

"You don't know the half of it, yet," he said in her ear, and rubbed harder. Down to her shoulder blades, her lower back. Val turned so he could reach whatever spot she—er, *he*—needed. He caressed both sides of her back, one with each hand, and she relaxed further, slumping into the bed, her head landing on the pillow.

Gil sat next to her, working the stress out of her back, down to her hips, her legs, even removed her shoes and rubbed her feet. Magical. Sirens sounded in the distance, but she didn't care. A warming feeling rose from her groin, spreading everywhere, especially when he worked his way back up to her legs, caressing her calves, her thighs, her hips—

A crashing sound in the house startled them, and she darted upright. Blue and red lights flashed through the windows. She called out, "Dad?"

"S'awright," her father replied, and Val's heart sank at the slurred voice, the extra volume.

Gil patted her hand. "Assume nothing."

The door burst open, and Dad stumbled into the garage, steadying himself with one hand on Beth's shoulder, his face flushed, his eyeglasses askew. Even from a distance, he smelled like a gas torch that continued to spew fuel after the flame had gone out. "I see you've got comp—" He burped. "Company," and he then fell face-first onto the floor.

***

Beth recounted her successful search for Val's father, finding him stumbling toward his SUV in the parking lot of a nearby whiskey bar. She'd driven him home, escorted by a pair of Clayton cops—friends of Travis's, alerted by his APB. Val walked her outside to say goodbye.

"He wasn't much trouble." Beth played with the brown curls behind her ear—her worst tell for when she lied. "My boy-toy gave me more grief than your dad did."

"I owe you big time." Val hugged her tight. "Thank you so much."

Beth returned the hug. "Speaking of the boy, I have a favor to ask of you, too."

"Anything."

Beth looked left and right, then leaned closer and whispered, "Can you hook me up with a bona fide set of police handcuffs?"

Val laughed so hard, she almost fell. "You got it," she said, hugging her once more.

"I'm glad to see Gil here," Beth said, breaking the embrace. "Are you two still hot and heavy?"

Val paused, wincing a bit. "I don't know that I'd call us 'hot and heavy,' but yeah, we're still seeing each other."

"Still haven't slept with him yet, then?" Beth asked in a low voice, her tone sympathetic.

"We've...*slept*," Val said. "I'm still working up to the rest of it."

Beth squeezed her shoulder, cocked her head. "It's a big decision," she said. "Don't rush it. You'll know when the time is right." She leaned in and whispered, "As will he, if he's truly the right guy for you."

"Thanks, Beth." She gave her another tight hug. She wanted to say more, to pump her for advice, but she didn't even know what questions to ask.

"Call me if you need to talk," Beth said, then got in her car and drove away.

Back inside, Gil made coffee while Val picked Dad off the garage floor and plopped him in her bed. No small task—her father outweighed her by at least sixty pounds, all of it sloppy dead weight in her arms. She found a puke bucket, then pressed Dad's finger onto his phone's sensor to unlock it. No surprise, his sponsor's number appeared atop his Favorites list: "AA—Jerry."

She called Jerry to fill him in. He advised her to give Dad water and bland food, help him avoid conflict and stress that could trigger an even greater relapse, and offer encouragement as best she could.

"Encouragement about what?" She escaped into the living room to get out of Dad's earshot. "To not drink?"

"Just steer the conversation away from drinking and from his triggers," Jerry said. "Things like his ex-wife, your job, and his brother. If he blames himself, change the subject. I'll be there in twenty minutes."

Val glanced at the clock: almost 9:00 p.m. Chad would still be awake and he needed to be told. He answered on the second ring.

"He fell off the wagon?" Chad exploded a minute into her explanation. "For God's sake, Val, that's what you were supposed to prevent by moving in there!"

"Yeah, well, great plan, bro," she said, her voice as rough as her dark mood. "I especially love the part where you send his abusive ex-wife over to fuck with our minds. That's so smart. I bet every alcoholic responds with perfect sobriety to that! We're lucky nothing happened to him."

"I didn't *send* her. I kind of let it slip where you were, and—hell, Val, I'm so sorry. It's not my proudest moment, for sure."

"Dumbass!"

"I *said* I was sorry."

"Oh, well, that fixes everything."

"What do you want me to do? Just a minute." Chad's voice grew muffled, as if he'd covered the phone, but Val made out the words. "Kendra, it's my sister. I'll just be a minute."

Val stewed while his brother tried, and failed, to ease his wife's concerns. Gil slipped by with coffee and buttered toast, leaving her a cup, and disappeared into the garage.

"Okay, I'm back," Chad said. "Listen, there's a process–"

"Screw your process." Val's anger spiked again. "You need to get back here and help me deal with this. I can't do it alone."

"I can't, Val. I have meetings, clients—"

"Yeah, and I'm working double shifts through the holiday. You've told me a hundred times you could telecommute 90 percent of the time. That time has come."

Chad's heavy sigh filled her ear. A good sign—it meant he hadn't ruled out the idea. "I could come late tomorrow. Ali would love to see you. Maybe we could all see the fireworks show together?"

"I'm *working* the Fourth, Chad. You'll have to take her to the show without me, though."

"Deal. Okay, gotta go. Tell Dad I love him."

"Tell him yourself when you get here." Val's anger eased. At least Chad was stepping up to help, and she always loved seeing Ali.

"Let's do it," she said. "See you around three?"

Wednesday, July 3, 2019

Chapter Twenty-Six

Val woke up on the sofa with the first light of morning streaming in through the picture window of her father's living room. She sat up too fast, and a sharp pain shot up her back. The old sofa had endured too many nights of Dad's much-heavier frame, passed out in odd positions, and it had the lumps to prove it.

She expected to find Gil sleeping in the faux-leather recliner, and failing that, fussing in the kitchen, but no go. Instead, a note:

> *Val,*
>
> *I needed a firmer bed. Didn't want to wake you. Anyway, it looks like you and Jerry have things under control. Your dad's lucky to have you both. See you Wednesday?*
>
> *Love, Gil*

Jerry's note, left next to Gil's, was more succinct:

> *Mike's going to be fine. I'll check on him to-morrow. – Jerry*

Val peeked into the garage, where she found her father snoring, still dressed, in her bed. She let him sleep. He had nowhere else to be, anyway.

She made it to work by seven, and Grimes greeted her with a grunt and a wave. "Thanks to Super Agent Forrestal," he said, "Petroni wants us to look into these nutso political groups, see who's behind this rumored 'event' tomorrow. I called dibs on the enviro-freaks, fem-Nazis, and the rest of the snowflake left. Shannon has the anarchists, racial and ethnic groups like Black Lives Matter and the Zionists, and Antifa crazies. That leaves you the right-wingers." He thumped a thick file on her desk. "Here's what we've got on them. Happy digging."

"What about Price?" Val asked.

Grimes shrugged. "Damari got pulled off onto street duty. Poor bastard. It's gonna be a scorcher out there today." Grimes tossed his navy blazer over the back of a chair, yanked off his tie, and undid the top two buttons of his white shirt. "Let's hope the AC doesn't fail this afternoon."

Val glanced down at her police uniform, a much-too-heavy blue cotton shirt and polyester pants, and wished she'd have gone with civilian attire. Ah, well. Too late now.

She opened her browser and dove into her research. She started with Patriots Pride, recalling the rants of the group's leader she'd watched online.

She found nothing on the group's website or social media accounts indicating any specific or imminent plans for Independence Day. One item drew her curiosity, though: an op-ed in a local conservative newspaper in Illinois that decried the rising prevalence of "promiscuous women" in society. The writer blamed most social ills on "lesbo-feminism" and the promotion of equal rights for women. Women, he said, needed to be "re-educated in traditional, American ways." That, he insisted, was the only hope for America to return to its days of glory. Val's eyes rolled so hard she thought they'd get stuck on the top of her head.

Still, although Val couldn't find any direct evidence

online linking the group to an imminent attack, it had achieved a following. A crowd-funding widget revealed they'd raised over a quarter of a million dollars in the past month, and their social media pages showed several thousand likes and followers.

In one of their chat rooms, one phrase, repeated multiple times, stood out: a complaint about the government's "criminalization of traditional sex" between men and women. Val found that odd phrasing juxtaposed with the phrase "the world's oldest form of free enterprise" referring to prostitution. The discussion focused on how Clayton police were "wasting time and public resources" with their streetwalker crackdown, and argued for legalizing prostitution. That seemed odd for a group that otherwise lamented a decline in "traditional moral values." The page cited another group's "findings" as evidence to support their argument. However, when Val searched for it, she found only secondary references and opinion pieces. No direct links, no actual data.

Such groups, she concluded, wouldn't dare show their faces on the traditional web. Val would need help from the department's IT group to look into the "dark web," where underground organizations conversed more openly about their ideas and plans. She submitted a formal request for dark web access, marking it Urgent, and hoped for the best.

Val broadened her search, finding links to other groups with similar messaging and priorities, such as the Ku Klux Klan and the Oath Keepers. There she found far more than she had ever hoped. She cross-linked them to the ones in the file Grimes had shared with her, and discovered that most of the ones in the file fell into two categories.

The first category, the better-funded organizations such as Patriots Pride, fought the complaints lodged against them in court, often with great success. Sympathetic judges, it seemed, were not hard to find at the federal or state levels. Even liberal justices leaned toward allowing extremists great latitude in the expression of their First Amendment rights.

The second category, the less well-funded and less sophisticated, more or less disappeared after being sued or charged with crimes. The crime accusations often focused on political activity: illegal contributions, unlawful assembly, lack of permits, and so on. After disbanding, most regrouped under a new name within weeks or even days, often with only the thinnest of disguises. Others merged with or dispersed into one or more similar groups. Individuals named in cases would flee the state, sometimes emerging in another city. By creating an almost inexhaustible run of distinct corporate entities, they eluded any serious heat from law enforcement. The governments in question lacked the resources and the will to pursue the matters once the groups went away, at least on paper.

Two things gnawed at Val, though. One: the groups would need sophisticated legal representation to continue to get away with such maneuvers. She guessed they retained specific, sympathetic lawyers or firms to provide such help.

Two: that would cost money, even if many of the lawyers donated their services. Court costs, filing of corporate papers to establish or dissolve an organization, web access, office space—it all cost money. Where were they getting it?

In the words made famous by the Watergate scandal, she knew what to do: follow the money.

***

Grimes swung by Val's desk around mid-morning, weariness etched across his face. "I got nothing so far," he said, taking a seat and propping his feet up on a nearby chair. "All the lefties are planning their usual sign-waving crap, complaining about what a war-hungry nation we are.

They filed for permits, so we can track them easily enough. O'Reilly's just getting started. What've you found?"

"Lots of smoke, no fire," Val said. "One group asked for a parade permit. The applicant had a recent firearms violation, so no go. I'm waiting for approval from IT to bypass the firewall and search 'dark' sites. I'm betting we'll find more clues there."

"That'll never happen," Grimes said. "A, they'll need to do a background check on you to make sure you won't piss your day away on snuff sites. B, half of the IT group is off today and the rest of the week. I'd be shocked if they even reply by Monday."

"I have friends over there," a familiar voice said from behind Grimes. A handsome man with broad shoulders, a square jaw, and wavy, dark hair appeared behind him. Gil rested his crutches against Val's desk and grinned. "Maybe I can help."

Val's jaw dropped, and she nearly trampled Grimes's stretched-out legs in order to dive into Gil's outstretched arms. "What are you doing here?"

"I got myself reinstated," Gil said. "With the all-hands request Brenda made, and so many guys off on vacation, they were all too eager to approve my early return."

"That's awesome! They put you on the WAVE Squad?"

Gil shook his head, a sad frown creasing his face. "They assigned me to Central Precinct down on the second floor, answering phones. My shift doesn't start until 1:00, though, and I wanted to see you. So, give me something to do. Keep me busy."

Grimes pointed a thumb over his shoulder at Petroni's office. "Check with Brenda. My guess is, she won't want you two love-birds working together. Because, natch, she'd actually want you to get some work done."

"Actually, Gil, I kind of like the idea of you taking orders from Dawes," Petroni said after Gil and Val explained the situation. "I know you outrank her, Kryz, but—"

"Meh." Gil waved her off. "It's only for a few hours, and I should probably get used to it."

"Are you calling me bossy?" Val said in mock indignation. "Wait until we get home, buster."

"Promises, promises."

"This," Grimes said with a roll of his eyes, "is why couples don't get assigned together."

True to his word, Gil worked his magic with the IT shop, who promised to expedite Val's request. "They'll have to set up a secure workstation with special software," he said after hanging up the phone. "It might not happen until the morning, though."

Val sighed. Bureaucracies.

"On another topic, I stopped by your father's house on my way in," Gil went on. "Jerry was there, getting ready to take him to an all-day AA meeting. Your dad didn't look too bad off. From what I gathered, he didn't drink all that much."

"One drop is too much. Thank you. I'll check in on him over lunch."

Grimes set Gil up with a workspace near Val's desk, and Gil took on some of Val's online searches. They hadn't gotten far when the sound of Grimes slamming his phone into its cradle startled them.

"Dawes," he called over to her. "Remember Destiny Mathers?"

"The way you say that, in past tense, makes me nervous." Val pushed her chair away from her desk.

"Not yet," Grimes said, "but close. She's back in the hospital. Someone used her as a punching bag, and I'm betting it's our friends from Saturday night's raid. They already posted bail. Come on, I'll drive. Sorry to break up the honeymoon, guys."

Val cast a pouty glance at Gil.

He shrugged. "It was fun while it lasted. I'll email you my notes."

Val nodded and swallowed a huge lump that formed in her throat. Seeing Gil back at work after so many months, and being a part of it for the first few minutes, made up for all the other crap she dealt with in this job. At least at HQ, he'd be out of the line of fire if something crazy happened. She felt confident about that.

Chapter Twenty-Seven

The nurse at Mercy Hospital warned Val and Grimes that Destiny's heavy sedation levels would leave her groggy at best, uncommunicative at worst.

"She's in stable condition. Please try not to upset her," the nurse continued. "We'll be monitoring her. If anything goes out of whack, the interview is done."

"We'll keep her as calm as the waters of Lake Woebegone," Grimes said.

The nurse responded with a puzzled expression, then glanced at Val, who shrugged.

Destiny groaned when she spotted them next to her bed. "I told them, no fucking cops. You're liable to get me killed."

"Don't worry, we snuck in the back way," Grimes said.

Val shot him the most annoyed look she could muster, but he refused to look at her. She steeled herself for a rocky interview. He'd asked her to let him take the lead, but she couldn't risk it. When Grimes got into one of his smart-aleck moods, only the worst could happen.

"We wanted to check in, see if you're all right," Val said.

"I'm fine. Now leave." Destiny closed her eyes again.

"You're listed in 'fair' condition," Grimes said. "In hospital-speak, that means not too hot. You didn't get that way by tripping over the dog. Who did this to you?"

"Go away," Destiny said. "I'm tired. I just want to sleep."

"We'll only be a couple of minutes, I promise," Val said. "Destiny, do you remember me?"

"Pfft." Destiny worked her lips and tongue for a few moments, as if trying to form words without success. "I remember both of ya'll. Unfortunately."

"Miss Mathers," Grimes said, "we'd like to help you by finding the guys—"

"Help me?" Destiny opened her eyes and laughed. "Because of you I got busted, and because of that, I'm here right now. That's how you 'help.' No thanks." She turned away again.

"If you don't assist us by identifying—"

"Detective Grimes," Val said, out of patience, "could you give us the room for a minute?"

Grimes glared at her, then opened his mouth to speak again. Val shushed him with an upraised index finger. "It worked once before," she whispered. "Give me another shot with her."

He huffed, but nodded and exited, shutting the door behind him.

Val sat next to the bed and remained quiet for a moment.

After a few seconds, Destiny rolled over and spotted her there. "I thought you left."

"Soon. Sometimes, he can be a little suffocating, and I just need some space."

"I hear that."

"Mind if I hang in here with you for a few?" Val said. "You'd be doing me a huge favor."

Destiny's brow curled. "I guess so. Just be quiet, okay?"

Val crossed her heart. "Promise." She waited a minute in silence, then two, then five.

Destiny huffed out an impatient breath. "You still here?"

"I'll just be another sec."

Another loud exhalation from the bed. "I can't give you his name."

"I know."

"He'll kill me."

"I don't want that to happen."

"He'd kill me if he even knew ya'll were here."

"Seems he ought to expect it, given the injuries you suffered. Concussion, bruises all over your body, internal bruises, broken finger—"

"What are you, freaking Chicago Med?"

Val laughed. "I've never watched that show."

"My boyfriend used to like it."

Val paused a moment. "Used to?"

"He gone. Ain't seen him in weeks."

Val nodded. "Miss him?"

Destiny chuckled. "Nah. He was as bad as—the, ah, dude who did this."

"Bet if we told him about this, he'd bust the guy's ass," Val said.

"Pfft. He's a pussy. He only hits women and kids."

Val sighed. "You're right. A man that won't stick up for you isn't worth missing. Remind me to kick his ass next time I see him."

Destiny laughed. "You a tough little bitch, aren't you?"

"I've been called worse." Val stretched and stood. "Well, I feel better. Thanks."

"Wait, you leaving?" Destiny sat up and leaned on one elbow. "Just like that?"

"Why not?" Val took a few steps toward the door. "You don't want our help, and I got my few minutes of alone time away from Grimes, so..."

"Wait." Destiny fingered the neckline of her hospital gown, biting her lower lip, then met Val's gaze. "If I give you a name, what are you gonna do with it?"

"Depends. We'll track him down, ask him a few questions. If he gets too sassy, we'll cool him off in jail for a day or two. That ought to ruin his Fourth of July."

Destiny laughed. "I'll say. That'd piss him off good. And a lot of other people."

Val returned to her bedside. "What other people?"

Destiny lay back down, folding her hands across her stomach. "He's planning some shit for tomorrow, some kind of protest. Him and some out-of-town folks. I don't know their names."

Val's skin tingled. "The guys we arrested in the raid? The pimps and traffickers?"

Destiny's eyebrows curled. "You and your terminology. They're just dudes, man. Doing business. Helping girls make money, giving us a warm place to crash. But yeah, them guys. The one who hit me, and...all of 'em. Hell, half of 'em just got out of lockup. You all couldn't have timed it better, letting them go."

Val cursed to herself. They could only hold suspects up to 48 hours without charging them. Once charged, suspects could make bail and escape the overcrowded facility in under a day. Which they'd clearly done. "Any idea where I can find them right now?"

Destiny shook her head. "All I know is, they ain't where you busted 'em Saturday. Sorry."

Val grabbed Destiny's hand and held it. "Thank you, Destiny. You've been a huge help. And if you change your mind about naming the guy..."

"Don't hold your breath." The girl rolled over to face away from Val again.

***

Petroni convened an all-hands meeting when Val and Grimes returned. She included Gil, who'd lingered in hopes of seeing Val again, and Damari Price, recalled from street duty.

Petroni stood in front of the whiteboard in the bullpen area, black erasable marker in hand. "Let me try to summarize what we've found so far," she said. She'd already outlined the basic points on the board and tapped them with her pen as she moved through the list. "We suspect some sort of 'statement' event will take place sometime tomorrow, which will either involve direct violence, or is intended to incite violence. We believe that an extremist group is behind it, but we don't know which one."

"Nor do we know where or what time," Grimes said, wiping sweat off his balding scalp.

"We can narrow that down," Petroni said, "at least, the most likely places. They want this thing to be visible, which means lots of people need to see it."

"Or the media," Val said. "They might just want TV coverage."

"Or," Gil added, "a combination of the above. Say, a splashy, noise-making protest that draws lots of media and police attention, while their primary target may be elsewhere."

"Like the Armory," Petroni said. "Which we already plan to protect with a big police presence. Where else?"

"City Hall?" Val said. Petroni wrote it down, though she looked doubtful.

"The big new real estate developments along the Waterfront," Gil said.

"The power plant, or the water treatment plant," Grimes said.

"Banks," Shannon O'Reilly said, without a lot of confidence. "But they'll be closed and have lots of security already, so..."

The room went quiet. Nobody could think of any other high-profile targets in Clayton.

"Okay," Petroni said. "So, what are the high-visibility targets that would draw media attention? The parade route during the day comes to mind."

"Fireworks party on the Waterfront," Price said. "And the live concert leading up to it."

"The annual police vs. fire department softball game," Grimes said.

"I dunno," Gil said with a grin. "I might catch that one on ESPN." The room erupted in laughter.

"Come on, think about it," Grimes said, growing more insistent. "Lots of law enforcement all in one place, a decent-sized crowd, a downtown park, and enough armed men to bring down a banana republic."

"Let's add it to the list," Brenda said. "My guess is, we won't need to add staff for that one."

"They ought to cancel it, given our staff shortage." Shannon shook her head. "What a waste."

"We'd have to forfeit, and no way we're letting the fire department break our five-game winning streak." Grimes's face grew red. "It's bad enough we don't have Gil batting cleanup this year. How about you, Dawes? You're pretty athletic. Want to take his place in left field?"

"Manage your baseball operations on your own time, dammit," Petroni said, glowering at Grimes. "Another word, and I'll schedule you for guard duty at—when is first pitch?— 9:00 a.m."

Grimes mimed zipping his lip and sulked in his seat.

"Our number one priority is figuring out who, where, and when," Petroni said. "Our hottest lead is the sex trafficking bunch, so let's start there. O'Reilly, Price, and I will hunt down the whereabouts of the men we locked up this weekend. Grimes, you and Dawes—and Kryzinski, while he remains available—follow up on what you learned from Destiny Mathers. Regroup here at 1:00. Go!"

***

While Petroni, Price, and O'Reilly dispersed to their desks and phones, Val, Grimes, and Gil remained at the meeting table.

"Like Val mentioned earlier," Gil said, "we need to follow the money. How does an activist group get ahold of the cash needed to organize something like this? In particular, how do they funnel it from a criminal operation like the one you all raided on Saturday to a legit political group?"

"Without getting caught," Val added. "So they have to launder the money somehow."

"That's easy," Grimes said, sitting upright in his chair. "Cryptocurrency."

"You mean like NFTs?" Val said.

"I've heard of those, but I've never understood how it worked," Gil said. "Explain."

"I'll do you one better," Grimes said. "I'll bring in our resident expert."

One phone call later, a short, slender woman with thick, spiky black hair and a faint mustache stood at the head of the table, dressed in a form-fitting button-down shirt and bright blue Capri pants. Broad-shouldered, with a narrow waist and hips, she looked like a compact bodybuilder with nerd glasses. "Team," Grimes said, "meet Shelby from our IT Security Department. She helped me track down some perps in a gun-running case about a year and a half ago where they used crypto. Could you summarize how that worked?"

"Bitcoin and its competitors are forms of virtual currency, otherwise known as digital money," Shelby said in a rushed, high-pitched voice. "It's created online by private parties, and it's the currency of choice among criminal organizations."

"Why bother with that?" Gil said. "What's wrong with good old-fashioned cash?"

"Because there's no government involved," Shelby said. "Since it's all virtual, there's nothing physical to trace. All the transactions are anonymous."

"Where does the money come from in the first place?" Val asked.

"If they follow the same pattern, here's how it all goes down." Shelby erased a small section of Brenda's notes on the whiteboard, then wrote: *I. Raise cash.* "Step one: they raise 'real' money, somehow. In the gun-running case, they sold drugs."

"Here, it's prostitution and sex trafficking," Grimes said.

"Wait, so you're saying the sex ring is just a fundraising operation?" Gil scratched his stubbly jaw. "Seems like the tail's wagging the dog here."

"Could be, or maybe it's the main objective," Grimes said. "Doesn't matter. The point is, that's where the money comes from."

"I get how the sex trafficking could work that way," Val said. "But are you saying the johns also pay sex workers with crypto?"

"Not a lot of ordinary people have crypto to spend," Shelby said. "So, here's what these guys do." She wrote: *II. (Optional) Convert to commodities.*

"Commodities?" Gil said. "Like corn futures and pork bellies?"

Grimes scowled and threw his pen at Gil's head, missing by two feet.

"And you're the pitcher on the softball team?" Val chuckled. "I'm betting on the firefighters."

Shelby laughed, earning an angry stare from Grimes. "Not ag futures, but easily fenced and useful items, like burner phones, designer clothes, laptops, or prepaid debit cards. All legal and almost as good as cash."

"They're doing laundry," Grimes said. "Creating distance between the money they get and what they spend, as crooks have been doing for years. The crypto part is the new piece."

Shelby scribbled: *III. Fence the goods.* "Right. They liquidate the goods, as crooks have always done, either into cash, or straight into crypto. Then, for even greater security, they engage in further crypto transactions, often blending the money with legit sources—celebrity investors, for example. That's called 'chain-hopping,' and it helps erase the transaction trail. Or muddy it up, anyway."

"Celebrity investors are in on it?" Gil frowned. "People like Gwyneth Paltrow and Tom Brady?"

"The investors have no idea what the brokers do with the money, and we don't know whose money is used where. It's all fungible," Shelby said. She scribbled again on the whiteboard. "Finally, they pay off the original party—gun-runner, sex trafficker—using crypto transactions. They can now use the funds in legit ways, including political donations."

"Corporations aren't allowed to do that," Val said. "That violates federal campaign financing laws."

"They could disguise the money as legitimate donations to those groups, funneling it through private individuals, say," Grimes said. "Easy-peasy."

"Sounds complicated," Gil said.

"It is. And, it's super-fast," Shelby said. "Since it's online, they can process all of this in hours, or even minutes. Even automatically."

"How the hell are we ever going to unravel this?" Val said. "If it's all so invisible."

"The good news," Shelby said, "is that while the transactions themselves are anonymous, they are all recorded somewhere and can be tracked. Unfortunately, that's the part that takes time."

"Unless we can short-circuit that process," Grimes said. "Which is where Destiny Mathers comes in."

Val got excited. "Are you saying that if we can ID one of the parties—"

"Then we can subpoena their records." Grimes grinned. "Then it all falls right into place."

"That's good," Val said. "Because time is the one thing we haven't got."

"In fact, I have none," Gil said. "It's time for me to report to my real job. Let me know how I can help from there. This is cool stuff, and I hate to leave it behind."

Val walked him to the elevator and held him in a long, warm hug.

"I'm so glad we're at least working in the same building now," he said. "I was hoping we could do lunch together, but it looks like we worked right through."

"We'll bc lucky to get dinner breaks, at this rate." Val stood on her tiptoes to give him a kiss. Her buzzing cell phone interrupted her. "I'd better take this, in case there's news on Dad." She glanced at the phone, and didn't recognize the number.

"Go ahead anyway," Gil said. "It might be his AA sponsor or something."

The elevator door opened, and Gil hopped on board. Val answered thc call as the doors closed.

"Valorie?" The woman's voice sent a chill down Val's spine. "It's your mother."

"I'm working," Val said. Damned Chad! How dare he give her Val's number! "Can you call me back later?"

"Sure, but before I hang up..." Her mother fumbled with the phone, and a moment later, a child's voice greeted her.

"Valorie? This is Sammy. Can we get together today to play?"

Chapter Twenty-Eight

Maggie took the phone back from Sammy when his big, silly grin turned upside-down into an about-to-cry-hysterically grimace. Probably because his own sister couldn't muster a decent reply to his simple request.

"So?" she said into the phone, cradling the boy's sniffling face into her bosom. "Can we see you today?"

"Uh...I'm working," Valorie said. "Until late. But I'd love to meet my little brother. Chad ought to arrive by 5:00. Perhaps we can all get together for a quick dinner?"

"Chad will be here by two," Maggie said. "Sammy's looking forward to meeting his niece *and* sister. I'm not available after four, so you'll need to make other plans."

"I can't make other plans!" Valorie shouted. "Do you understand how police departments operate?"

All too well, dammit. "The kids want to go to Dinosaur Park in Rocky Hill. We'll meet you at your father's house at 2:00. Don't be late." She hung up, in no mood for an argument.

"She won't show," Mac said. He lay across the motel room bed—*her* bed, the lout—reading an old issue of *Guns & Ammo*. "Your daughter's like you: contrary by nature." He snickered, and Smiley, absorbed with her cell phone in the corner, flashed that strange vampire grin of hers.

"She'll show," Maggie said. "Valorie won't pass up a chance to meet her little brother."

"What if she doesn't?" Mac's voice slurred a little.

"Then I adapt," Maggie said, irritation growing. "Smiley, please take Sammy to your room and entertain him for a while, would you?"

Smiley grimaced for a moment, then emitted a nervous laugh and showed that stupid grin again. "Come on, Sammy. I have some Go-Gurts in my fridge."

"Bandana flavor?" Sammy asked.

Maggie cringed at the kid's malapropism, then at Mac's chuckling at him. Bad enough the kid was slow, but encouraging him by laughing? Such an unfit father.

"All kinds of flavors!" Smiley said. "You can pick."

"I want bandana kind!" Sammy sang, running in circles until he got dizzy and fell, laughing.

Maggie sighed. The kid's high-energy antics and constant need for attention was a key reason why she hadn't rejected Mac's demand for custody in the divorce.

After Smiley and Sammy left, Maggie turned to Mac, all business. "Get up. We've got work to do."

"Later. I'm tired." Mac tossed the magazine aside and lay back in the bed. A trickle of blood dripped from one nostril.

"Mac, have you eaten today?" Maggie said.

"A beer or two, a handful of peanuts." He scratched at a patch of dry skin on his face, and the web of blue capillaries appeared more prevalent on his cheeks.

"Mac, look at me."

"In a minute. I'm resting."

"Mac!" Maggie crossed the room and sat next to him on the bed. She grabbed his elbow, and he jerked it away. Only then did she notice the bruises on his forearm.

He sat up, swearing, and rubbed his arm where she'd grabbed him. "What the hell?"

She focused on his eyes. Sure enough, the so-called whites of his eyes appeared yellow. His skin did, too, though it was hard to tell in the dim light of the motel room. "Did you see the doctor before you left Florida?"

Mac waved her off. "Yeah, yeah."

Maggie gritted her teeth and peered closer. His face seemed more haggard than a few months before. He'd bragged about losing weight, even though his ankles appeared more swollen than ever. "What did the doctor say?"

"Don't drink, don't smoke, blah, blah. Same old bullshit."

"It's your liver, isn't it?"

He shrugged. "Like I said. Same old, same old."

She tossed her head back in frustration, staring at the ceiling. Mac contracted hepatitis C from a prostitute several years before. Thank God their sex life was over by that point. In a vain attempt to hide his condition, he'd delayed getting treatment until cirrhosis destroyed his liver.

"Have you been taking your meds?" She hadn't seen him take any since he arrived.

"They don't help," he said.

Idiot! She took a calming breath. "Any blood in your urine?"

He waved the question aside and coughed, a phlegmy, raspy sound.

"Mac. What did the doctor tell you?"

He turned away without a word.

"Should I go ask Sammy, then?" Maggie stood and headed toward the door. Still no answer. The door loomed closer. Ten feet. Five—

"Three to six months," he said in a low voice. "That's all I got."

She stopped, turned in a slow rotation toward him. "Why didn't you say something before? We could've arranged for treatment."

"There is no treatment. It's too late. All they can do is make me suffer longer."

"That's not true. They can prescribe antivirals. They can—"

"Mags." He sighed. "It's too late."

She stared at him, realization dawning. "It's not really three to six months, is it?"

He stared at the floor, shook his head. "Not anymore. My liver's just about gone."

"You've known this—"

"For months, yes. They wanted to tie me to a dialysis machine, and, well, screw that." He sighed. "I don't want to go out like that, Maggie. Never have, never will."

She sank into a chair. "That's why you wouldn't sign the divorce papers. Or the custody agreement."

A heavy silence filled the room.

"Does Sammy know?" she asked after a minute or so.

Mac shrugged. "You never know."

Maggie turned away, unable to look at him. He'd lied—or, at least, withheld critical information from her—once again. And, through self-denial, from himself. A fatal mistake—literally.

***

Val listened to dead air on her phone for a good ten seconds before setting it down on her desk. The nerve of her mother! First she breezes back into her life after nine years of abandonment, acting as if she'd merely stepped out for a cigarette. Then she drops bombshells, one after the other, in a blatant attempt at manipulation, all the while making unreasonable demands. As if Val had no job, no life of her own to manage. As if nothing about Val's needs mattered. Then she tops it off with using her little brother as a weapon.

In some ways, nothing *had* changed between them in nine years.

"Got a minute, Dawes?" Grimes thumped his body down into a chair next to her desk, spilling coffee from an open mug onto the floor. He brushed about half of the spilled liquid away with his shoe, creating an even larger wet spot, and sniffed in satisfaction.

"Sure, what's up?" she said, driving the conversation with her mother out of her head.

"Just heard that IT is sending someone up to install some new software on our computers," he said. "Is that what you requested?"

"Not exactly," she said. "I only asked for it on mine. They're doing yours, too?"

"The entire team." Grimes set his mug down on Val's desk. Again, coffee sloshed over the sides, and he wiped it to the floor with the side of his hand. "They need to kick us off our computers for an hour or two. Got anything else to keep you busy?"

"Not if I can't use my computer."

"In that case, come help me with some field research," he said, already up and moving toward the door.

Val stood, glanced in irritation at the coffee cup he left on her desk, then patted her empty holster. "Wait, I'm not cleared for field work."

"I said *research*." He held the door open, waving her through. "Anyway, I'm armed enough for both of us. Come on, time's wasting!"

Try as she might, Val couldn't pry any details out of him, other than their destination: the Clayton Armed Services Historical Arsenal, better known as the Armory. While she drove, he spent the entire trip on his phone, haranguing last-minute drop-outs from the next morning's softball game and scrambling to recruit replacements.

"We're going to get killed," he said after his final call. "No left fielder, no shortstop, and our starting catcher might be giving birth at game time. You sure you can't help out in the morning?"

"I've never hit a ball with anything smaller than a pickup truck. And I wouldn't know a referee from a break dancer."

"Baseball doesn't use refs, we use—wait. You're putting me on, aren't you, Dawes?" He groaned.

Val grinned. The truth: she'd promised to spend the early part of the day with Gil before their shifts. "Tell me what we're doing here," she said, parking the cruiser in a visitors spot. "I hate going in cold."

"We've got some intel that Antifa may stage an illegal protest here tomorrow," he said. "We gotta find out what the staff know and help them prep."

The Armory's Security Director, a short, scrappy man in his forties by the name of Ryker, met them at the door and gave them a tour of the grounds first. Ryker had an unsmiling, leathery face and the build of a salt shaker. "We give annual tours of the facility on the Fourth, and we require people to register in advance, for screening," Ryker said. "Two names popped up with recent arrests for unlawful protest— one for assault at an Antifa rally. We think they're leaders of the group."

Val rolled her eyes. "You know Antifa's not a 'group' per se, right? More of a shadowy network of—"

"Organized or not, they have criminal records," Ryker said. "We won't be letting them on the tour." He walked them around the perimeter of the building, a two-story brick structure with a small parking lot and acres of green space. A plaque near the front door boasted a construction date of 1837 and a designation in the National Register of Historic Places.

"Wait, hold on," Grimes said. "Are you sure you want to do that? We don't want to tip them off that we're onto them."

"Easy for you to say," Ryker said with a growl, stopping near a statue of a Revolutionary War hero that Val couldn't identify. "You're not guarding five hundred firearms displays. Many of the weapons are still operational, by the way. You want those freaks getting their hands on these guns?"

"What Detective Grimes is suggesting," Val said, "is that you keep a close watch on them during the tour—"

"I understand what Grimes is saying," Ryker said, snarling. "Listen to what I'm saying: I don't want them here."

"How about you let one of us take the tour with them?" Grimes asked. "Undercover, of course."

Ryker glared at each of them, then nodded. "Tour starts at 9:00 a.m. Be here by 8:30."

Grimes held up both hands, palms-out. "Gonna have to be you, Val. I've got the game."

Val swore under her breath. "Can you give me a preview? Not the spiel, just the physical layout and the route."

Ryker led them inside and walked them through the tour's paces, pointing to spots where the guide would stop for extended talks. The drafty old building's acoustics created a cacophony, even with only three sets of footsteps pounding its ancient wooden floors. Plenty enough sound to cover up sneaky, nefarious activity. Val noted some narrow corridors where a person could wander unnoticed into secure storage areas in the basement—targets of interest for a splinter group. Afterwards, they settled into uncomfortable chairs in Ryker's spacious second-floor office, one of the few rooms in the building with windows large enough to permit a decent amount of daylight. Ryker's diploma from West Point perched on the wall behind him, surrounded by an array of ribbons and medals. A noisy air conditioner blew cold air on Val's neck while they talked.

"How often does the tour guide take a headcount?" Val asked.

"At the beginning and at the end," Ryker said, impatience infusing his voice. "Why?"

"If someone wanted to slip away and hide out inside until after you close—"

"Something for you to monitor, then," Grimes said. "Now, there's also the matter of the mayor's speech at the kickoff ceremony outside. What's your security plan there?"

Ryker grimaced. "Not my department. I thought you guys were dealing with that."

Val nodded. "That's Travis Blake's detail," she said. "He asked me to help him out."

"What'd Petroni say?" Grimes asked.

"I haven't asked her yet," Val said.

"I doubt she'll approve," Grimes said, "unless Cyrus changes his mind and lets you carry your weapon."

"No weapons on the tour, or anywhere on your person while you're in the building," Ryker said, his tone heated. "Strictly prohibited."

Grimes smirked, but said nothing. Val glanced at Grimes and, sure enough, detected the shape of his shoulder holster bulging under his navy blazer.

Grimes and Val thanked Ryker and stepped outside, where they inspected the dais being set up by city crews for the morning event. "There are no freaking barricades, nothing to restrict the flow of people in or out," he groused. "A security nightmare."

Val's eyes widened. "You think someone plans to take a shot at the mayor? She's a lame duck. Why would anyone–"

"Our intel says there may be some false flag ops going on here. Maybe some fights, or a few incendiaries—smoke bombs, nothing serious," he said. "A sideshow, designed to create a public panic and keep us occupied. I don't think this is the real thing."

"You think the folks hiding inside are the main event?"

Grimes shrugged. "Or, they want to steal the weapons for their shitshow later in the day. Either way, we can't let anything slide. We have to respond to, and prepare for, every possibility." He strolled toward the squad car, saying over his shoulder, "You'd better put in your morning reassignment request to Petroni ASAP."

Val nodded. Travis would be pleased. Gil, not so much.

Chapter Twenty-Nine

When they returned to the office, Val found Shelby standing at her desk and pecking away at her keyboard.

As always, Val had locked her workstation with a password before leaving, so the sight of a virtual stranger accessing her accounts filled her with alarm. "Excuse me?" Val said. "Can I help you with something?"

Shelby answered without looking up. "I'm here to set you up on the VPN."

"What's a VPN, anyway? And why?"

Shelby turned and cast Val an impatient frown. "Virtual private network. You requested dark web access, didn't you?"

"Oh. Yes, of course." Val knew next to nothing about computer networks and had hoped it would all be ready before they got back. "How long will that take?"

"Another hour or two," Shelby said. "We also need to install and configure Tor, and set you up with an anonymous login. Then I gotta reconfigure the router to let you access the stuff we usually don't permit. Then you sign some release forms, promising you won't look at anything *too* nasty." She smirked and wiggled her eyebrows at Val. "I'll also set up the other workstations the same way. No sense doing all this work for just one special person."

"Is there a book or manual or something on how to use this 'dark web' thing?" Val asked.

"No, sorry. Give me a minute and I'll show you a few things." Shelby clicked a few more keys while Val pulled up another chair, then pulled a laptop and some paperwork out of a backpack lying on Val's desk. "If you think of the web as an information superhighway, then the dark web is a network of undocumented tunnels with no GPS, no directions, not even a map."

"What's Tor, then?" Val asked. "Is that the VPN?"

"Tor is a browser, like Chrome or Safari. It's stripped of the usual safety features you'd find in those browsers. If Chrome were a car, Tor would be like driving a 1960s dune buggy on an unknown country road at night with bad tires, no headlights, and no speedometer."

"And Tor lets me onto the deep web?"

"First, there's a difference between the deep web and the dark web," Shelby said. "Both are hidden from mere mortals like us. The dark web is illegal stuff, while the deep web is secret personal data that shouldn't get exposed, like medical and financial records."

"Is that what that WikiLeaks group goes after?" Val asked.

"Exactly. By contrast, most of the so-called dark web is child porn, snuff films, crap like that. That's what you have to promisc not to waste time on—unless..." Shelby wiggled her thick eyebrows and play-punched Val's arm. "Go on, tell me your case requires it."

"We're looking at secret terrorist sites with a link to sex trafficking," Val said. "And any record of financial transactions—crypto or otherwise—to finance it."

"Then you'll need pretty broad access." Shelby scribbled on the "Additional Information" section of the forms. "Although, unless you know what you're doing, you're unlikely to find anything on the financial stuff. That can take years to find, even by experts."

Val's heart sank a little. "I don't even know how to find the basic stuff. I doubt they'll run ads to recruit underage sex workers."

Shelby glanced up from the forms and slid them toward Val. "They do, if you know what to look for," she said with a wicked smile.

"Which I don't." Val scanned the form, which demanded she promise not to peruse any site outside her specific area of research. "How the hell can I sign this? I don't know where to begin."

Shelby opened her laptop and fired up her Tor browser. "The best place to start is an add-on called DuckDuckGo. That, along with the VPN, hides your searches from prying eyes like mine." She laughed. "Then go to Torch.com, which is kind of like Google for the dark web. I'll set all that up for you." She showed Val the website and entered a simple search. "See all the ads popping up?"

"What lousy graphics," Val said. "The ad copy's even worse."

"That's because the words aren't the actual message. Read between the lines. OK, you're looking for sex traffickers?" Shelby typed "Night jobs for underage girls" into the search bar, and a whole new set of ads showed up. "See that 'Work from home and earn $$$' ad?" She clicked on it.

A page appeared with clearly underage girls flirting with handsome, wealthy-looking men in their thirties. "*Make $$, Meet interesting people*," Val said. "I see what you mean."

"None of them will come right out and say 'Earn money through crime,'" Shelby said. "You gotta poke and dig, and it's not quick work. OK, are you ready for me to mess up your workstation?"

Val nodded and Shelby returned to Val's keyboard. For several minutes, Val watched in silence, but soon grew bored with her machinations. "I heard there are all these secret websites and chat rooms where terrorists plot their nefarious schemes," Val said. "How do I find those?"

Shelby grunted. "You mean, like right-wingers and John Birch Society idiots?"

"For example, yes. People like that."

"The easiest way is to post some crap about how much you love gays, lesbians, and trans people," Shelby said. "Trust me, they'll find you."

"I don't have a lot of time," Val said. "Is there a faster way?"

Shelby cocked her head, nodded. "Start with the nutcase social media, like Telegram and Parler," she said. "You'll want to create fake accounts, and good luck with staying anonymous. Some of 'em cost money, and no way the city will pay your fees. You'll need to learn a lot more about them, learn how they talk to each other. Use their vocabulary: 'libs,' not liberals, for example. 'Femoids' for feminists, and so on. You'll need to get conversant with it, or they'll out you and shut you down."

"How? This is all Greek to me."

Shelby opened her email app and sent Val a file. "This glossary will get you started. Hey, I'd love to stay and help you more, but I'm in a time crunch. Plus, the sooner I get your computers set up, the sooner you can put these creeps behind bars for the rest of their lives. Which I hope you'll do. So, can you give me an hour or two?"

Val glanced at the clock. Maybe she could hang out with Sammy today after all. "Shelby, thank you so much for doing this, and responding so quickly. It's a big help."

"Yeah. You too."

Val headed toward the door, but stopped when Shelby called out her name. She turned. "Did I forget something?"

Shelby glanced around as if to make sure nobody was listening and lowered her voice. "Once I get off my regular shift..." Her voice grew more animated. "If you want, I might be able to help you with some web searches."

"That would be amazing," Val said. "How can I ever thank you?"

Shelby sneered. "Catch those trans-hating motherfuckers. Then hang every one of those bastards by their scrotums. On a rusty nail." She laughed and returned to her workstation.

Val laughed a moment, too, then paused. Shelby assumed that the perpetrators behind all this were male. So far, Val had assumed that, too. But maybe they shouldn't *assume* at all.

***

While Shelby continued working on her computer, Val sat at another workstation and dove into the in-house database on past incidents with extremist right-wing groups. Besides a few minor skirmishes involving unpermitted protests and the occasional breakup of street fights, only one major case stood out. Three years before, Clayton PD arrested a local leader of the Heroes of Freedom, a now-extinct, self-described men's rights activist group, on kidnapping charges. The victim, a twelve-year-old girl, disappeared after having complained that "some weirdo" was following her. Already known for fantastic fabrications, her complaints went unheeded. She turned up outside Philadelphia several days later, malnourished, frightened, and wearing "age-inappropriate" clothes, but uninjured. After keeping him in custody for 48 hours, Clayton police released the accused and dropped all charges for lack of sufficient evidence.

The arresting officer and lead detective on the case: Mickey Mulroney.

She called his desk, expecting to reach voicemail, but he answered on the second ring. "Mulroney, Vice Squad."

"This is Valorie Dawes of the WAVE Squad."

"No kidding?" He laughed. "Speak of the devil. I had 'Call Dawes' on my to-do list today."

Val nearly dropped her phone. "Me? Why?"

"Ladies first," he said. "Besides, you called me, so you must have something to say."

"Yes, I do. You handled a kidnapping case a few years back, involving the leader of a right-wing fringe group—"

"*Activist* group."

"Excuse me?" Val frowned at the interruption.

"Management says we can't call them fringe groups, or right-wing, or any of that crap anymore," Mulroney said in a mocking tone. "We gotta be all politically correct these days and use, how do they call it, 'neutral terms,' I think, is the phrase."

"Neutral. Right." Val swallowed her frustration. No doubt Mulroney learned this the hard way. No reason she had to. "The guy ended up going free. Do you remember why?"

"Yeah, that was a real circus." Mulroney's volume dropped a notch, as if he feared someone might overhear him. "Turns out, the whole kidnapping thing was BS. All a big divorce custody dispute. The kid's old man tried to take her from her mother, hide her at his girlfriend's place in Philly."

"Wait. The suspect was the girl's father?"

"That's what I said, isn't it?" Mulroney's voice dripped with sarcasm, his pronunciation veering toward the vernacular: *idn'it?*

"Right. Just clarifying." She cleared her throat, scanned the case file for another moment. "Isn't that still kidnapping?"

"Technically, yeah," Mulroney said. "We don't like to dive too deep into those family dispute cases. The accused, what's his name again?"

"Bosco Nicorelli," Val said.

"Yeah. Him and his ex-wife worked something out, and we didn't see any need to pursue it any further." *Enny furder.*

"The prosecutor's office signed off—"

"For Christ's sake, Dawes, read the damned report," Mulroney said. "There was nothing there. No ransom, no threats, nobody got hurt, and the mom changed her mind. So we dropped it. We can't force people to testify when they don't believe their own story."

Val sighed, unease settling over her. All too often, an overworked detective or prosecutor declined to pursue an unwinnable case. Still, this seemed a little too abrupt, given the facts stated in the file. A little too *neat.* Arranged.

Or, the result of political pressure? The local district attorney had a well-earned reputation for his conservative politics. Did that play a part in letting a messy case slide off his radar?

"Was there anything else?" Mulroney said, his impatience showing.

"No. Thanks for your help. If there's anything I can do to return the favor—"

"Actually, there is. Can you meet me outside, at the coffee cart, in five minutes? It won't take long."

Val's alarm bells rang. Why outside the building? That didn't pass the sniff test. "Can't you just ask me on the phone?"

"I would, but it's kind of personal," Mulroney said. "Come on, I'll buy."

Against her better judgment, Val agreed, if only to assuage her conscience. Mulroney had helped her, after all. Sort of.

***

Val arrived first at the coffee cart, which, for perhaps the first time in history, had no line of caffeine-starved officers waiting. She turned toward the front steps of the Headquarters building to watch for him. A minute, then two...he was late. For his own damned meeting. Where the hell—

"Hope you like it black." A thick paper cup with a plastic lid appeared by her side, the arm holding it extending behind her.

She took the cup from the plump, fiftyish man in an ill-fitting, light gray suit, his salt-and-pepper crew cut revealing a sunburnt bald spot on the crown of his head. She sipped the coffee, wishing it contained cream to mask its stale bitterness. "Thanks. What's up?"

"Let's walk." Mulroney strode away from her at a fast clip, not waiting to confirm that she'd followed. He turned at the corner against the light, cursing at honking cars swerving around him.

"We're setting a fine example," Val said, reddening. People might not make Mulroney for a cop in his civvies, but she wore a standard dark blue uniform and a visible silver badge.

He led her into a small city park, two blocks square with sidewalks crisscrossing it and circling its perimeter, occupied by a handful of dog-walkers scattered about. He found a park bench and perched one foot upon it, peeling off the lid of his cup and sipping his coffee. "You working tomorrow?" he asked.

"Isn't everyone?" She stood next to him, facing away from the police building, same as him.

"Yeah. Bunch of bullshit." Mulroney blew on his coffee. "A lot of nonsensical hysteria."

"Let's hope so," Val said. "We have to be ready, just in case, though, right?"

"Pfft." He shook his head. "I heard what they got. Which is nothing. A couple of protesters. So what? Last I heard, people got the right." He set his cup down on the bench, steam rising from it, and rested his elbow on his bent knee.

"You don't think they'll get violent?" Val said.

"It's the same bullshit every year," he said. "Good, patriotic Americans demonstrating their love of country and expressing their disagreement with the way things are going. That pisses people off—people in charge. Makes 'em afraid, and who's the one that's gotta work overtime to make them feel safer? You and me, that's who." He shifted his weight. His foot bumped his coffee cup, spilling its contents across the bench and onto the ground. He didn't seem to notice or care.

"You don't think there's anything to this alert, then?"

Mulroney rolled his eyes and stared off into the distance. "People shouldn't have to ask permission to express their First Amendment rights."

"Agreed." Val grew uneasy, like he'd tricked her, somehow. "But you didn't ask me here to discuss constitutional law. You said you wanted to ask a personal favor?"

Mulroney glanced down at his coffee cup, lying on its side on the bench, and righted it. "How's the department treating you so far?"

"Fine." But as soon as Val said the word, contradictions floated across her mind: Dr. Cyrus's distrust of her, and the resulting loss of her weapon. Petroni reprimanding her a few months ago for a leak that she later admitted knowing Val hadn't done. Four partner reassignments in her first year. Her on-again, off-again status as a member of the WAVE Squad.

Mulroney's squinty-eyed, doubtful expression made it clear he knew about some or all of that.

"As with every person in any job, there've been some down moments," she said. "What's your point?"

"You think the department's looking out for you?" His tone implied that he expected "No" for an answer.

"The department isn't a sentient being," she said. "It's a collection of people. Some better than others."

His face took on an air of bemusement. "Are the ones making budget decisions putting your personal safety and future first?"

"I think so, yes."

"Yeah? Well, forgive my saying so, but your uncle thought so, too."

Flashes of anger and sadness competed for control of Val's response. Sadness won out, as a hard lump formed in her throat. Her words came out hoarse and raspy. "The department didn't kill him. Some asshole carrying a gun into a shopping mall did."

"True. But..."

She glared at him. "But what?"

"He was a good man," Mulroney said. "A damned fine cop."

Val's impatience grew, along with her sadness. "Yes, he was. And...?"

Mulroney shook his head, as if in disgust. "A lot of us feel he didn't have to die that day."

That struck home, tapping an emotion Val had held for over a decade. Fighting to retain control, she heaved a deep breath. "Of course he didn't. What's your point?" When Mulroney didn't answer right away, she thought a moment longer and asked, "Why do you say 'a lot of people feel that way?' Do people still talk about it?"

Mulroney shrugged. "Some." He wiped sweat off his forehead, a reflection of the day's growing heat. "A lot of guys think things haven't improved a lot since then, either."

Val sipped her coffee, which seemed to taste even more bitter now. "Meaning?"

Mulroney shot her a sideways glance. "Why did he go in alone that day?"

"To confront the shooter? I don't know." Something she'd always wondered, herself.

Mulroney grunted. "Do you think he had proper backup in that situation? Is that the case today? If we run into goons carrying guns tomorrow, will we be ready?"

Val recalled the occasions where she'd confronted armed suspects. Too often, she'd faced them alone, with backup slow to arrive. Even the raid the week before had felt under-staffed.

But with nearly the entire force on duty for July Fourth...

"Wait a minute," she said. "I thought you said that to-morrow would be no big deal. A non-event."

"Maybe." He smiled. "But maybe we're on the wrong side of whatever happens tomorrow. Busting people for carrying signs and chanting slogans, like we did last year? Does that seem right to you?"

Val scoffed. "My understanding is they gave people tick-ets for failure to obtain parade permits. Nobody went to jail."

"Nobody?" He laughed. "Don't believe what you read in the papers. Or blogs, or whatever the hell you kids get your news from these days."

"Mickey, what do you want from me?" Val tossed out the rest of her nasty coffee and crumpled the cup into her fist. "If you're looking for a promise not to arrest someone who's just expressing their opinion, sure. Easy enough. But I'm a rookie. Seems to me you should lobby someone higher up the food chain."

"That's a good start," he said. "I'm glad to hear it. Look, Dawes, the higher-ups are under a lot of political pressure. They don't listen to folks like you and me. Guys—and gals—who face the real scum of the earth every day, who get shouted at, spit on, and shot at. Hell, you've been here less than a year, and how many have taken aim at you?"

Val grimaced. He was right, of course. "Too many."

"So, let the captains and chief hold their meetings with the mayor and issue their statements to the press," Mulroney said, turning to face her. His eyes burned with earnest intensity, locking onto her gaze. "You and me, we need to make the call on the street. Let the average Joe say his piece sometimes. If they break a few stupid rules about where they're supposed to stand or how many can gather in one place, what the fuck do we care? We got bigger fish to fry. That's what I'm saying."

Val considered his impassioned plea. It sounded reasonable on its face, and appealed to her own semi-libertarian, rebellious nature. "I won't crack anyone's head open for demonstrating without a permit. However, if things get weird—"

"Just consider who's making it weird," he said. "Your friends and neighbors in the crowd, or a bunch of bureaucrats making stupid rules we get stuck enforcing? If that means letting people blow off a little steam, so what? If people do a bit of pushing and shoving among themselves, well, a lot of guys are saying, let 'em have their fun. We shouldn't be the ones getting our heads kicked in. Save it for the low-lifes who deserve it, am I right?"

She nodded, then stopped. He'd pushed his point a bit too far. Something about it seemed...off. "You're not asking me to disobey orders or look the other way if people riot, are you?"

"Of course not." He smiled and clapped her on the shoulder. "You're a good egg, Dawes. Just like your uncle. He'd be proud." He shook her shoulder once, in a too-friendly way, and gave it a firm squeeze. "Thanks. I knew I could count on you."

He ambled away, humming some sort of patriotic marching tune. Val stared after him, wondering what he believed she'd agreed to.

Whatever. She had, as he put it, bigger fish to fry than to worry about Mickey Mulroney.

Chapter Thirty

Maggie waited at the coffee cart until her daughter left the park and returned to police headquarters, then strolled to the center, where the sidewalks crisscrossed. She sat on a bench and lit a cigarette, waiting. At one point, a young woman approached walking a precious little white dog on a leash and sat next to her. Maggie blew smoke in her direction a few times, and in less than a minute, the woman hustled away, shooting Maggie the stink-eye.

Minutes later, Mulroney returned to the park, glancing all around as he walked. Nervous fuck, that one.

"Don't worry, she's gone," Maggie said, patting the seat next to her. "What'd she tell you?"

"She's good," he said, his breathing labored from his fast walk in the humid summer heat. "On board, at least in concept."

Maggie took a final drag of her cigarette and flicked it onto the sidewalk, taking delight in the array of glowing embers spreading across the concrete. "That doesn't sound too definite. Did she say 'I will help you,' and volunteer to recruit others?"

"Not in so many words," Mulroney said, wiping sweat from his brow. Too bad he couldn't dry his armpits, which sported wet spots and stains the size of St. Louis. "But I think I got to her."

Maggie pursed her lips. She knew her daughter well enough, even after a ten-year lapse. Stubborn and definite. If she didn't say Exactly X, then she didn't mean Exactly X.

Which meant she'd need to work her hard this afternoon. Lay it on thick with the kid. Make her love the dumb little tyke. Willing to do anything for him. "What about the others?" she asked.

"Twenty, maybe thirty, firm and committed, eager to help out," he said. "All over, too. Armory, parade, and the Waterfront. They know what to let slide, and who to let go, where to direct attention—away from us."

"Twenty out of three hundred?" Maggie sighed. Knowing Mulroney, that meant ten or fifteen. "I guess that'll have to do."

"It's enough, given where and who they are," Mulroney said. "Especially in the morning. There's this annual softball game with the firefighters. A good twenty guys will be miles away, reliving their glory days from high school. Another few dozen there as spectators. And, get this." He leaned close enough that she could smell stale coffee on his breath. Coffee, and what? Something gross. Lox and bagels from hours before. "I got another surprise."

She glanced at him, doubtful. "I don't like surprises."

"You'll like this one!" He giggled like a kid. "Remember me saying the FBI swooped in and took over the trafficking investigation?"

"Yes." Heartburn. That had *not* been a pleasant surprise.

"And how they're tying the local response all up in knots?"

"Yeah, yeah. Come on, spill. The suspense is killing me and I have work to do."

Mulroney glanced around again, then whispered, "You know those twenty to thirty I mentioned? On the inside?"

Maggie waited. Damn it, he was enjoying this too much. Then it dawned on her. "One of them is FBI?"

He nodded, jiggling above the neck like a bobble-head. She wanted to swat him.

But she had to admit. That *was* good news.

***

Val made it home with time to spare before her mother arrived. She changed out of her uniform into shorts, sandals, and a sleeveless top and slathered on some sunblock. No sign of Dad, and he didn't respond to her texts. That meant, she hoped, he'd gotten immersed in his AA meetings.

A GMC Yukon parked in front a few minutes later, and Chad's BMW pulled in right behind it. Chad got out and stood by his car, holding Ali's hand, staring at the Yukon. After a minute that seemed like eons, Val's mother pushed open the door of her SUV, and a young boy climbed out of the back seat.

Gazing out the big picture window of the living room, Val recognized the boy from the photo with her mother at Easter. The boy resembled her older brother as a kid: slightly chubby with light-brown hair, round-cheeked, and shy. He stayed a step behind her as they followed Chad and Ali up the sidewalk.

Val opened the front door to greet them, not sure what to say.

Her mother filled the brief silence with her usual flurry of verbal force. "Come on, everybody move it, we're not air-conditioning the outside," she said, waving everyone toward the door.

Chad and Ali entered first, group-hugging Val with tight, wordless squeezes. Chad pulled back and locked eyes with Val, a pleading look that seemed to say, *Give her a chance.*

Val's response: an involuntary squint of her eyes, and a forced, quick nod.

"Good to see you again, darling," Mom said, thankfully not offering a hug. Come to think of it, she had never been much of a hugger. Like Val. That similarity bothered her a little too much.

Without missing a beat, her mother pulled the boy in front of her. She held him by the shoulders, as if presenting him to Val. "This is your brother, Samuel," she said. "Sammy, this is your big sister, Valorie."

Sammy glanced at her with serious brown eyes, then curled into his mother, wrapping his arms around her legs.

"Sammy," Mom said, pulling his arms off her leg. "Say hello, like we taught you."

He shook his head and stared at his feet.

Val crouched down to one knee and extended a handshake. "Hi, Sam. I'm Valorie. You can call me Val. Is it okay if I call you Sammy?"

After a long moment, Sam nodded and accepted her handshake.

"How old are you, Sammy?" Val said, guiding him inside the house with a hand on his back.

"Eight and free quarters," he said. "My birfday is August eleventh and then I'll be nine."

Val ran the mental math. Her mother left in February 2010, six months before giving birth. Which meant, when she left, she was three months pregnant.

"What grade are you in?" Val asked.

Sammy's face took on a troubled expression. "I don't go to regular school."

"His father and I homeschool," Mom said.

Val winced, turning away from them. Sammy seemed immature for his age. Whether congenital or due to neglect...right away the latter explanation seemed to fit. Homeschooling from Rita Dawes? Sheesh.

"Everybody use the toilet before you all go," Mom said, pointing to the two kids. "It's almost an hour's drive to the park."

"I just went!" Ali said, whining.

"Me too!" Sammy said. Nevertheless, he grabbed at his crotch, as if he needed to pee that instant.

"Go." Mom pointed down the hallway. "Ali, honey, can you use the upstairs bathroom, since you know where it is?"

Ali rolled her eyes and cast a silent appeal to her father for support. He crossed his arms, frowning, and off she went.

"So, Mom," Chad said when the kids were gone, "did I hear you right? You said 'before *you all* go.' Aren't you coming with?"

"I thought I'd give you kids some alone time together." Mom took a seat on the sofa and fumbled through her purse. She fished out a few twenty-dollar bills and laid them on the coffee table. "Get to know each other. Me, you already know, right?"

"Not really," Val said. "I mean, it's been a long time..."

Her mother waved her off. "I'm still the same old Mom you knew ten years ago," she said. "I haven't changed."

"Nine," Val said, her frustration growing.

"Excuse me?"

"Nine years ago, not ten. When you left."

Mom cocked her head, amusement crawling across her face. "Is it? I was never so good at math."

Val sat across from her in the easy chair. Chad remained standing, arms crossed, his face clouded, lips pursed. Val leaned toward her mother and lowered her voice. "Here's another bit of math for you, then. You were pregnant when you left, and you knew it."

Rita's smile faded a moment, then returned with what Val read as false bravado. "So?"

"So, who was the father?"

Chad gasped. "Val!"

"That's none of your business," Mom said.

"It is too," Val said. "Whose kid is that?"

"I'll remind you I was happily married to your father—"

"Yeah, so happy that you ditched him for a fucking rapist and child molester!"

"Val! Sh!" Chad waved his arms and pointed upstairs. "The kids don't need to hear this!"

"Absolutely not," Maggie said. "Thank you, Charles."

"But I do," Val said. "Since they could return at any moment, I suggest you talk fast. If that were Dad's kid, you'd have insisted on child support and you wouldn't have left and ghosted us. So, tell me. Is that Milt's baby? Did he rape you, too?"

"Valorie Dawes!" Her mother stood, her eyes wide, breathing hard. "How dare you!"

"I have a right to know!" Val jumped up and stepped toward her.

"Val! Sh!" Chad patted the air with his palms. "Keep it down!"

"All you need to know," Mom said, her nostrils flared, "is that Samuel is *my* child, just as you are, and Chad. And I love you all very much."

"Give me a fucking break." Val kept her voice down out of respect for Chad.

"Stop it!" Mom stepped back from Val and pointed down the hallway. "That's your brother in there. If you have any decency in that cold little heart of yours, you'll set aside the hate you feel for me and give him a chance."

"A chance? For what?"

"To be part of your family." Mom's voice softened. "Valorie, I realize I've made mistakes with you, and Chad, and Sammy, too. God knows I did with your father. That's not Sammy's fault. Don't take it out on him."

"What do you want from me?" Val kept her voice even. A struggle, given how little she trusted the woman standing in front of her.

Mom drew in a deep breath, licked her bright red lips. "Spend the afternoon with him. Give him some brother-and-sister-and-niece time. Let him know he has a family, beyond what this busy old lady has to offer. A family who loves him."

Val gritted her teeth, counted to five to calm herself. She glanced at Chad.

"I'm okay with it," Chad said. "I mean, we're all here, right? What's a few hours?"

Val cursed to herself. Her damned obsequious brother, always the Momma's boy. Always such a pleaser. For a change, though, he'd stepped up to help, and didn't just volunteer Val for the dirty work.

"Okay, fine," she said.

At that moment, Sammy returned, his pants still down to his knees, his white underwear wet in front. "Mommy," he said, tugging at Rita's dress, "I had a accident."

A little girl's laughter broke the tension in the room. Ali jumped up and down and nearly fell down the stairs, pointing at Sammy. "I see his underwear!"

Panic spread over Sammy's face and he hid behind Maggie from Ali, a sad moan erupting from his mouth.

"It's all right, Sammy," Mom said. "We brought extras." She patted his shoulder and said to no one in particular, "I'll be right back. I need to get a change of clothes for him from the car." She started toward the door, but the boy wouldn't let go of her.

"Ali," Chad said, "please go back upstairs for a moment." Ali scrambled out of sight, still giggling.

Val crossed to Sammy and again got down to one knee. "Hey, big guy. You want to know a secret?"

He bowed his head, thumb again inserted into his mouth, and nodded.

Val leaned closer and whispered, "I think I just had an accident, too."

His eyes flared wide, his thumb dropping to his side. "Really?"

Val made a face, as if mortified, and whispered, "I need to go change my undies, too."

Sammy opened his mouth wide and laughed, a gurgling sound so infectious, Val and Chad both burst out laughing, too.

"How about, when Mommy comes back with your fresh clothes, we race to see who can change the fastest?" Val said.

"Yeah! Winner gets a popsicle!" Sammy pulled up his pants and ran in circles around the living room, yelling "Popsicle! Popsicle!"

Mom headed toward the door, paused to flash a grudging smile at Val, then disappeared outside.

Sammy finished his final lap and crashed into Val, wrapping his arms around her waist. He gazed up at her, a smile filling his tiny face. "Val," he said, "you're an awesome sister."

She tousled his hair and hugged him back. "Yeah, well, you're an awesome little brother," she said.

What surprised her was, she meant it.

***

Chad drove, as his BMW offered much greater comfort and space for the four of them than Val's cramped, aging Honda. Ali and Sammy rode in the back, taking turns playing on her Leapfrog. Despite being three years younger, Ali took on the role of leader and teacher, showing Sammy how to play the various games and what strategies to use.

"They play together so nicely," Val said after a while. "Did we ever get along that well at that age?"

Chad chuckled. "When you weren't being a total brat."

"Me? I lost count of the number of noogies and wedgies you gave me." She smacked his upper arm. "How about the time you gave me Oreos but replaced the creamy center with toothpaste? I still can't eat those things!"

"The best part of that was, you dipped it in your milk first," he said, laughing. "I made five bucks off Ronnie Delgado over that!"

Val laughed along with him and glanced back at the kids. "They're about the same age difference as us, too."

Chad glanced at her, side-eyed. "Really? I thought they were closer in age."

She shook her head. "Mom let it slip that he was born only about six or seven months after she left."

He lowered his voice. "Val, don't hold it against Sammy. None of this is his fault. He couldn't choose his parents, any more than we could."

"Yeah." She sulked down in her seat. "I hope they have a happier childhood than we did."

Chad grimaced. "You especially. Val, I'm sorry I wasn't there more for you. I had college, then the wedding, and kids, and—"

"I'm not blaming you. I just don't have a lot of great memories of my childhood." She sat up straight again and turned on the radio. "Enough of all that. I don't want to spoil our afternoon by complaining about Rita."

Chad shot her another glance and smirked. "She prefers 'Maggie' now."

"I don't care what she prefers."

He chuckled. "You complain about her and say you hate her, but you're more alike than you'll ever admit."

"Shut up. I am not." She turned the radio volume up way too high.

"See? You're both argumentative as hell," he said.

"Am not." She laughed. "Okay, maybe a little. So, you've got one thing."

"You're both strong-minded."

Val scoffed. "Opinionated, you mean."

Chad laughed.

"What's so funny?"

He cocked his head to one side. "That's another similarity. You're both tenacious as hell. Neither of you takes any crap from anyone."

"Come on. You got anything else, or are you just going through your mental thesaurus for 'strong and opinionated?'"

"Well, beautiful, of course." He smiled.

"Don't kiss up. Be honest with me."

Chad pressed his lips together for a moment. "You're both idealists."

Val rolled her eyes and collapsed into her seat. "Mom? An idealist? The one who ditched her family and hooked up with my rapist? What 'ideal' does that represent?"

"I didn't say you shared the *same* ideals. She has a definite view of how the world ought to work, and how people ought to be, and she lives her life accordingly. So do you."

"If what she pursues is 'ideals,' count me out." Val crossed her arms. "To me, an idealist is someone who wants to improve the world for others, not screw it up for her own selfish ends."

Chad shrugged and drove in silence for a bit, taking a moment to glance at the kids in the back seat.

Val glanced back, too. The two kids remained glued to their gaming console. "What else?" she said to Chad.

"Well," he said, "that right there illustrates another similarity. Neither you nor Mom shy away from conflict. You hit it head-on. Dad and I..." His voice trailed off.

"You're conflict avoiders," she finished for him.

He chuckled. "I prefer the term 'peacemaker,' if you don't mind."

"Appeaser."

"Negotiator."

"Touché." Val smiled. "Which is why you're an excellent lawyer."

"Thanks." Chad drove in silence again for a bit, while Val stewed on what he'd said. More than once, she wanted to challenge his observations, but the right words wouldn't come. Her difficulty with his claims shook her up more than she cared to admit. By the time they reached their exit, her stomach had tied itself into knots.

"That's our exit," he said, pointing to a green highway sign. "Almost there, kids."

"Yay! Dinosaurs!" Ali said, clapping.

Sammy, following her lead, clapped too. "Dino-sewers!"

Ali broke up laughing. "Dino-sewers! Dino-sewers!" they chanted together.

Val spoke in a low voice to Chad, hoping the kids' chants would distract them from her question. "Do you really think I take after Mom?"

He patted her shoulder. "It's not an insult."

"I know, but...really?" Her stomach boiled again.

He stopped at the end of the highway exit and afforded her a long glance. "I'm sorry to upset you, Val. But yeah, really. You share a lot in common, and I don't mean just in your DNA. Now, which way to this damned dinosaur park?"

Val stared out the window. She pretended to look for signs to the park, but she couldn't focus on anything other than the disruptive boil bubbling up from her heart.

Chapter Thirty-One

Rid of the kid for a few hours, Maggie drove to the Clayton Waterfront to meet up with Mickey Mulroney again. His very presence made her cringe, but he'd left her a cryptic message on her burner, claiming "big news." She harbored serious doubts. Mulroney exaggerated all of his accomplishments and invented them when he had nothing real to brag about. However, he'd called this a "game-changer," something Maggie desperately needed at this point.

She found Mulroney eating a hot dog loaded with chili, cheese, and onions, leaning against the green painted railing that prevented only the least industrious scofflaws from accessing the river's rocky shore. As if he had all the time and not a care in the world. No responsibilities to either the city that paid his healthy salary and benefits, nor to her organization, which would soon ensure he wouldn't have a financial care in the world.

"Don't eat that too fast." Maggie stepped up next to him, leaning her elbows on the railing. "I need you to live at least another twenty-four to thirty-six hours. After that, if you want to die of a heart attack, it's on your dime."

"It's always on my dime," Mulroney said with his mouth full. He swallowed and chugged a huge gulp of soda from a twenty-ounce Coke cup. "You want one?"

"No, thanks. What's the big news that you couldn't share on the phone?"

Mulroney swallowed and opened wide to chomp another mouthful of hot dog. Maggie stayed his arm. He glared at her, but let her push the hot dog away from his mouth. Damned thing smelled like vomit.

"See that barge?" He pointed with his Coke cup to the flat-bottomed boat docked to a commercial pier a few hundred yards downriver. "That's our girl."

"Our 'girl'? What the hell does that mean?"

Mulroney burped, sort-of covering his mouth with the Coke cup. "Center stage for tomorrow night. They fire off everything from the middle of the river. For safety, you know." He laughed and snuck in another bite of hot dog. Only a quarter of the disgusting thing remained.

"Okay. Why is that good news?"

"*That's* not. The good news is, they load it up tomorrow morning, under the guard of Clayton's finest." He grinned. "Our boys and girls in blue. Hand-picked by yours truly."

Maggie cocked her head, and for the first time all afternoon, she smiled. "That *is* good news. So we need to make sure our detonator gets loaded on board along with it."

He nodded. "The boat anchors about a thousand feet out from the edge of the water. So your signal needs about a quarter-milc rangc, to be safe."

"Any chance you can bring it closer, just in case?"

Mulroney squinted at her, sipped at his Coke, which yielded that familiar slurping sound of a straw running out of available liquid amid a cupful of ice. "I don't control the boat. Even if I did, are you sure you want that? When that thing blows, shit's gonna fly in every direction. The closer it gets, the more likely you encounter collateral casualties."

"Spcak plainly to me, Mickey. I hate puzzles."

An exasperated rush of air escaped his mouth, along with the disgusting aroma of chili dog. "People are gonna be sitting on blankets and lawn chairs, right up to the edge of this fence, all up and down the river. Someone's gonna get hurt."

Maggie fixed him with a withering gaze. "That's kind of the point, Mickey."

He wiped his forehead, drenched with sweat. "That may not be such a good idea. I mean, I understand putting on a spectacle and disrupting the city's stupid little party to make a point. But—"

"Freedom isn't free, Mickey." Maggie returned her gaze to the river's flowing current.

"Yeah, I get that, but—"

"Don't tell me you're getting cold feet," she said with an edge to her voice. "You know how I hate flakes."

"I ain't gonna flake." Mickey took another noisy, futile sip of his drink. He glanced at his hot dog, seemed to consider taking another bite. Instead, he removed the lid from his cup and shoved the rest of his food inside, then crushed the entire mess into a ball. He stared at it, then glanced back at Maggie. "Keep my name outta this, you hear? Nobody ever knows, other than you."

"Of course." She smiled, this one as fake as saccharine. "You'll have your money. Crypto, none of it traceable. We will send the key to you before midnight tomorrow."

"Good." He seemed to grow angrier with every passing second. Without warning, he heaved the food-filled Coke cup into the river, then stomped away, never once looking back.

Maggie stared after him, her amusement building. Such a trusting soul.

***

Val held fond childhood memories in her heart of Dinosaur State Park in the small town of Rocky Hill, Connecticut. Her parents brought her there a few times, and each represented a special day for her, rare opportunities for the entire family to play and explore together. Chad always loved the outdoor trails, where he'd search for fossils and pretend to be the first person ever to discover the site's famous dinosaur tracks. Val preferred the museum, with its lifelike replicas of the ancient reptiles, and the hands-on activities like creating plaster-of-paris casts of dinosaur footprints. She wondered which features would appeal to Ali and Sammy, or if they'd find the whole excursion a crushing bore.

She needn't have worried. Sammy and Ali raced through the trails and exhibits, shouting out the names of "dinosaurs" they spotted and arguing over the name of the long-necked, ferocious-looking beast that left the gigantic three-toed tracks everywhere.

"Daddy, wasn't it a Dilophosaurus?" Ali asked.

"It's a Ceratosaurus. I know my dino-sewers," Sammy insisted.

"Daddy!" Ali said, hanging on his arm. "Who's right?"

"You're both right," Chad said, winking at Val. "A Dilophosaurus is a kind of Ceratosaurus. Right, Val?"

Val smirked at her brother. Such a conflict avoider. "I bet if you asked the park rangers, they'd tell you," she said.

"I wanna make track casts!" Sammy said, already moving on from their argument. "Help me, Auntie Val?"

"Okay," Val said, her heart warming. She'd wanted to make one again, too. "But I'm not your auntie. I'm your sister. You can just call me Val."

"That's okay," Sammy said, taking her hand. "I like calling you Auntie Val, like Ali does. She's wicked cool!"

"You're wicked cool, too," Ali said, draping an arm around his shoulder. "Come on, I want to make a cast, too. Daddy, will you help me?"

As it turned out, neither child needed the slightest bit of assistance from the adults. With Ali reading off the directions, Sammy cleaned and oiled the track and cast the ranger gave him. He sang and danced while mixing the plaster in an orange five-gallon bucket, and the two kids poured it into the mold as a team. While the casts dried, the kids raced each other through the trails again, each finding "cool rocks" they wanted to bring home.

"We can't bring those home, but maybe we can buy one in the shop," Chad said. "You can each spend five dollars. Okay?"

A few minutes later, Ali pulled Val aside and showed her a polished agate, which, of course, carried a ten-dollar price tag. "Please can I have this? It's so-o-o pretty!"

"It's not up to me," Val said. "It's up to your father." She gritted her teeth at her brother's uncharacteristic miserliness. Or maybe he simply didn't know what things cost.

Ali pouted and set the stone back on the shelf. But Sammy snatched it back and handed it to her. "Don't worry, Ali. Mommy gave me twenty dollars. I'll buy both of ours."

It was all Val could do not to break into tears of joy and swoop him up in a smothering hug. The only thing that stopped her was the memory of how much she hated it when adults did that to her as a kid.

"Ali," Chad said in a lecturing tone when he saw the kids at the checkout register. "I thought I told you no."

Sammy put his hands on his hips and faced Chad. "I'm buying Ali's rock and giving it to her as a present," he said. "And you can't stop me. You're not my boss and you're not my father." He grabbed Ali's stone and threw his money on the counter.

"You're the best uncle ever!" Ali sang, hugging him tight.

Chad turned to Val. "Help?"

Val laughed. "Face it, bro. He outsmarted you. Unless you're going to go all Grinch-face and insist that her favorite uncle can't give her a present."

He sighed, gazed at the ceiling a moment, and walked out of the store.

Val, laughing, waited while Sammy completed his purchase. She saw a lot of her mother in him.

And, reluctantly, she admitted: she saw a lot of herself in him, too.

***

For the first half of the drive home, Ali and Sammy seemed more wired-up than they'd been in the park itself. They recounted every attraction and activity, proclaiming each one their "favorite," and then devolved into roaring their best dinosaur impressions. Those got more and more ridiculous, especially when Chad joined in, and soon the two kids were giggling out of control. They laughed themselves silly…then, without warning, both fell asleep within minutes of each other.

"Works every time," Chad said. "If you ever want to put an audience to sleep, ask me to do my best impressions."

Val nodded in agreement. It had turned out to be a great day, after all. Just the distraction she needed.

Gil called Val a short while later. "How soon will you get back? Rumors are flying around here about who's pulling stunts tomorrow. Grimes is convinced it's Antifa, and the FBI seems to agree."

"They're both wrong," Val said. "Or, at least, Antifa won't be alone. I have a strong suspicion that it's Patriots Pride, or their allies. But where?"

"We're hearing that the Chief wants a full show of force at the parade," Gil said. "The FBI insists the focus should be the mayor's speech at the Armory. Possible assassination attempt, even. The mayor's having none of it, though."

"That doesn't really narrow down who's behind it," Val said. "She's made enemies on both sides."

"True. But that's not why I'm calling. Because of all this, I'm hearing rumors of some nasty turf battles going on over who's in charge tomorrow. You won't want to be out of the loop on this one."

"I don't care who's giving the orders," Val said. "I just want to know what mine are."

"You don't care if you're stuck babysitting parade-goers in the scorching sun?" Gil said. "Or putting your unarmed body in the way of angry protesters?"

"Okay, you're right. We're on our way back now. Call me back if you hear anything specific."

"I thought you wanted to spend the afternoon with us, get to know Sammy a little better," Chad said.

"I'm supposed to be working right now. You, Mr. Workaholic, ought to understand that better than anyone. Come on, let's head to her hotel and drop Sammy off."

"I don't know where she's staying."

"Oh, for God's sake." She texted her mother and read the message aloud to Chad: "Dropping Sammy at Dad's. Pick him up there in 30 minutes."

Her phone pinged with her mother's reply: *Can't you watch him another hour?*

She texted back: *No, sorry.* "Don't you undermine me on this," she said to Chad. "Don't let her manipulate us into doing her damned job here."

Val ignored her mother's angry replies, and as expected, her mother's GMC Yukon appeared in Dad's driveway ten minutes after she finished changing back into her uniform. Ali, not to be outdone, changed into a "police girl" costume that she'd packed for the trip. She lent Sammy her hat and toy gun so he could play, too.

"We're the cops and you're the bad guy," Ali said to Chad. "Go hide and we'll find you!"

Chad laughed and ran upstairs. Ali counted to ten, but only reached five before Mom pushed open the front door.

"How was Dinosaur State Park?" Mom asked Sammy, peeling his arms away from her legs moments later. "Did you see a Tyrannosaurus Rex?"

"Of course not," he said. "T. Rex was Mesozoic. Dino-sewer Park is all Jurassic." He shook his head, arms crossed, as if everyone ought to know that.

"I never could keep that stuff straight," Mom said, ruf-fling the boy's hair. "Good thing I have you here to keep me informed. Now, can you and Ali go play for a few minutes? I need to talk to your sister."

He nodded and chased Ali up the stairs in search of Chad the Bank Robber.

"Sammy likes you," her mother said when they were alone.

"I like him, too," Val said. "He has a good heart."

"Maybe you and he could spend some time together tomorrow?"

"Probably not," Val said. "The department wants me at the Armory by 8:00 a.m. Wait, why are you making that face at me?" Her mother, usually as poker-faced as they come, looked shaken up for a moment.

"N-nothing. I was hoping we could get together for breakfast, and, like I said, I need someone to watch Sammy..." She took a quick breath, as if calming herself.

"I'm pulling a double tomorrow," Val said. "So is the entire department. The fire department, too, but that's always the case for them on the Fourth." She watched her mother's face. Mom seemed to be fighting for control of her emotions. "Have I said something wrong?" Val said. "Other than 'no,' I mean."

"No, no," she said. "Perhaps if I took Sammy to the ceremony in the morning, or perhaps to the parade in the afternoon, we could, um, see you for an hour or two? He wants to see you in your uniform—"

"He just did." Val gestured to her dress blues.

"At work, I mean. Where else might we be able to find you?"

"I'm pretty sure I'll be at the Waterfront for the fireworks show. Perhaps we can talk there. Mother, what's wrong?"

"N-nothing, nothing." Mom paused for a moment, then sat. "Valorie, I need to ask you a favor. It relates to Sammy."

"I told you. I can't babysit tomorrow. At all. Okay?"

"Not babysit," Mom said. "Honey, this job of yours. It's so dangerous. But Sammy, he's like his little niece. They only see the uniforms, and the glorified version of police work on TV. He doesn't understand the risks."

"You let a nine-year-old watch cop shows?" Val said. "You wouldn't let me watch until I was twelve, and even then, I had to sneak half the time."

"Don't be silly," Mom said. "It's just that, well, if your entire department is pulling double shifts, that tells me that tomorrow may not be the safest day for you to be working. Or for Sammy to be watching the fireworks or parade, and–"

"So don't take him," Val said. "Anyway, I need to get going. Can't we discuss this later?"

"But he'd be so disappointed," Mom said. "And...oh, maybe I'm worrying too much. Do you think anything bad will happen tomorrow? Is that why your department is on such high alert?"

"We don't know, to be honest," Val said. "Last year there were a few isolated incidents. The country's so divided right now along political lines. So, maybe something might happen. Where, when, how big, we don't know."

Mom's face relaxed, as if a great weight had been lifted off her shoulders.

"That's so good to hear. Valorie, if anything bad were to happen tomorrow, and you must choose between risking your life or maybe just letting people, you know, blow off a little steam—"

"I'll do my job," Val said, "and enforce the law." Yet something about what her mother said bothered her. It sounded familiar—almost word for word what Mickey Mulroney had discussed with her in the park.

"Please don't risk your life over some silly protester getting out of line." Tears filled her mother's eyes. "I mean, if they want to fight over stupid politics, why should you get hurt over it? Don't follow in your uncle's footsteps and try to be the hero. Just let them punch each other, will you, dear? Please? For your brother, Sammy, who already worships you, if not for me?"

Mom's tearful plea took Val aback. She'd never once seen her mother cry, not even at Uncle Val's funeral. Of course, Val thought nothing of it, then—she hadn't let herself cry that day, either. Two stoic women, refusing to let the world see how it injured them. Showing strength, not emotion.

Another resemblance that left Val uncomfortable.

Her mother's pleading reminded Val of her tenth birthday, when Uncle Val bought her jiu-jitsu lessons. At first, her mother refused to allow it, declaring martial arts "unfeminine." At the time, Val accepted her complaint at face value. Now she realized her mother's real concern: it would, and did, further cement Val's close ties with her uncle, and ensure she'd follow his path into police work. Ten-year-old Val begged, promised to wear dresses more (she didn't), and that she would use her skills to protect the family. Her mother chuckled at her naiveté and, in an uncharacteristic moment, relented. Val recalled how happy that had made her, and how worried her mother had been about this career path all along.

Val drew in a deep breath. "I took an oath to defend and serve. But I won't be stupid about it, okay? I'll do what I can to keep the public safe...and keep myself safe as well."

"Thank you, dear. That's all I ask," Mom said. "Thank you, on behalf of me, and your little brother."

Her mother stood, and for a moment, Val feared she might try to hug her. Instead, she fished her keys out of her purse and called out, "Sammy! Time to go, son." She smiled. "I hope to see you tomorrow, Valorie."

After they left, Val stared out the window after her. Something about her mother's appeal seemed off. For the first time since she could remember, her mother thought of someone other than her own damned self. Why did that bother Val so much?

Val pondered the question a moment longer, then shook it off. She's a mother. Of course, she cared for her daughter's safety, and her son's. Val resolved to think nothing more about it.

Chapter Thirty-Two

Val arrived back at the WAVE Squad to find Grimes, Shannon, and Price huddled around the coffee pot. They spoke in hushed tones and cast worried glances at the closed door to Petroni's private office.

"What's up?" Val asked.

"Shush!" Shannon tamped the air with open palms. "Come here and we'll fill you in."

Petroni's door burst open before she could reach them, and the two FBI agents, Forrestal and Powers, traipsed out with smug grins on their faces. Petroni followed them with her arms folded across her chest and a deep scowl on her face.

"Listen up, peeps," Forrestal said, clapping his hands together. He looked like he'd spent a week in a spray-tan bakeshop, his face a ghoulish orange with reverse-raccoon white circles around both eyes. "We've got new intel to share."

"What new intel?" Grimes said, refilling his coffee cup. "From where?"

Forrestal flashed a Cheshire-cat smile. "Our anti-terrorism unit believes Antifa is planning a major raid on the Armory tomorrow morning to steal up to five hundred functioning firearms and several thousand rounds of ammunition. We believe that will be the major focus of their activities tomorrow. At least, if we're successful in stopping them. Which we will be."

"And if not?" Grimes leaned back against the coffee counter.

Forrestal sneered at Grimes and locked eyes with Powers, who smirked and shook her head. Val wondered if the woman ever spoke aloud in Forrestal's presence.

"There is no 'if not' scenario," Forrestal said. "Because we *will* succeed."

"How do you know that for certain?" Val asked. "No plan is perfect, after all."

"I'm sure that's been your experience with planning here at the local level," Forrestal said. "At the Agency, our plans work."

"Humor me," Grimes said. "What are the details of this failsafe plan?"

Sighing in exasperation, Forrestal gestured to Powers with an open palm. "Agent Powers, would you do us the honors of briefing Officer Mayberry here?"

Val rolled her eyes. Forrestal couldn't even get his insults right.

"First, we're locking down the Armory and canceling all public access for the next forty-eight hours," Powers said. "No tours, no restroom access, nothing. We're doing it without public announcement, so Antifa won't know until it's too late."

"Assuming they don't know already," Shannon muttered.

"Second, the Armory is securing their ammo into armored safes and functioning weapons into a secure state facility, which we won't disclose here for security reasons."

"What?" Grimes slammed his cup onto the counter, spilling its contents everywhere except, by some miracle, on himself. "You aren't even telling us? What, you expect someone here is going to go blab to freaking Antifa?"

"Doesn't moving the munitions expose them to even greater risk?" Val asked. "All they'd need to do is hijack a single vehicle—"

"And face a convoy of armed federal marshals? Doubt it," Forrestal said. "But hey, that's not a bad way for this to go. Somebody call Antifa and suggest that. We can end these bastards once and for all."

Val, disgusted at Forrestal's ethics and baffled by his scrambled logic, hung her head in dismay.

"Third," Powers continued, "we're doubling down on patrols. All available hands will be assigned shifts and issued riot gear. We want a show of force strong enough to discourage even the craziest of terrorists."

"Oh, good Lord," Val said under her breath.

Forrestal shoved his hands into his pockets and ambled toward her. "Got something to say, rookie?"

Val met his gaze and stood with her hands folded behind her, feet apart. "With all due respect, Agent Forrestal," she said, "doesn't this play right into the hands of Antifa?"

"Explain." A shred of doubt crept into Forrestal's voice.

"Antifa stands for 'anti-fascist.' Their message is one of suppression by a fascist dictatorship. Doesn't the presence of armed riot squads facing off against unarmed civilians support their narrative? If they want to incite public terror—which is, by definition, every terrorist's goal—wouldn't it serve their purposes to instigate a shootout between citizens and police?"

"Especially nutcases who don't mind sacrificing a few human bodies to advance their cause," Grimes said. "Great point, Dawes."

"You're assuming that they'll control the narrative." Forrestal's face reddened. "Which they won't. We're releasing info to the press now, warning of Antifa violence planned for tomorrow. Anything that happens reflects badly on them, not us."

Val glanced at Grimes, Shannon, Petroni, and Price. The expression on each face reflected her own feeling: Forrestal was delusional, if not downright stupid.

"We'll post duty sheets within the hour," Forrestal said. "Good news for you union schmucks. All of you will earn plenty of overtime this week." He laughed and earned a half-hearted grin from Powers and eye rolls from each of the locals.

"What's your communications plan?" Shannon asked. "Assuming we find something, how do we alert the other squads as to what's going down?"

"We'll coordinate all comms via your dispatch unit. Anything you hear, report in through regular channels, and vice versa."

"Coordinating?" Grimes laughed out loud. "You mean taking over."

"Potato, tomata," Forrestal said. "Speaking of which, Agent Powers, we need to head down there next." They strutted out the door, Forrestal in the lead, chatting in low voices and laughing.

Val, disgusted, kicked the door shut behind them. She expected a rebuke from Sergeant Petroni for the outburst, but when she turned to face the WAVE team, they surprised her by clapping. All of them—including Petroni.

***

"What a moron!" Grimes said when the team gathered for a debrief. "Brenda, are you on board with this nonsense?"

"For the record, I'm not," Petroni said. "Chief MacMahon is, though, and last time I checked, he outranked me."

"Which shift is he taking?" Grimes said, spittle flying. "Midnight to 4:00 a.m., like Dawes and Price here?"

Val's eyes widened, but she relaxed when she saw the gleam in Grimes's eyes.

"Dawes and I visited the Armory earlier today," Grimes continued. "No way a terrorist group wants their ancient junk. Especially if the building is locked down."

"The mayor's speech and the ceremony are still of concern," Petroni said. "Again, our opinions don't matter. Orders are orders."

"So, it looks like you'll be hanging out with your boyfriend here at HQ tomorrow," Grimes said to Val. "That's good. You guys can keep an eye on Agent Orange in Dispatch."

"Actually, Dawes, you'll be at the Armory, at Sergeant Blake's request," Petroni said. "Probably directing traffic. Nothing too lethal."

"I think Forrestal is dead wrong about tomorrow, anyway," Val said. "If this group is after publicity, the Armory event is too small potatoes to serve that purpose. What'd they draw last year, maybe a hundred people?"

"Half of those were the mayor's staff," Shannon said, nodding. "What arc you thinking, then? The parade?"

"That makes sense," Grimes said. "It's so spread out, we couldn't possibly cover it all."

"Again, if they seek publicity, the parade won't cut it," Val said. "At any given spot you'd have a hundred or two people, tops, and virtually no media. The big gathering is the fireworks show at the Waterfront. That's where they can make the biggest statement."

"If that's the case, they won't want to scare people off with smaller displays of force during the day," Grimes said.

"We can't afford to ignore any of it," Petroni said. "We assume everything is a target and defend accordingly. So, I'm afraid our friends from the FBI are going to get their way.

Everyone's on duty, round the clock except for brief meal and sleep breaks. Sorry, gang."

"Crap." Grimes plopped down into a chair. "There goes our softball game."

"If it's any consolation," Petroni said, "you won't have to forfeit. The fire department's on full alert, too. The whole Armory thing has City Hall spooked. It wouldn't surprise me if they call in the National Guard, the Navy, and the freaking Boy Scouts."

Frustrated, Val returned to her desk to resume her research. Despite Forrestal's obsession with Antifa—or perhaps because of it—she redoubled her focus on right-wing groups. Before she got going, though, she noticed a text message from her brother: *Dinner tonight with Mom?*

She texted back: *Can't, have to work. Bad stuff going down.*

After a long pause came his reply: *Mom asking: What stuff? Should we be worried?*

You're with Mom? Why?

Val glanced across at Grimes, already working the phones with his softball team. She wondered how much she should tell her brother and how to warn him without causing him needless worry. She thought about how much Ali and Sammy looked forward to the parade and fireworks, and about Mickey Mulroney's grousing about the department overreacting to the prior year's minimal protests.

If anything should happen to Ali or Sammy, she'd never forgive herself.

Skip the Armory thing. The parade should be OK, she texted. *Maybe watch the fireworks from a rooftop somewhere?*

His instant reply: *No way. Kendra insists on the Waterfront. See you at the parade. Good night!*

She set down her phone. No point trying to convince her stubborn brother otherwise, at least until she had something solid. Which, at the moment, she did not.

But her gut told her she needed to keep him, and her entire family, within easy reach for the next twenty-four hours or so.

***

Gil stopped by the WAVE Squad office at 8:15 with sub sandwiches and convinced a starving Val to join him for a sunset dinner in the park. "I'd hoped we could enjoy this fine warm evening with some grilled steak on my back patio," he said. "With a bottle of Cabernet and an early bedtime."

"I'm glad I get to see you at all," Val said. "Don't give up on me yet. Save that wine and steak for, say, Friday night?"

"You've got a date." He took a big bite of his Italian sub. "By the way," he said around a mouthful of meat and bread, "I met your pal Forrestal today. What a piece of work."

"Isn't he?" Val tasted her own turkey breast sub, savoring the spicy chipotle sauce. Gil chose well for her, as usual. "Lucky you. You get to work with him tomorrow on Dispatch."

"I might just kill him," Gil said, "if he calls us 'local schmucks' again."

"At least he talks to you. He refuses to share any information with us that isn't a direct order."

"Ah. Then it's good you have a mole in his makeshift organization now."

Val nodded. "I think he's figured this whole thing wrong, anyway."

"What makes you say that?" Gil said. "Besides his shoot-first, ask-questions-later mentality." He chuckled. "He's the worst example of a federal agent I've ever met. Most of 'em are pretty sharp. That guy's not only the dullest knife in the drawer. He's a damned soup spoon."

Val, laughing, spewed tiny bits of turkey all over the sidewalk.

"Sexy," Gil said, grinning.

Val washed down some Doritos with lemonade. "For starters, he's got the perps all wrong. He keeps calling Antifa an 'organization,' which is a stretch. I've explained that until I'm blue in the face, but he doesn't listen."

"What difference does it make? Terrorists are terrorists, no matter what their politics."

"It matters because we ought to understand who we're up against and what their tactics are," Val said. "Antifa is as disorganized as it gets when it comes to protests. There's no actual leader, no real plan. It's random, which is why their activities rise only to the level of vandalism and rock-throwing. If they're behind this—and Shannon, who did our research on them, doesn't think so—we should prepare for window-breaking and looting downtown, not an attack on the Armory."

"So, who is it, and what should we prepare for?"

"I think it's the alt-right groups, such as Heroes for Freedom and Patriots Pride," Val said. "A holiday like Independence Day, with its focus on individual liberty and blowing things up, is right up their alley. I spent the last few hours on some dark web sites, and it appears they're getting pretty revved up for something tomorrow. Not just here, either. The FBI expects events all along the East Coast."

"What events?"

Val frowned. "They're too vague, at least at the level I've gotten into," she said. "I only got access today, and I don't know what I'm doing. Plus, a lot of the sites require you to create new accounts and passwords, which take hours or days. Probably to shield what they're up to from people like me."

Gil rested his hand on her knee. "I'm sure you'll find something useful. You're awesome at research."

"Fat lot of good that will do me in the morning at the 'Antifa attack' at the Armory."

"Wait. They're putting you in the field? Without a weapon?"

She sighed. "Travis requested me. I'm sure it'll be fine."

Gil slid his hand up to her thigh and squeezed. "Do me a big favor tomorrow."

"Name it." She rested her head on his broad shoulder.

He held her tight and whispered, "Don't die."

"Okay." She held him even tighter as the sun set over the western hills.

Chapter Thirty-Three

Val and Gil walked back to police headquarters hand-in-hand until they reached the steps. She hugged him for what felt like mere seconds, but when their embrace ended, the sun had disappeared over the horizon.

"Sorry to make you late getting back," she said. "That's sure to impress your bosses on your first day."

"You can make me late for work anytime," he said, smiling. "And soon again, I hope." He gave her a tender kiss goodbye, running his hands down her back to her hips.

"Careful," she said between smooches, laughing. "Don't let my mother see you do that."

"Ah, yes, your mother's back. When will I meet this mysterious woman?"

Val's heart lurched, and she could tell from Gil's reaction that she hadn't hidden her reaction from him. "Let's sleep on that."

"I look forward to that," he said with a sly grin. "Okay, back to work for me."

He limped up the stairs, and Val couldn't help feeling she was making a mistake at that moment. But she couldn't pinpoint how. Only that she didn't know when she'd see him next, and it bothered her.

She drove to her father's house, and found it dark, with his SUV parked in the driveway. After changing into running shorts and a T-shirt, she tiptoed past his bedroom. The door was ajar, so she poked her head in. He'd fallen asleep with his reading light on and a Philip Margolin novel splayed open on the mattress next to him. Val turned out the light and gave silent thanks to his AA sponsors for getting him home, safe and sober, another night.

She returned to Headquarters, parked in the employee-only lot, and jogged to her favorite running path, a well-lit trail that brought her to the Waterfront pedestrian loop. The warm night and impending holiday seemed to draw people out, at least on the downtown side. Couples promenaded down the brick pathway overlooking the water, customers jammed cafés, and bicyclists weaved in and out around families strolling with children and baby carriages. Cheerful vendors busied themselves setting up temporary sidewalk shops, hawking handmade crafts, cotton candy, ribs and burgers and fries, ice cream and sodas. Already she could smell the grease and almost taste the sweet concoctions. A small crew fenced off a beer-and-wine garden. One of the men offered her a sample, which she declined with a smile.

"Rain check?" he said with a grin. She pretended not to hear him.

Crossing the pedestrian bridge, she appreciated the extra illumination provided by festive red, white, and blue string lights the city had hung for the next day's celebrations. Garish, but safer than the usual dim yellow street lamps, many of which spent a substantial portion of their existence burnt out or broken by vandals.

Across the bridge, she rejoined the running trail along the east side of the river on the edge of the Alphabet Soup District. Not so well-lit or well-maintained, darkness prevailed in sections where overgrown shrubs leaned over chain-link fences and overhead lights flickered on and off, or simply stayed off. Small groups of twenty-somethings, mostly Black and Latino, eyed her with suspicion until she passed.

No doubt the "Property of Clayton PD" T-shirt didn't help matters.

Upriver sat the Eastside pier. Built in the 1940s to support the war effort, the pier remained active for recreational craft and small commercial ships, with impressive supporting infrastructure. An asphalt parking lot connected the running path to the pier, and a paved entrance for boat-towing vehicles fed the lot from the far end. Warehouses dotted the perimeter, some of which backed up to the river's edge. Wooden decking extended from the paved area out over the water, supported by gigantic wooden columns, beams, and flotation supports. Gangways and ramps led to slips where a few dozen small boats could dock.

A barge was moored a hundred yards offshore, one she recognized from years past as the launching pad for the fireworks show. Something about the barge raised goosebumps on the skin of her neck, despite the slick sheen of perspiration she'd generated with her mile-plus-run.

She slowed down to examine the barge. Unlit, and with no apparent onboard activity, nothing about it justified her sense of unease. Armed private security guards strolled the pier, smoking cigarettes and gazing with mixed levels of alertness at passersby. One shooed away a loiterer, a homeless man Val often saw around town asking for money. Nothing unusual.

She ran on.

At the end of the pier, a stack of shipping crates blocked her path. She veered off into the busier streets of the Alphabet Soup District, home of tattoo parlors, liquor stores, pawn shops, and a few rough taverns she'd entered once or twice to haul away troublemakers. These streets, like downtown, seemed busier than normal, and less innocent. Men walked alone or in pairs, glaring at the world as if spoiling for a fight. Clusters of women hustled from one shop to the next, casting nervous glances over their shoulders. No families. Few couples. No mingling among the various groups in transit.

On impulse, she turned away from the river on East Fourth, heading up the progression of streets named for long-gone trees: Ash, Birch, Cedar, Dogwood. As she neared Elm, a small group of women occupied the well-lit corner, all dressed in short skirts or tight shorts, skin-tight and low-cut tops, and high-heeled shoes. Lots of makeup, some wearing cheap wigs. Unlike the others she'd seen, these women engaged with men walking by, or stopped to chat with drivers of cars that paused at the curb. Sex workers, no doubt. Out in force on the warm, busy night.

One woman looked familiar. Tall and slender, with a silver wig. Young. White. Smiles fading into exhaustion.

Destiny Mathers.

***

Val jogged straight for the group. The women scattered, one by one, until only Destiny remained, chatting with a man wearing a cowboy hat and boots, who ran away as soon as he spotted Val approaching. Only then did Destiny seem to notice Val. She made a half-hearted attempt to escape, but in her three-inch heels, she stood no chance. She gave up and leaned against the brick wall of the nearest building, lit a cigarette, and blew the smoke skyward.

"Officer," she said in greeting when Val stopped a few feet away.

Val took a moment to catch her breath and rein in her surprise. Destiny's heavy makeup almost hid the bruises on her face and arms, and her rheumy eyes betrayed her poor health.

"I'm surprised to see you out here, working already," Val said. "A few hours ago, you were hooked up to an IV drip."

"I got better." Destiny sneered at her. "But you look like hell."

Val glanced over her own body, sweaty in all the expected places, and figured the minimal amount of makeup she'd applied that morning had run or smeared in unattractive ways. "I thought you'd be at Mercy for at least a few more days," she said.

"You guessed wrong," Destiny said. "Anyway, I don't have time to chat, so unless you got some business to conduct..." She coughed into her fist, then again, harder.

"You sure you're okay?" Val edged closer and reached out.

Destiny batted her hand away and strutted in the other direction, taking another drag on her cigarette before stomping it out on the sidewalk. "It's these damned cancer sticks," she said. "I really gotta quit."

Val followed her, noticing a serious limp in the woman's stride. "I'm glad I ran into you. I've been wondering if you'd changed your mind about naming the guy who—"

"Chrissakes, beyotch!" Destiny whirled around to face her. "You think I want to tell you his name? Would I be out here tonight, if I ratted out the dude who done this to me? Who do you think pulled me out the hospital and set me on this damned corner? Santa Claus? Now get the hell away from me 'fore he spots us and gives me another damned beating!"

Val stopped in her tracks, stunned, and chided herself for pressing too hard once again. "Listen. As a cop, I could bust you right now, and we both know where that would lead. Nowhere, right?"

Destiny cocked her head, crossed her arms, said nothing.

"But you've been through enough, and I've never been on board with the whole crackdown-on-sex-workers thing while we let the johns walk. What I'm trying to say is, I appreciate the situation you're in. Really, I do."

"Great. Thanks for the pep talk. Good night." Destiny turned to leave.

"Look," Val said, "I need your help. You know things, and I bet some of those things relate to the violent crap going down tomorrow. So if arresting you is the only way to get you to talk...well, why would you force me into making that choice?"

Destiny glared at her for several seconds, uncrossed her arms. "You can't bust me. You ain't seen me do nothing."

Val scoffed and she channeled her inner Bobby Grimes. "Come on. If I dragged your ass downtown right now, which member of Clayton PD would take your word over mine? Huh?"

Destiny heaved an angry breath and stared off into space. "Fine. What you wanna know?"

Val stepped closer and lowered her voice. "A name. A place. Any detail at all that can help me keep people safe tomorrow." A beat passed. "Anything at all."

Destiny bit hcr lip, watching Val with intense eyes. "No names, okay?"

Val nodded.

"This dude, he comes by the hospital to spring me, says I gotta work tonight over here, and tomorrow night over at the Waterfront. Everybody's got to. Even me, all beaten up. A show of force, he says. Whatever that means."

"A show of force." Val mulled over the words. "Of sex workers? Why?"

Destiny shrugged. "They got themselves some other shit going down and maybe they didn't want ya'll focused on any of that."

"Why would we focus on you gals when we—wait a minute. The *Waterfront*?"

"That's what he said."

"Where the big outdoor concert and fireworks show is going on."

"I don't know. That ain't my scene."

Val thought a moment. "With families, kids, all that. Not over here, where we'd ignore you."

"I guess."

Val rubbed her chin. "Any idea of what they're planning? What the event entails? A riot, or an attack? Guns, explosives, anything?"

Destiny shook her head. "They don't share the details with the peons."

"What time?"

Destiny glanced around, as if fearing someone might overhear them. "They said to start work by sunset or earlier. And not to be shy about it, if you catch my drift. Now, I gotta go, okay?"

Without waiting for a response, she limped into a nearby doorway to a darkened nightclub. When Val approached, a scary-looking bouncer with muscled, tattooed arms, a buzz cut, and an angry face blocked her progress.

"Sorry, we're full," he said in a gravelly voice.

Val considered playing the Cop card, but she had no ID on her, no badge, and no backup. Besides, Destiny had given her what she would, and could, share. No point in creating trouble for her.

She jogged back to the running path, resuming her lap around the developed area and onto the north-end bridge. She picked up the pace until she reached sprinting speed, as if finishing the last lap in the long-distance relay at a track meet. Excitement built within her. Destiny's intel confirmed her intuition that the fireworks show would play a big part in the attack the next day. But was it the main event, or just another distraction? She needed to find out more.

***

Val barged into the WAVE Squad office minutes later, sweating from every pore. Sergeant Petroni, standing at the whiteboard by the large conference table with marker in hand, gazed at her in surprise. "What are you doing back? You're not due in for another two hours."

"I got a tip," Val said, breathing hard, as much from her sprint up the stairs as her three-mile run. "It's the Waterfront. At least, I think so. I need to verify."

Petroni glanced at the whiteboard, which contained squad assignments for various locations around town. "How solid is this info?"

Val sprawled out in her chair, wiping perspiration from her forehead. "She has no reason to lie to me."

Petroni picked up an eraser and wiped several names off under the "Armory" heading. "Verify away," she said. "And keep me posted."

Val fired up her secure browser and, with much trial and error, navigated to the Parler social app. There she discovered her account had been activated. She clicked around, joined some chat groups, and found, to her chagrin, that those, too, required further admin approval before she could read the ongoing discussions. Same for Gab and the other apps she'd signed up for.

More mysteries, more walls. Where were the doors, and the keys to unlock them?

Thursday, July 4, 2019

Chapter Thirty-Four

Val emerged from a far-too-brief three-hour slumber in her own bed, heat and sunlight already filling the lonely space of her garage bedroom. She'd dreamed of holding Gil close, hearing his deep baritone murmur reassuring words into her ear. Instead she woke up hugging her pillow, five minutes ahead of her alarm.

Ah, well. At least she didn't dream of right-wing terrorists and unfriendly chat rooms.

She texted "Good morning, handsome" to Gil. When he didn't answer straight away, she remembered their staggered shifts. He'd worked from 2:00 to 6:00 a.m. and would return for a twelve-hour shift at noon, so he wouldn't rise for another hour or two. She needed to be at the Armory by 8:00, so she slammed down a quick breakfast, showered, and dressed in her Clayton PD uniform.

On her way out the door, though, she peeked in on her father, still asleep in his own bed. He'd mentioned attending some of the day's festivities, and that sent a shiver down her spine. Val wanted to warn him off without revealing inside information that could compromise their investigation.

Recalling her run from the night before, inspiration struck. She wrote him a quick note:

> *Saw lots of beer/wine/etc. vendors setting*
> *up at the Waterfront - no doubt at parade*
> *too - maybe best to celebrate at home this*

year? Have fun today. Love, V

She needed a different reason to keep the rest of the family away from danger. Given how stubborn they could be, she'd need a good excuse. None came right to mind, and she didn't want to be late to work. She made a mental note and drove to the Armory.

Travis Blake, a giant cinderblock of a man with short, sandy-colored hair graying at the temples, waved her into an "Official Use Only" parking area. "Dawes!" He hustled over to greet her once she parked and gripped her hand in a power-shake. "Glad you could make it. Wait, what the hell? Where's your sidearm?"

Val clapped him on the shoulder and freed her hand from his grip. "Cyrus still hasn't cleared me. Will that be a problem? Petroni said you'd planned something non-lethal for my assignment."

"Damn, I had you on sniper duty," he said with a grin. "Okay, I guess you can stand next to the mayor and take her bullet."

"Glad I wore my Kevlar. So, give me the lay of the land here."

Travis walked her over to the dais where the mayor and a handful of other local dignitaries would deliver patriotic, cliché-laden speeches about freedom, prosperity, and the American Way. "We posted guards inside the Armory and at the shooting range out back. Sentries guard both sides of the stage and the tech area, and we put at least one near every statue and memorial plaque. They'll handle crowd control."

"And my role?"

"Escort Mayor Iverson to the podium and stand behind her during her speech, watching for suspicious activity." Travis paused. "If you spot anything that poses a threat, or if anyone radios you to that effect, get her under cover. Shield her with your own body, if you must."

"Gotcha."

"The podium's bulletproof glass shield will protect her from the front, with about 180 degrees of coverage. She'll be much more exposed while getting on and off the stage." He paused and cocked his head. "You all right with this? I could put you in the command-control-communications trailer—"

"I'm fine with the detail. It's just that I haven't seen or talked with her since I arrested her husband for murder a few months ago. Things could get a little awkward."

"She's a politician," Travis said. "She'll be fine. Make small talk. I hear she's really into the Red Sox."

"Great. I know zip about baseball."

"You'll think of something." Travis checked his watch. "Things get rolling at 9:00. The mayor's speech begins at 10:00. Until then, monitor the crowd. Anyone looks weird, kick 'em out. Got it?"

A black sedan with federal plates rolled up next to them and parked right in the driveway. The window powered down, revealing the haughty orange mug of FBI Special Agent For-restal.

"I told you idiots to shut this thing down," the agent said without making eye contact.

"You must be Forrestal," Travis said. "So it gives me great pleasure to tell you to move this car the hell out of here and go complain to someone who cares."

Forrestal's face, already spray-tan orange, turned bright red. "Where's the CCC van?"

"The officer staffing the official parking lot will direct you there," Travis said. "Now get this tin can off my scene before I start busting headlights." He readied his baton and made a show of taking aim at the sedan's front grille. After a moment's hesitation, Forrestal slammed the car into reverse and burned rubber.

"Watch for pedestrians," Travis called after him in a soft voice, then smiled.

"I thought they only shut down the building's interior today," Val said. "Tours and such."

"Yeah," Travis said, grinning, "but wasn't that fun?"

***

Val spent the next hour roaming the Armory grounds. Spectators dribbled in at first, and the early arrivals—mostly local media—took the shaded seats under a canopy in front of the stage. With temperatures already in the low 80s and climbing, the standing-room-only crowd on the unshaded lawn behind the canopy would suffer obstructed views as well as a real danger of heatstroke.

The event kicked off with City Council members delivering welcoming remarks and handing out public service awards to local dignitaries. Val, camped out in the VIP tent next to the stage, browsed Parler, Gab, and Telegram on her phone, gratified to see that they granted her access to a few alt-right chat groups. She found some lame banter about how July Fourth belonged to the "true patriots" and how the "snowflakes will melt in this heat." None mentioned anything about events planned in Clayton. She glanced around at the crowd every few minutes, but saw nothing that concerned her.

Around 9:45, her phone buzzed with a message from Travis: the caravan for Mayor Iverson had arrived, mere minutes before her scheduled speaking time.

Val stood and waited by the entrance to the tent. Moments later, a caravan of three black sedans parked in a line at the curb. Black-suited security guards emerged from the lead and rear cars, and the mayor stepped out of the middle car. Iverson's blue and white sheath dress accentuated her tall, thin figure, and her wrinkle-free, tanned face looked years younger than the age of 47 given on her website bio.

Two staffers climbed out of the car after her, and the threesome speed-walked the twenty yards to the VIP pavilion, heads down in conversation. When Iverson spotted Val, her entire demeanor changed.

"What the hell are you doing here?" the mayor snapped, then blew past her into the tent, with her staff scrambling to keep up.

"I'm your on-stage security detail, Madam Mayor."

"Unnecessary," Iverson said over her shoulder. "I brought my own." Sure enough, four of the black-suited men entered the tent behind her staff, taking positions in pairs near each exit.

"Nevertheless, I'll need to escort you on stage—"

"I'd sooner take the bullet," the mayor said.

The on-stage speaker, an AM-radio talk-show celebrity, exhorted the crowd to "show your patriotism today" and urged them to support a fringe candidate for governor in the next election. Iverson frowned and muttered that "speeches weren't supposed to get political today." She caught Val staring at her and glared. Val returned her attention to the speaker.

"We must continue to *fight* for our *freedoms!*" he shouted. "Fight! For! Freedom!"

"Fight! For! Freedom!" the crowd chanted back, growing louder with each repetition.

Someone screamed something in response, a lone voice. The crowd's chants drowned out the protester.

A louder rumbling sent Val back to the tent's opening near the stage, where she peeked out at the crowd. Angry shouting interrupted the chants, followed by sounds of flesh hitting flesh. Val couldn't spot the commotion at first, so she stepped out onto the stage. Deep in the crowd, behind the shaded seats, a fight had broken out between two men, and others joined in. Uniformed police struggled to push through the onlookers to break it up, while clueless rubberneckers continued to vie for a better view, obstructing the officers' progress. The fighting spread to a few more audience members, several of whom were dressed in camouflage, and their opponents in all black, with face coverings. More shouts, more pushing and shoving. The police, rather than moving closer, got pushed back. For a moment she wondered whether they'd break out tasers or tear gas, and guessed that the prospect of harming innocents outweighed the potential crowd control benefits.

They needed more police bodies. Lots more.

"What's happening?" Iverson said from inside the tent. "It sounds like a riot out there."

Val radioed Travis: "Should I get in there and help?"

"Negative," Travis said. "You're unarmed. Get back in the tent with the mayor."

"It's getting out of hand," Val said. "We're outnumbered out there!"

No sooner did those words leave her mouth than a wave of heavily armed bodies in army-green uniforms wedged its way through the crowd. A few fired shots into the air. One screamed something about "Get down!" or "Get out!" to the crowd. People scattered, including those trading blows. One man in particular stood out: a short, wiry guy wearing all black with long, purple locks and a scraggly beard flowing around a black face mask. Purple Hair ran through the thinning crowd, throwing punches and knocking people down on the way to making a successful escape.

Val glanced back at the VIP area. One of the black suits in there shouted, "To the car!" Moments later, the entire entourage hustled to their black sedans.

Val spotted Purple Hair again and started to chase him, but stopped when Travis's orders to stay put echoed in her head.

Seconds later, the army-green contingent pushed through to the few remaining fighters, knocking them to the ground and standing on their shoulders, guns pointed.

"Who the hell are those guys?" Val radioed Travis.

"Feds. And National Guard. Forrestal's gang. The dumb son of a bitch called out the freaking cavalry."

Within minutes, they'd cuffed the brawlers and a few dozen random others face-down in the grass. One by one, the feds dragged suspects on their bellies into the police vans on the perimeter. Someone on stage announced to the disappearing crowd that they'd canceled the remainder of the event.

"The mayor's car skedaddled," Travis said over the radio. "Come help me with traffic control. It's a freaking mess down here."

Val joined Travis a few minutes later near the public parking lot. They spent the next hour sorting through the chaos of honking horns, shouting drivers, and vehicles that somehow got turned the wrong way, snarling traffic for blocks in all directions. When the flow of cars returned to normal, they huddled near the communications trailer, sipping iced coffees.

"What a mess," Travis said.

"Was anyone hurt?" Val asked, downing half of her coffee in one gulp.

"A few cuts and bruises, nothing serious, and mostly the fighters, from what I hear," Travis said. "We'll know more once they sort through the arrests downtown. We should head there to help out."

"No need," boomed a loud voice behind them. They turned.

Of course: Forrestal.

"They're all going to our facility in Hartford," Forrestal said. "We'll keep all of 'em under wraps for at least 24 hours. By nightfall, they'll all be singing like choir boys. By the time tonight's fireworks fly, there won't be a radical in the state available to throw a punch."

Val rolled her eyes. "You're sure this is an Antifa attack? Why? Did one of them surrender their membership card?"

"You saw how they were dressed," Forrestal said. "You may not want to admit it, but they threw the first punch, started the whole damned thing." He laughed. "And I ended it. You guys and gals in blue will thank me, because I just saved your town's Fourth of July celebration. You'll get the day off because of it."

Val shook her head. "Even if you're right," and somehow didn't add, *but you're not*, "a bunch of them got away. What makes you think they'll stop here?"

Forrestal made a face at her, as if deciding whether to respond. "Because," he said in a condescending tone, "they're cowards. They'll run home to their mommies' basements and hide there for a week, where we'll find them once their comrades talk. And," he went on, his tone growing even more self-assured, "we stopped their raid on the Armory. They needed the guns for their attacks later today. We've foiled their plans. They're done."

He paused, checking his cell phone, and laughed. "There's your mayor now, calling to thank me. Excuse me while I talk to someone who matters." He strutted away with the phone to his ear.

Val turned to Travis, who'd remained quiet, arms folded. "What do you think, Sarge? Is he crazy, or am I?"

Travis shrugged. "I've known all along that you are. I've also known you to be right, even when you're crazy."

"So, do we continue on, or go home, like Forrestal suggested?"

"That's above my pay grade," Travis said. "For now, we do what the Chief ordered. But it wouldn't surprise me if those orders change soon."

Chapter Thirty-Five

Val helped Travis unsnarl the gridlock that clogged the streets around the Armory after the abrupt end to the morning's ceremony. They'd just gotten traffic flowing again when Sergeant Petroni called.

"As soon as you can get here, we need you at HQ for a debriefing," Petroni said. "I don't trust the reports I'm getting from Forrestal's people."

"Go on, I've got it from here." Travis paused traffic in all directions to let her car escape the parking lot, and she made it to the WAVE Squad office in fifteen.

Sitting across from Val, Petroni's haggard face looked like she hadn't slept in weeks. A few times during her quick summary of the events at the Armory, Val wondered if her boss had nodded off.

"I trust your instincts as much as Travis does," the sergeant said when Val finished. "The chief reversed his double-shift-for-everyone order, but he's letting individual commands make their own call. I say, let's stay vigilant and keep our eyes and ears open." She yawned, then grinned. "If we can, that is."

Val stood to leave her boss's office, then cleared her throat. "Are you all right, Sergeant? Have you even been home in the past 24 hours?"

Petroni blinked up at her through bleary eyes. "I caught a quick catnap here and there," she said, gesturing toward a worn sofa and fuzzy blanket off to the side of her office. "I'll catch up once this thing is all over. On that note: if the light's off in here, don't knock, okay? Close the door on your way out." She gave Val a weary smile and stretched her arms over her head.

Val, seated back at her desk, glanced over at Petroni's office minutes later. Sure enough, the room had gone dark.

A message popped up in her email from Shelby, containing a list of right-wing websites she should explore. Energized by the help, Val dove back into her dark web research, finding her way around with more ease as her familiarity with the sites grew. In Parler and Gab, she discovered photos of the skirmishes at the Armory already posted, many with captions blaming Antifa for starting the riot. A few other posts reported fistfights and vandalism spreading elsewhere in the city—again, blaming Antifa.

But she also found some contradictory clues to what happened, including this back-and-forth chatter in one of the chat rooms:

> SgtFreedom: When is go time?
> ForceP: No set time. Wait for the signal.
> Raven: Who starts, then? Black or green?
> ForceP: Black 100%.
> SgtFreedom: What about the tours? Are we getting in?
> Raven: Canceled!
> ForceP: Remember, no weapons this AM. None!

Val's spine tingled. While the contributors to the chat never said outright what "go time" meant, in context it appeared clear: disrupt the Armory event. Create chaos. Digging further into the histories of the contributors' previous posts and chats, she found racist comments, complaints about the "criminal radical left," and images of swastikas, Confederate flags, and Aryan crosses. One praised Patriots Pride by name in a comment posted a few days before the raid.

She glanced at Petroni's door. Still dark through the

semi-opaque frosted glass panel.

Moments later, her partner arrived, dressed in his usual black suit, but without the tie, his white dress shirt unbuttoned partway. "I heard you had quite the morning over at the Armory," he said.

"Bobby, look at this." She showed him the chat.

He stood behind her, reading over her shoulder. "So, what's this from? The anarchists' chat room?"

Val shook her head. "The other end of the spectrum. Authoritarian militants. Followers of Patriots Pride and that ilk. Bobby, I think they staged this morning's riot as a false flag operation, and a diversion from what they're really up to."

"Namely, what?" Grimes sat next to her and took over the keyboard, scrolling through the various posts. "I don't see anything specific."

"It's all in the subtext—code, of sorts," Val said. "They use words that mean something specific to those in the know. Like 'MGTOW.' That means, 'Men Going Their Own Way.' 'Clay-Town' is their derogatory term for Clayton, and taking the 'black pill' means, basically, tearing the whole system down."

"So when they say they're targeting 'TPTB', what does that mean?"

Val checked the file Shelby sent her. "That's 'The Powers That Be.' The establishment. Us!"

"We'd better tell the feds," Grimes said. "As much as I hate them, they're in charge of this right now, and they're gonna have to own whatever happens." He picked up Val's desk phone and dialed. "Yeah, Forrestal, this is Detective Grimes, Clayton PD. We found some—what? Yeah, sure." He mouthed to Val: "On hold."

"They're planning something tonight, too," Val said. "Destiny—"

Grimes held up his hand to shush her. "Yeah, Forrestal. Dawes found some stuff online—what? Hell, I dunno. Hold on." He put Val's phone on Speaker. "Tell our good friends at the FBI what you found, and where."

"I was looking at posts on Parler, Gab, and—"

"Whoa," Forrestal said. "Freaking Internet sites? *That's* your source?"

"Right-wing chat rooms," Val said. "There's clear evidence they orchestrated—"

"Who orchestrated what?" Forrestal's impatient exhalation filled the speaker. "Come on, name names. Be specific."

"We don't know names," Val said. "Just 'handles'—online identities. We'd have to subpoena the sites' records to get their real names and so on. Anyway, these groups clearly staged this morning's riot, and—"

"Antifa? Yeah, we know that."

"No, not Antifa," Val said. "Alt-right groups. Paramilitaries, authoritarians, and white supremacists. I'll send you a screen shot."

"No need," Forrestal said. "We have them under wraps, and we'll get identities and confessions from the perps. We don't need their Facebook posts of puppies and kitties."

Val hung her head in exasperation. "These aren't cute puppy pictures. It's actual plans, for—"

"Quit wasting my time," Forrestal said. "Go home, like your mayor and police chief ordered." The line went dead.

Grimes stood, his jacket slung over his shoulder. "What a moron. All right, let's bring Petroni up to speed."

Val glanced at the sergeant's office. "She's taking a quick catnap. Let's learn a little more and brief her all at once, okay?"

"Agreed." Grimes strolled to his desk and slipped his jacket onto the back of his chair. "I've got parade duty in an hour. Sure you don't want to join me?"

Val pointed to her empty holster. "Not yet. I'll keep researching, okay?"

She resumed her search.

***

Following Shelby's advice, Val traced through several other accounts, linking one to the next and alternating between chat groups and the profiles of individuals who participated in them. One account, identified as "BigPete," made a candid admission:

> GirlyQ: Why the girls gotta work 2nite?
> BigPete: It's just the plan. Do your job.
> GirlyQ: Nobody's buying. Everybody's watching fireworks.
> BigPete: Zactly. We need attention on you from boyz in blue, not on the show.
> GirlyQ: Don't expect any green. Dudes gonna be with wives and kids. Ain't nobody looking our way.
> BigPete: You all dress right, they look.
> GirlyQ: Stop saying YOU. I aint turning anymore, Im too old.
> BigPete: No, you mine, now.

Excited, Val scanned the room. Grimes had left already—she vaguely remembered him announcing his departure some time before. Meanwhile, Petroni's office remained dark. Frustrated, she drummed her fingers on her desk. She needed to share this, get perspective. Val knew one trusted soul who'd just come on duty who always had the clearest mind on things.

She grabbed her cell phone and called her favorite number.

"Good morning, beautiful," Gil said moments later. "Breaking for lunch?"

"Not today." She filled him in on her discovery. "Gil, I think they're planning mini-riots all day, trying to tie us up in knots while they carry out their big hit, whatever it is, unnoticed," she said. "The Armory was the beginning. The parade is next, then the fireworks. Then, who knows?"

"The parade started a few minutes ago," Gil said. "I'll tell the officer-in-charge, and see if we can scare up a few more bodies. It'll be tough, since the chief let everyone skip their second shift after this morning's big arrest."

"Petroni's keeping us active, and Grimes is down there now. O'Reilly and Price are there, too," Val said. "I'll see if Travis is willing. I wish I could head down there. Damned Cyrus!"

"I can go," Gil said.

"No way. You're not cleared—what the hell was that?" Val said, interrupted by a clatter in the background on Gil's end.

"My stupid crutches. I knocked them over."

"I thought you don't need them anymore."

"I kind of overdid it yesterday," Gil said in a sheepish tone. "Things hurt a little this morning. So, for insurance, I brought them in today. I've *barely* needed them, Val. Really, I'm *fine*." He grunted.

Val recognized that sound: Gil, trying and failing to hide his pain. "Please don't go down there. It's bad enough for guys who *aren't* on crutches."

"They need help. I'm not doing much good here."

She drew a deep breath, held it. He could be so thick sometimes. "Tell you what. My lunch break is in an hour. If you stay, I'll bring you something?"

He chuckled. "Dirty pool, young lady, bribing me with a visit from your smiling face. Okay, dammit, I'll stay. But let's both work on recruiting some additional help. Deal?"

"You got it." They exchanged sweet goodbyes and she hung up, with a warm feeling tingling up inside her. In the time she'd known him, Gil never, *ever* pulled back from danger.

Until now. Until his relationship with Val entered the picture.

She knew that wouldn't—couldn't—last. They were cops, after all. Danger came with the territory. She didn't shy away from risk, either.

But this one time, having him choose her over a stupid parade felt amazing.

She returned to her work, sleuthing around further on dark web sites, looking for clues to what might happen later in the day. She found some photos of black-clad, masked individuals carrying anti-fascism signs. Some demanded "special rights," in the words of the contributors, for gays and women and Blacks, with captions deriding their "femoid, snowflake agendas." Other photos showed angry faces and more fights, again blaming "Antifa." A series of posts claimed that "leftists" and "transtrenders" threw rocks and bottles at the police. However, no such incidents had come across her desk, either from the scanner or via email.

As her lunch hour drew near, an image caught her eye. A short, wiry man, dressed in camouflage, "defended" a woman from an "attack" from "Antifa." From Val's perspective, it appeared the woman was pushing against her "defender" from behind, shouting and pointing at her "attacker." As if she, not the other man, was spoiling for the fight.

What caught her eye, though, wasn't the woman, nor her attacker. It was the "defender." In particular, his long, flowing hair and scraggly beard, both dyed a bright purple color.

Like the "Antifa" rioter from that morning who ran away. Only now he was dressed in camouflage. And he'd been fighting someone who looked an awful lot like the guy in Antifa black in the current photo.

As if the whole fight, in both cases, was staged.

She glanced at the caption again. The person who posted the photo used the handle "SuperPowers." Underneath, in the comments, came a thumbs-up from another user: "Tricky Mikey."

She checked their profiles. SuperPowers described himself as A Man of Law, Agent of Freedom, With a Vision of Liberty. His posts often defended the use of force by police, yet derided local cops as "idiots." Others blamed everything from child porn to the rising price of gas on Antifa.

For his part, Tricky Mikey spoke of "Glory Days" when "crooks didn't run America" and "women knew their place." He wore his views, he said, like a "badge of honor." His profile picture was the national flag of Ireland. No, wait. Not the Republic of Ireland— the province of Ulster. Northern Ireland. But not the true flag. It contained, in its center, a phrase: "14 Words." She looked it up: shorthand for a 14-word white supremacist slogan.

Her mind spun, making connections. Tricky. Mikey. Women in their place. Ireland/Ulster. Glory Days. 14 Words. Badge. What did all that signify?

Wait. She scribbled the words on scraps of paper, reorganized the scraps in various ways. Mikey. Badge. Ulster. Glory Days.

She shook her head. Nothing.

She set it aside and tried it with the other user's keywords: Super Powers. Idiots. Man of Law. Antifa. Agent of Freedom. Something clicked, and she rearranged the words.

Agent. Powers.

Could it be? Agent Powers? As in Special Agent Forrestal's partner?

She rearranged the pile of word scraps again, and another one fell into place.

Mikey, from Ireland, with a Badge of Honor.

Among those contributing to the plans and attacks from the alt-right that day were none other than Clayton Detective Mickey Mulroney, and FBI Agent Powers.

Chapter Thirty-Six

Val's first instinct was to knock on Petroni's door, but the sergeant yanked her door open before Val took two steps. "All hell broke loose at the parade," Petroni said. "We need all hands down there, ASAP."

"Even unarmed?" Val said.

Petroni waved her toward the door. "Cyrus didn't ban you from using your taser, right? Or your martial arts skills, or driving a vehicle. Come on, I'll find a role for you."

Val grabbed her taser out of her desk, checked its charge—full—and followed Petroni to the door. On the way out, she glanced at the clock: 2:25 p.m. Dammit! She'd promised Gil lunch at 2:00. She texted him: *Sorry, time got away...now Petroni's taking me into the field. Rain check for lunch?*

Gil's reply: three emojis. Sad face, worry, and a red heart.

Val grimaced. She didn't deserve a man that patient and understanding.

"Looks like you were right and Forrestal was wrong about the Armory not being the 'big event' of the day," Petroni said while driving the short distance to the parade route. "We have fights and vandalism going on left and right around this city."

"There's a reason Forrestal was wrong," Val said. "I found activity on those alt-right sites, posted, I'm pretty sure, by his trusted partner, Agent Powers. And Mickey Mulroney as well."

The car lurched, brakes squealing, and Petroni stared at her, wide-eyed. "You found proof?"

"Well, not proof, but—"

"Enough for a warrant or a court order to stop operations of the site?"

Val squinted, grimacing. "I'm not sure what the standard is."

"Dammit, I should've made you stay behind and nail that down. Oh, well, this is more urgent, and no judge is working today anyway." Petroni faced back toward traffic and the squad car rolled forward again.

They intercepted the parade on MLK Boulevard, and Petroni blipped her siren to part the crowd. Drums boomed and brass instruments blared in the distance, getting louder. "We're ahead of the lead float," Petroni said. "Trouble's brewing more toward the end. It's a U-shaped route, so we can take a quick shortcut." She blew the siren again and security staff moved the barricades so she could cross the blocked-off boulevard. They raced down the empty one-way street, where more crowds loomed ahead.

"This is close enough," Petroni said, screeching the car to a halt against the curb about twenty feet away from the crowd. Another marching band's song floated in over the gentle, warm breeze.

They got out and raced toward the gathering. Shouts rose over the din to the right, near blue-and-red flashing lights. Through the crowd they could see police struggling to separate men exchanging blows and swinging broken bottles. Four officers against over a dozen brawling guys, with onlookers screaming and pushing and throwing rocks. About half wore all black and face coverings; their opponents, a mix of camo, red-white-and-blue, or army green.

"Just like this morning!" Val shouted to Petroni. They drew their batons and headed for the nearest fighting pair.

When they got close, Petroni blasted an air horn, startling the two men enough that they paused their exchange of fisticuffs for a moment. Raising her baton, Petroni shouted, "Enough! Back off, now!"

The man in the red, white, and blue T-shirt and jeans bolted right. The man in black dashed left—right into Val's arms. She brought him down with an easy foot sweep move, and he landed on the pavement with a loud grunt. Val rolled him over and strapped his wrists together behind his back with zip-ties.

"Over here!" Petroni shouted. She'd approached another fighting pair, who tried the opposite tack: instead of running, they each grabbed Petroni by one arm and delivered round-house punches to her midsection.

Val kicked one behind the knee, and he went down in a heap. The other guy raised a fist, but Petroni escaped his grip and elbowed him in the mouth, knocking him on his butt. Petroni knelt on his chest and pressed her baton against his throat, ordering him to stop resisting. After a moment, he did, and seconds later, they'd zip-tied both men's hands and feet.

"You okay?" Val asked.

Petroni grunted and tapped her chest. "That's why we wear Kevlar."

After that, the fights seemed to disintegrate. A few others lay cuffed on the ground, while several ran away. A few in the crowd shouted "Police brutality!" and similar complaints, but Val and the other officers ignored them.

"Thanks, you two!" said one of the other four officers, all male and all larger than both Val and Petroni. "They outnumbered us until you two showed up."

Val considered pointing out that twelve-to-six still counted as "outnumbered," but she held her tongue.

"Who's in charge of this unit?" Petroni asked.

"That'd be me," said a tall, barrel-shaped man with a sweaty, ruddy face walking toward them. As always, Mickey

Mulroney wore a suit he'd outgrown twenty pounds ago, sweat staining both armpits halfway to his waist.

"Where the hell have you been all this time?" Petroni said, an edge to her voice.

Mulroney glanced at the cuffed suspects lying on the ground. "Holding back the parade from running us all over, and crowd control. What the hell happened?" His glare at Val accused her: *You promised restraint.* Or was that her overactive imagination?

"Some people got a little carried away with their fun," Petroni said. "Come on, let's get these perps out of the way so we can roll the parade."

They paired up and dragged the detainees by the armpits to the sidewalk, and the parade rolled past again. A float sponsored by a large hardware chain store tossed hard candy into the crowd, followed by a 1950s-era convertible transporting a smiling, waving candidate for governor.

"Let's bring these guys downtown," Petroni said. "I'll call for a wagon. Crap, hold on." She answered her cell phone. "Yeah, Bobby, where are you? Okay, we're on our way." She called Mulroney over. "Mickey, you'll have to mop up here. Dawes and I, and anyone you can spare, need to go help Grimes with another brawl."

"I can't spare anybody," he said. "Like everyone else, we're short-handed."

Val followed Petroni down the street, passing the parade participants and then breaking into a jog. "You trust him with that?" Val said.

Petroni tossed her hands in the air. "What choice do I have? Besides, just because he chats on weirdo social media doesn't mean he can't do his job. Especially with four other officers watching."

They caught up with Grimes after a few blocks, in time to see him tase a black-clad man into submission while his opponent fled. Two other fights broke up seconds later, one man running into Val, and she used a lapel drag take-down to bury his face into the pavement. Petroni grabbed another guy for a moment, but he slipped away with the others.

"What the hell's gotten into people today?" Petroni said. "I haven't seen so many fights since the last Bruins-Flyers hockey game."

Val's radio blasted static. She turned down the volume and recognized Shannon O'Reilly's voice. From what Val could tell, a group of self-described "leftists" carrying signs spouting pro-socialist and pro-environmentalist slogans tossed some unsuccessful Molotov cocktails at the local wastewater treatment plant. Shannon and Price were chasing them and needed backup.

"Pretty lousy environmentalists, if that's their tactic," Petroni said.

"Sounds like another false flag op," Val said. "Can we help?"

"Too far away. Dispatch will send someone."

"Who's left to send out?"

"Not our worry. If they want us there, they'll—dammit!" Petroni's phone chirped. "Petroni here...hey, Forrestal." Her eyebrows arched. "Is that so? Interesting. Who's stupid enough to attack a gathering of war veterans? Antifa? Uh-*huh.* Well, I'd love to chat more, but we've got our hands full down here, quelling your 'foiled' threats to public safety. Yes, at the parade. What's that? You're breaking up. Oh, *darn.*" She hung up, a Cheshire-cat grin spreading across her face. "I hate that guy."

Val laughed. "I'm glad I'm not the only one."

"Come on, let's help Grimes clear the scene." They yanked the captured brawlers off the pavement and force-walked them to a nearby squad car. Along the way, onlookers pointed cell phone cameras at them. Some shouted "State-sponsored terrorism!" and "What about their rights?" Val, like Grimes and Petroni, ignored the taunts.

Except one short, wiry, thirty-something guy, dressed in ripped jeans and a long-sleeved American flag T-shirt, with long flowing locks and a scraggly beard...both tinted purple.

"Hold on to this guy!" Val shoved her perp at Petroni. She ran into the crowd after the purple-haired guy, and he took off running. With her track speed, she narrowed the gap between them to within a few yards. She thrust her baton between his legs, tripping him to the ground, and he rolled several feet to a stop. But she lost her baton, and he regained his feet with surprising agility. He lunged at her, his foul breath catching her by surprise. As she drew her taser, he swung something at her: her baton. Val ducked, but he landed a sharp blow to the side of her head.

Moments later, everything went black.

***

The South Clayton High School band marched down Albany Avenue, erupting into a John Philip Sousa tune, trumpets and trombones blaring ten feet from where Maggie stood with her son and grandkids. Dressed in gaudy maroon and gold military-style uniforms that reminded her of a third-world dictator's personal guard, the band's lackluster performance reflected the mood of the crowd, melting in the humid, 90-degree heat. Except that it was loud. *Really* loud. So loud, she almost missed the call from one of the few numbers exempted from her phone's Do Not Disturb list.

"You better be standing over a dead body or a bag of hundred-dollar bills," Maggie said, hustling away from her family and the noise, "to interrupt my extremely limited time with my grandkids."

"It's a body, but it's not dead," Mulroney said.

"One of ours?" Maggie cursed to herself. They couldn't afford any more losses.

"You might think so." Mulroney paused. "It's your daughter. She got into it with some of our street folks, and, well, she got the worst of it."

Maggie's eyes widened and she covered her other ear with her free hand, seething. "Did I hear you right? One of your goons took down my daughter?"

"*My* goons? You mean *your own* goons. My guys are—"

"Dammit, I thought you said she was with us! I *knew* you were lying."

"*She* lied to *me!*" Mulroney said. "What am I supposed to do?"

"What good is a detective who can't tell when someone's lying?" Maggie said, mad enough to spit. "Where are you?"

"About mid-route, on MLK. Don't come here—I'm surrounded by cops. Let's meet down by the water, at the Founder's Statue."

Maggie hung up and waved at her older son, a good twenty feet away, then mimed having a full bladder and pointed in the opposite direction. Chad nodded and turned back to the parade.

Ten minutes later, Maggie spotted Mulroney's rotund figure resting against the base of the statue of the town's founder, Nathaniel Clayton. The statue's grim stare over the waters of the Torrington River attracted birds from miles around, judging by the discoloration of his marble face and head. A few tourists wandered the grounds, one or two at a time, none within fifty feet, none looking their way.

"She's alive," Mulroney said as soon as Maggie got within earshot. "She's getting checked—"

"Idiot! I said to recruit her, and failing that, sideline her. I *never* said to harm her." She lit a cigarette.

"I didn't touch her," Mulroney said. "She picked a fight with that Bosco guy—tried to club him. He defended himself. Anyway, if you wanted her sidelined, this little bump to her head ought to do it. We won't see her back today—and that's a good thing. My sources say she was getting too close."

"Why do you keep talking when everyone knows you're lying?" Maggie took a deep drag of her cigarette and blew the smoke at him.

"She's the one who lied," Mickey said. "Why are you getting so bent out of shape? You're the one who waxed all poetic about how 'sacrifices have to be made.' Now the shoe's on the other foot, and you're the one having to sacrifice. Well, boo-fucking-hoo!"

She caught him off-guard with a slap to the face, knocking him backwards a step. "Don't you ever, *ever* again try to equate the losers and scum of this world with a member of my family."

Mickey lunged at her, grabbing her hair and jerking her head back, sending her cigarette flying. He spoke in ragged breaths, his face close to hers, his other arm tight around her waist. "Lay one finger on me again, and I will break you in half!"

"Let me go, you disgusting slab of corned beef," she said, spittle hitting his cheeks. He complied, shoving her back into the statue. "Tell your *people* to keep her away from the Waterfront tonight," she said through gritted teeth. "Hell or high water. Even if you have to tie her up and lock her in one of your stupid jail cells."

"Concussion protocol will take care of that," he said, calming. "She won't be around, whether she likes it or not. But that's not our only problem, or even the biggest one."

"Well? Don't leave me hanging. Come on, I'm missing out on grandkid time here." Such a useful card to play with a family man like Mickey. Maggie hoped she hadn't overdone it.

"Our trigger man for tonight got swept up in the city's response," he said. "He, ah, won't be available tonight. Unless your daughter really takes his place in city lockup."

"Fuck!" Maggie lit another cigarette, blowing the smoke skyward. "What the hell was he doing on the street, anyway? Critical resources like that must be protected. You're so damned stupid sometimes!"

"I'm not in charge of your street lackeys," Mickey said. "That, I believe, is your useless husband's job."

"One of your people will have to do it," Maggie said. "They're the only ones close enough."

"Hell, no. I want no part of that."

"If this doesn't get done," Maggie said, frustration mounting again, "then the mission fails. *You* fail. If you fail, you don't get paid. Do *you* hear *me*?" She sucked a deep drag on her cigarette, enjoying the burning sensation in her throat and lungs.

Already red-faced from exertion and sunburn, Mickey's face darkened even more. "If I don't get paid *tonight*," he said, tapping the badge clipped to his suit jacket, "I will make sure that you never see the light of day again. I'm not talking city lockup, either. I'm talking hard time for conspiracy, attempted murder—"

"If I go down," Maggie said, her voice cool despite the anger welling inside her, "you go down with me."

"We'll see about that!" Mulroney stomped off, pausing about ten yards away to shoot a wordless glare over his shoulder.

Maggie took another deep drag on her cigarette and called her husband. "Mac," she said. "Mulroney's getting cold feet, threatening to take us down, like you said he would."

"It brings me no joy to say I told you so," Mac said. "What should we do?"

"You know what you need to do." Maggie finished her cigarette and flicked it at the statue.

"I can't. But you can."

Maggie rolled her eyes. "Why me?"

"You're close to the drop point. I'll text you the info."

She expelled a violent breath. Things were spiraling. "By the way, I think we need to operationalize the next element of the plan a few hours earlier than expected."

"What? That's crazy. Mags, we timed all this out. First, we get them running around and spread out—"

"I'm not saying right this minute. I'm saying early. Say, six or seven o'clock?"

"Why?" Mac huffed and continued, "That creates some logistical issues on my end."

Maggie's stomach churned, stress mixing with the bad street food she'd eaten all afternoon. "They're closing in, Mac. If I had to guess, I'd bet my daughter's largely responsible for that."

"Ironic," he said. "But you're right. She's a smart cookie. And cute, like her mother."

Maggie's stomach flipped, pain searing her abdomen. "Don't be such a fucking creep, *Mac*." She resisted calling him Milt, as her daughter's accusations returned to mind. She shook her head to force them out. "The point is, if we don't get it done soon, we won't be able to. That's unacceptable."

After a long pause, Mac exhaled a long, steady breath. "You're the boss."

"That's right," she said, her confidence returning. "And don't you ever forget it."

Chapter Thirty-Seven

When Val opened her eyes, the sweaty, concerned face of Bobby Grimes filled her view. Behind him, white puffs of clouds phased into focus, framed by blue skies. The sounds of beating drums and clashing cymbals drowned out whatever Grimes tried to say. She attempted to sit up, but dizziness and nausea forced her to lie back down. Grimes's rough hands caught her and eased her to the ground.

"Easy, champ," Bobby said, leaning over her.

The overwhelming aroma of stale coffee flooded her face. She coughed and turned her head to the side, in case the churning in her gut came to ugly fruition.

"Looks like you took a knock to the noggin," Grimes said, and the stale scent washed over her again. "Can you hear me all right?"

Val nodded and raised herself up onto one elbow. "Did the purple-haired guy get away?"

"Purple-haired guy?" Grimes shot her a puzzled, amused smirk. "You must've taken quite a knock to the head, after all."

"I'm not making him up." Val's nausea grew stronger. She closed her mouth and breathed through her nose. After a few beats, she continued. "He's the one that hit me. With my baton."

"Ah. That explains why it's gone missing from your belt." Grimes leaned back and squatted on his haunches. "Maybe you can look at some mug shots at HQ, try to ID him."

"After she gets checked out," Brenda Petroni said from somewhere behind Val. She moved into Val's field of vision, her face filled with worry. "You may have a concussion. I want the doc's opinion to be sure."

Val's nausea erupted again, interrupting her protest. This time, bile scorched the back of her throat and coated her tongue. It would be pointless to argue, anyway. She nodded and Grimes helped her into a squad car parked on the curb.

An hour later, she sat shivering on an examination table, dressed only in a light blue paper robe. A young Asian-American man in scrubs shined a light into her eyes and tugged her eyelids open.

"Any blurry vision?" he asked, switching to the other eye.

"Not until you blinded me with that flashlight," she said, smiling.

He chuckled and put the flashlight away. "Please read line four of that eye chart on the wall for me."

She rattled off the letters and numbers. "And you're Dr. Park," she said, reading his name tag.

He smiled. "Good. Let's check your reflexes." He bopped her knee with a hammer. Her lower leg jerked outward. "How does your head feel?"

"Fine, except where he cracked my skull," Val joked. "That's a little tender."

Dr. Park laughed. "I see your sense of humor is intact." They ran her through a battery of additional tests, checking her hearing, balance, coordination, and short-term memory.

"My best guess is," Dr. Park said some time after they finished, "you suffered a mild concussion. I recommend you rest for the next 12 to 24 hours, avoiding any intense physical exertion. If the headaches or nausea worsen, if the dizziness returns, if you notice a loss of smell or taste, a ringing in your ears, or if you can't sleep, then you should return here immediately for further observation and testing. Is there anyone at home who can keep an eye on you?"

She nodded. "My father."

After Dr. Park left the room, Val got dressed and wandered toward the exit. She had no intention of going home, but she knew not to admit that out loud.

***

When Val reached the hospital lobby, Petroni stood to greet her, as did a short, spiky-haired woman with nerd glasses and a faint mustache.

"Shelby's offered to give you a ride home," Petroni said, "which we appreciate, given how short-handed we are."

"I was thinking I should return to HQ and help there."

"Didn't the doctor order bed rest for you?" Petroni said, eyebrows raised.

"Desk work *is* resting, for me." Val's tone sounded more irritated than she felt. "Come on, I'm fine. The doc's being over-cautious. Didn't you want me to ID Mr. Purple Hair from mug shots?"

"If he's being cautious, so am I. Mug shots can wait a day." Petroni turned to Shelby. "Take her home, or to McDonald's, or anywhere except a police precinct. Understood?"

"Yes, ma'am," Val and Shelby said in unison.

Val followed Shelby to her car, a shiny new SUV with a roof rack, spoiler, and black tinted windows. Clearly IT staff earned more than rookie cops. "So, where'll it be?" Shelby said, blipping the car open with her fob. "It's way past dinner time for me. So, fast food, beer joint, or the Dawes Mansion?"

"How about someplace with Wi-Fi? I assume, with a job like yours, you keep some sort of laptop within reach at all times."

Shelby snorted. "Wi-Fi I've got, right here in the car. You'll have to provide your own laptop."

"Home, then. At the very least, I should change out of this uniform."

When Shelby started the car, the radio blasted Metallica, and Val's head nearly exploded. "Sorry," Shelby said, turning it off. "I like to crank tunes while I drive. Got a preference?"

"Love it, but my head won't take it right now." Val shaded her eyes from the low-lying sun on the horizon. "How about regular old conversation?"

"Wow, so the gossips are right. You *are* a throwback." Shelby pulled into traffic at high speed.

"I am not! Who says that about me?"

Shelby laughed. "Don't worry, they mean it as a compliment. Anyway, you rock, in my book. I love this case you're working on. Have you found anything new?"

"A few things. I'm not supposed to talk about it."

"Fair enough." Shelby took a corner way too fast. "I can share stuff I know with you, though, right? I mean, if I have evidence relevant to your case, I'd be legally obliged to disclose it, wouldn't I?"

"Like, what?" Val grasped the hand grip with white-knuckled fingers.

"Well, you were looking into those freaky alt-right groups, right? That's kind of a hobby of mine, too, given how miserable they make my life every day."

"Makes sense. What do you know about them?"

"That one group you guys busted last week—Patriots Pride? They're one of the worst," Shelby said. "They hate everybody: minorities, women, gays and lesbians, liberals, and especially trans people. Which means they hate me the most of everybody." She grinned. "I'm also a quarter Mexican."

"What do they do?" Val said. "Besides brainwash angry blue-collar men."

"For one thing, they shut down a youth counseling organization with their stupid protests, a group that helped

LGBTQ kids who were getting bullied in school," Shelby said. "They've also gotten 'dangerous' books banned from libraries, and recently shut down two Planned Parenthood offices. A couple of years ago, they even got public officials fired for being 'anti-white' or 'anti-straight.' Last month they went around trying to 'find' illegal immigrants at restaurants to get them deported. They're scary people."

"They sound horrible, but I can't arrest them for that." Val's words sounded hollow, even to her. She must be missing something, a connection, something important. Her foggy thoughts wouldn't clear, though.

Shelby grimaced. "What if I can show you they're planning something today? Something...violent."

Val's pulse quickened. "Related to the stuff going on around town today?"

Shelby nodded. "And more...I think."

Val's mind seemed to sharpen a bit. "That would be a tremendous help. How?"

Shelby's GPS told her to turn onto Val's street, and she obeyed. "You said you have a laptop and Wi-Fi at home?"

"Yeah, but none of that VPN stuff."

Shelby grinned. "Leave that to me."

***

Val and Shelby arrived at Dad's a few minutes later, where she found he'd left a note on the back side of the one she'd left him:

> *Heading to Jerry's for a while, then going down to join Chad et al at the Waterfront for fireworks. Looking forward to seeing Ali and Dar, it's been so long. Hope to see you there. - Dad*

Val and Shelby set up their laptops side-by-side at her father's kitchen table. Before rebooting Val's laptop, Shelby plugged in a USB drive from a black case she'd retrieved from her car. While Val fixed turkey-and-provolone sandwiches, Shelby fired up some apps stored on the drive. When Val rejoined her, Shelby's screen displayed a strange website called 'FreedomBros,' with its text and very limited graphics all rendered in black and white.

"These guys have gone by all different names over the years," Shelby said, munching her sandwich. "But they've kept the same domain name. From what I can tell, it provides a bit of a smokescreen from prying eyes like ours." She barked out a harsh laugh. "Little do they know, I'm practically a charter member."

"*You* are?" Val choked on her words. "You hate everything they stand for."

"My idiot brother doesn't, or didn't, and I hacked his account ages ago. When he moved on to greener pastures, I kept his profile alive." Shelby's fingers flew over the keyboard, and moments later, a photo of a floating barge appeared on the screen. "Recognize this?"

"The fireworks barge," Val said. "Is it theirs?"

"No, but you'd never know it from all their chatter. Watch." Shelby scrolled down and highlighted an exchange of messages, then turned the screen to Val.

Soldier4God: Security is in place.
SuperPowers: 100% ours?
Tricky Mikey: Enough. Th others won't be a probelm.
SuperPowers: So, the package?
Soldier4God: Delivered.
SgtFreedom: What about the trigger?
BigPete: Working on it.
Tricky Mikey: Not in place? YET???
BigPete: WORKING ON IT.
Tricky Mikey: BossGal wont be hapy.
BigPete: WHO DO YOU TIHNK IS WORKNG IT?

A patina of perspiration sheened Val's brow, and she set aside her almost-untouched sandwich. Too dry, anyway. "I recognize a few of these names from my research," she said. "I know who some of these people are!"

"How?" Shelby sat back, her arms folded. "These guys are serious about protecting their identities."

Val pointed at the screen. "Things they say. For instance, I'm not 100% certain, but I think SuperPowers is none other than FBI Agent Powers."

"Isn't Powers that quiet Asian woman?" She frowned. "I'm pretty sure SuperPowers is a guy. He's a racist, misogynist asshole, at least in a lot of his posts." She wolfed down the rest of her sandwich and drank a long gulp of water.

Val's confidence ebbed, and her voice showed it. She pointed at the last few lines of text. "Okay, maybe not then. And, for what it's worth, I think that guy is a Clayton cop."

"The guy with all the typos?"

"No, Tricky Mikey. I think he might be Mickey Mulroney."

Shelby cocked her head. "Working undercover, or for real as a member?"

"I never considered the possibility of him working as a mole," Val said. "It's not like I can ask him. He'd deny it either way, unless they read me in on the case."

Shelby pursed her lips and nodded. "Nah, I think you're right. He can be a real pig. In person, I mean, *and* on here. So if that's him, he's for real. Anyway, what do you make of all this?"

Val studied the text again, and the unease she'd felt while running the night before returned. "I think they're plotting something with the barge. They seem to feel they control its security detail, so they have every opportunity to...what, I'm not sure."

"I thought Clayton PD provided security down there."

"They do. I saw them down there last night. Which means…" Val's head grew dizzy, and she recalled her odd meeting in the park with Mulroney. "They've infiltrated the department. Dammit, it *must* be Mickey! He's in on it! He's one of them!"

"And," Shelby said with triumph in her voice, "Look at this. What I told you about before: something about a 'trigger.' What do you suppose that's about?"

Val's mind whirled, dizziness ebbing away. "An attack, that's what," she said, alarm rising. "They're going to attack the barge!"

"That doesn't add up if they put their own people on board. Maybe they're using the boat to launch their own attack?"

Val rubbed her temples. "Either way, it puts everyone down there at risk—thousands of people. I've got to tell Sergeant Petroni!" She grabbed her cell phone and called her boss.

Or tried to. "All lines are busy," the robotic female voice said after three tones sounded. "Your call cannot be completed. Please—" She hung up, tried again. Same result.

"Can I borrow your phone?" Val asked. Shelby slid it toward her and resumed typing. Val tapped Petroni's number into Shelby's phone. Same result. "Something's wrong. I can't get through on either of our phones."

"Does your dad have a landline?"

Val sighed. "I convinced him to drop it a few months ago to save money. Dammit!" Then she paused. "Speaking of my dad, I should warn him not to go down there." She sent him a quick text. Waited…it didn't send. Then she noticed that her earlier text to him had also bounced. She tried calling. That failed, too.

"There's been a denial of service attack on the local cell carriers," Shelby said, her face buried in the laptop screen. "Guess who's responsible?"

"Patriots Pride?"

Shelby mock-grimaced. "I was hoping you'd waste a guess or two."

"So all cell service is down in the city?" Val asked, incredulous.

"As far as I can tell, the entire metro area. It's an attempt to further complicate police response."

"That's unbelievable. What kind of operation are these guys running? It must be huge!"

Shelby shook her head. "Not at all. Base Transceiver Station hacking is Anarchist 101-level stuff. With the old tech deployed on most of Clayton's cell towers, flooding and overwhelming the system is child's play. The amazing thing is that it doesn't happen more often."

"I need to warn Petroni, and—shit! My whole family is down there!" Val said. "Wait. Wi-Fi is working. Can I message them over the Internet?"

"If they're logged in to a Wi-Fi data network, yes. But if you're thinking SMS messaging, no. They need a cell carrier for that. You could email them, but even then, unless they check their inbox a lot, they'd miss it."

"I've got to go downtown, then," Val said. "Right now. Can you drive me?"

Shelby grinned. "I always wanted to get some field work. And with lines down, you can't call an Uber. Weren't you going to change out of your uniform?"

Val caught herself halfway to the front door. "Damn, I almost forgot." She ducked into the garage and changed into street clothes, and slid her badge into her purse, just in case. A moment later, she grabbed the radio and clipped it to the waistline of her jeans. Without cell service, it'd be the only way to stay in contact with Petroni and Grimes. And Gil, for that matter.

She considered wearing the Kevlar vest, but she couldn't hide it under her light, short-sleeved top. And Kevlar hadn't protected her earlier that afternoon.

She lay the vest on the bed and waved Shelby out to the car.

Chapter Thirty-Eight

Reclining in Chad's metal-framed canvas beach chair, Maggie sipped a cold strawberry lemonade and listened to the children play behind her. She zoned out of the argument her son carried on in hushed tones with his beautiful, high-maintenance wife all afternoon, who hadn't said two words to Maggie since arriving that morning. She checked her cell phone for the time: 7:05 p.m. Sure enough, still zero bars of reception. Good job, Mac.

Her messaging app, though, showed missed texts from before the service interruption, including a few marked Urgent. She scanned them and realized her worst fears: the operations had begun to fall apart. Most critically, Mac hadn't found anyone to deliver and operate the detonator. She'd have to pick it up herself, then convince him to walk it close enough and push the button. Maybe one of the girls—the local one, Destiny-what's-her-name. Anyone but Maggie. She planned to be far from the blast zone by that time.

"Mommy, I need to pee again!" Sammy popped into view, clutching his crotch, his shorts already displaying evidence that he'd realized this about five minutes too late.

Maggie heaved an impatient breath and turned to Chad, playing with Dar on the blanket spread over the grass. "Would you mind taking your brother—"

"Chad has his own children to watch," Kendra snapped from the other side of him. "Sammy needs his *mother* right now, don't you think?"

Very well then. "Of course," Maggie said, easing her frame out of the low chair. "I just thought they might enjoy some brother time." No matter. This gave her the excuse she needed to leave them for a short while. She led Sammy by the hand toward the port-a-potties a hundred feet up the gentle grassy slope behind them.

After the boy finished his business and washed his hands, she led him further from the action with a firm grip on his shoulder.

"Mommy, we're going the wrong way," he said, pointing back at Chad.

"Mommy and Sammy need to go on a little adventure first," she said. "Don't worry, the fireworks don't start until after sunset. Remember when that happens tonight?"

"Eight-thirty," he said. "Firecrackers at nine."

"Right. So, we have almost two whole hours. You don't want to sit still for two whole hours, do you?"

Sammy shook his head. "What kind of a-venture?"

"You'll see." She checked her missed messages from Mac again: *Check the PO Box.* Maggie's anxiety level climbed another ten notches. Please, God, say it ain't so. Surely he didn't send the detonator through the US Mail.

The good news: the post office was downtown, only a few minutes' walk. She dragged Sammy up the sidewalk in that direction.

"Mommy, I'm hungry," he said in a whining tone. He'd eaten like a pig all day, but the kid had a hollow leg. They passed a street vendor who supplied a hot dog with ketchup and a root beer, and Sammy seemed happy. For a minute.

The post office was closed for the holiday, but the PO boxes remained accessible. She retrieved a letter-sized envelope and tore it open. The envelope contained a single piece of paper, folded, and a small key with a number on its thick plastic handle. The note read:

Where we met. - MM

Maggie smiled, recalling the occasion. Over two decades before, she'd picked up her first husband from the train station after a business trip to New York. Mike asked if she could give a ride home to his colleague, Milt McCloskey. His fierce gaze and electric energy captured her attention from the start. They'd met at the station café a few times before their affair caught fire. So fitting, then, this choice.

The walk to the station took twenty minutes, and it cost her another potty stop and an ice cream at McDonald's for Sammy. Otherwise he made it without complaint. She found the locker, inserted the key—

The damned thing wouldn't turn.

Maggie tried again. Twisted on it harder. Wouldn't budge.

Cursing, she removed the key from the lock, checked the number. With a sigh of relief, she realized she'd tried the wrong locker. She moved one column over and tried again.

Success!

Maggie removed the package from the locker, a heavy rectangle of black plastic and metal the size of a cell phone. On the back, Mac had taped one of those black-and-white scanner codes. She scanned it, and her phone tried to download an app, and failed. No service, of course. Now what?

A noise startled her. Someone else coming in to check their PO Box. She needed to hide the detonator—where? It wouldn't fit in her tiny clutch purse.

Of course. Sammy's backpack. "Come here, son. Mommy needs you to carry something for me."

"Is it part of the a-venture?" he said with a devilish smile.

"It sure is." It felt good not to have to lie for a change.

Now, to get it close to the barge, and in the hands of a competent operator.

***

The drive back to the Waterfront took Val and Shelby almost an hour—three times normal—because of congestion arising from last-minute fireworks-show traffic. Val groused that she could have run there faster, and part of her wished she had. But her growling stomach begged to differ. She'd left most of her sandwich on the kitchen table and otherwise hadn't eaten since 7:00 a.m. Her head throbbed, too, where Mr. Purple Hair clocked her with the baton. Running would have been painful.

Once there, they discovered that all downtown parking lots had filled hours before. Shelby must have sensed Val's growing anxiety, because after the tenth "Sorry, we're full" sign, she pulled to the curb. "You go do what you need to do," she said. "I'll park wherever I can."

Grateful, Val didn't argue. She crossed the busy sidewalk, lined with vendors, and picked her way through the crowd to find her family. Sure enough, she spotted them where they spent every Fourth of July celebration: a hundred feet in front of the largest collection of portable toilets. Not too close to suffer the smell, not so far that they couldn't reach them in an emergency, and with an unobstructed view of the fireworks.

Val arrived at the same time as her mother, tugging Sammy along by the arm, smudges of chocolate and ketchup all over his shirt. She smiled, despite the urgency of the situation. They'd had a good day. He did, at least.

"Val!" Chad stood to hug her, a plastic smile affixed to his sunburnt face. "I thought you had to work. Hey, what happened to your head?"

"I fell." She glanced at her mother, who shot her a puzzled look. Whatever. Mom didn't offer a hug, but Kendra did, a tight squeeze that spoke of fraught emotions left unexpressed. "Look, everyone—wait. Where's Dad? I thought he was going to join you?"

"We haven't seen him," Chad said. "And he hasn't called."

"We need to find him. And everyone—you have to go. Now!"

"Go? Where?" Kendra snatched up Dar, their toddler, who'd chosen that moment to undertake his newest favorite activity: running toward strangers. "The fireworks aren't scheduled for another forty-five minutes."

"Trust me." Val kept her voice low. "In a few minutes, everybody's going to try to get out of here, and it'll be a stampede. Go now, while you still can." She scooped up an empty chair, folded it, and grabbed a second one. Chad grabbed its other arm and tugged it away from her. Behind him, Mom glared, frozen in her spot, holding Sammy's shoulders.

"We're not leaving until you tell us why," Chad said. "We drove all the way from Danbury for this, and the kids have looked forward to it all day."

"I don't want to miss the fireworks!" Ali said.

"Me neither!" Sammy shouted, clutching his mother's leg.

"Please?" Val clutched her hands together, conscious of the seconds ticking by. She still needed to contact Petroni and Grimes—after she got her family out ahead of the inevitable mad rush that would accompany an emergency evacuation. "Please do as I ask you this one time. It will all become clear soon."

"But why?" Kendra said. "Can't you please explain what's happening?"

"I can't." Val's head decided to spin at high velocity at that moment. Coupled with a bout of nausea, it almost knocked her down. She leaned against the chair folded in her hands to remain upright.

"Val? Are you okay?" Chad stepped closer, rested his hand on her shoulder. "Should we call a doctor?"

"No!" Val's shout made her head throb. "It isn't safe, okay? Please, go!" She met Chad's eyes, saw the worry there, then more of the same in Kendra's. Then her mother's, whose expression she couldn't read. Not worried, exactly. More...angry?

"Perhaps we should listen to Valorie," Mom said. "After all, she is a police officer. If she says it isn't safe..."

"Excuse me, why isn't it safe to be here?" A brown-haired white man in his thirties, dressed in an unbuttoned Hawaiian shirt and Bermuda shorts, whipped off his sunglasses and stepped closer. "Are we in danger? What's happening?" A few people on blankets nearby sat up to listen.

Through her haze, Val's panic rose. The situation could soon get out of hand. "Please step back," she said in a loud voice, making her head pound more. "We...have a medical situation here, and we need to leave. Please, give us some space."

"What medical situation?" Chad asked. "Yours?"

Val grabbed her brother's shirt and drew him close. "Chad. Please. Trust. Me." Each word echoed inside her head, each echo a blast from a hammer against her skull. "Go. Now. Take. Ali. And Dar. And Kendra." She pushed away from him, and bile rose in her throat. She bent over at the waist, her breaths coming in hot, harsh blasts.

"I should take you home," Chad said. "Kendra, you and the kids—"

"NO!" Pain seared Val's skull. She straightened and spun her brother around, pushing him toward their ice chest. "Pack up. Go. Now. Don't argue!"

Kendra's eyes widened and she nodded. Still holding Dar, she gathered up their belongings into the center of the blanket, except the ice chest and chairs. She tied the corners of the blanket together, and slung it over her back. "Let's go,

Chad, kids." She turned to Val's mother with an expression of distaste. "You, too."

"I'll wait here," Mom said. "Why don't you take Sammy with you? He'll want to stay near Ali, and I—"

"As I've already explained," Kendra said through clenched teeth, "our hands are full taking care of our own children. You should take care of yours. Come on, Chad." She marched off, carrying the blanket bundle over one shoulder and Dar on her opposite hip. Around them, families began gathering up their own belongings, fear on their faces. One childless couple chased after Kendra, leaving their stuff splayed all over the ground.

Chad's gaze flickered from Val to their mother, back and forth, a look of helplessness on his face. "Mom, why don't you and Sammy come with us? We'll find another fireworks show somewhere, on TV at the hotel if we must. Come on, it'll be fun."

"We'll be fine," Mom said. "You go on ahead."

Chad knelt next to Val, still bent at the waist, breathing hard. "Val? You coming?"

"After I find Dad. How about you pick us up at the Founder's Statue?" Val had no intention of leaving, but if she found her father, that gave her a place to send him.

"Chad?" Kendra called from the port-a-potties. "The kids need to use the toilet. Are you going to come help me?"

"Mom, I've gotta go," he said, grabbing the ice chest. "Can you get those chairs back to me later?" He huffed up the gentle slope toward Kendra.

"Go on, Mother," Val said, her breathing returning to normal. "You need to go, too."

"Why don't we both stay and spend some family time together?" Mom smiled, a sickly expression. "I'm sure we'll all be fine if we stay together."

"You don't understand. It's not safe. For anyone. Please, bring Sammy and go."

"Val?" Chad's voice cascaded down the slope. "Come on, I'll help you up." His voice drew nearer as he spoke.

Val turned. Sure enough, Chad left the ice chest on the ground near his wife and started downhill, probably at Kendra's urging, to retrieve her. "No!" Val waved her arms, directing him back up the hill. "Go!" *Damn*, how shouting made her head hurt.

Still, he kept coming. Damn him! At the top of the hill, Kendra waited with Dar. No doubt Ali had ducked into the restroom. They weren't leaving! And Val's mother still refused to.

Screw her, then. At least she could save Chad and his family. She forced herself upright and charged uphill, meeting her brother halfway. "Chad," she said. "I can't leave yet. But you've got to, okay? Take the kids and go. No questions, no arguing. I promise, I'll explain later."

Ali emerged from the restroom and started down the slope. Val cursed and dragged her brother toward her, grabbing Ali on the way. Reaching Kendra, she shoved them toward the street, ignoring their protests. Next she'd force her mother to leave, then find her father. Then she could warn Petroni and help with some sort of orderly evacuation.

When she turned to face her mother, Mom and Sammy were gone.

Chapter Thirty-Nine

Maggie huffed to a halt and set Sammy down on the running trail, fifty-five pounds of squirming petulance—worse than dead weight. Fifty-seven, with the stupid backpack and its contents. But the kid refused to come on his own, and Valorie wouldn't remain preoccupied with Chad for long.

Amazing, though, how fast she could move when motivated, and how easily she could disappear into a crowd. She removed the oversized straw hat that she'd stolen from an unoccupied blanket along the way, fanned herself to cool off, and put it back on.

She risked one look back at Chad, still arguing with his wife. Come on, son. Show the world how stubborn you can be. Keep her busy.

Resuming her escape, her eyes fell on a familiar face. Her first ex-husband, dressed in a ridiculous get-up of a Hawaiian shirt, Bermuda shorts, and Panama hat, wandered through the crowd, as if searching. For Val and Chad, no doubt.

How serendipitous.

"Michael!" She waved at him.

Mike startled, followed the source of her voice with his gaze. He cocked his head, his mouth gaping open, and responded with a quick wave. She pointed at a pod of food vending trucks segregated from the festivities with a three-foot white picket fence and headed toward them, away from Valorie and Chad.

He glanced around again, doubt etched on his face, soon replaced by resignation, and he trudged over to the vending carts. Which, as it turned out, sold not food, but beer, wine, and sugary mixed drinks. Talk about serendipity.

They met outside the fence, an awkward four feet apart. "So, you're still in town," Michael said, disappointment weighing down his voice.

"Don't be so damned excited about it," she said. "Have you sobered up yet?"

He straightened with pride. "Almost six months, until—Oh, Rita. You don't really care, do you?"

"My friends no longer call me Rita. Call me Maggie."

"We're no longer friends." He wiped sweat from his brow.

"Sure we are. Come, have a drink with me." She pulled Sammy toward him.

Michael backed away, hands up in a defensive posture. "Don't be cruel. You know better than to offer a drink to a recovering alcoholic."

She smirked. "According to Chad, that ship already sailed." Speaking of which, it took all of her willpower not to look at the barge, mid-river. Instead, she glanced at the rear wall of the nearest drink truck, which advertised *Best Mojitos North of the Border*.

"Where are Valorie and Chad?" he asked.

"Waiting for me to bring back some mojitos. But I need to bring Sammy to the toilets. The ones uphill have long lines. Do me a favor and bring them?"

He frowned, puzzled. "Bring them what?"

"Hold the boy a moment." She darted through the opening in the fence, smiling-not-smiling at the guy checking IDs, daring him to ask. He didn't.

"Get back here!" Michael shouted. Sammy edged closer to the gate, then tried to dart through. The ID checker grabbed him, and Michael pulled him back, apologizing.

Maggie laughed and ordered two mojitos. The vendor plopped a pair of sweating plastic cups with clear lids and yellow straws onto the counter and took her money. She made sure the ID checker wasn't looking and ducked behind the mojitos truck, setting the drinks on the ground next to Michael.

"You can't take drinks out of there," Michael said.

"I'm not. You are." Maggie walked back through the gate and grabbed Sammy's hand. "Valorie and Charles are at the top of the hill. Be a dear and bring these drinks to them? Thanks, love." She yanked Sammy down the sidewalk. Mike was always a sucker and a pushover. No part of her doubted Michael would deliver the drinks and further delay Valorie's pursuit of her. Or he would drink them, which could have the same effect.

With cell service out, she'd have to bring the detonator closer to the barge—a few hundred feet—so its built-in radio transmitter could get the job done. That meant crossing to the east side of the river, to the pier. And soon: they'd start the fireworks show in less than a half hour. She needed the explosives detonated before that.

Getting that close posed a greater risk for her, of course, if any of the rockets strayed off in her direction before she escaped to their new headquarters nearby. Bad enough it would take out a handful or more of their sex workers patrolling the streets on both sides of the river. But, as she and Mac demonstrated in the past week, the girls were replaceable.

Sammy in tow, she hustled up the ramp to the pedestrian bridge, heading toward the Alphabet Soup district, and the culmination of all her planning.

***

Val scanned the crowd for a tall, fiftyish, brown-haired woman walking with a young boy. She focused on the street-side edge of Waterfront Park, Rita's most likely path of escape. Hoping, anyway, that she'd headed that way. After a few minutes, she gave up. She'd warned her mother that she should leave. Whether to comply was up to her. In any case, Val still needed to find and warn her father.

Back in the days when her parents brought them down for the fireworks display, they often disagreed about where to set up their blankets. Mom always won the argument, and they'd set up right where Chad had that evening: in front of the port-a-potties. Dad always argued for a spot in the shade, near the trees on the far edge of the park. She headed in that direction.

"Look, Mommy! That lady has a walkie-talkie, just like me!" shouted a young boy, pointing at Val. The boy spoke into his walkie-talkie in a low voice, his eyes locked on Val.

Of course! Her police radio. In her concussed haze, she forgot to turn it on. She couldn't return the boy's message—she had no idea what channel he'd used—but she could inform Headquarters about what she knew.

Gil was working Dispatch. Maybe, just maybe...

She flicked on the radio, and a blast of chatter greeted her. Officers and Dispatch trading details, reporting and responding to a myriad of situations. She waited for a quiet moment, which never seemed to come. In the meantime, she searched, stepping with care around blankets, chairs, and sprawling legs.

She needed to get the warning out. Soon. She also had to get her father out before he got trampled by the mad rush.

She glanced at her cell phone. Still no signal. Thirty minutes until the fireworks start.

A familiar voice came over the radio. The voice she loved above all others, sending a pair of officers to a downtown intersection to clear it of suspected sex solicitation.

Downtown?

After the officers confirmed their intention to respond, Val pressed "Talk" before anyone else could cut in. "Gil? Ah, I mean, Sergeant Kryzinski, this is Officer—"

"Val? I heard you took a bop to the head." Alarm rose in Gil's voice. "Are you okay?"

"I'm fine." A wave of nausea passed over her, and she stopped walking.

"Where are you?" Gil said. "Wait, let's switch to a private channel so we can talk. Use, um…twenty-two."

She switched channels and smiled at the boy, who pressed his walkie-talkie tight against his ear. "Gil? I'm at the Waterfront. Patriots Pride is planning an attack on the fireworks barge tonight. It could get pretty ugly."

"I'll pass the word, see if we can beef up security," Gil said. "Are you sure you're okay? Your speech is a little sluggish."

"You're imagining things." But she felt dizzy enough to plop down in an unoccupied lawn chair. A young woman lying on an adjacent blanket glared at her and started to say something. Val flashed her badge, then ignored her.

"I'll send someone to come get you," Gil said.

"Send backup instead. To the pier. I'm heading over there as soon as I locate my father."

"If they attack that barge, it'll be a catastrophe," Gil said. "We'll need to evacuate, shut the event down. Val, you need to get out of there. In your condition—"

"Give me five minutes. If I don't find him by then, I'll assume he left, too, or that he will when you give the orders. Please?"

"What do you mean, 'he left, *too*?' Who else did you tell?"

Val's heart rate accelerated as she realized her breach of protocol. "My brother and my mother," she said. "I didn't reveal anything, except that they should leave. Which they have."

"Good. Don't tell anyone else. Let this go through channels. Call me when you reach the east side. Over." The long silence that followed let Val know he'd switched back to the main dispatch channel.

The woman on the blanket waved her hands to get Val's attention. "What's going on?"

Val drew a deep breath. Gil told her not to tell anyone else anything, but she didn't feel she should lie, either. "We're recommending that people move away from the river's edge," she said. "For safety."

"Why? What's wrong?"

"Nothing." Val rose out of the chair, steadying herself before strolling on. She passed close to the young boy with the walkie-talkie and changed channels to the one most popular among toy devices. "Breaker One, this is Firecracker One," she said, and almost jumped out of her shoes when it echoed back to her from the kid's radio. "What's your handle, good buddy?"

"Um...Firecracker Two, good buddy," the kid said, a grin spreading across his face. "What are your orders, Firecracker One?"

"Change to channel nine and keep your ears open." Val switched to the police band while the kid fussed with his controls. When she heard emergency channel banter coming over the kid's speaker, she breathed easier. The announcement to evacuate would come first over that channel. She gave the boy a thumb's up and moved toward the shaded area to search for her father.

No dice. By the time she reached the trees, a buzz emerged from the crowd, and scattered clusters of picnickers began gathering up their belongings. Her tip to the kid was a mistake: the warning had already come out. Navigating the crowd would become much slower and more hazardous, particularly in her condition.

She turned around and headed toward the closest pedestrian bridge. More groups stood to leave, and many others added to the buzz surrounding a potential threat. She could no longer see over the crowd, and needed to fight against the tide to reach the running path that led to the bridge. She neared a set of food trucks and realized there'd be no safe way to evacuate those vendors, much less the massive crowd heading in multiple directions on foot.

Especially if the crowd panicked. And the moment the attack started, panic would be a near certainty.

Chapter Forty

A few minutes later, her father's voice cut through the din. "Valorie! Over here!"

Val spotted him near the short white picket fence by the beer garden, holding two plastic cups, one in each hand. She rushed toward him, and when she got close, she recognized the drinks as mojitos. "Dad! What are you doing with alcohol? Throw those away and get out of here!"

"Your mother bought them for you and Chad." Dad's lips hovered near one of the straws.

She grabbed the cups and tossed them into a garbage can. "Chad left, and—wait, you saw Mom?"

He nodded. "She headed that direction." He pointed at the pedestrian bridge. "Why is everyone leaving? The fireworks are about to start."

"There won't be any fireworks," she said. "You need to go. Now!"

"No fireworks?" He shook his head in confusion. "Why not?"

"Trust me. Please?"

"Wait, did you say they canceled the fireworks?" a man exiting the beer garden asked. "Why? Are you sure?"

"No, I'm not sure." Val's headache returned. She winced in pain.

"Valorie, are you all right?" Her father leaned closer and touched her head, close to the bruise. "You're injured."

Val jerked away from his touch. "I'll be fine, Dad. Please leave. How did you get here?"

"I took an Uber."

She checked her cell and cursed. With phones still down, rideshares weren't an option. "Go to the Founder's Statue. Chad will pick you up there. Hurry!" She shoved him in that general direction and hurried off toward the pedestrian bridge. The doctor had told her no exertion, and she'd already experienced enough symptoms to confirm a concussion. She walked at the fastest pace she dared, and her shadow faded from long and faint to nonexistent. Darkness was setting in. If the barge didn't get word, they'd be firing off a spectacular show of airborne explosives in a matter of minutes.

A crowd loomed ahead of her—people leaving the event early, the ones who got word and believed it. A major bottle-neck formed at the ramp to the bridge, bringing movement to a halt. She threaded through the throng as best she could, but her progress slowed to a crawl.

"Police!" She waved her badge. "Let me through!" With some pushing and shoving, some of it returned by an increasingly grumpy crowd, she forced her way to the front of the throng, about halfway across the river.

She glanced at the crowd behind her. If the explosion happened in the next few minutes, the people on the bridge would be sitting ducks, much closer to the barge than those still crowding the grassy riverbank.

Approaching the east side exit ramp, Val's breathing grew labored, and she stopped to rest, leaning on the guard-rail. From that vantage point, she had a clear view of the running path all the way to the pier. Lots of physical stuff, but few if any people. Most of the boat slips appeared empty. No doubt those craft had secured front-wave seats, so to speak, for the fireworks show on the water.

Still no sign of her mother and Sammy, and nothing on her radio about reinforcements.

She radioed in. "This is Officer Val Dawes. What's the status of adding backup on the pier? Over."

A male voice, not Gil's, responded. "Roger that, Dawes. We assigned that to East Precinct. We're, ah, having communications issues. We sent a unit out from downtown and another from Liberty Heights, but congestion has blocked both downtown bridges to auto traffic. How close are you?"

"Five or six hundred yards." Val resumed her quick pace up the path. "Any word on delaying or canceling the fireworks?"

"Not to my knowledge. That's the county Fire Marshall's call. Gotta love the bureaucracy, eh?"

Val gripped her radio tight in frustration. "What about boats?"

"What *about* boats?" Dispatch replied.

"Can't our backups find someone to ferry them across?"

After a long pause, Dispatch answered. "Checking on that. Good idea, Dawes."

"Thanks. Hey, where's Kryzinski?"

"Not sure. Want me to find out and get back to you?"

"Please." Val re-clipped the mic and quickened her step. Her breathing became difficult again, and she slowed down to normal walking speed.

She checked the time. Twelve minutes until the scheduled start of fireworks. She had time...she hoped.

***

Maggie parked the stolen electric car—more of a golf cart, really—against the curb nearest the pier. She gave silent thanks to the Parks Department for leaving the vehicle unattended back on the west side. That saved her a good ten or fifteen minutes, particularly with Sammy in tow. "Wasn't that fun?" she said, helping him down from the passenger side.

"Yeah! I never rode in a 'lectric car before," Sammy said. "Look, I see Daddy!" He ran toward the rotund, balding figure leaning against a post on the far side of the pier. Sweat drenched the sides of his white polo shirt from his armpits down to his khakis.

Maggie caught up with them at the end of their long hug. "Glad to see you could make it," she said to Mac. "Where did all the security guys go?"

He waved a hand. "Our boy let them go. For their safety."

"Damned idiot Mulroney! What if the authorities come? We have no defense!"

Mac chuckled. "First off, wrong boy. Nobody's heard from Mickey in hours. This was the work of our Special Agent in Charge. Second, do you think city cops would defend us against their own? We're better off with them gone."

Maggie's furor cooled. Mac, for once, was right. She knelt beside Sammy. "Please let Daddy take your backpack for a second."

"Why?" Sammy gripped both straps in tight fists. "It's mine!"

"Yeah, why? What's in there that—Oh, no you don't." Mac moved away from them. "I'm not pushing the button."

"Why not?" Maggie grabbed at the backpack. Sammy eluded her and ran across the pier, back to the electric cart. She cursed and started after him, then stopped to face Mac again. "Dammit, Mac. Someone's gotta do it. Why didn't you bring one of the crew, like I asked you?"

"They're all deployed elsewhere."

"One of the street girls, then?"

He scoffed. "They're running the diversionary op, remember? And it's not like I can go out looking for them. Not in the condition I'm in."

She fumed and indicated Sammy with a toss of her head. "We can't risk having *him* this close. What if something goes wrong?"

"Nothing will go wrong," Mac said. "Anyway, this is on you. We need to get a long distance away, and I'm a lot less mobile than you right now."

"Mac. Sammy can't be here, and he needs me. Come on, it has to be you."

"He needs *someone*," Mac said. "How about I'll bring him with me, you set the timer—"

"Mac." Maggie stepped up next to him, slid an arm around his waist. He stiffened and tried to pull away, but she grabbed his belt and tugged him close. "Your *condition* is why you ought to take the greater risk right now. Know what I mean?"

Mac wrinkled his nose at her, an expression of disgust. "You mean, I'm expendable."

She drew a steadying breath. "You said you have, what, two, three months, tops? Most of which will be in a hospital bed. So what if it's under prison guard? That's only if they catch you."

"If I stay here, all they'd catch is tiny bits of flying, bloody flesh."

Maggie brought her lips closer to his. "Don't be melodramatic."

"I'm being serious."

"In that case, think of Sammy. He needs one or both of us to survive this. At least, have a high chance—"

"No way." Mac threw her arm off his waist. "Besides, the rest of the operation depends on me. The troops are waiting on *my* orders. *I* signal the attack."

"The explosion signals the attack, and you know it. Your orders come into play only if that fails. You're Plan B, Mac. This," and she pointed to the barge, "is Plan A."

"So, execute your damned plan. You do your part, I'll do mine."

They glared at each other a moment, interrupted when the golf cart began rolling down the street. Sammy shrieked in laughter. "Mommy, Daddy, look!" he said. "I'm driving!"

Terrified, Maggie broke into a run. She'd never close the forty-yard gap between them in heels. "Stop, Sammy! Stop the cart!" she screamed.

"I don't know how!" Sammy's laughter turned into terrified shrieks. The cart veered onto the opposite sidewalk, then back across the street, into the path of oncoming head-lights—

Brakes squealed and tires screeched, rubber burning. The car skidded to a halt just in time. The cart did not, slamming into the front grille of the sedan with a loud *Bang!* Sammy's backpack slid from the passenger seat onto the ground and rolled to a stop against the car's front tire. The cart's motor choked to a halt, and the sedan's engine cut off as well.

"Sammy! Sammy! Are you all right?" In seconds, Maggie reached the wailing boy and scooped him into her arms. "Are you hurt anywhere?"

Sammy wrapped his arms tight around Maggie's neck. "My...tummy hurts," he said between sobs.

The driver of the car, a thirty-something man with dread-locks, jumped out of the car. "I'm so sorry, I didn't see him! Is he okay?"

Maggie whirled to face him. "You maniac! What the hell? You're gonna kill someone!"

"I—I didn't—"

Furious, Maggie set Sammy down and pulled a .22-caliber pistol from her purse. Of course the incident was Sammy's fault, and therefore hers, but she needed this guy gone. "Get out of here before I blow your fucking head off!"

The man's eyes widened. He scrambled back into the car and burned rubber getting out of there.

Maggie tried restarting the cart. No go. The best she could do was roll it, with much effort, to the side of the street. That done, she looked for Sammy—and found him next to Mac, holding his backpack.

"We got a problem, Mags," Mac said when she came close. He waved his walkie-talkie at her. "Cops are heading this way. Real ones, not our boys. We're out of time. We've got to get this done, and now."

Footsteps sounded on the pavement behind her. She turned to identify the source, and her heart fell.

Chapter Forty-One

Walking along the east side path, Val cursed the dizziness and nausea that slowed her pace. The day before, she'd run this entire three-mile loop in under eighteen minutes. It might take her half that long to walk the quarter-mile from the bridge to the pier.

On one side of her, the river flowed, and on it floated the fireworks barge, surrounded by a flotilla of small, private vessels. On the other side, a wall of dark, decaying buildings lined the path, interrupted by narrow streets connecting the running path to the area's transitional business district. Loud music emanated from a few of the clubs, attracting crowds uninterested in the family-style entertainment offered by the city's fireworks show.

Out of nowhere, tires squealed nearby, followed by a *Bang!* and loud voices. Sounded like a car accident. She should investigate.

Except she had higher priorities at that moment. Val trudged on.

Tires squealed again, and a car engine raced. She glanced down the alleyway that led into the Alphabet Soup district and saw it whiz by. Hit and run. She should call it in.

Except. Except.

Moments later, she rounded a bend, passing a clump of trees, and the pier came back into view. Not a cop in sight, nor any Coast Guard or even private security staff. Just three people: a tall, slender woman facing away from her, a large man, and a kid in shorts, clutching the man's leg.

Sammy!

Val recognized the woman, even from behind, fifty yards away, as her mother. And the man...

Him.

Despite the urgency of the situation, seeing Milt McCloskey stopped Val in her tracks.

The nausea she'd battled all afternoon and evening rose again, and this time she lost the war. Val dropped to her knees, and her insides emptied into the dirt and weeds lining the path. Val remained there for a solid minute, breathing hard and spitting hot bile, wishing she'd brought a bottle of water.

When the retching stopped, she rolled into a sitting position and wiped her mouth, then cleaned her hand as best she could on a patch of grass. Over the radio, Dispatch issued a Code 982 and ordered the Explosive Ordnance Disposal Team to the east side pier.

The *bomb* squad.

Then, a follow-up. A 10-22: *Disregard. False alarm.*

Val recognized the voice. Not Gil's, and not the officer she'd spoken to twenty minutes before. A haughty, commanding voice.

Special Agent Forrestal. Why would *he* be handling dispatch? Why would the FBI override—

She realized her mistake. Shelby was right. Agent Powers wasn't the mole. It was Forrestal, shutting down the city's response to the threat.

Nobody else would come. If Val didn't intervene in time, the attack would succeed. She had to make it. Had to.

She regained some strength and straightened up onto her knees so she could see the pier again. Rita—er, Maggie— and Milt continued their conversation. She couldn't decipher the words, but their voices sounded angry.

Their presence here made no sense. None at all.

Val couldn't distract herself with that. She needed to stop the attack, in whatever form it would take. Somehow.

She got back to her feet and, despite the headaches and nausea, she ran toward them, taking long, clumsy steps that echoed off the walls of the buildings beside her. She didn't get far before her mother turned toward her. Rita's face registered surprise, which made sense, as much as anything made sense right then. Then it changed, showing...what? Anger? No. Fear, perhaps? Shock?

"Val!" Sammy jumped up and down, clapping his hands. "Val's here, Daddy! Mommy, look!" He ran toward her. Maggie caught him by the shirt collar, and he tumbled to the ground, still in his mother's grip.

"Stay back, Valorie," Maggie said, and that didn't make any sense, either. "Turn around and go back to...wherever you go. Don't argue. Just go."

Val slowed to a walk and caught her breath. "Mother," she said, surprising herself that she didn't call her Rita. "It's not safe here. You...need to leave. And Sammy, and..." She pointed at Milt, but refused to make eye contact with him.

"You're the one who's in danger, Valorie," her mother said. "Didn't your little whack on the head today clue you in to that?"

Confusion clouded Val's thinking. "How...did you know...about that?" Dizziness overtook her again, and she stopped walking, bending over at the waist to keep from falling over.

Maggie laughed, a sound of genuine surprise. "A mother always knows. Sammy, settle down, please!" She pulled him up off the ground and brushed dirt from his shirt.

"Maggie," Milt said. "It's time."

"Mother," Val said, "there's a dangerous situation developing here. *We all have to clear out.*"

"You see?" Milt said. "I *told* you! We've got to make our move. *Now!*"

Val's head pounded again. She winced in pain, dropped to one knee, tried to shake off the dizziness. Sirens sounded in the distance. Backup would arrive soon, if they could fight through traffic.

Still, Milt's words didn't jive with what he *should* have said. Instead of saying, "we need to move," he said they should "make their move." Figure of speech, or...?

Her mother turned toward Milt. "Abort. There's no way to do this without undue risk to at least one of us."

"No way!" Milt moved toward Maggie. "Absolutely not. We've put too much into this."

Val stared at them, and a fresh wave of dizziness swept over her. "Put too much into *what*? What are you doing? Why are you even here?"

"See?" Maggie chuckled. "What did I tell you? She has no idea."

Val's radio announced an ominous statement. "Sensors at the pier are picking up a radio signal of some sort, very close to Ground Zero," Dispatch said. Not Gil, and not Forrestal. "We're guessing a transmitter of some kind."

"Fuck!" Milt said. "Maggie, it's time. If we plan to live through this," and he nodded toward Sammy, "and if we want to, say, continue being parents to this boy?" With that, he shot Val a baleful stare, then lunged for the boy.

But instead of grabbing Sammy, he snatched away his backpack, then shoved him back into Maggie's arms.

"What are you doing?" Maggie yelled at him. "You can't do it now. We're too close!" She spun Sammy by the shoulders to face Milt. "*He's* too close!"

Milt sneered. "You're the one who decided I'm expendable, that I should push the button. Well, I'm pushing it now. And you're going down with me." He laughed. "What is it you always say, Mags? *Sacrifices must be made.* Now it's your turn."

"Mac, wait. Think about this. You're really willing to sacrifice your own son? For what? A *job*?"

"A job?" Val said. "You're here because of a *job*?"

"What's the difference?" Milt said. "You're leaving me, and taking Sammy. I have so little time left. I won't spend it without you, Mags, and without him. I can't." He reached into the backpack and removed a black rectangular object, about the size of a cell phone.

Val's heart skipped a beat when she realized what the device was: a radio transmitter.

For blowing up the barge.

***

Val realized in that moment what they meant by the "job." She cursed herself for her blindness, for not seeing the obvious truth this whole time. Her mother and Milt planned the attack. They planted the bomb. Milt and her mother were about to kill or maim thousands of people, including Val and her nine-year-old brother that, until a few days ago, she didn't even know she had.

And she had no idea why they wanted to do this.

"What are you talking about?" Maggie said, continuing her argument with Milt. "I never said I would take him from you. Hell, I'd *rather* you keep him. But you said yourself. You're out of time."

"So are you." Milt poised his finger over the transmitter, and he glanced at Val. "So is *she.* And...all of us." His face grew sad. "Sammy boy, I'm sorry."

"Why are you sorry?" Sammy said. "You didn't do anything wrong."

Val climbed to her feet. Must. Stop. Him.

"How much time?" Maggie asked. "Once you press the button."

"The signal gets sent sixty seconds after," Milt said. "Then, instant detonation. Not enough time to get away."

Milt's finger remained a few inches above the device. He hadn't pressed the button yet. Val lurched toward him—

Her mother stepped in front of her, aiming a pistol at her chest. Ten or twelve feet away. Too far for Val to reach and disarm her. Too close to miss. "Stop, Valorie."

Val met her mother's gaze. Pure steel shone from her dark eyes. "Really, Mother? You'd shoot your own daughter?" She gestured at her little brother, clutching Rita's leg. "Would you kill Sammy, too?"

"Sammy's innocent. You..." Mom spit. "Tell me, daughter. What would you do to stop me? Would you sacrifice my life to save the lives of all those people over there?" She swept an arm toward the bridge, the boats in the water, and the crowded west-side Waterfront. "Tell me. I want to know."

"I'll..." Val swallowed. Her mother always could tell when she lied. "I'll do my job."

Mom scoffed. "Thought so. You're too far gone, Valorie. Such a believer in the all-powerful State, here to save us. You're brainwashed." She shook her head. "I didn't want to believe it, even as late as yesterday. But seeing you has changed my mind." She waved the gun at Val. "Back up. Slowly. Now."

"Pushing the button in five seconds," Milt said. "Count down with me. Five, four..."

"Three-two-one!" Sammy shouted, laughing. "Ready or not, here I come!" He let go of Mom and ran to Milt, slamming into him. The transmitter flew out of Milt's hand and clattered across the parking lot. Milt cursed and twisted his body around, searching for it. His legs got tangled up with Sammy's body, and he fell with a heavy *Oomph* onto the pavement.

"Sammy!" Val shouted. "Get the phone! Quick!"

"Shut up!" Mom stepped closer to Val. "Sammy, run somewhere safe. Run and hide!"

"Yay! Hide and seek!" Sammy laughed and ran in circles. "Who's It?"

"Sammy, wait," Val said. "Hide the backpack and win a big prize!"

"No!" Mom grabbed for him, but he eluded her grasp.

"I wanna win!" Sammy scooped up the transmitter, shoved it into his backpack, and zipped the device inside. "I win! I get a big prize!" He ran toward the water's edge.

"Don't just lie there, go with him!" Mom yelled at Milt.

"I...can't," Milt said. "I mighta pulled a hammy or something. Help me up."

"Oh, for God's sake." Maggie turned toward him. "Don't be so damned useless!"

Val saw her opening and took it. She dove at her mother, going low, staying under the gun's line of fire, and slammed into her knees. Maggie crashed to the ground with a loud grunt, Val landing on top of her. The gun skittered across the pavement, inches from Milt's outstretched hands.

Val untangled herself from her mother and stood. And...fell. The world spun around her, a feeling not unlike the Tilt-a-Whirl at the amusement park. With the same intense nausea that ride always gave her.

She lifted her head. Milt's hand stretched toward the pistol. So close. She couldn't let him get to it.

Finding strength from God-knows-where, Val crawled on hands and knees across the asphalt. Breathing hard. Belching. Aching.

Val reached for the pistol, missed. Milt's hand closed around the handle. He drew the gun in toward his body, aimed it at her. She lunged toward him, her hand reaching for his wrist as she fell.

Then her insides exploded again. Not, as she feared at first, from a gunshot wound. The other kind, the kind that plagued her all day, from the inside. Hot bile and vomit gushed out of her and onto Milt's face, into his open mouth and eyes.

He gagged, spit, swore, and rolled onto his stomach, with Val tumbling along for the ride. She couldn't reach his pistol hand, but she had other options. She raised her body into a crouch, jumped up, and landed on his back with both knees. His body slammed onto the pavement. Air whooshed out of his lungs, and a satisfying *crack* sounded from his ribcage. He screamed. Val pushed off of him, finally able to stand.

Milt rolled over, holding his ribs. His legs splayed out, providing an easy target. One that Val had waited ten years to destroy.

With all her might, she pulled back her leg, one that kicked countless soccer balls and cleared endless hurdles, and drove her toe hard into his crotch.

Val ignored his howls of pain and whirled around in search of her mother. She spotted her twenty yards away, running, gun in hand, more or less in the direction in which Sammy had disappeared.

Chapter Forty-Two

Maggie rounded the corner of the nearest small warehouse building and leaned against it, breathing hard. She listened for telltale signs of the ongoing scrape between Mac and Valorie—or, failing that, footsteps. Mac's continued howls of pain told her the fight would soon come to a close, and, no surprise, her martial-arts-trained daughter would emerge triumphant.

She checked the pistol in her hand and discovered the safety still on. The whole frigging time. Rookie mistake. She shoved the gun into her purse.

Maggie needed to find Sammy before Valorie did, and she'd gotten off to a lousy start. She'd chosen the wrong building, and moving to any of the others would expose her. She couldn't outrun Valorie. Hell, she couldn't outrun Sammy. Where did he go?

Footsteps approached—not Milt's. A woman's. Valorie's. Time to move. She crept along the rear of the warehouse, a small rectangle with ribbed sheet-metal siding, and reached a door. Tried it. Locked. Crap.

Maggie continued to the end and turned the corner. More wall, and this time, no door. Not even a window. Exposed to the running path, not the parking lot or the water.

Still no Sammy, and no detonator.

She felt bad for abandoning Mac. If she'd stayed, though, Valorie would've subdued her, too, and the entire plan would fail. Which could not happen. Mac was right: aborting was not an option. They'd all go to prison for life. Which for Mac meant only a few months, but still. Not for her.

Poor Mac. Maggie doubted he'd get away at this point. So he *would* go to prison. Not Maggie, though. And unless he operated the detonator...well, that made him dead weight. Yes, expendable.

Valorie wouldn't give up. She'd sacrifice her own life if necessary to stop the attack. That saddened her, yet also made her proud. Her daughter stood for something. A stupid cause, of course. The tyranny of the state, and its power to crush freedom-loving citizens, like herself and Mac. At least she believed in it, and fought for it. Took bold risks. She respected that.

Not enough to let her win or to put them all in prison...or worse. But still.

Engines revved nearby. Not cars or trucks, though. It came from the river. Boats! The flotilla surrounding the barge started to float upstream. Why? Were they leaving? Maggie checked her watch. The show should have begun already. Was the barge moving too? Or was the show canceled?

She crept back to the corner of the warehouse and peeked out at the river. The barge remained in place, but a tugboat approached it. Of course! Barges don't move on their own. But the tug would get there soon. If it reached the barge before they detonated, it might push the damned thing out of range.

Or...back to the pier...closer to her!

Voices drifted in over the sound of the engines. Valorie's and Sammy's, from behind another building, closer to the water. Dammit! Valorie found him first.

A gangway led from the deck around each side of the structure. A walkway with no rails continued around the back, toward the water, near some vacant boat slips. The slips would soon fill with returning, disappointed fireworks show-goers. A means of escape for Valorie, Sammy, and the detonator.

Time to move.

***

The roar of engines echoed over the water, drawing Val's attention. Boats on the move. She ought to know what that signified, but she couldn't suss that out in her condition. Stay focused, girl. Where did Sammy go?

Something slammed into her from behind. Her knees buckled under her, and she pitched forward. She stopped her face from slamming the pavement with outstretched palms, at the cost of some painful road rash. A large body—Milt's—landed on top of her, his hands groping for purchase, and landing in inappropriate places.

"You're all grown up now," he grunted in her ear, his breath rancid. "Shall we finish what we started ten years ago, darling?"

Enraged, she tore his hand from her breast and crushed his fingers in hers. "We didn't start anything, asshole." Val swung her elbow backward, clubbing his nose and eliciting a satisfying *Crack!* He screamed and let go. She bucked him off of her and rolled to her feet.

Milt stood a few yards away, holding his nose, now gushing blood. "You bitch!" He lunged at her. Val dodged him and, capitalizing on his momentum, tripped him to the ground. He landed hard, head-first. He rolled onto his back, tried to sit up. She kicked him in the throat. His head pounded the pavement again. Milt's eyes glazed, then, moments later, fluttered shut.

Val glared at him, catching her breath. The entire fight took maybe half a minute, but those seconds seemed precious, with Maggie chasing after Sammy and the detonator. At least with Milt out cold for now, she'd only have to worry about one nemesis.

She refocused and tried to think like a nine-year-old: where would Sammy hide? He'd keep it simple, ducking behind one of the buildings.

Val stumbled off toward the water. One of the larger buildings had a walkway all around it, newish, made of those fake wooden planks popular on patio decks. Sammy would prefer that over the older, scary-looking wooden decks. She would've, anyway, at nine. She veered off in that direction, opted to take the long way around, figuring he went the short way. He'd be looking back the way he came, so she could approach him from behind, surprise him. Also, it led her away from the direction her well-armed mother had gone.

She rounded the rear edge of the building, and sure enough, Sammy stood at the far end, peeking around the corner. She crept toward him, appreciative of the solid construction of the deck. No creaking, no loose boards to rattle. She drew within twenty feet, then ten. Five—

Sammy turned, saw her, and yelled. "Aah!" Then he laughed. "I found you first! I win!" He wrapped his arms around Val and squeezed. "That was fun! Do you want to hide now and I find you?"

"I think we should celebrate you winning," Val said with a big smile. "You're the champion!"

"I should get a prize! A big one!"

"Okay." Val walked him toward the far end of the building. "Let's keep our voices down, though, okay? Your mom hasn't found you yet. You don't want to give your hiding place away, do you?"

"Okay," he whispered. "What's my prize?"

Val shot a glance over her shoulder. No sign of her mother. "How about a nice big ice cream cone?"

"No!" Sammy laughed. So much for quiet. "I want a phone!"

"A phone? Why a phone?"

"My mom won't let me have one. But I won, so I should get one. Like the one in my backpack!"

"That's not a very good phone. How about we get you a nice one at the store?"

"No!" he shouted. "You think I'm stupid. I'm not stupid. I want this phone and you can't take it from me!" He ran down a ramp leading to some vacant boat slips.

Val panicked. The deck there lacked any sort of handrail. He might fall in, and she didn't know if he could swim. She chased after him. After a few head-pounding steps, she had to stop.

Sammy sat on the edge of a boat slip, holding the detonator in his hands, examining it with a puzzled expression. "How do you turn it on?"

Val stumbled to her feet, took slow, plodding steps. Must reach him before he pushed any buttons of consequence.

Something blurred by her. No, not something—some*one*. Her mother reached him, grabbing the device from his hands. Sammy wailed in protest and grabbed at it, but she held it out of his reach. "Settle down!" Maggie said. "Mommy has to work!"

Val forced herself to take steps toward them. Maggie looked up and drew her pistol from her purse. "Stop, Valorie. Don't take another step."

Val stopped, considered sitting. Didn't. "You won't shoot me." She took another step.

Rita's eyes grew wide. "Stop right now! Don't test me, daughter. I will pull this trigger."

Val willed her foot to step forward. Paused. Took a second step.

"Last chance! I'm warning you!"

Val lifted her foot—

A shot rang out, and a gash appeared in the decking a foot away from her, plastic splinters flying everywhere. Sammy screamed, his hands over his ears.

"Another way that we're not alike. You're a terrible shot." Val set her foot down a half-yard forward, paused. Ten, maybe fifteen feet separated them.

"I get better, the closer you get." Rita's hand shook, and with the other hand holding the transmitter, she couldn't use it to stabilize her aim. The roar of boat engines grew louder.

"We'll see." Another step.

Sammy, crouching next to Maggie, suddenly leaped high in the air, his hand reaching for the transmitter. He missed, but his leap and her evasion forced Maggie to take her eyes off Val.

Val summoned her last ounce of strength and ran at her mother. She reached for the pistol, instead grabbed a handful of flesh, just below the wrist.

Mom struggled to free Val's hand, failed. She swung her other hand, smacking Val's chin with the transmitter. The device fell to the ground. Sammy scooted away toward the warehouse.

Val gripped Rita's gun hand with both of hers, twisting and bending her mother's arm backward. Her mother held on. Another shot fired, this one into the air. The loud report hurt Val's ears, and her head pounded. Her resistance faded, and her mother punched her in the side with her free hand. It hurt like hell. Maggie hit her again, and Val struggled to hold on.

Val's anger and frustration mounted. While her mother stood a good three or four inches taller, Val always stayed in top physical shape. If not for her concussion, she would have had no trouble overpowering her.

Another punch to the midsection, and Val would have vomited, except she'd emptied her system onto Milt. She should hit back, use her martial arts skills.

Her mother's gun hand shook free. The nuzzle pressed against Val's neck. She grabbed at it, squirmed away, as the roar of the boats seemed to envelop them—

A *thud* sounded, something hard hitting flesh. Her mother cursed and stumbled backwards, waving her arms...and fell, screaming, into the water.

A speedboat splashed to a halt. A man holding a metal crutch like a baseball bat stood on the edge of the boat, panting.

"Gil," she said. "I thought you'd *never* get here."

"When you said 'send backups,' I assumed you meant me," he said, grinning. His smile faded a moment later. "Where's the detonator?"

Val's head swiveled, first on the deck, then to the walkway, where Sammy sat, fiddling with a black device the size and shape of a cell phone.

***

Splashing reminded them that Val's mother remained in the river. She thrashed about, bouncing above and below the surface of the water. "Help!" she said on one of her above-surface bounces. "I can't swim!"

"We'll get her," Gil shouted from the boat. "You get the device!"

Val ran a few steps, then almost collapsed again, and settled for a brisk walk over to her brother. "Sammy," she said, "if you give me that phone, I promise to get you a better one. Here." She offered her own cell phone. "You can use mine until then."

Sammy pouted a moment, then held the device out to Val. "I can't get it to work anyway."

Val traded her phone for the transmitter. A robotic voice sounded from its speaker, nearly causing her to drop it. "Twenty seconds," it said.

She checked the display. 00:19, it read. 00:18.

Shit! He'd somehow pressed whatever button set the damned timer in motion. It had two on each side and one on the top edge. "Sammy, which button did you press?"

"All of them," he said, playing with Val's phone.

"Which one did you press to make it start counting?"

He shrugged. "I don't know."

"Ten seconds," said the robotic voice.

Val pressed all the buttons. Eight seconds. Seven.

She set the device on the deck and stomped on it.

"Five seconds," the machine said. "Four..."

Val raced to the edge of the deck, finding speed within her somehow, and heaved the transmitter into the river, as far from the barge as she could. As it flew, the robotic voice continued counting: "Three, two..."

The slender device knifed into the water, disappearing from view.

Val waited. One second passed. Two. Three...

A loud blast erupted overhead, and the sky lit up with bright colors. Red, white, and blue streams emanated from a series of explosions in the sky. Across the river, the crowd broke into a loud cheer.

Fireworks.

Just fireworks.

"Got her!" Two men in the speedboat—Gil and a balding man in a dark suit—pulled a sputtering, coughing Maggie from the water. Val's partner, Bobby Grimes, waved to her, as did the boat's pilot, a short Asian woman Val recognized as Agent Powers.

"Happy Fourth of July," Gil deadpanned, and the speedboat motored to a halt next to the deck.

Chapter Forty-Three

The fireworks continued, even as a small fleet of speedboats ferried members of the Clayton PD to the barge. Several minutes later, they deboarded, carrying a package about the size of a bushel basket, and they carted a few men off in handcuffs.

"So, tell me," Gil said, sitting next to her and Sammy on the pier, his arm around her waist. "How did you know that throwing the device in the water would disable it? I would have guessed it to be waterproof."

"Physics 101," Val said. "It's a radio transmitter. Radio waves don't travel underwater. That's why they use things like sonar on submarines. I gambled that the actual detonation signal wouldn't transmit until the timer completed its countdown."

"It's amazing you could remember that in your condition," he said. "I couldn't, and all my faculties are intact."

"Debatable," she said with a sly grin. "Question for you, now. Why didn't you shoot her?"

"With you two tangled up like that, and with us in a moving boat, we couldn't get a clear shot." Gil hefted one of his crutches. "Lucky for us, I brought along ol' trusty here. Of course, I only needed them because I overdid it yesterday and could barely walk this morning. Besides," he went on, grinning, "killing your mother might be the worst way to begin a new relationship."

"She'll live," Grimes announced behind them. They turned in time to see paramedics load Maggie into an ambulance. "In fact, she's in much better shape than her husband. What happened to him? You and he get into a family squabble, Dawes?"

"He's not my family," Val said between clenched teeth.

"Are you talking about my mom and dad?" Sammy said, looking up from Val's cell phone.

Seeing the apprehension on his face, Val regretted her tone. "Your mom and dad are going to the hospital to get checked by a doctor."

"Can I go too?" Sammy said. "Sick people like having company."

"Sure."

"Will you take me?" Sammy asked.

Val struggled to answer. She hadn't even thought about visiting her mother in the hospital. Sadness weighed on her, as well as exhaustion, and her headache returned with a vengeance.

She made up her mind. "Bobby, can you find someone to drive us?"

"On it," Grimes said. "Quick question. Do you want this collar? You've earned it, but I'd understand, either way."

"All yours—no, wait. Tell you what," she said. "You book *her*. I want McCloskey's. I'll swing by later to do the paperwork."

"Deal." He hustled off.

"Can we watch the rest of the fireworks first?" Sammy said.

Val laughed. "You betcha."

Sammy clapped his hands. "Yay! You are the best big sister ever." He wrapped his arms around her legs, squeezing hard.

She gazed down at him. Hard to imagine such an innocent child being raised by the likes of Maggie and Milt.

Maggie had raised her, too. As difficult as it was to reconcile sometimes, the little boy hugging her was her younger brother.

Val hugged him back, as tight as she dared. What a family.

***

Val, Gil, and Sammy arrived at the hospital an hour later. On the ride over, Val noticed that cell service had returned to normal. She called her brother, who met her outside their mother's room.

"Can we see her?" Chad asked the attending nurse.

"Seriously?" Val said. "After all this?"

"She's still our mother," Chad said. "You should, too."

"We'll see." At that moment, Val couldn't imagine seeing her mother and not strangling her.

Val rested in the waiting area for a short while, enough to take the edge off her headache. When the nurse allowed Chad to bring Sammy in for a brief visit with Mom, Val got checked again, and the doctor confirmed the diagnosis of a moderate-to-severe concussion. "Go home," he insisted. "Doctor's orders."

"I will, I promise," she said to Gil after filling him in. "Chad's right, though. I need to at least try to talk to my mother."

She arrived back at her mother's hospital room moments after Chad exited, shaken, tugging Sammy along by the hand.

"They gave her a painkiller, and she's a little out of it," Chad said. "Val, I've never seen her like this. She looks...I don't know, *broken.*"

"He didn't hit her that hard." Val rolled her eyes. But a sedated Maggie was welcome news if it loosened her tongue a bit.

"Yeah, well, she's not herself right now," Chad said. "She says she doesn't want to see you. You might want to wait a few—"

"It's not up to her this time." Val brushed past him, not looking back. She found her mother propped up in her bed, with an IV drip hooked to her arm.

Mom cast Val a withering stare and turned away from her. "I guess you didn't get the message," she said, her voice a bit slurred.

"I got all the message I needed on that pier," Val said, "when you fired your pistol at me, and then tried to blow us all up. Along with a few thousand other innocent people."

"Innocent? Bullshit." Mom faced Val again. "Coming from you, of all people. You with your guns and uniforms. You, Valorie, have blood on your hands. The blood of patriots. Oh, yes, I heard all about what you've done."

Val flashed with anger, then recalled the sight of the man she'd shot the weekend before, bleeding and screaming on the floor. Her nausea returned, and she sat in the guest chair next to the bed. "That was in self-defense—"

"Self-defense? How?" Maggie said, snarling. "You and your little army invaded private property, armed to the teeth, and opened fire on a group of men—for what? Exercising their freedom of speech?"

"For breaking the law." Val's voice rose. "For trafficking the lives of underage girls, selling them into slavery—"

"They did nothing you didn't do at the same age," Mom said. "Using your youthful body to lure good men into what we all know is their fatal weakness, their desire for sex—"

"For God's sake, mother! I did *not* 'lure' Milt into bed with me. He *raped* me, overpowering me in my own bed—"

"Liar!" Mom swung an open palm at Val's face, which Val dodged with ease. "He would never do such a thing!"

"Oh, please, shut up!" Val shouted at her. "Keep your delusions to yourself. Oh, why did I even bother trying to reach out to you here? Screw it. You're both going to prison, and good riddance!" She stood and marched toward the door, then whirled around to face her mother again. "I don't even understand why you came back here. What were you thinking, that we'd somehow pick up where we left off as a family?"

Rita's face registered surprise, and she burst into laughter.

"What's so damned funny?" Val said.

"You think I came here for *you?*" Mom laughed again, wiping tears from her eyes. "Oh, that's a good one."

Val gritted her teeth, counted to five. "Not me, per se. The family. Chad, Ali, Dar..."

Her mother's bemused expression stopped her. "Okay, Mother. Why did you come back? Please explain it to me. Was it this stupid job you and Milt talked about?"

Mom coughed into her fist. "Why don't you find me a cigarette?"

"You can't smoke in a hospital!"

"Why the hell not? They're my lungs!"

"And the lungs of a lot of other people! There are rules, Mother, and they apply to everyone—including you."

Mom pointed a finger at Val. "See? This is how we're different, Valorie. You're all about what we can't do—what the *government* says we can't do. But you'll use your guns to make sure nobody can break *your* stupid little rules. Mac and I, we're all about what we *can* do—what we should all be free to do. *That's* why we came back to Clayton, my dear. Because our country needed us."

"Needed you to do what? Kill people?"

"Whatever was necessary to take back this country, from the immigrant mob and their socialist apologists in government. To restore this country to—"

"Spare me the pseudo-patriotic, libertarian bullshit," Val said. "How is blowing up a fireworks barge 'liberating' people, other than freeing their bodies from their souls? How is killing children and tourists helping Clayton? Come on, Mom. Educate me." She stood with her back leaning against the closed door, arms crossed, eyes burning a hole in Rita's skull.

"The barge wasn't the point." Mom kept her tone light, as if discussing the weather. "Or at least, not the main point. Yes, we wanted to put on a show, to wake people up about their performative pseudo-patriotism. To remind them that freedom is won with blood, not with pretty fireworks shows. But that wasn't the primary target."

Val waited. No further explanation seemed forthcoming. "Okay, I'll bite. What was?"

Mom smiled. "The fascists-in-arms, defending the government and its tyranny over the people. With the police and military preoccupied—"

"The police?" Val pushed away from the door, advancing on her mother's bedside. "You mean me?"

Rita's smile deepened, her eyes showing no mirth. "Yes, my dear. You. All the people like you. Like your uncle, whom you view as a hero. Trust me, daughter. Valentin was no hero, and neither are you."

Val fell back, as if punched, and steadied herself with one hand against the wall. Her head swam with the preposterousness of her mother's claim. "What...what are you saying?"

Mom rolled her eyes. "I'm saying that when the armed forces of the government bring their guns to a knife fight, the people have a right—no, a duty—to respond in kind. That the aggressors—you, your uncle—are not heroes when they pick those fights, win or lose." She turned away again, this time rolling onto her side and covering her head with a pillow.

Stunned, Val backed away from her until she bumped into the door. Then she fumbled with the door handle and stumbled into the hallway.

"What's up?" Gil said, standing nearby on his crutches. "You look like you've seen a ghost."

Val rushed to him, holding him close. "Not a ghost, per se. Safe to say, though, the mother I once loved—and thought I knew—is dead. The woman in there..." She glanced toward Rita's hospital room. "Her soul left her long, long ago."

Dizziness and grief swept over her, and she held onto Gil until the feelings passed.

***

Back in her father's kitchen later that evening, Val filed a preliminary arrest report for Milt for conspiracy, attempted murder, and illegal transport of explosives across state lines. She considered adding the ten-year-old rape charge, as Connecticut had no statute of limitations for underage rape. But she knew it would get dropped, which infuriated her.

On the other hand, she expected that Agent Powers would add a slew of federal charges. In the meantime, Val's filing would ensure that he stayed in custody. Once word got out that he'd raped a young girl, his fellow inmates would provide prison justice, of sorts. At least, if she could believe her more experienced colleagues' rumors to that effect.

Grimes called as she finished up. "Good news. Milt McCloskey ratted out Forrestal and Mulroney—and a host of other perps, all over the East Coast."

"Sex traffickers?" Val asked.

"That, and a vast network of nut-right conspirators, planning more extensive attacks," Grimes said. "The blowing up of our barge? That was the real 'signal' you and Shelby found. Other groups were primed to stage greater attacks on strategic sites—including a return to our now-undefended Armory."

Val considered that, but still harbored doubts. "You'll want to verify all of that. McCloskey's a liar who'd say anything to save his own ass."

"We will," Grimes said. "Starting with Forrestal. He's in jail, and we're putting the fear of God in him. Mulroney's on the run, but we'll find him. Mickey better hope it isn't me that catches his fat ass."

"How will you do that?"

"Follow the money. And there's always money involved."

"Check with Shelby," Val said. "She's a whiz at all this dark web, cryptocurrency stuff."

"Already have," Grimes said. "Get some sleep—and I mean, from now until Monday. I don't care what Petroni says."

Val hung up and turned off her phone. She wrapped Gil in her arms. "Let's head to your place. I don't want any more interruptions."

"Agreed," he said, and held her close.

Before their rideshare arrived, Chad dropped off her father, who'd stayed at their hotel room all evening. After a round of tearful hugs, Dad excused himself to go to bed.

"Can we talk a minute?" Chad said to Val.

Gil scowled. "One minute, no more. Your sister needs rest."

"Sammy's going to stay with us at the hotel tonight," Chad said. "Val, we need to talk about what happens to him, and soon. He's about to lose both of his parents, for all intents and purposes."

Val squeezed Gil's hand. "Not tonight. I'm in no condition."

"Understood," Chad said. "He can stay with us until we sort all this out."

"That could take a while," Gil said.

"What about Kendra?" Val asked. "How does she feel about all this?"

"She says she's cool with it," Chad said, "but we have a lot to work out."

The Uber arrived, and they all walked out together. Chad stopped them before they got in and held Val's arms. "Val, I just want to say I'm sorry. You were right about Mom all this time. I was so blind, because, well, she's our mother, you know? Biologically, and in other ways, she's still a part of who we are, like it or not." After a long, awkward silence, he got into his car and drove off.

Getting into their Uber, Val pondered Chad's parting words. She wondered which parts of her she'd inherited from Rita.

She didn't like the answers that came to mind.

Friday, July 5, 2019

Chapter Forty-Four

Val woke in Gil's bed to the smell of fresh coffee and sweetbread and the faint, off-key humming of some classic rock tune. Bright light filled the room through sheer curtains, not quite closed.

She sat up, testing her body for dizziness, headaches, and nausea. None. No blurry vision, either. In fact, she felt great. She pulled on a pair of jeans and padded out to the kitchen.

"Lunch is ready." Gil stood at the stove, spatula in hand, wearing an apron over a T-shirt and loose-fitting shorts. The outfit showed off his muscular physique, but the frilly apron made her laugh.

"Keep laughing and you'll be eating leftover Taco Bell instead of my patented banana pancakes," he said. "Coffee?"

Val sidled up to him and wrapped her arms around him, breathing in his scent. A little musky, in a good way. "If you *don't* give me coffee," she said, "I'm going to join Patriots Pride and help them blow up your house. What time is it, anyway?"

"11:30." He added with a grin, "A.M."

"I slept for thirteen hours?" Val pulled two coffee mugs from the cupboard and filled them.

"Another hour and I would've called 9-1-1, or the morgue. You are one talented sleeper, my dear."

She stirred cream into their coffees and sipped hers. Mmm. "I could sleep thirteen more. I hope that's not a bad sign."

"Doc said to watch out for that." His expression turned

serious. "Overall, rest is a good thing. How are you feeling? Not just physically. I mean, everything—your mom returning, all of it."

Val reflected a moment, taking a long sip of coffee. "Relieved. Like a giant weight's been lifted off my shoulders."

"How so?" Gil brought the pancakes to the table and set out plates and silverware.

"For years," Val said, words catching up to her thoughts as she spoke, "I thought I hated my mother. Leaving us when she did, and how she did it—I didn't understand. Mostly, I didn't understand why."

"Learning her reasons helped?" Gil's eyebrows rose. He filled their plates and sat across from her. "Shacking up with Milt?"

"Yes, because now I know it wasn't my fault." Val poured syrup onto her plate. "Then, yesterday, when we fought, I learned something else. Something important."

"I'm listening." Gil waited, fork in hand.

Val dipped a chunk of pancake into a pool of maple syrup, swirling it around to soak up maximum sweetness. "I learned I didn't hate my mother after all. When push literally came to shove on that pier, I couldn't hurt her—even in self-defense. Something inside wouldn't let me do it."

"You had no problem hurting Milt McCloskey," Gil said with a smile.

"Nope. Not one bit. Him, I *do* hate." She paused, thinking. "With my mother, it was anger—at someone I once loved. There's an enormous difference." She stuffed the syrup-soaked wedge of banana pancake in her mouth and savored its sweetness. So unhealthy, and so good.

"How does that help?" He dug into his food.

"It's liberating." Val prepared another bite of pancake for its syrup bath. "For years, I didn't trust my emotions. I believed love would always, inevitably turn to sadness and hate. I think that kept me from opening up my heart to others." Her vision blurred, and she blinked away tears. "Kept me from trusting myself in love."

"And now?" Gil rested his hand on hers.

"Now," she said with a sad smile, "I'm on the road to trusting myself again." She leaned across and kissed him, tasting the sweetness on his lips. "Yum. Can I have you for breakfast?"

He laughed and kissed her back.

They devoured the pancakes along with slices of pineapple, and her healthy appetite was a good sign, Gil said. Despite the coffee, the heavy dose of carbs made her drowsy again, and she lay back down to rest after lunch, this time sleeping fitfully.

Her phone vibrated on the bedside table late in the afternoon, and she checked her messages. Her father had left a few, wondering how she was. She found Gil in front of the TV.

"Ready for that steak dinner and massage I promised you?" he said, standing.

"More than you know. But I need to go to my dad's," she said. "He's worried about me. Also, I need a change of clothes and a shower. Or that hot bath you also promised me." Val paused a moment. "Gil, weren't you supposed to work today?"

He nodded. "I took a personal day. No way I was leaving you alone." He tossed her his car keys. "Let's go. Maybe we should pick up some dinner on the way, and have that steak tomorrow instead?"

"Steak I can wait on," she said, "but I'm not forgetting about that massage."

They picked up enough takeout Chinese food to feed the entire neighborhood, as everything sounded delicious to Val and she couldn't choose. That turned out to be fortuitous, as

Chad was there already, talking to Dad in the living room.

"I'm so glad you're okay," Dad said, wrapping her in a tight embrace. Too tight. Dad had never been the best hugger, due to a lack of practice. "I've been worried sick about you."

"We've been discussing the Sammy situation," Chad said after they all dove into the various scrumptious dishes Gil and Val had brought.

"What Sammy situation?" Val asked.

Dad set down his chopsticks, his face glum. "There's a strong possibility that the state may try to step in."

"No way a stranger is raising my brother," Chad said, slamming the Szechuan chicken container onto the coffee table.

"Agreed," Val said around a mouthful of tangy broccoli with beef. "So, what are the options?"

"We don't know," Chad said. "The best option for now is for him to stay with us until they make an official determination. Having said that..." He drew in a deep breath, held it. "We need some help from you."

Val hesitated, catching Gil's eye. He gave her a solemn yet encouraging nod. She swallowed hard and set down her kung pao. "What kind of help? Financial? I'd be happy to pitch in, but on a rookie cop's salary—"

"Sammy wants to get to know you, too," Dad said. "He's joined Ali's superhero worship club, and you're the designated superhero."

"He wanted to live with you," Chad said, "although we didn't expect you'd be up for that. We're thinking maybe spending a weekend or two a month with you?"

"I'd love that!" Val said. "I, um, need to chat with Gil first—"

"I'm on board," Gil said. "I'll help any way I can."

"Awesome!" Val said, relieved. They discussed the details and decided that Sammy's visits would also include time with Dad when possible—and they'd arrange similar visits for Ali.

"There's something else I want to discuss with both of you," Dad said once they wrapped up the Sammy plan. He swapped out his orange chicken for Val's kung pao and took a bite, then set it down and clasped his hands together. "I apologize for keeping you isolated from your mother all these years. As you discovered, she tried to stay in contact. She sent letters, tried calling, even sent Christmas gifts one year."

"Hey!" Chad said in mock indignation. "I *needed* a pair of underwear that year!"

Val laughed. So true. Mom *always* gave them undies and socks at Christmas. *Always.*

"I'm being serious," Dad said. "At the beginning, I think I *was* right to keep her from you. Once you came of age, though, I should've let you decide for yourself. I got all caught up in what I thought was right, and...well, you and I weren't on good speaking terms, anyway."

Val gave thought to his words. Dad was right, of course. Plus, he spent most of the past ten years plastered on booze and what-not. Even if he'd said something, she might not have believed him.

"I let my anger at her interfere with your relationship with her," Dad continued. "I can only wonder if what I did helped set her on this path she's on now..." His voice broke and trailed off.

"Don't blame yourself," Val said. "Remember what you told me last weekend? She was always kind of wacko in her politics."

"Still. It was wrong of me. I'm very sorry."

"Thank you, Dad," Chad said. "Apology accepted. I appreciate how hard it must be to say that."

"Ditto," Val said. "Although I'm not as sure that we needed to stay in touch, considering how she turned out."

"Uh, yeah. There's another element to all this." Dad took another deep breath. "I knew she'd taken up with Milt McCloskey, and by then, I knew he was...not a good guy." He paused. "Val, I wish I'd listened to you about him. In fact, I found out years later from mutual acquaintances that he was a suspected sex offender." Tears flowed down both cheeks and he wiped them away with his bare hand. "I knew then he had hurt you, Val, and..." He stopped and choked out a loud sob, covering his face with his hands. "I...didn't want him around either of you. So I thought it best to make it a clean break, and...I'm so sorry." Sobs wracked his body and echoed in the silent room.

Val ached to see him in such pain. All this time, she'd interpreted his distance from her as him blaming her for breaking up their marriage. Even a week before, she'd ascribed selfish motives to him for hiding the letters. To learn now that he'd done it all to protect her and Chad broke her heart.

She left her seat and knelt by her father, one hand on his arm. "Dad, you had a tough choice to make. I think you made the right one, and I thank you for it." Behind her back, she crossed her fingers for Chad's and Gil's benefit, and hoped her father wouldn't catch her in this little white lie.

"Me too," Chad said, wrapping an arm around Dad from the other side. They remained in that awkward position, tears flowing on every face—including Gil's, seated a few feet away—until long after their food went cold.

***

"What a night," Gil said on the drive back to his house.

"Never a dull moment in the Dawes family," Val said.

"For what it's worth, I think you guys came to the right answer regarding Sammy."

"Thanks to you," Val said. "You jumped in at the exact right moment with that neutral outsider perspective and helped us navigate a tough discussion."

"Glad to help. By the way, Grimes passed on some news while you slept the day away. That guy Milt? Acute liver failure. He has months, maybe weeks, to live."

"So, he'll likely die in jail, before he even goes to trial," Val said. "I don't know how I feel about that."

"I do. It sucks. I hoped to attend his execution."

Val's eyes widened.

"Kidding," Gil said. "Actually, I wanted to chop his balls off with a rusty spoon and watch him writhe in pain. But they've outlawed that in Connecticut."

"You're worse than Travis with your ghoulish humor," Val said, but she laughed along with him.

She pulled into Gil's driveway and offered to help him inside. He waved her off. "My hip's better," he said, and proved it by carrying his crutches instead of walking with them.

"It's good to be home," she said once they got inside, then realized her error and covered her mouth. "Oops, I mean—"

"My home is your home." Gil took her into his arms. "Anytime, all the time."

Val rested her head on his shoulder. "About that. Gil, I didn't want to say this earlier, but...I can't live at my dad's house. It's too weird. I mean, he needs me for now, especially with Sammy coming to live there. Once Chad moves back and can help keep an eye on him, though, I'm going to need my own place. Is that awful of me?" She looked up into his eyes, which smiled down at her.

"Your own place is a fine idea. Or, like I said. *Mi casa es tu casa, Señorita.*" He kissed her forehead. "No rush, but that invitation remains open, and will until you wise up and say yes."

Val's heart pounded. "That's a very intriguing suggestion. Are you sure?"

"I'm sure," he said. "Val, for me, you're The One. I've known for much longer than I care to admit. So, yes. One hundred percent sure."

"But we haven't even..." She swallowed. "Slept together."

"Again, no rush," he said.

Val smiled, kissed him. Relished the excitement that built inside her every time they touched. That had come so close to erupting a few days before, when their mutual touch grew intimate.

How she wanted it to feel. How she imagined it could feel.

"So much for *long term* plans. As for the short term, as in, this evening..." Val let the words dangle, spun on her heel, and drifted toward the bedroom. Pulled off her shirt, her shorts, and her bra along the way. She stopped at the bedroom door and turned back to face him. He'd followed her, stripping off his own shirt and pants, and stood an arm's length away. A sheen of sweat reflected in the dim light off his muscular chest.

Val slipped her hand into the waistband of Gil's boxers and slid them over his hips. They fell to the floor. Her underwear landed on top of his.

Val met his gaze. Shivered, despite the heat. His lip quivered as well. Their bodies drifted closer, inches apart. Heat from his body warmed her skin.

"Third base again?" Gil said in a quiet voice.

Val smiled, took his hand. She reddened, wanting to say it, but not sure how. Then it struck her. "I don't do sports analogies. But I'm thinking, in honor of the holiday...fireworks?"

Gil smiled, and Val led him by the hand into the bedroom.

From The Author

Thank you for reading *Mother of Valor*. If you enjoyed reading it, won't you please take a moment to leave me a review at your favorite retailer? And please, tell your friends!

Questions to consider when posting a review:

What made me first decide to read this book was...

As I started reading, the first thing that drew me into this book was...

What I liked most about the main character was...

What I liked most about the plot was...

What I liked most about the author's writing style was...

My favorite part of the story was...

Compared to other books in this genre, this book was...

__ Among the best __ Better than most

__ About average __ Not as good __ Among the worst

I would / would not recommend this book to a friend because...

ACKNOWLEDGMENTS

One of the most common questions asked of authors is, "Is this autobiographical?"

It most certainly is not. But it is very much drawn from events of the world around us.

Mother of Valor originated fully in the projected experiences of the main character. Which is a fancy way of saying, once I'd finished *A Better Part of Valor*, "What's next for Val?"

Val's family is nothing like mine. Thank God for that! My family has always been there for me, starting with my parents, my eight brothers and sisters, and our extended family. (Which has, unlike Val's, grown quite large.) They're usually the first to buy any new book that comes out and to then ask, "What's next?"

This entire series could be credited to my family. My father, Donald Corbin, first dreamed up the basic story of *A Woman of Valor*, the book that inaugurated this series. He pitched it to me, and I loved it from the start. We wrote the first draft together. Unfortunately, we weren't able to get it into publishable shape before he lost his battle with lung cancer in 2006. It took years for me to get past the emotional wall that kept this project tucked away in a drawer for over a decade. I hope, Dad, that the result does you justice.

Dad and Mom helped in an infinite number of ways, but not least was driving me around Hartford on one of my infrequent visits home so I could revisit their old haunts. That exploration led to the creation of Clayton, Connecticut, and the neighborhoods in which the action of this novel occurs.

Several members of the Hartford Police Department assisted me in my background research for this book, and helped ground this fictional story in reality. In particular, Detective Buyak and Officers Mulroy, Kent, and King gave generously of their time, expertise, and personal perspectives, and I thank you all. The *Valorie Dawes Thrillers* would not have happened without you.

When I started *Mother*, I knew very little about sex trafficking and, thanks to spending over a decade earning undergrad and graduate degrees in political science, only slightly more about right-wing fringe groups. But a few high-profile sex trafficking cases hit the news cycle at that time, and the rise of violent right-wing fringe groups over the past decade is well-documented—if not legitimized by the election and behavior in office of our 45th president.

But a writer is nothing if not a reader, and I turned to some published sources for self-education. Cynthia Miller-Idriss's *Hate in the Homeland: The New Global Far Right* (Princeton University Press, 2022) contributed significantly to my understanding of how fringe groups operate and create the image of legitimacy in a free society. Bob Woodward's *Peril* (Simon & Schuster, 2021) and *Rage* (Simon & Schuster, 2021) happened to be sitting on to To-Be-Read pile and added significant depth to my understanding of how those groups infiltrated their way into the halls of power. Katariina Rosenblatt's chilling personal account of her victimization in *Stolen: The True Story of a Sex Trafficking Survivor* (Revell, 2014) provided vivid examples of how sex trafficking organizations lure young, vulnerable girls and women into this brutal trade, and how the organizations themselves are linked to other crime syndicates.

Special thanks goes out to my critique group partners—Erick Mertz, Jenny Furniss, and Laura Mahaffey—whose scene-by-scene critiques improved this story on a weekly basis.

Thanks also to my Beta Readers—Judith Bottorf, Danielle Faucheux, Erick Mertz, and Kate Kort—who gave me invaluable late-in-the-game feedback. You found the holes in this story just in time and gave me the perfect advice I needed to fix them. If any holes remain, it is because I am too stubborn sometimes. (So, maybe Val is a *little* bit autobiographical?)

No writer can survive without a great editor, and I have two. The keen eyes of Laura Lee Bennett and Patsy Silk caught many errors long after my own eyes glazed over. If errors remain, they are my fault, not theirs.

I can never give kudos enough to Steven Novak, whose creativity and patience with me once again yielded an amazing cover design.

Nobody contributed more to my writing career than my dear mother Patricia Corbin, who awakened in me the love of books and reading, and always encouraged my love of writing.

Many other friends, colleagues, and family members—too many to count or even remember—have contributed ideas, feedback, critique, encouragement, and love. I thank you all.

But most of all, thanks to Renée, the kindest, most patient, most beautiful person I've ever known, whose smile lights up the darkest night and brightens the sunniest day. We met fifteen years ago, and every day feels fresh and new. Without you, I'd be lost. I love you.

Book Group Discussion Questions

Characters

1. What do you think of Val? What terms would you use to describe her? Do you think you would like Val if you met her in person?

2. Which of the other characters did you like? Which did you dislike? In each case, why?

3. What do you think happens between Val and her mother after the end of the story?

4. Do you think that the author—a middle-aged white male—portrayed Val, a young woman who struggles with her memories of abuse by older men, authentically and sympathetically?

Scenes and plot

5. Which scene or scenes stood out to you? Why?

6. Were you satisfied with the conclusion of the story? How would you describe the state of Val's relationship with her father and mother at the end of the book?

Personal connection

7. For the most part, what emotion(s) did the story evoke in you as a reader?

8. Did you identify with Valorie? Any other character? How did that affect your enjoyment of the book?

Writing

9. *Mother of Valor* crosses genres, blending some character-driven aspects of literary fiction with the plot-driven aspects of police procedurals and crime novels. Did this work for you, as a reader?

10. If you could change something about the book, what would it be and why?

11. Describe what you liked or disliked about the writing style.

General

13. Name your favorite thing overall about the book, and your least favorite.

14. At what point in the book did you decide if you liked it or not? What helped make this decision?

15. If someone asks you what this book is about, how would you answer them?

About The Author

Gary Corbin is a writer and playwright in Camas, WA, a suburb of Portland, OR. In addition to eight published novels, his creative and journalistic work has been published in *BrainstormNW*, the *Portland Tribune*, The *Oregonian*, and *Global Envision*, among others. His plays have enjoyed critical acclaim and have been produced on many Portland-area stages.

Gary is a member of the Willamette Writers Group, Nine Bridges Writers, the Northwest Editors Guild, PDX Playwrights, and the Bar Noir Writers Workshop. He serves as treasurer of *The Pulp Stage*, and participates in workshops and conferences in the Portland, Oregon area.

A homebrewer and home coffee roaster, Gary is a member of the Oregon Brew Crew and a BJCP National Beer Judge. He loves to ski, cook, and root for his beloved Patriots and Red Sox. And when that's not enough, he escapes to the Oregon coast with his sweetheart.

Connect with Gary Corbin

Keep up to date with the latest at
http://www.garycorbinwriting.com

Follow me on Twitter:
http://twitter.com/garycorbin

Follow me on Facebook: https://www.face-book.com/garycorbinwriting

Follow my Amazon Author Page (and review this book!)
http://smarturl.it/GaryCorbinAuthor

Favorite me at Smashwords: https://www.smash-words.com/profile/view/GaryCorbin

Also by Gary Corbin

Valorie Dawes Thrillers

In Search of Valor

*The action-packed prequel to **A Woman of Valor***

Valorie Dawes fights an international kidnapping syndicate on behalf of a new college friend—and harbors serious doubts about her future as a police officer.

Anxious to prove herself worthy as a cop and a friend, Val puts her own life on the line, and discovers the kidnappers will stop at nothing to get rid of obstacles like her.

ISBN: 978-1-7346152-0-3

A Woman of Valor

A rookie policewoman, who had been molested as a young girl, pursues a serial child molester—and struggles to control the anger his misdeeds awake in her.

Can Valorie overcome the trauma she suffered as a child and stop this dangerous criminal from hurting others like her—or will her bottled-up anger lead her to take reckless risks that put the people she loves in greater danger?

ISBN: 978-0-9974967-9-6

A Better Part of Valor

While jogging off duty along the riverfront, Val discovers the dead body of a teenage girl—and ignites a manhunt for a serial killer.

The Shoeless Schoolgirl Slayer has remained a step ahead of the Clayton, CT police for months. All of his victims drowned. All were found barefoot. And all bear the same strange, fresh tattoo.

Then rookie cop Val Dawes notices patterns that eluded the department's more traditional senior detectives. Following her intuition, she discovers clues that convince her she's closing in.

But is she? Or is the clever and elusive Slayer laying a trap to make Val the next victim?

ISBN: 978-1-7346152-4-1

*All **Valorie Dawes Thrillers** are available in hardcover, paperback, audiobook, and all eBook formats at garycorbinwriting.com, and at your favorite local retailers.*

The Mountain Man Mysteries

The Mountain Man's Dog

In the small town of Clarkesville, in the heart of the Oregon Cascade Mountains, Lehigh Carter, a humble forester, stumbles into the complex world of crooked cops and power-hungry politicians...all because he rescues a stray, injured dog on the highway.

ISBN: 978-0-9974967-1-0

The Mountain Man's Bride

In this thrilling sequel to *The Mountain Man's Dog*, Lehigh's wedding plans get put on hold when the authorities arrest Stacy for the murder of popular acting Sheriff Jared Barkley. Mounting evidence of a secret affair causes Lehigh to wonder how innocent Stacy really is.

ISBN: 978-0-9974967-3-4

The Mountain Man's Badge

Appointed to fill out the unexpired term of disgraced sheriff Buck Summers, Lehigh battles the mistrust of the community's powerful elected elites, the sheriff's department he leads, and his own wife—until he finds shocking evidence of who really killed Everett Downey.

ISBN: 978-0-9974967-7-2

*All three **Mountain Man Mysteries** are available in hardcover, paperback, and all eBook formats at garycorbinwriting.com, and at your favorite local retailers.*

Lying Injustice Thrillers

Lying in Judgment

A man serves on the jury trying a man for the murder that he committed!

Peter Robertson, 33, discovers his wife is cheating on him. Following her suspected boyfriend one night, he erupts into a rage, beats him and leaves him to die...or so he thought. Soon he discovers that he has killed the wrong man—a perfect stranger.

Six months later, impaneled on a jury, he realizes that the murder being tried is the one he committed.

ISBN: 978-06926426-8-9

Lying in Vengeance

Peter's worst nightmare comes to fruition: Christine, his beautiful and charming fellow juror, knows his dark secret and uses it to blackmail him.

The price of her secrecy: Peter must kill again, this time to stop Kyle, the man who torments Christine and threatens her very existence.

ISBN: 978-0-9974967-5-8

*Both **Lying Injustice Thrillers** are available in hardcover, paperback, audiobook, and all eBook formats at garycorbinwriting.com, and at your favorite local retailers.*

Chapter One

Stafford Allen Ray squinted his right eye shut and peered through the scope with his left. At first, he could see only red brick and the reflection of the sun on tinted windows. He adjusted his aim downward and to the left, and the building's heavy metal front door came into view. He turned the magnification ring counterclockwise to broaden the view so he could read the inscription on the door: "Helen's Orchid—Family Planning." Perfect.

He lowered the rifle a moment. At this distance, about 500 feet, he could make out distinct figures and objects in front of the clinic: two wooden benches, five or six feet wide, one on each side of the door. Azaleas, long since out of bloom, lined the sidewalk in front. Four parking spaces, two currently empty, the other two occupied by SUVs. No people yet in sight.

The angle, the view, and the time of day all satisfied him. Assuming good weather, the afternoon sun behind him would shroud his face in shadow—assuming anyone looked his way—and cast his targets in a favorable light. His rooftop perch on the six-story building across the street from the clinic afforded a clear shot to any target of his choosing.

A third vehicle approached and pulled into one of the two vacant spaces. A new "customer" of the clinic. Like the others, a potential baby killer. Hate boiled inside him.

He peered back through the scope. All three of the cars bore Connecticut license plates. From the third vehicle, a woman opened the driver's side door and stepped out. She didn't appear pregnant. But that could mean she was still in her first or even early in her second trimester. The fact that no man emerged from the car with her told him that she, like so many murderous would-be mothers, had excluded the father of the baby from her impending decision. She, and only she, would decide whether to kill the innocent child growing in her womb.

Correction. She, and her abortionist doctor, hiding safely inside the brick fortress.

He focused his aim on her, adjusting his magnification ring clockwise until she filled his view. She fussed with something in her purse, holding open the car door, and the breeze swept her long blonde hair in front of her face. He swept the scope downward, from head to toe, analyzing her body shape. Curvy and busty, in the way women get when their body responds to the responsibility of hosting another human being. Her loose blouse, ruffling in the slight breeze, could hide an early-stage baby bump with ease. Her jeans stretched tight over wide, baby-bearing hips. Low-heeled sandals revealed swollen feet and ankles.

Conclusion: Pregnant, three to four months along. Her body had expanded faster than her clothes-shopping habit could keep up. Definitely someone contemplating becoming a customer of the baby-killing factory down below.

She shut the car door and walked toward the door. He followed her in his scope, counting the seconds between her vehicle and the building. Eight, maybe nine seconds, with her brisk gait. A slower walker, someone further along in their pregnancy, might take twice as long. This one, probably still in the first trimester.

She paused at the door, her head down, as if praying. She remained still as he centered his aim on the middle of her back. He steadied his breathing, recalling his training.

He inhaled, exhaled, readied his trigger finger. Inhaled another breath, then exhaled, then held it. Squeezed the trigger.

Click.

A perfect kill shot. A would-be murderer, denied.

Or would be, when the moment came, when he returned with ammunition loaded into his rifle's magazine.

He drew another deep breath and lowered the weapon. A good practice run. He hadn't flinched, his hands remained steady, his aim true. He'd found the right clinic, the right time of day, the right vantage point. He had a few things left to figure out: how to escape undetected topping the list. But those details would come, and soon. After that, he would review his plan with his mentor, get the green light, and push forward with God's work.

Today's work was done.